The Magical Bookshop No. 1

The Tale of Silvia & The Big Sweet Bear

by

Ella Outlaw

ISBN: 979-8-9918378-1-1

Published by Uncommon Pages LLC

First Edition: October 2024

Book Cover by Lisa Austin

Dedication

To Brennan Lee Mulligan, the cast, and crew of Dimension 20.
For reminding me how much I love storytelling. For showing me
that it's still okay to use my imagination & share it with the World.

Also, to all the smut authors out there...
What have you done to me?!

Trigger Warnings!!!

I want to reassure you that this is indeed a COZY romance. That being said, there are a few topics that I want to make sure you are comfortable with before diving into this adventure.

- Sexual content and acts

- Abduction/kidnapping

- Going N/C with family member

- Non-consensual biting

- Imprisonment

- Drugs/drug addicts

- Mention of selling body parts

- Being drugged

- Negative/abusive self talk

- Stalking/following

Chapter 1

Silvia

Don't cry, don't cry, don't cry. It's only a torn umbrella, nothing major. Just a busted umbrella, during a downpour, one week before your period, on the day you up and quit your shitty ass call center job.

Damn it, I'm going to cry right out here on the street.

No, breathe...just breathe. You can do this, Silvia. At least until you're alone. You can break apart once you're alone.

I know I'm not going to make it home. In fact, if one more thing happens to me today I am going to absolutely lose it no matter where I am.

Breathe, just breathe!

Why, why does everything make me cry? I'm happy, I cry. Sad, I cry. Angry, I cry. Too many emotions to process, I cry. It's infuriating, and if I'm honest the crux of many a failed relationship. "Too emotional," they say. "Using your tears against me," they say. Trust me, if I could be stoic and keep my emotions on the inside I would, but that's never been in the cards for me.

Breathe, just breathe. In through the nose, out through the mouth.

I need to find someplace private soon, a bathroom, a corner, a dressing room; hell, I'd take a phone booth at this point. Hmm, are phone booths still a thing? Funny how you don't really notice things are gone till you want it or it's pointed out to you.

That's right Silvia, distract yourself with phone booths! When was the last time you saw one in person? Maybe you saw one while driving? Where would they be anyway? On corners, at bus stops, near shopping centers? Wonder if there is one around my office building and I never noticed because I didn't need one. I should look around the place next time I....oh crap.

No, no, don't go down that line of thinking. Phone booths, phone booths, phone booths, bookshop.

Bookshop? I don't remember there being a bookshop around here. I've walked down this street many times before. How could I not notice a bookshop? Me, cozy girl extraordinaire, book fair lover since grade school. Heck, I am still a card-carrying public library regular. How have I missed this?!

It certainly doesn't appear to be new. Even through all the rain, I can see the slightly worn paint, the well-trafficked tarnish of the brass door handles, and the scuff and age on the wood facade. The warm glow of the lights from the front windows pulls me across the street to peer inside. It looks so inviting, especially compared to the rainy gloom of the outside world. In fact, now that I'm standing in front of this shop, the orange glow from the lights within seem to be the only illumination around. Behind me feels only of darkness, of sadness, and almost like despair. I don't just want to go in, I need to go in! If only to embrace that light, that warmth, to escape the crushing darkness behind me.

I'm standing on the other side of the tall wooden doors ogling the sights in front of me before I even realize what I've done. I don't remember reaching out my hand, pressing down on the thumb latch, opening the door, or stepping inside. I don't remember the weight of the door or hearing the bell above my head chime. But it must have, because it's still swinging lightly as I gaze up and around. All of that should bother me more, as should the fact that I'm dripping wet.

But my senses can't seem to get enough of the absolute treasure of the place that is before me. The warmth of this light is equally matched by the warmth of the space itself. Not just the physical warmth radiating from the crackling flames dancing in the fireplace to my left, but also the emotional warmth this place is emanating. It's like I've been wrapped up in one of my grandmother's handmade quilts, fresh from drying on the line in the sun. The aroma of the fire mingles perfectly with the smells of books, leather, old wood, and something else. Tea perhaps?

The bookshop itself is arranged as a two hundred year old book shoppe from Europe should be. Books of various shapes, sizes, and colors cover the walls from top to bottom. Big solid wood shelves are all along the walls and in rows on the floors, which themselves are covered in an assortment of rugs. And when I say covered, I mean covered! Overlapping rugs abound. The only way I know that there are wood floors under it all is the small patch in front of the door that I'm currently leaking on and the shine I can see directly in front of the fireplace.

The books themselves are absolutely gorgeous, but odd. All of them are leatherbound, each sporting a single solid color with gold or silver embossed on the spine and cover, which wouldn't be odd if this was some kind of collectors shop or antique book dealers, but all of these books seem new. Brand new, in fact. Feels weird to see a store with all new books but no cover art in sight, no book jackets either. Maybe this is some kind of specialty bookstore? I didn't look for the name of the shop before I was compelled to come in.

As I gaze around searching for store branding of any kind, I notice a flicker of movement to my right. A remarkably tall woman has come in through a doorway that is hung with a linen curtain instead of a door. She stands behind a long curved wooden counter, her focus on the tea serving tray she carries in her hands. Her mahogany brown hair is long with a bit of wave and lays perfectly down her back, slightly past her waist. Her skin is as pale as mine but unlike the chaos of freckles I sport, hers is totally without blemish or mark. And did I mention how tall she is?! Even from this distance, I can tell she would tower over my five-seven frame.

It's at this moment, while I am open-mouthed and wild-eyed, drinking in the vision of this heavenly representation of Woman, that she turns and notices me. I stop breathing as her eyes lock onto mine. Despite their color being that of vivid amber, the depth they hold seems fathomless, almost terrifying in their vastness. I have never seen eyes like these. I have never been held in a gaze in this way. I have never felt so overwhelmed in my life. Then, she blinks and I feel as though I have been released from a hold that lasted countless hours, but must have only been a moment.

"My goodness, look at you! Poor thing, you are soaking wet. Here, let me help you," comes her soothing, almost melodic, voice.

I don't know where she got the towel, I don't know when she put the laden tray down, and I don't know how she appeared at my side so quickly, but I'm almost immediately being wrapped up in the largest towel I've ever used. It actually overlaps my body, my very curvy body, which isn't something that's been able to happen since before puberty. Going to have to ask her where she bought this towel from, as I need at least eight now.

It's not until she's helping pat me dry that I realize I have created quite a puddle of water on her beautiful hardwood floors. Water that is starting to make its way to a nearby rug.

"Oh gosh! I am so, so sorry," I begin. "Look what I've done to your poor floors! I did not realize what a mess I was making. If you have a mop or any drying cloths handy, I'll clean it all up right now then be on my way. I can't believe I did this."

"Dear, I'm not worried about my floors or my rug, I'm worried about you. You've been crying." As she says this, she gently places a flawless finger to my cheek where I do, indeed, feel tears sliding down. Of course, it's at this moment that I burst into full-on sobs. How embarrassing.

This saint of a woman pulls me into a hug I feel like I've needed my whole life. A hug of true kindness and patience. It's so darn soothing I practically melt into her. She rubs my back and pats my hair, which is probably a frizzled mess by now. My poor curly hair must look a wreck. First, doused in pelting rain, then hurriedly tousled dry in a towel. Not at all how it's been getting treated these last few years, not now that I know how to properly handle my lovely red locks. But as this woman holds me, I continue to literally cry into her shoulder. I can't even bring myself to care as much as I usually would. Yet another issue to deal with on an already stinking heap of a day.

"Come," the shop owner says gently as she steps back from me, placing her hands on my forearms. "Let's get you a dry blanket and set you in front of the fire." She steps to my side, links arms with me, and guides us towards the fireplace. In front of the crackling flames sits a high wingback chair and a very inviting antique loveseat.

"Oh, no," I protest while shaking my head, "I couldn't sit. I'm still pretty wet and don't want to ruin your furniture. I already feel bad enough about the floor and rug." Dang, I knew that water puddle was going to make it to one of those rugs but it still made me grimace when she mentioned it. There's no way I want to repay this person's kindness with a big cleaning bill.

"Objects dry, and I will not have you getting sick or being uncomfortable in any way while you are in my establishment. You are my guest and I intend to treat you as such. One does not deny someone their guest rights over some rainwater. Now, let me take that wet towel," she swiftly removes the wonderfully large towel, "and here is a nice warm blanket. Take this seat by the fire, and I'll grab us some tea."

Before I can utter any more protests a new fluffy blanket appears from what again seems like nowhere, and it is indeed warm. She promptly wraps the blanket over my shoulders and gently sets me in the loveseat close to the fire.

"Now, you make yourself comfortable, perhaps even take your wet shoes off, and I'll return shortly with some fresh tea for us to drink. Then, you can tell me all about your woes while you dry off and rest your weary bones." With a graceful turn and swish of her dress, she's gone.

Since I had forgotten to swap out my nice business casual flats for my more comfortable walking shoes when I stormed off in anger from work, I now realize how thoroughly soaked and painful my feet truly are. I remove my shoes and wonder how my day could have taken such an odd turn as I place my probably ruined shoes in front of the fireplace. I never really liked those shoes anyway, only had them for work due to some outdated dress codes. So I'm going to remove that worry from my list and simply throw them out once I get home. It'll be a cold day in hell before I take another call center job, that's for sure.

The job had started off so well; I breezed through the training, learning as much as I could about 'our' products and services. I had heard call center horror stories, sure, but this was inbound calls. The people calling us wanted help, and I was here to help them. I had learned so much in order to help them. So logic told me they wanted my help. I wasn't calling them to pester or nag, to pressure them into buying something, or collecting a debt. So why had so many people been so rude, so mean, so nasty when I was here to help them? I knew I should have quit the first time a customer made me cry, but my coworkers said it would get better. Well, maybe for those who aren't emotional criers, but for me it only got worse. I tried to be indifferent when they called me names, I tried to be stoic when they yelled, but that's not who I am I guess.

I told my supervisor I was struggling. I asked for help, tips, and suggestions. But he only complained about how often I went to the bathroom, and once he berated me for hanging up on a customer who had me sobbing on the phone. No help or support was offered or given, only more irritation and anger, which I already had plenty of from those people who called in. Oh, there were nice ones at times. People who were kind, thankful, and a pleasure to talk to. But we were trained to wrap up calls as quickly as possible so we could get on to the next. Wonderful callers were few and far between and overshadowed by the 'Karens' of the call center world.

Let's not dwell on that awful job anymore. Time to think ahead, to the future, and maybe a little thought to the here and now wouldn't hurt. How did I even get here? I know this place wasn't here last week when I walked this route after work. If it had been, I would have come in for sure. I mean, places like this are my cup of tea and I would have made a beeline to it. But all these books and furniture couldn't have been moved in over the weekend, could they? It truly looks and feels so well lived in. Oh gosh, am I lost?! Did I get turned around in the rain storm? That totally seems like the kind of thing that would happen to me today.

"Penny for your thoughts?" a voice says next to me.

"AH!" I jump in surprise to see my lovely hostess sitting on the loveseat next to me, tea tray on an adorable vintage rolling tea service between us. "S-sorry," I stammer. "Didn't hear you come back." Golly, someone should put a bell on this woman. How does she move so fast and so silently?

"Clearly," she says with a slight smile tugging at the corner of her lips. "I did not mean to startle you my dear. I hadn't realized how deeply into your thoughts you had gone. Tea?" She gestures to the tea cups, which I now notice are mismatched, as if she's gone to thrift stores or estate sales to find designs she truly enjoys instead of simply buying a matching set. For some odd reason this makes me like her even more. Knowing she's gone to the trouble of giving these unique and separated pieces a new home, a new life.

"I would love some, thank you. The perfect thing for this rainy day and this damp woman." I manage a little chuckle as I gesture at myself.

"Is orange-spiced okay? I saw it on my shelf and thought it would be perfect for you." I look at her with what must be the widest of eyes.

"Are you kidding me? Orange-spiced is my favorite kind of tea. How did you know?"

"Well, seems like this is your lucky day after all. I came upon it last time I tried a new tea shop. I haven't had the pleasure of trying it myself. But if it's your favorite I bet it is delicious. Do you like it with sugar, honey, or milk?"

"Oh, I love it with a little spoon of honey. That's how my grandma always made it, and I guess that's how I've always done it too." I still can't believe she made me this tea, the same tea which my grandma used to always make me when I was feeling down. Those memories alone bring a lump to my throat. Maybe my luck is turning around after all? Maybe my grandma led my steps to this place, to this kind woman who somehow has the exact tea I needed on the day I needed it most. All of this feels too perfect for it to be a coincidence.

"So my dear, why don't you tell me what happened to make you cry on a stranger's shoulder while dripping wet from the rain?"

And just like that, I feel awful again. Ugh, lucky day my ass. Sorry Grandma.

I shouldn't be burdening this divine creature with my silly sob story. But after she pours our tea, fixing both cups with spoons of honey, she hands me one, then leans back on the arm of the loveseat, gazing over her cup of tea expectantly. I dawdle by looking intently at the design on my tea cup, an ivy of some kind encircling the rim. I take a sip then close my eyes as the all too familiar and soothing flavor coats my tongue. Tastes exactly the way it did when Grandma made it for me all those years. Wonder if it's the same brand?

In a strange way this woman across from me seems to carry the same sage aura of wisdom that comes from age, though she appears to be no older than my thirty-six. She could be forty I suppose, but that would be stretching it in my opinion. Perhaps she carries the wisdom and knowledge contained within all these books, all these words, all these voices. Or maybe she's lived a completely different life than it seems at first glance. Everyone has a past I suppose.

"I promise it will help if you talk about it," her voice breaking me from my thoughts. "Get it all out in the air and released from your body. However, if you don't feel comfortable talking about it to a perfect stranger, I understand and will not take offense. Though," she leans in closer while giving me a conspiratorial look, "who am I going to tell that matters to you." She winks at me as she leans back, getting comfortable again.

That little gesture and the choice she gives puts me more at ease than she could know. So I take a deep breath, order my thoughts, and prepare to tell this stranger my terrible, horrible, no good, very bad day. I tell her a little of the lead-up: how terrible my job was, how it makes me feel, and how my supervisor only makes things worse. How I have recently been given a much younger girl to train and how I feel a little protective of her due to her sweetness and youth. She's my responsibility, and I don't want her to feel crushed the way I do. Then, how today my new trainee got her first 'Karen' customer.

"I could hear this grown-ass woman yelling through the headset," I continue. "Then Jasmine turned and looked at me with wide-eyed shock. When I saw the beginnings of tears in her eyes, I lost it. I took the headset off my protégé, cut this woman off mid tirade and calmly, yet firmly, told her that this was not how you spoke to a fellow human being who is honestly trying to help with your problem. I might have also questioned her upbringing, the state of her home life, and offered my sympathy for her husband and children. Not my finest hour. I admit I should have stopped much sooner, but it all just came pouring out of me."

"Well," the shop owner interjects while sitting up straight once more, "I say good riddance to those people and that position. I can hardly believe you were able to stand such a terrible vocation for as long as you did. I would have done much worse much sooner, believe you me," she says with a slightly wicked grin and a wink. And though she has been nothing but wonderful and kind, I know to my core that she is indeed capable of being...wrathful? Why does wrathful seem like the exact right word? I make a very important mental note to never ever get on this woman's shit list.

"I do commend you for sticking up for your pupil, though perhaps you should take a page from your own book and stand up for yourself a bit more, dear."

Yep, nothing feels better than having a complete stranger pinpoint a major failing of yours so quickly and so bluntly. Ouch. I'm brought up so short that all I can manage is to blink at her, repeatedly. Finally, after what seems like eons, I stammer out a, "T-thanks," and a weak, "I'll try," since I realize some form of response is expected of me. Having tough conversations I'm not really prepared for is not exactly my strong suit, but given a bit of time I could most certainly craft an eloquently written response. Too bad all conversations aren't crafted over text or email. If that were the case, I would be crushing it.

"How about we move on to more enjoyable topics?" my companion shifts. "Tell me about your family and friends. Who will you be celebrating this big change in your life with?"

While I am more than grateful for the topic change, she must have sensed my freeze up there and showed me mercy, the new topic chosen is not much better. My father was never in the picture, I went 'no contact' with mom years ago, and both my wonderful grandparents have passed. No real close friends to speak of, only acquaintances, and there hasn't been a man in my life since I offloaded my man-child of a boyfriend some years ago. Celebration, party of one, over here.

"Oh, I don't really have anyone close anymore. Pretty much all alone at this point in my life. Besides, I don't feel much like celebrating quitting my job without a plan, to be honest. It was so stupid and rash of me. But what's done is done, and I have no desire to go back."

"I believe that when we are faced with a major change in our lives we should honor that time in some way." Locking her eyes with mine, the shop owner continues, "You are now standing at a crossroads where a new adventure begins, a new way of life, a new path forward. Cherish this newness and embrace the change and transformation that is to come from it. For on the other side, you shall be a whole new person. One should reinvent themselves as often as the chance arises." She says all this with so much vehemence that I'm somewhat taken aback.

"Don't know if it will be that much of a transformation to be honest," I eventually reply. "I'll probably find some other not so great J-O-B as quickly as I can so Harvey and I aren't kicked out of my apartment."

"And who is this Harvey that lives with you? I thought you said you didn't really have anyone in your life, but if this Harvey lives with you then you must be close." Is she upset with me about this? She's asked these questions as though I've lied to her about being utterly alone and now she's disappointed in me.

"Sorry, um, Harvey is my cat. He's a chimera tortoiseshell actually, very special. Acts like an opinionated old man sometimes, though he's only 3. Didn't really think he would be down for partying, ya know. Though he will deign to comfort me when he senses I'm in distress as I'm sure I will be tonight. So I guess he and I will be cuddling on my couch later as I play my current cozy game fixation and cry on and off." Oh gawd, I am rambling. I'm rambling and oversharing. "I'm sure that's not the kind of celebrating you meant, but honestly, that is what's going to happen. I totally agree that life events should be acknowledged, for sure, but I'm not there just yet with this one." Stop talking. Please stop talking! "I guess if I had some close girlfriends they would take me out for drinks as a way to say farewell to a terrible job and demon boss, like you see in movies. But I don't really have that kind of relationship with anyone and it's not exactly my scene. So it'll be just me and my cat."

Fortunately, this wonderful human being gently places her hand over mine in my lap, putting a stop to my nonsense before I continue to devolve into what a sad and sorry life I have. Real smooth, Silvia.

"My dear, you may choose to commemorate or process this transition in your life however you see fit. You shall have no judgment from me on that score. I merely thought that I was missing a big piece of the puzzle that is you. I did not mean to put you on the defensive with my questioning. Harvey sounds like an admirable feline, who lives up to the mystique and aloofness that cats are famous for."

Okay, complimenting my baby is definitely a good way to put me back at ease and feel more comfortable talking with this stranger. Stranger?! Oh my gosh, I don't even know her name and we've been talking all about my woes and troubles. I never even introduced myself. Grandma would be ashamed of my poor manners.

"Sorry, I tend to go on and on when I'm nervous or if I feel like I've disappointed someone, or heaven forbid, not explained something clearly. Harvey is my cat and my name is Silvia, Silvia Sanders." I say as I hold out my hand for a handshake. She encloses my outstretched hand with both of hers.

"It is a pleasure to make your acquaintance, Silvia Sanders, owner of a marvelous chimera cat. You are most welcome in my humble little bookshop." I only barely register that she does not provide her own name before she continues. "Let us move on to a more enjoyable topic. What types of books are your favorite? Which stories do you have a hard time putting down once begun?

What tales leave you so entranced that you lose yourself and all sense of time?"

She asks these questions while still holding onto my hand and looking directly into my eyes. I feel as though she is seeing right into my very core. Before I can even think about what I am saying, the truth bubbles up from the depths of my being, a truth I would never tell a stranger. Particularly one who, I suspect, is intentionally withholding her name for some reason.

"Fantasy!" I blurt out. "Especially YA fantasy with a love story." Squeezing her hand I emphatically continue, "I need there to be magic, adventure, and romance! With a 'happily ever after' at the end." My eyes go wide as I realize what I have just confessed. I can feel my cheeks, ears, and neck turning red from the embarrassment. Why would I ever say that out loud? Those aren't the kinds of books a grown-ass woman reads. I never even told my own grandmother I still read the 'juvenile' books. What is this proper lady and business owner going to assume about me now?

As my internal struggle begins to ramp up, the shopkeeper gets that slightly wicked half grin again, tilts her head down, and gazes at me through her eyelashes.

"An amazing adventure with an amazing amount of spice. A girl truly after my own black heart." Whoa! I didn't say anything about spice. I've never even read one of those before! As I get the courage to correct her, she claps her hands together in excitement.

"Oh, I have the perfect adventure for you," she proclaims. "Do wait right here, drink your tea, get cozy and warm, and I shall be right back." With a twinkle in her eye she gracefully spirits her way into the rows of shelved books.

What could she mean by 'black heart'? The woman I've been talking to has anything but a black heart, in my opinion. She's been nothing but caring and understanding since I walked in. Someone with a black heart does not hug strange women who are crying while dripping water all over their rugs and floors. I really shouldn't be burdening her with my troubles and wasting her time.

Ugh, I actually shouldn't be wasting my time either. Need to start making future plans and updating my resume. At least this downpour seems to be keeping other customers out for the time being, so I don't feel too bad. I really don't want to walk in it either.

Despite the darkness on the other side of the windows, it really is still early in the day. I didn't even make it to lunch before the incident at work. So, since I'm all nice and snuggled in here on the couch, finally feeling dry and warm, I might as well stay for a bit. Bet my hair is a hot mess. I chuckle to myself, envisioning what I must look like right now. Frizzy red hair and a blotchy red freckled face poking out the top of a, what is this thing, a comforter?

"Ah yes, this will do quite nicely." I hear the woman say a short distance away before appearing around the corner of a bookshelf.

She deftly takes her seat on the cushion next to me once more and reverently hands me the leatherbound volume. I hold it with both of my hands, trying to show the same amount of respect for the book she passes to me. It is weighty, but comfortably so. It's very obvious it was made well, and to last. The leather covering has been dyed a lovely forest green with accents of gold filigree. It feels so monumental in my lap.

I run my hand along the spine and front. Feeling the textured divots and grooves of the natural leather and embossing. I carefully open the front cover and am rewarded with the crackling sound of new pages and bindings unused to movement. The smell of cured leather, book pages, and dye is heavy in the air as I glide my hand over the first blank page.

Before I can continue to inspect this treasure further, my hostess places her hand on mine once more and, when I look up, gazes deeply into my eyes. She has a smile of true happiness upon her face, a face I couldn't believe could be any more beautiful, but this smile has proven me wrong. I'm in awe of the grace that emanates at this moment, a moment that feels enormous for some strange reason.

"I'm going to leave you alone while you get acquainted with your new adventure. Please feel free to stay as long as you desire. Get yourself good and comfortable. I shall come back to check on you after a while."

Before I can even ask her what the book is about, she's gone again, around the register, through the curtains, and into the back. How does she move so quickly without making any sounds? I'll have to ask her if she was trained in the art of ninjutsu when she comes back. I would love to be able to move like that. Maybe she'll train me if I ask? I chuckle to myself as I think of learning to walk quickly and properly with a stack of books upon my head, finishing school style, while wearing all black ninja garb.

I turn my attention back to the precious item now resting in my criss-cross applesauce lap. To no one in particular, I say, "Let's see what this book is all about, shall we?" as I nestle a bit more into the couch and comforter cocoon I've made for myself. This really is the perfect reading situation: warm fire, cozy loveseat, wrapped up in a big blanket, and my grandma's tea on demand. The only thing that could make this better would be having Harvey curled up at the other end with me. Maybe some kind of snack, as well? I bet it's around or past lunch time at this point, and I haven't eaten since my overnight oats this morning. Though you can bet I am not about to say anything to the owner about food. I've put her out so much already today. I wonder if there's a tip jar up front? If there is, she's getting all the cash I have on me and five star reviews on all the apps.

As is my custom, I pick up my 'new adventure,' hold the text block at the top corner, and quickly skate my thumb across all the pages to fan the scent of the book into my face. Nothing else in the world can match the smell of a book. It has its own unique aroma. Old or new, constantly used or shelved to be forgotten for a time, books smell absolutely divine. I can't seem to read one without smelling it first. This one, as expected, smells of new paper, leather, and that special bookish kick. My eyelids flutter and I moan in pleasure as the aroma makes its way deep into my nose and wafts across my face.

But as I gaze down at the book, my brain registers something odd. I set the book down on my lap once more for a closer inspection. I flip open to the first page, then a few past that, searching for a title, but they are all blank. I must have it backwards then. There's no title on the cover, so it's hard to tell which side is which. I turn the book over, again looking for the title page. Okay, now I am confused. Grabbing more pages, I quickly fan through them and realize they are all blank. There are no words printed on any of these pages. That is so odd. The shop owner must have picked up the wrong book by mistake. This has to be a journal or something that looks similar to the book she meant to give me. I'll just point it out once she comes out of the back room.

A large yawn erupts from me at this moment. Man, I guess the events of the day are finally catching up to me and being so comfortable has really ramped up the sleepiness factor. I yawn once more while lazily flipping through the pages of this journal. As I let my eyelids drift closed, I swear I see a bright flash of light. I dimly think that it must have started to lightning outside. I'm also pretty sure I feel a whoosh of wind, but I'm so bundled up I can't be certain. Everything must be fine though, what could possibly be happening in a bookshop?

Chapter 2

Silvia

Are those birds chirping? The rain must have stopped, and the sun has to be out because I can feel the light on my face and see it through my eyelids. Gosh, the birds sound like they are inside this bookshop. Is that a breeze on my face? No, that's silly. There must be a fan or A/C on, perhaps both. Oh that was such a good nap and exactly what I needed. It has been a strange day, for sure. But I guess I need to get up and make my way home. I'll buy that book she meant to let me read, then thank her profusely for her care and attention. Maybe try to sneak in one more heartwarming hug before getting back home to Harvey.

This loveseat is no longer as comfortable as it was, which should make getting up easier. I must have twisted wrong, or am I now laying on that book? Something hard is definitely under me, pressing into my lower back. It's starting to get painful actually.

I lurch up into a seated position, getting away from that discomfort, and rub at my eyes as I'm hunched over my legs. Not a very ladylike posture. Straightening up and doing a bit of a backbend as I reach my arms high overhead, I yawn one last time, stretch my fingers wide, and finally open my eyes...to a forest dappled in sunlight.

It is at this point I think my brain has short-circuited, so I blink about a hundred times in rapid succession. I'm in a forest? No, no, that's not right; that would be silly. I must still be asleep, and I am in a dream. A super realistic dream, but a dream nonetheless. See, look over there, a unicorn is getting a drink of water from a little pond. And since unicorns aren't real, this is one hundred percent a dream.

"Isn't she gorgeous?" a voice says directly behind me. A startled scream is about to erupt from my throat when she continues, "Shhh, we don't want to startle her, my dear." Somehow, I am utterly silenced.

I turn my head to the left and see the shop owner towering over me. Did she get even taller or is it just my perspective right now? I very ungracefully make my way to my feet, trembling from head to toe. This can not be happening right now! This is the kind of thing you hear about in the news or on all those murder podcasts we women devour for tips so the same situation doesn't happen to us. But, I mean, you never really expect it to be another woman. Lesson learned, I guess.

"D-did you drug me?" I ask in a squeak. "W-what did you put in my tea? Did you bring me out to this forest to murder and bury me? Is that why you were asking about the people in my life, making sure I wouldn't be missed and reported quickly? Oh no, oh no, this can't be real. You seemed so nice, so kind, but I guess that's how you get your victims huh? Lure them in with your honey and tea and hugs." I'm rambling again, but this time I don't care, anything to prolong my life. It wasn't a perfect life, but damn it, it was mine, and I was mostly happy and content. I'm trembling so hard I can hear my teeth chattering. I...I think I am going to pee myself.

"I have no intention of murdering you, nor of burying you in these woods, and I most certainly did not slip anything untoward into your tea." As if that was the most outrageous part in all of my accusations. "While I do admit I did pry into your social life to see if you would be missed by anyone, it was not for any kind of nefarious purpose. I merely wanted to make sure you were fully available for this grand adventure. My compliments for picking up on that facet of our interaction. Most people never do." She gives me a small handclap, which I hate to admit does feel like a reward for a job well done. Damn, I do love recognition.

My brain is working a million miles a minute, racing along every scenario of fight or flight. I know my eyes are darting around, looking for the best way to run. That way has a big log, no good. Can't go forward unless I want to fight this Amazon of a woman. I do have the solid mass upper hand but she has the reach and, lets face it, the confidence to take me. I don't see any pathway or clearing aside from the one with the pond the unicorn is drinking from.

"No, you must have drugged me because I am seeing a unicorn over there," jutting my arm and finger out rigidly, I point. Yes, that's a great idea Silvia, distract the woman, and maybe you'll get an opening when she looks away trying to see your hallucination.

"You are seeing a unicorn over there because there is a unicorn over there, my dear. An extremely thirsty female, it seems. Any interest in petting her? I believe it would help to calm you down. They do have a fondness for young women and, of course, you are in my company which is also a boon."

"I'm not young enough to tempt a unicorn, I'm thirty-six. And I'm no virgin so I doubt the 'unicorn' would be very enticed by me. Now, please let me go-" Before I can finish my desperate plea for release, the shopkeeper gently laughs into the back of her hand while looking me up and down.

"Well I should sincerely hope that a person's sexual status isn't the kind of thing a unicorn takes into consideration when sizing a person up. Goodness, where do you people get such odd notions? Trust me Silvia, a unicorn isn't going to care if you have been with zero sexual partners or one hundred. They prefer people who are gentle, kind, and good-natured. Plus, they enjoy a woman's presence due to that spark of the Divine Feminine we all carry. The potential life force that resides within. And you, my lovely, have all of these in spades. All things considered you are still quite young, relatively speaking, as many of the residents and creatures of this realm can live to vast and countless ages. Now come," she reaches out her hand to me, "let us stop being rude and introduce ourselves to our new friend over there. She has been quite patient with us so far, don't you agree?"

"And, and you swear you didn't drug me? You can really see that unicorn too? You're not just placating the delusional person into following your orders? There really is an honest to goodness unicorn right over there?" I tilt my head and flash my eyes to the opposite side of the pond from where the unicorn is standing. Taking in a patient breath, the bookshop owner turns her head to the correct side of the pond.

"The unicorn is about ten yards from us, just there at the edge of a small pond whose source of water is bubbling up from deep underground. The unicorn is about four feet nine inches tall, making her an adolescent. Her coat and mane are the typical snow white, though the ends of her tail are a bit dirty, and it looks as though someone has put a small cornflower next to her ear. Ah, and her horn is around eleven inches long and gleaming beautifully." Crossing her arms in front of her chest, "How's that? Do you now trust that I too can see what you are seeing?"

Everything she said is spot on, even the little blue flower I now see tucked in the mane next to the ear. I'm trembling again, but for a very different reason. I close my mouth, realizing it's been hanging open for who knows how long, and swallow. There go my eyelids again, blinking uncontrollably.

"Can...can we really pet her?" As I say it, my arm and hand start to rise in anticipation. Seizing the opportunity, she links my arm with hers and gently smiles down at me.

"Of course we can, dearheart. Come now, let's say hello. Finally." She arches her eyebrow at me on that last word.

I'm still trembling as she guides me over to the pond where an animal I thought only existed in fairytales stands, seemingly waiting, watching us walk over. Once we get a few feet away, my escort stops and bows her head slightly while bringing her unattached hand to lightly touch her chest. I mimic her gesture of respect, as this is all new territory for me. I do not want to fuck this up! I have never wanted to pet anything more in my life, and as a White woman and animal lover, that is saying something.

"Hello there, little one. My lovely companion and I could not help but marvel at your beauty and grace. We wished to come pay our respect to you and your kind. May we have the honor of bestowing some loving attention upon you while I explain some things to this young lady? She's new to these lands and has never seen one of your ilk before."

The myth makes a neighing-type sound and dips her head a bit. I guess that means yes? My companion takes my hand and gently lays it on the gleaming white coat. O-M-G! I have never felt anything as soft as this. I want to rub my face in it. I resist the urge, but just barely. I do, however, begin to pet the beast with both of my hands. I mean, come on, it's a freaking real-life unicorn and it feels like heaven. Then I get a whiff of something sugary. I bend down, getting my nose closer, and inhale. Is...is that cotton candy? Yes, this unicorn smells like cotton candy! Well, mostly. There's something else there too.

"It's ambrosia, my dear. Her scent is that of ambrosia."

I mutter a quick and breathless, "oh," and continue to pet and run my hands along her coat.

"Now that you seem to be a bit more composed, would you care to know where you are and what is going on?"

"Yes, please. I'm so confused. The last thing I remember was being in your bookshop on your loveseat in front of a fire and flipping through that blank book you gave me. Pretty sure I fell asleep, and when I woke up, I'm outside in a forest where apparently unicorns are a real thing. So yes, I could really use all the explaining."

"Well, my dear, you are actually inside that book I gave you. It was blank because it will contain your story, once you have your adventure, of course. Then, the pages will fill with your actions, thoughts, and deeds. Welcome to your very own Fairytale!" She says that last part with a flourish of her hand, waving vaguely at the forest around us.

I burst out laughing.

It might sound a little hysterical, and it might go on for a bit too long, but come on, she can't be serious?! Things like this don't happen in real life. Then again, I am fervently petting what seems to be a unicorn. This shop owner isn't quite like any person I've ever come across before either; so silent, so swift, definitely taller now than before, she has commanded me with her words more than once, and her eyes...There's a gentle touch to my shoulder, breaking me from my thoughts.

"Are you alright? I understand that it's a lot to take in?"

Oops, I can feel that my face has frozen into total blankness. People don't like my blanked-out face but that's just how it stays sometimes when I'm not thinking about it. Must be doubly upsetting now with the added tears from my hysterical laughter clinging to my cheeks.

"S-sorry," I stammer, "trying to take it all in. So, this is really for real, like for real for real? Not some joke or dream or concussive hallucination, right?"

"Oh, my dear, do you not feel the land beneath your feet and the breeze within your hair? Do you not hear the babbling brook and the birds around you?" She's cocked her head and is giving me a crooked, indulgent smile. "Can you not smell the divine scent of our magical equestrian friend here and the crisp clean air around you? Do you have so little faith in all your senses?"

A line from Scrooge immediately comes to mind regarding bad bread or cheese affecting said senses. Shaking my head of those thoughts, I take in a deep breath to calm and steady myself. The urge to cry is coming on strong, I can feel it bubbling up.

"Okay, I am going to choose to believe that all this is real until proof to the contrary is presented to me. I have been sucked inside a book to a magical fairytale land."

"Excellent!" she exclaims with a clap of her hands before I can continue, startling our unicorn a bit. Damn, this little lady must really love pets since she didn't bolt. Which is good, considering I haven't stopped this entire time.

"Now, I am going to need your verbal consent before we continue. So tell me, will you heed the Call to Adventure?!" she loudly proclaims while throwing her arms wide and looking expectantly at me.

"Um, ah, can you tell me what that means exactly? I don't really know what you expect of me, or what I should do, or what's going to happen if I say yes."

"Well the gist is this; if you agree to answer the call, you will set out from here onto whatever type of adventure or quest you fancy. Killing a foul beastie, plundering treasure, overthrowing a wicked king, helping out a village of townspeople in some way, training yourself in the arcane arts, falling in love," she says with a wink. "You know, the usual. Then, once your tale is complete, your goal reached, your 'The End' as it were, I will come back to collect you from your story and plop you back into your humdrum life once more. But heed this, once I leave you here, you will not see me again until your story is concluded. You will not be receiving undue Divine help from the outside source that is me. Once I leave, everything that follows is up to you and whatever friends, lovers, or companions you acquire." Fully ignoring the unicorn now, she continues.

"So what do you say, are you ready for a change of pace in your life? Are you ready to forge a new you and have some much needed fun and excitement, if you don't mind me saying?" She adds a slight smile in an attempt to take the sting from that comment. "When you were a child did you not ever wish you could dive into the books you were reading? Now is your one and only chance. For if you say no, we will immediately return to the real world, and you will never see me or my bookshop again. Choose wisely, my dear." She then steps back, giving me space and time to think.

She is right. I mean, who hasn't wished they could be whisked away into a magical land or help out the heroine in their latest binge-reading obsession, or heck be the heroine herself. And if I say no...I know I will regret it till the end of my days. I mean, what is the worst that could happen? The hero always makes it to the end, and I'm still not sure I believe this is real, anyway. I take a few deep inhales and exhales, smelling that sweet cotton candy from heaven. It's so hard for me to make decisions, and I usually take a long time mulling things over while making pros and cons lists. But it seems like I don't have that luxury with this one.

With one more quick breath through the nose, I straighten myself and draw my shoulders back. I've made my decision.

"I agree." My words seem to echo through the trees and a kind of zing goes through my body. Oh my, that felt ominous.

"Perfect! Now let's get you properly outfitted for your grand journey upon this land. First, let's get you some proper walking boots." I look down at my feet to realize I'm barefoot, chipped nail polish and all. When I look back up, she's holding a pair of boots out to me. Where did she get these all of a sudden?

"Put them on now. I want to make sure you know how to lace them up, so you can get them on and off by yourself in future." I begrudgingly say thank you and goodbye to the unicorn, then sit on a fallen log as she shows me how to wear the stockings I find inside said boots. She then gives me a quick tutorial on how to criss-cross the laces quickly and effectively. The boots fit perfectly. Next she snaps her fingers and I am suddenly wearing a Ren Faire-type top, skirts, and bodice. Wow! She then hands me a bag that also came from nowhere.

"Within, you will find two more changes of clothes and stockings, a cloak, a sleeping gown, a silk head wrap for that amazing hair of yours, toiletries, a few hearty apples, a container of water, and a bag of coin. You will need to find a way to make more, but what I have given will get you started. Here is a menstruation cuff," she slips a silver bracelet on my wrist that kind of hums with energy at first, then resizes on its own to fit me perfectly. "So you don't have to worry about bleeding or babies on your journey." Woah, this woman has thought of everything! No period and no babies? Perfection. No pregnancy trope for me. I chuckle at myself for thinking of all this in book terms. But if this woman is to be believed, a book is indeed what I am in. Creating a story for that blank tome she handed me.

The shop owner then touches two fingers to my forehead. I see a bright light and instantly get a bit of a headache. Ouch!

"That, my dear, was some knowledge you will need in order to move about these lands. How to speak and read the common tongue, how the money system works, etc. Unfortunately, your head may hurt for a time."

"Yes, I am feeling that already. But thank you, all this is absolutely amazing. It's like having my very own fairy godmother, to be honest." The shop owner lifts the back of her hand to her mouth again and kind of titters. Not quite sure what that means.

"I do believe that is everything. Come, I shall accompany you to the main road as it's not far. Don't want you to starting off your adventure by wandering around these woods all alone." She flashes that wicked half grin at me, but before I can ask her what it was for, she goes on, "Oh, here is some trail mix. You should probably eat up now."

Chomping down on this mix of nuts and dried berries, I recall the events of my day. What a wild ride this has been! The more I think on it, the more dream-like it sounds. I start the day at work, tell off a customer, then quit. I find a mysterious bookstore, get pulled into a book, am transported to a magical land while asleep, pet a unicorn, decide to go on an adventure, then get a new wardrobe and magical items. Yep, this definitely sounds like one of those all-night crazy dreams that blend one into another.

"Here we are! Now, my dear, which way will you choose? Left or Right?" I step out onto the dirt road and glance in either direction. They both look the same to me, long and flanked by trees on both sides.

"I'm not sure. Which way do you think I should go?" I ask while turning back to her, but she's gone. I do a couple of circles and walk back a bit into the woods, but can't see her anywhere. Guess it's time for me to start this new adventure of mine all on my own.

"Oh no, my cat!"

Chapter 3

Torben

"What are your plans for the day, son?" Ma asks while kneeling amongst her herbs in the garden. She's so entrenched that I can barely make out her shape within them. Her question catches me as I'm about to stride into the tree line, but I stop and turn in her general direction to answer.

"Um, going out to find an amiable tree for the Farris commission."

"Ah, well, if you find any fairy ring mushrooms while you're out, snag some for me. I haven't come across any yet this season and would love to have some."

"Of course. I'll keep my eyes peeled. If Uncle comes by let him know I've finalized the plans and will be starting on the project soon." I give my mother a wave that she doesn't see, and make my way into the forest.

What a perfect day to source some wood. Though Uncle and I have stores set aside, I've found that when taking on a special commission I have better success choosing a new tree specifically for that project. When the wood knows and agrees to what it's going to be transformed into, it just seems to work with you more easily. As if it's assisting in its own rebirth, rather than me forcing it into existence.

I have no particular spot in the forest in mind today, so I decide to let my feet carry me to where I need to go. Given that it's such a perfect spring day I may ramble along the all too familiar paths more than usual. It's after a little break where I sit to eat some wild berries that my entire life changes.

I can smell my Mate. I can smell my Mate! And she smells amazing!

I recognize them as a female from her scent, her wonderfully magical, enticing scent. I have dreamed of this day since boyhood. Asking my parents to tell the tale of their meeting over and over. Pestering every mated bear in the Clan for their story too. I wanted to learn as much about it as possible to make sure I didn't miss it. It's exactly like they all said; there is no mistaking this smell for any other.

I shift into my bear form and run in the direction of her scent. As a Grizzly, I can make much better time getting to her. I can't wait to meet her, to start our life together. I just hope I'm not a disappointment to her in any way, as that would be truly devastating.

I've been told before that I am a good-looking male. I'm big and strong, as any wood-splitter should be. My human form isn't overly hairy, though I have a beard and a nice patch of chest hair. My long hair is a simple brown with some lighter streaks from the sun. I also now have the slightest of tans from being outdoors. Goddess, I really hope that she finds me appealing and not too boring. There is nothing my Mate could do to be anything less than perfection in my mind.

I feel favored by the Fates already for pairing me with a female. Though I would have loved a male Mate with all my heart, I have to admit I've always been partial to females. My heart sings in my chest, my inner bear urging me on, *faster, faster!*

Her smell is running quickly my way. My heart flutters at the thought that she may be as eager as I am to meet. Is she riding a unicorn? I come upon the beast and stop it. Disappointment fills me as I realize my Mate is not with the creature, only her aroma. Goodness, she must really love petting unicorns for her scent is all over its left side. I quickly decide that this is a good thing. It means my Mate is kind and gentle and sweet. She must be all these things in abundance for an adolescent unicorn to allow such prolonged petting. They are usually quick to run off after only a few moments of attention. It's the older ones that truly enjoy affection, praise, and companionship.

I let the beast continue on its way as I resume running to my Mate.

A house, I must build her a house first thing! I have a few spots in mind, but I will leave the decision up to her. Wherever she wants I will build it along with all the furnishings inside. I may not be good at much, but carpentry is my trade and I will lavish my new Mate with any item she desires.

I'll make sure she has a garden, find that flower unicorns love, and plant them all over the perimeter of our homestead. I can't remember what the flower's called, but I will find it for my Mate who loves unicorns so much. There shall not be a day that goes by where she does not get to see or pet a unicorn.

I still can't believe this is happening. I mean, it felt the same as any other day in the forest, looking for the perfect tree to chop down. Maggie Farris has asked me to craft a new wooden tub for her and her mate. They are both getting older and the heat of a hot bath helps their joints, but their current tub is far too low now. Plus, I think they enjoy soaking together and want more space. I hope she doesn't get too upset about the possible delay. When a mating happens, other things slip away for a time, or so I've been told.

This couldn't be happening at a more perfect time. Spring has begun and all the flowers are in bloom. What a wonderful season for a mating ceremony! The Fire Festival will be coming up soon too. Wait, this means I'm going to have my Mate for the next Fire Festival! I don't know if bears can blush but I can feel heat in my cheeks, for sure. Though I am no stranger to coupling at a Fire Fest, to have one's mate to join with...it's a happiness I have much anticipated. Not that my previous partners for such events haven't been great, I've just never really felt that spark or the true connection I crave. Someone who loves, cherishes, and desires me as I am, flaws and all. Someone I'll actually be able to hold a conversation with. I pick up my pace.

There she is! I can glimpse her now through the trees. Looks as though she is walking to the main road, eating something, and in the company of another female. I'm not quite sure what the other female is though. My nose hasn't ever smelled anything like it, but I do sense she has power. Lots of power.

I begin to wonder that my Mate hasn't smelled me yet. So I slow down and stay back, don't want to barrel right into that being, or interrupt my Mate. Now that I've taken the time I suddenly realize the smell of my Mate is human, fully human?! Which is odd. There aren't many full humans anymore, at least not so far from their towns or the occasional one that pops up in the Fae Courts. Suddenly my heart sinks a little. Humans don't have mates, do they? This means she may not know about mates or mating bonds at all. I sit down roughly and stare at the ground feeling dejected.

I hadn't expected that. From the stories I've heard, all parties knew what was happening, what it meant. But if she doesn't know, if she doesn't feel it too, doesn't feel how I feel... There is a clutching at my heart and my inner bear rumbles at the notion of rejection.

Then we will make her feel it too, my inner bear interjects into my racing thoughts. *Make her fall in love with us, or ask her to become a shifter so she can feel the mating call. I like both options.*

"No," I quietly vocalize my reply, "if she becomes a shifter, it will be a choice she makes for herself, not for me. I will not pressure, trick, tempt, or convince her to do it. I will love her the way she is, no matter what she is." My bear takes a moment before replying.

Well, we will woo her then. Make her fall in love the human way.

"Easy for you to say, you're not the one who has to talk to her. You know how fumbled I get around females. Every partner I've had has pursued me. I've never been the one to initiate anything. How am I going to do this without scaring her off or weirding her out? How am I going to make her fall in love with me?"

But this isn't any female, this is your Mate! Whether she knows it yet or not. You will be able to woo her since she is the one you are meant to be with. It just turns out it's going to take more work than you thought.

My inner bear is right; we are meant to be together, and so I will be able to do this. I hope. My eagerness and resolve somewhat restored, I get back up and follow her once more.

I have slowly gotten closer, and in that time the powerful female has disappeared, which I am both glad and mad about. Glad that I won't have to try and deal with her and mad that she has left my Mate all alone in the woods. These woods typically aren't dangerous, but anything could happen! She's only a human without any magic or healing attributes that I can sense. What if she fell and broke her leg? No one would find her for a long time. What if something came along and ate her or took her? It's a good thing I am here now to watch over and protect her as she travels. I've decided to keep my distance and follow her for now while I think of a way to get her to like me. I'm sure having a big strange male, or a big bear, following her would not be a thing she would appreciate. I can't imagine having my Mate scared of me in any way. My heart aches at the thought. So for now, I will watch and wait till it's more appropriate to introduce myself.

I could watch my Mate walk all day. I've never seen a more beautiful female in my life. Her hair is red and wild and curly; bouncing as she moves. Flying away here and there as the wind catches it. She has a wonderful scattering of freckles all over her face, arms, and chest. I'm eager to see if they cover her whole body. My guess is they do, and I want to kiss every last one of them. The thought of kissing her all over makes me blush again, at least as much as a bear can blush.

Those thighs, so round and plump like the rest of her. I want to grab a handful and feel the give of them beneath my palms and fingers. Oh, how I would love to sink my teeth into her ass. That wonderfully round and meaty ass. And her breasts, did I mention her breasts? I sometimes quietly run past her so I can sit and watch them jiggle as she walks toward me. I can't decide which is better, watching her walk away from me, or watching her walk toward me. Either direction seems to set me off, to be honest.

I have never lusted or desired a person like this before. Never. I seem to have a one-track mind, and it hasn't been set on that topic so much since my body started down its path to adulthood. I think this is even worse. I'm having the hardest time even thinking about anything else but her. Oh, I want to drizzle honey all over those magnificent breasts then lick it all off while she squirms and moans beneath me.

Hmm, that sounds good to me, my inner bear chimes in.

I shake my head in an attempt to clear my mind of such thoughts. There will be none of that until she likes me enough to allow such things. I need to get to know her, to learn about her. I need to listen to everything she says. Thankfully, while she's walking, she is talking a lot. Some things I don't understand but I am getting a clearer picture of who she is as she seems to be talking out all of her inner thoughts. Of course, she believes she is alone, and I probably shouldn't be listening. But I need all the information I can get if I am going to have any chance of getting my Mate to fall in love with me. Plus, her chatter is so cute, I could listen to her talk all day.

She talks a great deal about hallucinations, which worries me at first, but after listening longer, I suspect she's just referring to magical things. Being transported, petting a unicorn, items being summoned, are all completely normal to me. This further proves my assumption of her being from a human city. My fears at being able to win her affections increase as it really sinks in that she doesn't feel the mating urges. If she did, she would have sought me out by now. I've been around her a good part of the day, and she hasn't even noticed anyone is following, let alone her mate.

You must be strong and not give up before even trying. My bear is right. The fight for my Mate hasn't even begun yet.

I keep my distance as I continue to follow her. Listening to her talk about hobbits, whatever those are, and other stories she's heard about or read. She also doesn't really seem to know where she's going, only that she's following this road. She breaks into a song about following a yellow brick road for a time, which lifts her spirits, though it only confuses me more. As far as I know, there is no wizard along this road, and I've never heard of a place called Oz. Hope my poor Mate hasn't become lost, been told lies, or led astray somehow by that powerful female she was with earlier.

Chapter 4

Silvia

Y ou know, in all those fantasy books I've read, they always talk about walking everywhere and how long it takes to get from point A to point B. But I've never really appreciated how long and how awful it is. Until now. I have been walking for what feels like FOREVER! I have not seen one other person, cart, horse, or any sign of civilization since I set foot on this road. Nothing but trees, forest, flowers, birds, and that one mountain way over there. Not even any signs pointing to, "Such-N-Such Town" or saying, "X Miles to Whatever Landmark."

Oh, it was fun at first. I haven't been out of the city in a while and haven't walked out in nature for even longer. As lovely as it is in games, there's nothing quite like having the experience in real life. For the first hour or so, I would marvel at the largeness of a tree, the cuteness of a mushroom, or the abundance of moss. In between my bouts of, "Oh my gawd, what have I done?!," and, "Is any of this even real?," or, "If I die, I am haunting my boss and that bookshop lady!" While the fresh air feels nice on my face, my feet have been killing me since that one-hour mark.

But my panic didn't really start sinking in till the sun began setting and the sky started changing colors. I don't know how to start a fire or build a shelter. I don't know what mushrooms or berries are safe to eat. And I certainly don't know how to kill or catch anything to survive. The closer the sun gets to the horizon the more certain I become that I am going to be sleeping out in the woods tonight all alone. Even thinking about that has my bottom lip quivering and tears beginning to form in my eyes. So, if the shop owner was telling the truth and this becomes a story that people read in the real world, take my advice and start training now. Go on some hikes, build up your stamina, learn some survival skills. Warning given, my conscience is clear. Oh, and maybe learn the best ways to use the restroom in the woods; now that was an embarrassing and humbling experience.

Just as I am about to totally lose it and start crying here in the road, I smell a fire. As I look up above the trees, I can see a single stream of smoke. It must be coming from up the road, hopefully not too far. Assuming it's a controlled fire since there is only a single small column of smoke, I pick up my pace down the road in search of its source and hope it is something friendly.

Then I see it, complete with a sign hanging out front with the name The Wandering Mead. It's a tavern or inn, hopefully both, and I've never been more relieved or happy to see a building in my whole life!

The door to The Wandering Mead is wide open so I walk right in. There is so much activity and noise going on inside that I pause for a moment at the threshold to take it all in. I first notice the big fireplace opposite the door on the other side of the building. In between it and me are tables of varying sizes, some for large groups and some just for two. A few more tables line the walls, as well as some in little alcoves. Oh good, introverts can hang out here too.

All along the right wall is a large, tall wooden bar complete with tapped barrels behind it.

Only after I notice the major features of the building do I finally take in the wide array of people...creatures...beings? I'm not quite sure what is appropriate here. There are wings of many varieties, tails of all kinds, and a wide range of sizes and colors. Many sport fangs, either a few or a mouth full. Pretty sure I get a glimpse of a woman with blue skin, but I lose her in the mass of bodies moving, talking, laughing, and eating. At least everyone seems to be jovial, which helps put me at ease. Mostly. I guess I really am in a fairytale book because I have certainly stumbled upon a real life Fantasy Tavern.

Since I must do something before I start getting weird looks for standing around and gawking at everything, I plaster a smile on my face and walk quickly to the bar. There are several empty stools at this end, so I claim one. It's a very clean bar, which is nice, and they have a few menus perched up here for customers. So I grab one and start perusing it. Yep, that is definitely a different language, but I actually understand what it says. Guess that little spell worked. Glad to know I didn't suffer an hours-long headache for nothing.

As I am marveling at my new reading abilities, the person manning the bar comes up to me. I first notice her light pink hair and linebacker frame with muscular shoulders and arms. Then I notice the rest of her looks to be a chestnut and white dappled horse with a white tail that also sports a streak of light pink. This barmaid is a centaur, a real honest to goodness centaur! And I am staring like I was raised in a barn.

"Love your pink hair. It really suits your tanned skin tone." Gosh, I hope that covers up for why I was staring. Plus, a compliment never hurts. Her hand automatically reaches up and fingers a lock of her hair. It's about shoulder length, beach curl wavy, and shaved on one side.

"Aw, thanks," she says kind of bashfully. "My name is Rosy, so it just sorta felt like the right color to choose. Your hair is also quite lovely. Is that your given hair color?"

"Yes, it is actually, but my poor curls are a hot mess right now. They are going to take a long time to sort out. But thank you."

"Well, I think you look absolutely ravishing, in that wind swept kind of way," an rougish male voice interjects. I turn my head to see a mostly transparent man has taken the stool next to me. Well, he's standing where the bar stool is, giving the impression he is sitting there. Ghostly white and slightly blurry on the edges, it appears he was dressed well when he died, and he sports a low ponytail held by a ribbon in a bow. Several inches shorter than me, with a small potbelly, he looks like a guy in his fifties. The phrase 'gone to seed' comes to mind. My eyes are definitely as big as saucers at this point, and my brows are now within my hairline.

"I know, I know, my sweetling, it's not everyday you get to see such a companionable ghost. But here I am. This is my tavern actually," he says while spreading his arms, gesturing about the place.

"Theodore, this hasn't been your establishment in a very long time," Rosy says through gritted teeth. "You know good and well that this tavern is mine."

"Yes, yes," the ghost waves his hand dismissively through the air, "technically, I guess it does belong to you now. But enough about us, I want to know more about this lovely creature. Tell me, where have you traveled from?"

"She's a full human, Theo," a wafer-thin woman with iridescent wings chimes in as she walks by. "Must be from one of their towns since she doesn't have a Fae escort or scent upon her."

"Oh my goodness, child!" the ghost exclaims. "Whatever are you doing so far from your home? Wait, don't tell me; you are off adventuring, aren't you?" I slightly nod, as he's not totally wrong. "I knew it! I knew it as soon as I saw your visage step through the door into my fine establishment. I said, 'Theodore, that's a lass who has taken her destiny into her own hands.' I took a couple years off for adventuring too after my schooling and apprenticeship. A fine and noble tradition, indeed. How goes it?"

"Well, actually so far it's been walking, walking, and more walking. Oh, I did get to pet a unicorn! That was amazing."

"Theodore," Rosy interjects while pinching the bridge of her nose, "can't you see the lady is hungry and exhausted? Go regale someone else with your stories, or better yet cross over already."

"Yes, you are quite right and prudent as ever Rosy, my sweet. Please get this fair girl a hearty meal and a place to sleep at once." With that he waft-walks over to a large table, full of patrons.

"Sorry about him," Rosy says. "Can't seem to get rid of him or convince him to move on. He died of a heart attack in his sleep but swears-"

"It was poison!" Theo declares from the middle of the tavern. "Someone poisoned me and I shall not move on till my killer is dead or brought to justice. To think my heart gave out on me is preposterous! I was as healthy as a horse, I tell you." Theo is quickly silenced by a glare that speaks of death and pain from Rosy. "No offense intended my dear Rosy, no offense." Under Rosy's intense gaze, Theo silently glides as far from the bar as possible.

Rosy directs her gaze back to me, thankfully no longer carrying the menace it had recently directed at Theo.

"Can I get you something to eat, honey, and do you need a place to lodge for the night?"

"Yes, and yes! I do need somewhere to sleep and hopefully a place to bathe as well, if that's possible? And I'm starving! What would you recommend?"

"All of our rooms have private washrooms and soft beds. I'll have our lad show you to one, so you can clean up while I get your dinner ready. Personally, I would recommend today's special: rabbit stew served in a bread bowl with a side of fresh apple pie as dessert. How does that sound?"

"It sounds amazing, actually," I say earnestly. I haven't had rabbit since before my grandfather passed. Plus I'm so hungry I could eat a...well, ya know. Rosy calls for a boy named Kor to show me up to my room. He quickly grabs a key and races up the stairs. I take them at a more moderate pace since I now feel like an extremely old lady, sore all over. I find him waiting in front of a door which must be to my room. He unlocks it, hands me the key, and dashes back down the stairs. How I wish I had his energy!

Inside, I find a cozy little room with a window. There is a full-size bed against a wall, a full-length mirror that I wish I hadn't glanced in, a little dresser, a chair, and a door to a washroom with a tub and an odd toilet. Once I use the toilet, I learn that it must be magic or something, seeing as how whatever goes in disappears and I don't have to worry about the flushing situation. The sink, which boasts a series of colored jewels at the top, has a new little bar of handmade soap upon it. Through some trial and error, I learn that a quick tap on the clear gem turns the water on and off, blue is for colder water, while red is for hotter. Easy enough. I wash my face and arms and do what I can with my hair.

Taking the coin pouch from my bag, I stuff it down my bodice, so I can pay without getting robbed in the meantime. Then, I make my way back down the stairs and to the bar. My dinner, water, and I'm guessing mead, is waiting for me at my spot along the bar when I get back down. It smells divine. Maybe the whole day hasn't been so bad. Though I do wish that big guy over there would stop staring at me, or maybe blink a little. Starting to get a little creeped out over here.

Sure, he's a looker, built like a lumberjack. His close-cropped full beard doesn't hide his strong chin and pleasant face. His chocolate colored hair is kinda cool, shaved on the sides with a man-bun on top. But as all us ladies know, a pretty face can hide danger too.

Chapter 5

Torben

I wait to enter The Wandering Mead since I don't want it to look like I am following her, even though technically I am. My bear wants me to go in right away, but I wait for as long as I can handle. Which ends up not being very long at all. I enter in time to see my Mate following a boy child up the stairs to the rooms. I want to follow her there too, but quickly realize that would be a terrible idea. I can smell where she was sitting at the bar, so I choose an alcove not too far away. Hopefully, here I won't be bothered by others but will be able to see her if she returns. I've been here a few times in my life and I might know some here, but I don't want them to distract me from my goal. I have to find a way to talk to her.

I absently order whatever the special is tonight and wait for my Mate to return. Her food gets set on the bar, which somewhat upsets me. They should have waited for her to return; what if it gets cold? She soon descends the stairs looking even more radiant than before. Her cheeks are all rosy from the wash she clearly gave her face, and her hair has been slightly rearranged and tamed. By the Goddess, I can't take my eyes off her!

I listen in as she occasionally speaks with Rosy, the owner. They seem to make easy conversation with each other and I wonder if Rosy knows my Mate, where she's from, her likes and dislikes, her name. I would love to know her name.

Not for the first time I find myself wishing I was more like my sister who can easily talk to anyone at any time. She has no problems speaking with people, even complete strangers. How would I even start a conversation? I've already been sitting at my alcove for a while absently eating my meal, so I can't move to the bar now. That would look too obvious and weird. I should have sat at the bar, not in this alcove. What was I thinking? The goal was to talk to my Mate, not ogle her. I've been doing that all day.

"Hey, Rosy," I hear my Mate whisper, "is that big guy still staring at me? He's been doing it since I came down, and it's kinda creeping me out at this point. Every time I glance back his eyes are on me."

Creep. My Mate already deems me to be some weirdo and I haven't even met her yet. I make eye contact with Rosy, who is now glaring at me, so I shift my eyes to my food and leave them there. This is going so terribly. How can I be doing everything so wrong already?! Finding your Mate is supposed to be an amazing experience, not this tricky mess.

"No, he's not anymore. So Silvia, have you thought about what your plans for your adventure will be? Anything you hope to come across or accomplish? I always thought that, if I ever went adventuring, I'd try sailing. I've never been on a ship but have always wanted to. I bet a centaurs strength would come in handy. You?"

Silvia, my Mate's name is Silvia. I can feel myself grinning like an idiot at my stew.

"No, I don't imagine sailing would be right for me. I get motion sickness too easily for a voyage to be fun. I do enjoy helping people though. I have always liked being useful to people or completing tasks. Nothing quite as satisfying as crossing off a to-do list, ya know? So maybe I'll come across someone needing assistance."

My Mate is so kind and honorable, wanting to aid others in need. Maybe there is a way I can help her help others? I am pretty big and strong, even for a bear shifter. Besides, I also enjoy lending a hand. Perhaps we could go adventuring together, walking the roads and hiking side by side. There goes my silly grin again.

"Hmm," Rosy looks deep in thought as she puts her hand to her chin. "Well, I do recall that Oakveil Village always seems to have signs and notices of Help Wanted or chores needing doing on their town board. It would get you started and could earn you some coin." My Mate's eyes and body seem to light up at that.

"Are you saying that there is a cute little town near here that has a real noticeboard where people can request help with things and anyone can accept to take on the job? Are you saying those really exist here?" Silvia then whispers to herself, "Totally like in my games."

"Yes? There are always things that people may not have the time, energy, or knowledge to do themselves. Sometimes chores are too much to do alone, especially during different seasons. It's not that uncommon, though I've never heard of it being a game before. But if you're willing, I'm taking some folks and things into Oakveil tomorrow. You could tag along."

"Let me sleep on it tonight, but I'm pretty sure I'll end up taking you up on that offer. What time are you leaving?" my Sweet Mate asks.

"Oh, we won't set out till after breakfast is finished and cleaned up. Mid-morning to early afternoon, I'd say. So you have some time to decide."

"Thank you so much, Rosy. For your offer and your time. I've really had the strangest day and your kindness has been super amazing. Sorry if I ended up keeping you too much from work with my talking and questions. Thanks for being so nice to the new guy." I can't help but steal another glance at my Mate after her words, so sweet and considerate. Rosy blushes wildly and has her hand on the back of her neck.

"Oh, don't worry about it at all. It's kinda my job to listen to people and serve them. Guess I like helping too." With that, Rosy moves down the bar to refill the mug of an Orc.

While feigning to gaze out of the tavern window, I watch through the side of my vision as sweet Silvia finishes her apple pie. Which she must find extremely delicious because she is rocking side to side, sometimes letting out a soft moan that does things to my nether region. I find that I must adjust myself several times. Mental note, always have fresh pie at home.

Once done, she says goodnight to Rosy and walks back up the stairs to her room. Since that is a sight I will never pass up seeing, and her voluptuous backside is now pointed directly at me, I dare to watch her fully once again. I must stare after her for a while because the next thing I know Rosy is at my table glaring down at me. Seeing how centaurs aren't known for sneaking around, I'm not sure how I missed her approach.

I know why you missed it, my bear intercedes.

"Torben, why are you staring after that female like she's a delicious meal and you're starving?" Rosy loudly hisses at me.

Because she is a delicious meal and I can't wait to eat her all up. Shh, I say to my bear.

"H-hey Rosy."

"Don't you 'hey' me! You made her very uncomfortable, and I know your mother raised you better than that. Explain yourself."

"S-sorry," is all I can stammer out. I don't really know Rosy and it's always been difficult for me to talk to people, especially females, I don't already have a relationship with.

"First off, that isn't an explanation. Secondly, I'm not the one who you should be apologizing to. Now out with it, what were you doing?"

"M-mate," I say quickly before I can think. "S-she's my Mate, Rosy." Why did that have to come out sounding so pitiful and dejected? And now she's looking at me all confused.

"What do you mean she's your mate? If she's your mate, then you two should...oh no!" Her hand comes up to cover her mouth, her eyes are wide. "She's human and they don't have mates, and you're-"

"Terrible at talking to anyone, but especially inept at conversing with the opposite sex," Theodore interjects as he slides into the alcove seat across from me. "But excellent catch there, my boy. A positively radiant and charming young lass. Now, aside from ogling her, what are your plans for courting the lucky lady?" I don't know why he is wiggling his eyebrows at me like that. I must be silent for too long because he continues, "Come come, don't be shy with us. We are here to help you, aren't we Rosy dear?" I look over to see that Rosy is now rubbing both of her temples while her eyes squeezed shut.

"Theo, he doesn't need your help. He merely needs to talk to her. Go away, please." She sounds truly exasperated.

"Nonsense! Of course he needs my assistance. Why, I have wooed and bedded many a young lady in my day. How many females have you ensnared, my sweet Rosy?" Now he is looking at her mischievously, and she is fully blushing from ear tips to cheeks.

"Torben, please follow me outside so we can have a more private conversation," she says through gritted teeth before turning to walk out the front door. As I get up to follow, I can hear Theo sputtering.

"Now, that's not fair! You realize I can't leave the building, and I can be of real help to the lad. I know my way around a female. Torben! Torben, my boy, come back and talk to me after she's done with you out there."

Rosy has taken a seat in the grass on the side of the road opposite the tavern. The moon is almost full so it's more than bright enough. The crickets are chirping, and the breeze feels good against my face. I take a deep breath in then sit down not too far from the centaur. Though I do stare at the ground instead of her, and pick up a blade of grass to fiddle with.

"Ok, so let me make sure I have everything straight here. You came across Silvia today and realized she's your mate?" I nod my head yes. "Then you realized she was fully human and therefore does not know what it means to find your mate or anything really about mating culture?" Again, I nod yes. "So when did you find her, at the Tavern or on the road?"

"The road," I answer simply. No need to discuss my run through the woods, the unicorn, or the powerful Lady.

"Torben, how long have you been following her?" I don't answer. "Torben?" she says more insistently this time.

"Since after midday." Rosy is quiet for so long that I sneak a peek at her face. Her mouth is open and she is staring at me.

"You have been following her for half a day?!" I quickly bring my eyes back down to the grass.

"I, I didn't want to scare her. She was alone, and I am a bigger male." Wow, look at me, two whole sentences. She takes in a deep breath.

"Yes, yes, you are right. You were put in quite a hard spot and did what you thought best. I can see your reasoning, but you can't keep that up. Now that there are people around, you will need to talk to her." She scrubs a hand down her face. "This is quite the pickle you find yourself in Torben, but I will help however I can, for both your sakes. Do you need a room for the night?"

"I had better not. I'll sleep in the woods. I would appreciate a morning shower though." I'm on a roll, three sentences this time.

"Right. Just come see either Kor or me in the morning and we'll get you cleaned up. I'm guessing if she decides to go to Oakveil tomorrow with us you'll want to tag along?" I nod yes. "I figured as much. Well, I wish you and Silvia all the luck. This will be an interesting courting." With that she gets up and trots back to the tavern.

I shift into my bear form and choose a spot in the woods where I can see Silvia's window. To make sure she stays safe during the night, of course. It doesn't hurt that from here I can still smell the sweet scent of my Mate.

Chapter 6

Silvia

Once I'm in my room, I empty my bag and lay out all my new items on the bed to see what I've got. After taking inventory, I repack the bag, leaving out a nightgown, silk head-wrap, bathing items, and a wide-toothed wooden comb. I also leave out the one dress I have, hanging it to prevent wrinkles. Since I'll probably be visiting a new town tomorrow, I want to make a good first impression. Considering I'll be riding in a cart instead of walking, and the dress being the nicest looking of my clothing options, it seems like the obvious choice for tomorrow.

Because I am a little paranoid, I sneak out of my room to see if that big guy is still here. As I peek, I see that Rosy and Theo are speaking with him. Good! I hope they set him straight. Before I get back to my room, I run into Kor. He tells me to put anything I want washed into the white bag I'll find in my room and place it outside my door.

Now that I feel a bit safer, it's long past time for a bath. Al-though, I do slide the chair in front of my door and wedge it under the knob. Can't be too safe. I am a woman traveling alone in a strange land after all.

The bath is amazing. My poor aching feet really appreciate the heat. Surprisingly, the soaps that the bookshop owner provided me feel divine. After some testing I find that some are great for my curls too, allowing me to give them some much needed TLC. I stay in that bath till the water is lukewarm at best before I drag myself out.

I sit criss-cross-applesauce in the bed as I work on my hair, absently rocking side-to-side. That's when I finally start to cry. It's been threatening to burst since I stormed off from my job, and I'm honestly surprised it didn't happen before; like in the street, in the bookshop, in the woods when I was all alone and frustrated. Heck, the bath would have also been an excellent place to let it all out. But at least it waited till I was well and truly alone. I let my tears fall as I reflect on my out-of-pocket day. Still hard to believe that all this happened in a single day, to be honest.

What exactly does the future hold for me? How am I supposed to complete this adventure and get to 'The End' the shop owner mentioned? I was never given any direction, and I haven't a clue what I should be doing. In books, there's usually a goal or a quest with a roadmap of some kind to complete. I mean, even in games, there's a main story directive. Should I wait around the tavern and see if something pops up? Maybe some other adventurers I can tag along with? 'Adventuring' seems to be a thing here, so maybe others will show up mid-quest.

Perhaps I can do some side quests while I wait for the main quest to find me? That town's noticeboard does sound right up my alley. Those types of tasks are usually my favorite in games anyway. That is, if there's anything on it I can actually do. I don't really have the type of skill set typical for a fantasy realm. No magic, no birthright, no special sword or ring, no family secret, no one died and left me a farm to save. I only have myself and my administrative and customer support background. Oh wait, I do know how to care for bees! I used to help out my grandparents. That's a skill that could be useful, if anyone in that village has a hive and needs help.

Once done futzing with my hair, I wrap it up in silk for the night, find the white bag in a dresser drawer, stuff my worn clothes into it, then set it outside my door. After replacing the chair in front of said door, I hurry back to the bed and bury myself into the covers. It all really does feel cozy.

Lying here, I remember the shop owner's comment about having a 'black heart.' I'm starting to grow concerned with who or what I've made a deal with. Aren't there loads of stories and parables about not making deals with certain creatures? Too late now, I guess.

My dreams this night take a very interesting turn. At first, there was the usual 'late for school and I didn't study for the test' dream. Then, there's one about an endless mall with stores of every kind, selling anything I could ever want or need.

After my three a.m. bathroom trip, however, I fall into a dream that mainly stars that hulk of a man from the tavern. It starts with him in my doorway, watching me, but for some reason I'm not scared to find him there. I feel more protected and looked after than anything. Then, I reach out for him and he gathers me into an all-consuming hug. He makes me feel all safe and small in his arms, which is not an easy feat considering my full figure.

When I wake up in the morning, it still feels like he is holding me for a time, all loved and warm. Wow, these are some really good covers! Wonder why my mind conjured him of all people? He did have big burly arms and a wide chest good for snuggling, if you're into that kind of thing. Which I totally am. Wish I had gotten a better look at him now that he's been in my dreams. I actively tried not to peek since he was staring so hard at me, plus he was somewhat hidden in that alcove. Maybe I'll ask Rosy more about him. We'll see how I feel after breakfast.

Speaking of breakfast, the smell of it is wafting into my room, making my tummy growl in annoyance and anticipation. Better get up I guess, but I'm finding it difficult with how comfy and warm this bed is. So exquisitely cozy. My bladder eventually wins out. I wash my face with cold water in an attempt to help wake myself up more. It only helps a little, to be honest. My hair is looking so good this morning! Sure hope I can find this stuff the bookshop owner gave me in a shop somewhere, it's amazing. I give my curls a quick tousle as I watch in the mirror. Not too bad, if I do say so myself.

I get my boots on, move the chair back into its proper place, and strut out the door ready for a yummy breakfast. But I end up walking face first into something else that's yummy. A towering shirtless beefcake of a man's chest.

"Oh my gosh, I'm so sorry I-" have now lost the power of speech. It's the guy from last night, and he's standing in the hallway wearing only a towel wrapped around his waist. One hand is clutching the towel and the other is holding my shoulder to steady me, while his clothes have fallen into a pile on the floor. Shame he dropped the clothes instead of the towel. Wow, where did that thought come from?

If I thought he was a big fella before, it's nothing compared to him actually standing right next to me. I'm no shortie at five feet-seven inches, but he's got to be well over six feet tall. His shoulders are so broad they take up much of the hall, and his muscular chest is covered in hair. The perfect amount to run your fingers through. Glancing up to his face, I see that his beard is full, cut close, and lined to perfection. This man knows how to take care of himself, I'll give him that. His damp hair is out of its bun, swept to one side and hanging loose about his shoulder. His eyes are such a dark shade of brown that they almost look black, and if I wasn't so close, I would think they were. And his smell, it's intoxicating! He smells of the forest, of clean air, sawdust, and something else that's all his own.

Great, now I have become the staring creep. Fantastic Silvia, what a hypocrite.

"S-so sorry about that," I manage to stammer out as I bend down to pick up his clothes. "Here're your clothes, sir. Again, I am really sorry I wasn't paying attention. Must have been trying to get down to breakfast too quickly. I'm not usually this hungry in the mornings, but it smells so good, and given how delicious dinner was last night, I know I am in for a treat this morning. Also, didn't expect there to be a half naked man in the hallway either." I nervously laugh and wish I would shut up, but I can't seem to stop myself. "Not that I'm complaining of course because the view is nice. Not that you're some piece of meat for a woman to ogle or anything. Seems you take really good care of yourself is all.

Um, why didn't you put your clothes on before you came into the hallway?" Oh gawd, what am I saying?! I really hope he didn't hear the part about me liking the view. He opens his mouth to answer just as Kor races up and interrupts us.

"Sorry sir, I think I gave back the wrong clothes." I now realize I handed him back a small flower-patterned dress. Yep, that definitely wouldn't fit this man.

"Oh, well, that explains it then," practically flies out of my mouth. "Sorry to bother you. Hope you have a great day!" With a speed I didn't know I possessed, I hightail it past Kor and down the stairs. My whole face turning beet red from embarrassment, shame, and okay yeah I might be a little turned on too. But I mean who wouldn't be?!

I claim a seat in an alcove then hide my face behind my hands. What is wrong with me? I see one mostly naked, smoking hot man and babble like a brook. Get yourself together girl!

"Gooood morning!" I jump in surprise as Rosy greets me. "Oh, didn't mean to startle you there. Everything okay?"

"Oh, I would say everything is more than okay with Miss Silvia this fine morning. Wouldn't you agree, you naughty little tease you?" Theo says with wiggling eyebrows as he pokes his head through the ceiling. "She got herself one hell of an eyeful of Torben in the hall upstairs as he was trying to find his proper clothes. She practically plastered herself on him! Gave him a long look-over too, and went on a spiel that included saying he was a 'nice view' and calling him a 'piece of meat.' Rather interesting flirting technique, I must say. Said it all at breakneck speed too." The ghostly form in the ceiling chuckles at me. I'm so embarrassed that I feel like I am about to burst into flames.

"Theodore, you are not helping. Please leave," Rosy tells him sternly. "Can't you see she's embarrassed enough without you poking your head into her business and spreading it around. Now keep your trap shut and buzz off."

Thankfully, Theo leaves without another word after a brief staring contest that Rosy obviously wins. Before she can ask any questions, I find myself confessing.

"I bounced out of my room without thinking and literally ran into him in only a towel, which wasn't his fault since it seems he had no clothes to put on. I tend to babble when I'm nervous, and he's, ya know, not hideous to look at, so I ended up looking too long. Then, words kept falling out of my mouth, and now I don't think I can ever be seen by that man again." I pause to catch my breath and hide my face once more.

"Well, that might be a little difficult to do, honey," she retorts. "How about you sit here, calm down, and I'll get you some cold water? The breakfast is buffet style, but I can make you a plate and bring it to you if you want."

"Oh my gosh, would you please? If it's not too much trouble, that is. I feel like I'm going to explode from sheer embarrassment." Rosy chuckles, pats my shoulder, and trots away as I do my best to merge into the seat.

I eat breakfast without incident, and the cold water really helps. Thankfully, I haven't seen the man down here. He's probably hiding from me now.

"So, have you given any thought to finding some adventure in Oakveil?" Rosy asks some time later. "We'll be setting out in about an hour or so, if you're interested." Looks as though everyone else has eaten and Kor is cleaning up now. I've been too afraid to leave my seat.

"Yes!" I say a little too loudly. "Yes, I would really like to give that noticeboard you mentioned a chance." That, and there is no way I'm sleeping here another night in case Towel Man is staying again. No more run-ins for me, no siree. I had already decided to go anyway; this is now simply an added incentive.

"Great, I'll introduce you to my friend Ellis. They own the bakery in the town center."

After thanking Rosy again I quickly make my way back to my room, where I find my clean clothes waiting for me. I pack my few belongings then make my way outside. Might as well get some fresh air while I wait for my ride. Plus, the morning is beautiful and there's a cute little garden in the back that I want to look at. Thankfully, the wait goes by without incident.

"Anyone heading to Oakveil Village and wanting to travel with us better come on now," Rosy calls out. "We're about to hitch up and head out."

Rounding the corner to the front of the inn I witness Rosy and another centaur connecting themselves to a cart. I don't know what I expected but it wasn't that. Makes sense though now that I think about it. Interesting.

"Hey Silvia, come on over and climb into the back. This is my brother, Pip; he's the cook. Here, can you hold this when you get settled?" Rosy asks while holding up a basket. I make my way to the front of the cart, take a seat, and hold Rosy's covered basket in my lap.

"Hello Pip," I offer happily. "It's nice to finally meet the cook. Your food has been delicious and a much-needed comfort."

"Oh, um, hello. I don't usually talk to guests. Rosy hogs them all to herself and hides me away to slave in the kitchen." He gives me a wink, and his sister backhands him in the stomach with an audible 'ooph' from Pip. Pip is only an inch taller than his sister and has long white-blond hair in a loose French braid. His coat colorings are the same as Rosy, minus any pink additions.

Just then a little old man and woman climb into the cart. And when I say little, I mean little. They can't be more than three, or three and a half, feet tall. I realize I'm staring, but I can't look away. They are so cute! A true little old couple. I have to remind myself I am in a fantasy land and I should start viewing such things as normal, because here they are. I'm probably an oddity. No, I know I'm the strange one given where I came from. This is my new normal, for now anyway.

"I know what you're thinking, little lady," comes a slightly squeaky voice. "What are these two old Knockers doing so far from any mines, and in daytime no less?" He chuckles to himself. "Even the other Knockers from back home reckon we are an odd sort, so I don't take offense to your surprise. But the only way most people seem to travel around here is during the day, so we are making do with your strange waking hours."

"Oh, I'm sorry. I've never met a Knocker before. My name is Silvia. It's a pleasure to make your acquaintance." I hold out my hand for a handshake.

"Shh, shh, little girl! You can't be giving out your name like that. No telling who or what's around that should want it and take it."

"Oh, you silly old male. There's hardly any folk who do that kind of thing anymore," the wife says while smiling at her husband.

"Better safe than sorry, my love," he retorts as he tucks a blanket around both their laps. "Now don't you mind us over here. We're going to have ourselves a little cat nap during this trip. We're really starting to get used to this retirement lifestyle, and old people do so love our naps, no matter the time." With that, they snuggle into each other and are both sawing logs before we even move.

"Alright Torben, if you're coming you'd better get in now or walk," Pips remarks. The whole cart shifts to and fro as the Towel Man himself climbs into the back of the cart. Just my luck, the one person I've been trying to avoid is not only going to the same town I am but riding in the cart with me too. Great. Here's hoping that the village is close. And big.

My saving grace is the old couple asleep in the cart with us. Seems like we are both being considerate in not talking to avoid waking or disturbing them. No matter what the real reason may be, I am grateful for this excuse. No way my mouth can run away if I keep it closed, and no rebuke can come from him either.

The cart ride turns out to be quite lovely; with Rosy and Pip quibbling back and forth like siblings do. The scenery is beautiful, and the weather is wonderful. We even cross a stone bridge over a lively river, which I get way too excited about. With the little old couple here, this almost feels like taking a road trip with family. I get the familiar ping of heartache as I remember my grandparents. They would have loved all this. And yeah, I might have to hold back some emotions for a second there. But for the most part, I am enjoying my second day of adventuring.

Though every once in a while, I do feel the gaze of Towel Man on me. I really need to stop calling him that. What did Pip call him earlier? Tore Ben? I think that's what I heard. I'll ask Rosy to confirm once he separates from us. Every time I try to catch him watching me, he quickly looks away. Though one time, I was still looking at him when he looked in my direction again. Could have sworn I saw him blush at that. Is this man...shy? No, that can't be right. He's probably still embarrassed by what I did and said in the hallway this morning. Great, now I can feel my ears turning red. I nonchalantly bring my hair forward to cover them up.

After riding past some homesteads we get to Oakveil Village in no time. It's a cute little town with cobblestone roads, and structures of various shapes and sizes. Some are made all from wood, some from stone or brick, and some out of that whitewashed stuff with exposed wood beams. In the center of town, there is a large water fountain with shops all around it in a circle. All the shops have flowers in full bloom displayed in the windows, and some have outside seating areas. It all looks so picturesque I sigh in contentment. Oh yes, I am going to love it here.

Rosy and Pip circle the fountain and park the cart in a little alley in between two shops, a general store and a bakery.

"Okay, all safe to disembark!" Pip calls out. The Tore Ben guy hops out first while I gently wake the couple.

"Excuse me, sorry to wake you but we have arrived." I have to shake them a bit before they actually wake up, and then I have to repeat myself.

"Oh yes, yes, thank you little lady. We are deep sleepers, aren't we my love?" The old man folds up the blanket and puts it in his wife's bag. He takes her hand and leads her to the front. "Oh, why thank you, young sir. Awfully considerate."

I look up at the comment and see that not only has Towel Man found a little set of stairs but he is also holding onto the woman's hand to steady her as she climbs down. Once safely on the street, he does the same for the man, who thanks him once again for the assistance then says something about being old and whatnot. To be honest I don't pay close attention because now I am calculating what's about to happen. Once he's done helping the old couple, what will his next move be? Will he offer to help me, or will he walk away? I don't need the help as they did. But if he offers, will I accept or climb down on my own? What if he doesn't offer, how will that make me feel?

Before I can run though all the scenarios, the old Knocker couple is walking away and a big hand is being offered to me, though its owner is staring at the ground. Well, it feels rude not to take it; plus, I don't want to fall and ruin my new dress. So I place my hand in his and use the steps he found. His hand is strong and steady, warm with a hint of callus. Not in a bad way though, more in a well-used way. A man who works with his hands but still takes care of them.

"Thank you," I say once I'm on the street. He continues to hold my hand loosely until Rosy asks for the basket I'm holding. I slip out from his grasp and walk to her. Once I pass off the basket, I glance back to find that he hasn't moved and is looking at the hand that once held mine. He closes his eyes, then opens and closes his hand. Was that a Darcy hand flex? Did I just get a Darcy hand flex?! My heart flutters in my chest.

Chapter 7

Torben

S he took my hand. I can't believe that all worked out. I may never wash this hand again. I covertly inhale, savoring her lingering scent upon it. It's the same hand I used to keep her from falling over when she ran into me in the hallway this morning. I will forever remember the feeling of how warm and soft she was. She looks even more beautiful today than she did last evening. I, again, had a hard time keeping my eyes off her. I know she noticed since she caught me a few times. I really need to stop doing that, and I should apologize to her too. Better do that now, while she is still close and I have some courage left.

I'm still in shock that my plan actually worked. I thought about it the entire ride over here, wondering if she would let me help her down. If she saw how gentle I was with the little folk, it might make it easier to take my hand. I was worried I blew it for sure when she caught me staring, but she took my hand anyway. I'm smiling again and I don't care who sees it.

I look up to see Rosy pointing out some of the shops around the circle to my Mate. I catch Rosy's eye and I nod my head toward Silvia. She must understand what I want.

"If you wait right here in the alley," Rosy says loudly, "I'll go get Ellis and see if their room is still available. Be right back." She trots around the back of the bakery to enter that way and tells Pip she'll be back to help unload. Now's my chance.

I walk over toward my Mate, making sure not to get too close, and wait for her to notice me. She's gazing around with such a look that I wonder what her villages are like if this one intrigues her so. I could watch her all day. No, no, I'm here to apologize for staring and making her uncomfortable, not do it some more.

"Pardon," I muster up. Her big, beautiful green eyes turn to meet mine, her ears and cheeks instantly go pink. I'd better hurry. "Sorry about staring. I didn't mean to make you uncomfortable yesterday or in the cart." Her mouth has formed an O shape in surprise. I'm guessing she didn't expect an apology.

"Oh, yes, thank you. It did make me feel a bit uneasy yesterday, having a big strange man I didn't know drilling holes into me with his eyes. But then I wasn't that much better this morning, was I? And I really am sorry about that. I usually am more considerate of other people's feelings and space. Yet there I was eyeing you all over while you were in your own situation. Glad you did get your real clothes in the end. Not that you weren't rocking that towel or anything. Did you end up eating breakfast? I didn't see you down after. Of course, I probably scared you off."

"I ate before I bathed," I interject before she can continue. My Mate rambles when she's nervous. It's adorable. I wasn't quick enough this morning to say anything. That and I was so stunned she was even speaking to me.

We enjoyed her rambling very much. Indeed we did.

"Oh, that makes sense. Much more plausible than you being afraid of little ol' me. Not that I'm little by any means, but compared to you, I almost feel small." She rushes on quickly past that statement, but I catch it all the same. "So what brings you to Oakveil today? Anything fun? It is a wonderful day, isn't it? And the weather is so nice. I enjoyed the ride up here too, all that beautiful scenery."

"Yes, a very beautiful view." I marvel at my own boldness. It makes her blush return even deeper than before. "Sorry again about staring. I find it hard to keep my eyes away from you. You are the most beautiful thing I have ever seen." I didn't mean to say that out loud, and now I'm the one blushing like a fool. Eyes fully absorbed with the ground again, I quickly mumble, "Gotta go," and walk away as fast as possible.

Too far, that was too far. I can't believe I said that the first time I actually spoke to her. I walk straight across the main circle and splash some water on my face from the fountain.

Why are you so upset? You only told our Mate the truth. And I think she's even more beautiful when she is flushed. Makes her scent stronger. No need to be shy with a mate. As true as that is, she doesn't know we are mates and may not even know what that means. I don't want to scare her off with how strongly I feel. We need to take this slow and that statement was anything but slow.

I catch a glimpse of her with Rosy and Ellis across the way. She's safe there with them, and I need to make some plans. Yes, plans will help with this whole situation. First, I will tell my family where I am and what is going on. Second, I need to find a place in the village to stay so I can be near her. Finally, I need to come up with ways to speak with her. Maybe some topics? I run my hands along the sides of my head feeling the texture of my short hairs along my palms. I wish I were smarter, I wish I was better at speaking with people I don't know, and I wish I knew what the heck I was supposed to do. Following her around hoping for an opening while listening and learning from her is all that comes to mind right now.

With crafting, everything is laid out step-by-step. There's a plan, an order of operations. And if you mess up along the way, you can either try to salvage it or start all over. In the end, you're left with your completed creation. So simple and easy; why couldn't finding my Mate be like that? That's how it seems to happen for others. I take in a deep breath and blow it out. Well, no use crying over cracked wood. I've got a project that won't go like the rest but I will make something beautiful and unique out of it. I have to, for both our sakes.

Maggie Farris's new bathing tub! That was the whole reason I was in the woods yesterday and I've forgotten all about it. Okay, at least this is something I do know how to take care of. I'll go talk to Emna, who has a carpentry studio here in Oakveil, and see if she can spare the tools and space for me to work on Maggie's tub. Then I'll find a place to sleep, tell Ma what's going on, and maybe follow Silvia around some. I can't really handle the thought of being away from her for too long. I may have apologized for making her uneasy with my staring, but I didn't say I would stop. She's the best view we've ever seen.

I walk down the road away from the circle and find Emna in her shop talking with a customer. Emna is a partial Orc who trained under my uncle for a while when I was still his apprentice. She was journeying around learning from different crafters to 'expand her knowledge base.' She even trained a bit under a smith and can make some stunning nails, pins, and various decorative finishes for her pieces. Uncle Ulric was glad she settled and opened up shop so close.

"Well, Torben, as I live and breathe!" Emna exclaims upon seeing me. "I haven't seen you in some time. How's your family? What brings you over to my shop?" She claps my back hard while giving me a bear hug, nearly lifting me off my feet. She's a hugger Emna, which is always something I conveniently forget till I'm in one again.

"Family is good. Uncle loves the last batch of nails you sent him. Almost used them all up already, I believe. And I've come needing a favor."

"A favor you say! Well, let's go into my studio to discuss it." She leaves her apprentice in charge of the store-front then leads me to the back where the actual work happens. Grabbing two mugs, she fills them with warm apple cider and sets them down at a work table, hooking a stool with a foot to pull under her as she sits. "Have a seat and tell me what you need." I pull up another stool and sit across from her at the table, taking the warm mug to hold it in my hands. Oakveil Apple Cider is never a thing to pass up.

"I've got a large tub commission for Maggie Farris, but need to stay in Oakveil for a while. Something unexpected came up but I don't want to let Maggie down. I was hoping you might have some space for me to work on it while I'm in town. I'd need to use your tools, as well, since I didn't bring mine with me."

"Is that all?! I thought your Uncle had sent you here to sweet talk me into doing some big project with lots of work. But if space and tools is all you need then that's no problem whatsoever. All I ask is that you clean up after yourself each day, trying to set a good example for the boy. Maybe show him how you do things when he's not busy with me or chores. I'll set you up in the back since it's a bigger piece." We shake hands and the deal is done. "You got a place to stay already?" she asks as she gets up and starts walking to the back of the workshop.

"No, not yet. Stopped here first." I follow her while sipping my drink. I wonder if my Mate would like this cider. Most everyone does. I should make sure she gets to try some while she's in town.

"Well, if you don't have a particular place in mind already, I have an extra apprentice room right now. Had another one but he decided carpentry wasn't for him," she shrugs. "I think you'll fit in the bed," Emna says with a wink and a grin. "You'll have a room to yourself but will share the bathing room with the boy." I notice she hasn't gotten out of the habit of calling all apprentices 'boy' no matter the age or gender. As though they don't get names till they prove themselves. "Have an idea of how long you'll be staying?"

"That sounds perfect, thank you. And no, plans are still up in the air right now." I finish off my mug and take a look around the area she's given me to work in. Good light next to big windows and a large barn door, which is currently thrown wide open. There's a big table, sawhorses, and tools neatly organized along the wall. As I peer outside I see the place backs up to the woods. "Is there any place around you would recommend sourcing a large tree from?"

"Hmm, there's some pretty big ones that should suit your needs about a fifteen minute run straight back that way," Emna points out the barn doors. "Run for me anyway, you might have to shift to make it in that time." She slaps my back while laughing. Thankfully, I'm sturdier now than when I was a 'boy' so I manage to stay in place, mostly. "Come, I'll show you where your room is. Got plans for the rest of the day?"

"Some." I mean, following my Mate is kind of a plan.

"Well, when you decide to search for a tree to fell for your project, let me know. I want the boy to see how you speak to the trees. I'll even come and help if you give me the leftovers from the tree. Waste not, want not! And whatever tree you choose is sure to be a good one." That unexpected praise does make me look down at the ground. "Still have a touch of bashfulness I see. One day you'll learn to take a compliment to the face." She laughs again.

Chapter 8

Silvia

He thinks I'm the most beautiful thing he has ever seen. I think I might ride this high for the rest of my life! No man has ever said that to me, especially a stranger. Not even as a cheesy pickup line. Given all the staring, our interactions so far, how he blushed and practically ran away after saying it, I'm inclined to believe that it wasn't a line but the truth. Things are starting to click into place a bit more now.

And that voice! I could listen to him read an instruction manual with that voice. I was so shocked at the depth of its tone that I know my mouth was hanging open. If I had a glorious voice like that, I'd talk all the time. Before I can ruminate on all our interactions and melt further into a puddle, I hear Rosy coming back to the cart.

"Hey, Silvia, this is the friend I was telling you about, Ellis. Ellis, this is Silvia." I almost don't hear the introductions as I am now entranced by the most beautiful being I have ever seen in my life. Better not let Tore Ben see them or I'd be replaced. This entity in front of me must be the Deity of Androgyny themself. They somehow embody both the masculine and feminine, perfectly balanced into one being, yet they are neither. I internally scan my face to make sure my mouth isn't open this time. Ellis would be the new 'It' model if they ever crossed over into my world, that's for certain. Tall, graceful, and poised, with flawless skin that glistens and shines with a hint of turquoise hue. Their perfectly waved, teal hair almost hides pointed ears, but I clock them. Oops, I've been silently staring too long again. Better say something.

"I'm sorry for staring, but you are absolutely marvelous. Nice to meet you, Ellis." I kind of give a partial curtsy as I hold out my hand to shake theirs. I don't know why I did that, now I feel oh so silly now. Ellis, to their credit, chuckles with a half smile and shakes my hand.

"It's a pleasure to meet you, Silvia. Thank you for the fantastic compliment. You are just as sweet as Rosy proclaims." Their praise makes my whole body warm. They think I am sweet. I'm on cloud nine today!

"Oh yeah," Pip shouts from the cart, "just stand around and talk. It's okay, not to worry, Pip will unload everything all alone. No, no, don't mind me, just over here slaving away as usual." Ellis and I can't help but laugh at this.

"Don't get your hooves in a twist; I'm coming. No one told you to start offloading by yourself now, did they?" Rosy stomps off to berate and assist her brother.

"Those two, whatever shall we do with them?" Ellis observes the pair with love in their eyes, as if they are looking at a family they adore. It melts my heart. "Rosy tells me you are adventuring and want to stay to help out our town for a time; is that so?" I nod in the affirmative.

"Yes, I hear Oakveil has a noticeboard that might have some tasks that need doing, and I'd like to see if I could help out at all.

I'm new to this whole adventuring thing, so I thought I'd start out slow and see where it takes me." But I notice Ellis's eyes have caught on my bracelet and have gone wide.

"Now where did you get that lovely little bobble? May I?" they ask so I offer up my wrist. "My goodness, what a powerful and curious Menstruation Cuff you have here! Appears to be blessed by a goddess if I'm not mistaken. How did you come to possess this?"

"Oh, it was gifted to me when I set out on my adventure. Why would a goddess bless a bracelet meant to keep women from getting pregnant or having periods? Can you tell what goddess? I didn't realize it was so precious."

"A gift?!" they say astonished. "A thoroughly impressive gift if that's the case. While most Menstruation Cuffs are highly effective and are usually only overridden by powerful magic or divine intervention, this one shall have no such failings. Not even the goddess who blessed it could, or would, override its directive. You shall have no pregnancies or flow till you decide otherwise and remove it. An extremely rare item indeed, and one usually kept within families. As to the goddess who blessed it, I can't be sure who it was. Sorry."

"Ah, it's okay. I was only curious. But thanks for telling me. I knew it was awesome, but didn't realize how precious it was." They gently release my hand.

"Of course. I also hear you are in need of a place to stay. If you don't mind an attic room on the third floor, I have an extra bedroom and full bath up there. I could let you use it while you're in town. In exchange, I'd ask you to help out in the bakery sometimes when my assistant is out or off. It used to be her room but she's moved in with her paramour, so it's currently free."

"Are you serious? That is so kind of you. Yes, it sounds amazing! And I'd love to help out anytime you need."

"Rosy, I'm going to show Silvia the room and bakery. Feel free to come in when you two are done." Ellis doesn't wait for a reply. Instead they link our arms and guide me in through the backdoor into the kitchen. They show me around the bakery, then lead me upstairs. The second floor is their living space and blocked off by a red door. At the top there are two teal doors sitting opposite each other. The left door leads to a bathroom for me to use, and the right is to the room I'll be staying in.

The room is small but cozy enough, with a bed, desk, chair, and a wardrobe to hang my clothes in. The two windows face the village circle and have box planters with an assortment of wildflowers in them. Gliding over to a window, they open it to let in a little fresh air as I put down my travel bag. I can hardly believe my amazing luck!

Ellis, Rosy, and I spend the rest of the day walking from shop to shop. Ellis introduces me to all the owners, and lets them know I'm up for odd jobs and will be checking the noticeboard later for tasks. Rosy also gets supplies for her tavern every now and then.

To my surprise, we run into Torben. Ellis said his name in greeting, so I had his name mostly right in my head. He's a carpenter from another village, working on a project here for a little while. My cheeks flush a bit at seeing him again so soon after his confession. I know Ellis sees it. While I'm looking at all the wood crafted items on sale in the shop, I notice Rosy and Ellis having a private conversation with Torben. Sure wish I could eavesdrop without being noticed. But Emna, the owner and artist, is a loud and boisterous talker who is very proud of her wares. They are gorgeous and expertly made. I'll give her that.

Once we are done with all the shops Ellis wanted to show me, we three head to the tavern in town called The Bobbing Apple for food and libation, as Ellis says. I try to hide the relief on my face when it's brought up because I am starving! My breakfast left me a long time ago, and the baked goods at Ellis's smelled so delicious it got my tummy ready for some food. I should have asked to buy something then, but I didn't want to be rude and they seemed ready to hang out and shop.

Thankfully the tavern put bread and butter on the table as soon as we sat down and confirmed we would be eating there. Freshly baked bread and handmade butter, I'm in heaven.

"If you think that's good, wait till you have some of Ellis's bread." Rosy chimes in. Guess I was making happy noises or something as I ate it. Oops.

"Can't wait to try it." I get out after swallowing my mouthful. "What do you suggest I get here? What's their specialty?" They both know their food, and I plan to trust their judgment on this.

"Actually," Ellis answers, "The Bobbing Apple is best known for their hot apple cider. It's the best in the area and people come from all around to purchase it by the barrel. The family owns the apple orchards around here too. Their apples are the best in my opinion. We all use them; it's a point of pride for the village." As if by magic, our waitress walks over with a steaming mug and places it in front of me.

"The gent in the corner booth wanted to make sure you got some of our cider." She winks and nods to the booth in question where Torben, Emna, and a kid are sitting and eating. He raises his mug at us, then quickly looks away.

"How thoughtful of Torben," Ellis says with a raised eyebrow. "Making sure that our lovely Silvia doesn't miss out on having the finest cider in the land." They are both staring at me and grinning so wide that I squirm a bit in my seat.

"He's just being nice," I manage to eek out.

"Oh yes, very nice indeed," Ellis continues. "He's such a sweet-heart thinking of you. Thinking only of you. Seems we don't warrant any cider, do we Rosy? If I didn't know any better, I'd say that male has a crush on our new little friend here."

"A crush at the very least," Rosy says under her breath as she looks away, but I still hear it.

"What do you mean? We've only just met, and he's said barely five whole sentences to me." I glance at them to see that they are now staring at me in wonder.

"You mean he's spoken to you, in full sentences, and more than one? When did this happen? What did he say? Tell us every-thing." Ellis now has their elbows on the table, hands cupping their face waiting expectantly. "Come on, you must tell us. In case you haven't noticed, Torben is known for being shy around females, especially if he doesn't know them. So to hear that he's spoken up to you, whom he's newly met, is like finding out that the clouds chat about our lives. I must hear the whole story."

So I tell Ellis about all the interactions from last night, and this morning. Then explain to them both what happened during and after the cart ride. I haven't gotten to gossip with friends in such a long time. It's really nice. They both listen to everything I say, gasping and oohing at the right moments. When I'm done, Ellis is slowly fanning themselves with a hand.

"Oh, I do adore a cute love story. I'm so glad this is going to unfold in my town. I love love for other people. Not my thing personally, but I enjoy watching it all unfold."

"Well, that doesn't seem fair," Rosy interjects, "I met her first and it started at my tavern. You have to promise to keep me up to date on everything that happens. Here, give me your message book so you can message me about it." The centaur digs out a cute little booklet with pink roses on it from her bag and reaches a hand out to me.

"Yes, we can have a group letter so she doesn't have to tell her stories over again or answer the same questions." Ellis also pulls out a little booklet but theirs is black with silver sparkles. They both look expectantly at me.

"Sorry, I don't have a message book. I don't even know what that is." Oh, now they are looking at me like I've grown a second head.

"What do you mean you don't have a message book? How are you keeping in touch with your family and friends while you are away? How do you not even know what it is? I thought even the full human villages and towns had them." Rosy peppers me with questions as Ellis stands up and starts to walk away.

"Hold that thought, Silvia. I'm going to remedy this gross oversight right this minute." When Ellis returns they have a little forest green booklet. "This is called a message book. It's a little booklet and pen that you can use to write messages to any friends, family, or acquaintances whom you have linked with. At the front of the message book, you have your new person write their name with their pen in your book, and you do the same in theirs with your pen. Best to do this near each other's booklets. Here, let me show you." Ellis then whips out their silver pen and writes their name in the front of my new little book with a flourish.

"Then if you want to write them a message you flip to a blank page, write their name at the top, scribble your message, then at the bottom when done write 'END' in all capital letters. The message will be sent to their book to read. You'll get a little vibrating buzz, similar to a bee, for every message you receive. Does all that make sense?"

"Oh my gosh, this is so cute. It's just like a text message system on your cell phone. Yes, I understand. We have something similar, but a little different where I'm from, and I lost my cell in the woods coming here." They both look a bit too relieved by my explanation. They must have thought I was some backwoods simpleton. Don't like that. "What do you do when you write a message, then change your mind about sending it?" There's no delete or backspace here, and I really need to know.

"That's simple enough," Ellis states. "All you do is put a line through the word or words you don't want sent and they will be omitted for the recipient."

We then link up our message books and test them out to make sure I understand how to use it. I accidentally send the first message in English instead of Common Tongue, which is a really weird thing to switch your brain over to, but it becomes easier as I continue.

We eat our meal then say goodbye to Rosy and Pip. Ellis walks me to where the noticeboard is so I can look it over. I find a few tasks that seem doable for me, so I take them. Ellis gets me a map of the town and marks off where the people are located that I would need to speak with. They suggest waiting till the morning to start. So, for the rest of the day they show me around their kitchen and explain what tasks they might ask me to do during my stay.

I dream of Torben again tonight. But now his smell envelopes me as I'm cradled in his arms. His deep voice washes over me as he tells me how beautiful I am. I wake up with goosebumps all over me and my nipples are peaked to the heavens. Goodness, now that was a good dream. Wonder if I'll see him again today?

Chapter 9

Torben

She was in my dream again last night. Second night in a row, not that I'm complaining. In this one I held her in my arms and told her all the things I wish I could tell her in real life. How much I cherish her, what a beautiful Mate she is, how soft her skin is, how sweet and kind she is. I talk to her all night and she snuggles into me and gives soft sighs of contentment every now and again. I can still feel her in my arms as I wake, her scent fills my nose. If I hadn't told Emna and the boy, whose name I discovered is Lestien, that I'd be choosing a tree today I would be trying to fall back to sleep right now.

But I gave my word, and the boy seemed very excited by the prospect. So up I get, though I do have to think of other things for a bit so my pants don't give my dreams away.

After we are all fed and dressed, I shift and Emna carries Les as we run to the area of woods the Carpentry Master at my side spoke about. When we arrive, she puts Lestien down and I shift back. I find I can feel the trees with my human hands better than my bear's. Though my uncle prefers his bear's nose.

I relay all that information to my new little pupil while walking around, touching and feeling trees of suitable sizes. After about thirty minutes of wandering around the woods, I find a tree that tingles my palms just right. I press both hands down upon the trunk, telling the boy to do the same. I ask if he feels anything, any difference at all. He doesn't, but I didn't really expect him to. Those of us who can feel out a tree have our own tells. Mine is tingling palms, my uncle gets an itch in his nose, and my grandfather's right eye ticked. I tell Les all this so he doesn't get discouraged, and it always makes kids laugh when I do my 'eye tick' impression. Now it's time to see if the tree is amenable to the task.

Placing both my hands back onto the bark of the tree, I set my forehead in between them. Though I usually do this silently, today I say it out loud.

"Hello, magnificent tree. My name is Torben, and I have a question for you. Are you still fully enjoying the life and serenity of a tree, or would you like to be transformed? To be carved into something else, to serve a new purpose? My friends and I here are carpenters seeking fine wood to craft into new pieces needed by folks. What do you say, are you ready for a change?" Then I wait.

The waiting doesn't take long for this tree. Very soon I feel the familiar warming of my palms that indicate a 'yes' for me. 'No' would be cold, and an 'undecided' answer would be no change at all. I sometimes will come back to an undecided tree later to see how they feel. But this tree is eager and ready for something new.

"Thank you. We promise to treat you with the respect you deserve." With a final bow, my companions and I begin our work.

It doesn't take long for an Orc and Bear Shifter to fell a tree. Les gets to work cutting off the branches while I look the tree over for the section I want. I quickly find it and we get started cutting it out.

"Can't believe you've taken your shirt off for this, Torben," Emna comments while shaking her head at me. "You are going to be picking sticky sap and wood splints from your chest hairs all week." This makes both Les and Emna laugh.

"I get hot, and that shirt is precious. Getting shifter clothes is no small feat. Have to go all the way to the big cities to find them. Can't wear regular clothes or they would shred when I shift and then I'd be a naked male walking around." I get a giggle from Les at that. "Plus, at this point, I know all the tricks for getting sap out of my hair and such."

"True enough. But aren't you itchy at least? Got me itchy just thinking about it." She gives a full body shiver that sets Lestien off again. She's a good mentor.

We take a lunch break together after a quick rinse in the stream. There were a lot of wood bits stuck to my chest hair that I did not want on me while eating. After we eat, we make a travois each to carry our goods back to the shop. I drag my trunk section, the boy a bunch of cut up limbs, and Emna has taken a section as well. She says they'll be cutting off the tree for a while so I agree to help them carve off some more sections tomorrow. Now that we know where the tree is, they'll bring a cart to help with hauling all this good wood. But for today a sled will do just fine.

We take a longer route on our return trip so we can travel on the main road, making dragging easier. We also stop at one point, giving poor little Les a break. He'll grow into some strength soon, even adults would have a hard time keeping up with Emna and me. He's doing very well and I tell him so. He beams at me for that.

It's as we are walking along the main road again, closer to town, that I catch her scent. My Mate is nearby. Why is she outside of town, and alone no less? I drop my burden and run to my Mate, despite the protests from my companions. I round a curve in the road and see her. Red hair blazing like fire under the sunlight, it's up in a nest atop her head with a stick of some kind in it. Which only adds to the nest like resemblance. Her skin is flushed and wet with exertion and she's puffing up the road toward me pulling a wheelbarrow behind her. I race forward to assist.

"Do you need some help?" I ask quickly as I run up to her. She starts and drops the barrel, dumping its contents into the road. Now look at what I've done! I knew she had her eyes on the road and didn't see me. Just because I am always aware of her presence does not mean she is of mine. "Sorry, that was my fault." I bend down to put the items back in the barrel. Turns out it's a bunch of old nails and scrap metal bits. At least nothing was damaged.

"Oh no, I should have been looking where I was going. Here let me. I've been going around town collecting scraps of metal for the blacksmith's new apprentice to practice on. The new smith can't find the time to get them before his pupil arrives. So I took on the...job." The last word is said in a whisper. She is staring fixedly at me now. I must look a real mess, sweaty, wood chips, sap, and no shirt. Wait, no shirt! I haven't put my shirt back on yet. Didn't want to until I had a real bath, and there's still dirty work to be done.

It's then I catch the scent of arousal coming from my Mate. I glance down at her face in time to see her lick her lips then bite the lower one just a little.

Our Mate wants what she sees, my inner bear growls in pleasure and I must as well because her eyes flash to mine. I let a low growl escape again and she lets out a little "oh" sound while bringing her hand to her chest. Now it's my turn to lick my lips. She looks so damn delicious right now.

Her hand then drifts from her chest to land on mine. My eyelids close at her gentle touch.

"Did that come from you?" she asks in a breathless whisper. I nod my head yes as I hold my body tight. This is no time to lose control. My Mate is touching me of her own volition, and she is smelling even more tempting than ever before. "Is it a good growl? Should I stop touching you?" She moves to lift her hand away, but I move faster and cover her hand with mine to keep it there.

"You can touch me as long as you want." It must be the right thing to say because a new wave of her arousal hits me. I growl again in satisfaction which once more elicits that sweet little "oh" sound.

"Hey Torben, why in Hades did you run off and leave your wood like that?" Emna shouts at me from behind. My eyes snap open while Silvia drops her hand like she's been caught doing something she shouldn't. Forgot we were in the middle of the road and I have people following me.

"S-sorry Emna, just helping Silvia here," I shout back as I hunch over and continue to pick up the metal I made her drop. It's also a great excuse for hiding my hard-as-a-rock cock from all these eyes as Les has now caught up too. I can feel my cheeks flush at the whole situation.

"Well, we left your trunk back where you dropped it. Best go pick it up before some other strong crafter finds it and steals it away." Emna lets out a guffaw as she and the boy continue on their way, Emna eyeing me as she passes.

"Oh, I didn't mean to interrupt you," Silvia says in a rush. "I can handle this now. You can go back to whatever it was you were doing. Thank you." She abruptly stands and tries to move away quickly but her wheelbarrow is full once more and clearly too heavy for her.

"I can carry that for you."

"No, no, this is my job and it sounds like you already have something to carry." I'm walking beside her now as she slowly pulls her little cart. She blows out a breath from the corner of her mouth in an attempt to move the strand of hair from her face. If I were a braver male, I'd tuck that strand behind her ear for her.

"Though I'll admit," my Mate breaks me from my daydream, "I wouldn't mind being even half as strong as you. Bet this wouldn't even feel heavy at all if I were stronger. I never enjoyed the whole going to the gym thing, all those people staring and judging me. I mean, isn't the point of going to the gym to lose weight? And don't I need it more given how big I am."

"But you are not big. And why would you want to lose weight?"

"Well, maybe I'm not big compared to you but I've got more fluff than most women. The beauty standard is 'smaller and thinner is better' after all. Then, of course, most men don't really lust after heavyset girls either."

"Those males are stupid." I'm getting angry at these people who tell my Mate she is too big. "They must also be weak, if they claim you are heavy. And blind." This makes her giggle.

"Well, aren't you being sweet. But I know I'm a curvy girl."

"Yes, you have delicious curves. I love to watch them when you walk." I did not mean to admit to watching her walk. Hopefully, she doesn't think I'm creeping again. "Um, here are my things. I'd better hurry to catch up."

I easily pick up my burden and hastily walk off. Why do I keep embarrassing myself in front of my Mate!? But before I'm out of range, I hear her say something under her breath about my "fantastic arm muscles" that puts a smile on my face and a bounce in my step. She likes how strong I am. Those weak, blind males from her past are clearly no match for me.

Quickly catching back up to Emna and Les I realize I must have a silly smile on my face, but I can't bring myself to care about that, or hide it.

"Sooo," Emna interrupts my pleasant thoughts of my delicious Mate. "What was all that about? You sweet on the new girl? Cause it sure looked like you were sweet on her to me. What do you think, boy? Does Torben like this new little lady?"

"Looked like she liked him too." Les says then giggles. "Isn't that the same female you bought a cider for?"

"You know, I reckon you're right, boy. That is the same girly from the tavern last night. Oh yes, she likes him too, that's clear."

"Really?!" I blurt out hopefully. "Do you think so? How do you know? She could just be being nice." Emna laughs at that.

"Oh, let's call it feminine intuition. She fancies you well enough, and I'm glad to see you actually speaking to a lady. Full sentences to boot! Though I never pegged you as a male that shows off his body to impress the females." Her eyebrows bounce up and down her forehead at that statement.

"You know I didn't do that on purpose Emna." Even if I have noticed it does seem to help. Emna laughs and teases me all the way back to the studio.

Once back, I set up my tree section and bench to start work tomorrow morning. Once I am done being messy for the day, I take a swim in the cold river nearby to help cool my searing hot thoughts. My Mate touched me, my Mate was aroused by me, and my Mate might actually like me too. The cold water doesn't help as much as I had hoped.

I pick up a small spare bit of wood to begin carving Silvia a gift before heading into town. And if I happen to keep within sight of Silvia as I work, well, that's simply a happy coincidence.

Chapter 10

Silvia

I've been in Oakveil for a few days now and no grand adventure has found me yet. So every morning I take on little odd jobs I find on the town's noticeboard. Guess rumor has spread that a sucker is in town. One who is willing to do the most random things and the people here are taking full advantage. So far I've collected and organized metal bits from all around town, helped water plants, found a lost goat, dug up so many potatoes, cleaned out and organized an old shed, and painted a fence. For Ellis, I help clean up at the end of the day then prepare for the next day of baking. Oh, and I have peeled so many apples I don't think I ever want to look at one again. This town is crazy for apples and apple by-products. To be fair, the apples are delicious.

At least I am making and saving up some money. Given this, I plan to go shopping soon around the town. Have myself a little day off. Ellis says there's a Market Day coming up, where vendors will be setting up booths around the circle to sell their wares and such.

I have to say, I am actually really enjoying myself, despite how sore I am most mornings. This has been like playing my cozy games times a hundred. I've been helping people, getting to know the locals, and I feel as though I have finally been able to decompress here. I didn't realize how burnt out I was in corporate life. But here there is no pressure, no stress, with so much fresh air and outside time. I could happily live the rest of my days this way. Maybe become someone's apprentice and learn a trade. I couldn't do one of the magical ones I've come across, like the plumbing or A/C systems. All those people are mages, and highly trained in the bigger cities. But I could do something non-magical, such as cooking or selling or something. I haven't really decided. Still greatly enjoying the non-pressure to be honest. Gosh, if I keep going at this rate the book shop owner will come back just to kick me out for creating the most boring book she's ever come across.

I'm still a bit miffed that she never gave me her name. I'm starting to think this was on purpose. No clue as to why, but I just know she deliberately kept her name from me.

Another plus is that I've seen Torben every day. Sometimes it's only from the corner of my eye, and sometimes we run into each other, either on purpose or not. I find that I kind of look forward to seeing him each day. I've come to realize he is really shy but is making an effort to talk to me. I've also seen him helping and talking with the apprentice boy Lestien. Torben's so kind and patient with the kid, it's adorable to watch.

Today I'm off to the infamous Crowcrest Orchard to help pick some apples. I've been tasked with bringing back a basket of their Special Reds. Not sure what makes them special but they are not the normal reds that Ellis typically uses for baking. Apparently, they are highly sought after and Ellis's shop is among the lucky few who get them.

The walk to the orchard is wonderful. I'm getting better at walking around now that I'm doing so more often. I bet I'd have lost a few pounds too if it weren't for all the tasty treats I get from Ellis's bakery. Guessing it's all balancing out in the end, more walking for more baked goods. A win-win in my book.

Just outside of town, I am able to hitch a ride to the Crowcrest Orchard with some other lucky souls who also plan to help pick some fruit today. I don't know any of them well enough to warrant more than a hello, so I enjoy the scenery as they chatter amongst themselves. They appear to be mostly teens trying to earn a little coin before the Market Day and it seems that Crowcrest Orchard pays well. At least better than most noticeboard jobs. I now feel a little guilty that I've taken these kids' source of income, but I don't take all the jobs so there's still chances for them if they wanted.

We arrive at the orchard, get a demo and instructions, which I am very thankful for, and head out with a few professionals to get to pickin'. Some of the apples are easy to get, others not so much. I now greatly envy the teens with wings, and the ones who have superior strength who can shake the trees. Glad this isn't a competition because I would be losing big-time. Maybe I need to find a way to get some powers? That happens in books a lot, right? They get a supposed curse, find a magical item, go to a magic school, or get a wish granted. Perhaps I should save a bit more of my money and head to one of the bigger towns I've heard mentioned a few times. Seems as though being a full human in this fantasy land is a bit odd and can sometimes be dangerous.

While I contemplate getting a magical boost of some kind, I realize I really do need to get up on this ladder to reach the next set of apples. I've been avoiding it, but now's the time. So up I get. After checking three times that the ladder is indeed secure and can handle my weight, that is. The sturdy wood ladder holds up just fine, turns out it's the person on the ladder that fails. As I'm reaching and grabbing and plucking, I get a little too confident and overzealous. Next thing I know, I'm losing my balance, flailing my arms, and completely missing the tree branch I try to grab.

In a flash I realize what's about to happen and accept my fate. It's as I'm praying that I don't break anything upon impact, I register that I'm no longer falling at all. Instead of eating dirt in a face-plant off this ladder, I find myself cradled in some seriously strong arms.

It's his intoxicating smell I notice first, letting me know who my savior is before I even look up into his face. Torben, my sweet and magnificent stalker puppy has caught me in his arms like in a movie, and all I can do is smile like an idiot up at him.

"Hi," I say as if I'm a nervous preteen calling out to her first crush in the school hallway.

"Are you ok? Did you hurt yourself anywhere? Twist your ankle or scrape your hands?" Gosh, I always forget how deep his voice is, and now being pressed to his chest I can practically feel it vibrate us both as he speaks.

"Oh, I'm fine." Damn, I still sound all dreamy. I'm both thankful and impressed he caught me. I didn't even realize he was at the orchard today. Sometimes I swear this man has a tracker on me or something. He seems to always know where I am and when I need help. Like when I couldn't open a jar when I was cleaning out that shed. One minute, I was struggling to open it, and the next Torben came out of nowhere offering to help. Or when I ran out of paint while refreshing that fence. I was about to get up and walk back to the house to grab the second pot, and boom, Torben was there, setting it down next to me and taking the old one away. It's like he's become my guardian angel or something. I wonder if those are real here?

Whoops! After that thought tangent, I have definitely been in his arms for too long.

"I'm so sorry. My mind went off into space there, and I know I must be heavy. You can put me down. I promise I'm fine, just lost my balance there." There's an interesting rumbling coming from him, and it takes me a second to realize he's laughing. I hadn't heard him laugh yet, and it now erupts out of him like he can't hold it down anymore. It's a rich laugh, pleasing to the ear and soul. "Are, are you laughing at me?" I ask with a smile on my face.

"You think you are heavy to me?" he asks through a chuckle. "You could be holding ten baskets of apples in your lap and you still wouldn't be a burden. I could carry you all day without a problem. To me, you are as light as a feather."

It's that last statement that makes me quickly kiss him on the cheek, right above his beard line. No one has ever referred to me as 'light,' and from him, it feels like the truth. I feel completely safe and secure in his arms.

At the kiss though, I notice he has gone stock-still and is looking straight forward like his mind is still processing what happened. It's so cute that I wrap my arms around his neck and plant another, longer kiss on his cheek.

"Thank you for saving me," I say with the biggest smile on my face. "You can catch me any time, but right now I do need to get back to apple picking."

He emits one of those sexy growls, holding me ever so slightly tighter. Damn, why do those turn me on, and so fast? A growl should not have me thinking such naughty thoughts about this truly sweet man. To my utter surprise, he bends his head down and sniffs into my neck, inhaling earnestly. His nose gently runs along the shell of my ear. It makes me shutter in the best possible way. Gawd, if he said anything into that ear right now with his deep-ass, sexy voice, I'd be putty in his hands for sure. Instead he just sniffs my neck again and lets out a low hum of pleasure. Oh geezus, that might be even sexier. I give a nervous laugh and shutter which has him lifting his head to meet my eyes with his.

"Sorry," his voice has taken on a grittier sound, "you smell so good, I did that without thinking. I'll remember to ask next time." Oh, you can sniff my neck anytime, is what I want to say but I know I shouldn't.

"It's okay. It was nice." It was nice!? What kind of a dork am I? It was way more than nice. This whole interaction is the sexiest thing that has ever happened in my life! And I say it was nice. I could slap myself on the forehead.

My words still make him smile even though they were wildly inaccurate. Slowly, gently, he sets me down on my feet. I may hold onto his arm for a moment to steady myself. Yes, totally doing it to steady myself. Not because I don't want to break physical contact with this man just yet. Yep.

He offers to help with apple picking and gathering, which I accept. We end up making quite the team. Turns out he is as strong as he's suggested and simply shakes the trees to make the apples fall out. I then grab the edges of the ground tarp and "we" lift and pour the apples into various barrels and baskets. I'd be lying if I said there weren't a few stolen glances and blushes between us as we work.

When done, we leave quite the hoard of apples in our wake. We are paid well for our haul, and I have to practically force Torben to take his fair share. He deserves more than half, but he seems appalled at the very idea. So I split the coin fifty-fifty and end up dropping it down his shirt so he's forced to take it. This tactic makes me giggle as he doesn't seem to know how to react, which is cute to watch. I do, however, let him carry Ellis's treasure of Special Red apples to the departing cart and then into the bakery itself. Ellis sends him on his way with a blueberry custard pie for his troubles to share with Emna and Les. Ellis says that growing boys need surprise treats every now and then. And so do ladies.

Ellis, of course, grills me as soon as Torben is out of the town circle and well down the street. So I tell them what happened, which seems to please them greatly.

"I'll be sure to tell Rosy about this new development in a message tonight," Ellis says. "I'd better put it in the group one, in case she has any follow up questions I didn't think to ask. Oh, the beginning stages of a romance, so delicious!" they proclaim with a wiggle of their shoulders.

Wait, am I in a Romantasy book!? The shop owner and I did talk about Romance but I told her I liked Fantasy the best...then she said something about spice. Oh no, I can't be in a smut book! I'm not sexy enough for that. No, no Torben isn't that kind of fast mover, and neither am I, really. I must be in a slow burn then. Okay, that might not be so bad, and Torben is very pleasing to all the senses.

"I'm going to wash up and head to bed early," I say abruptly. I need to analyze everything that's happened, also, I'll be getting up early for the Market tomorrow. "Unless you need me, that is." Ellis waves me away as I watch them furiously write a message to Rosy.

I dream of Torben again tonight, as I have every night since arriving in this land. But this time things take a decidedly naughtier turn. The dreams have all been the same so far; Torben comes into my room, gathers me into his arms, and cuddles with me while speaking soft sweet words.

But this time, when he comes into my room, there's a predatory gait to his walk. It instantly sets me ablaze. When he gathers me into his arms, his hands roam over my body with more daring. Gently, almost teasing at first, before they turn needy. I honestly can't decide which sensation is better.

And his words, oh his words, make me flush all over. He talks of how sexy I am, how he yearns for me, how he can't stand to not touch my soft skin. His voice works in tandem with a hand that slowly eases its way up my sleeping gown, skating over my sensitive skin to eventually find my breasts. The other hand grabs firmly onto my ample ass as he plays with my nipples in turn, whispering into my ear how marvelous my breasts are. How delicious my ass looks when I walk and how he can't wait to sink his teeth into it.

Warm lips graze my jaw as he pinches a nipple. He tells me how much he loves my little moans and how he can't wait to hear them grow louder. He nibbles on my neck as his hand slides from my ass over my thighs then slowly parts them. It doesn't take much convincing as I am more than willing to let him explore further.

"I can't wait to find out what you taste like," he practically growls into my neck. "If you taste half as good as you smell, I think I'll live between these heavenly thighs forever." His hand oh-so-slowly makes its way up my inner thigh to my sweet spot, the place I desperately need him now. He pinches my neglected nipple and I moan louder than before. I can feel him smile into my neck. So close, he's so close to my–

Bang, bang, bang! I'm jolted awake.

"Wake up sleepyhead," Ellis's voice croons from the other side of the door. "We've got to get you all dolled up for the Market today. I bet Torben's going to be there." They laugh as they walk away back down stairs. Well, he was almost there before you went and ruined it, I think angrily. I'm still so hot and bothered from that amazing dream I contemplate having a little morning masturbation time. But since I know Ellis is waiting for me, I decide against it and opt for a few splashes of cold water on my face and neck. It doesn't really help, but what's a girl to do?

Chapter 11

Torben

I can't hide my frustration at waking from my dream, no more than I could have hidden my massive erection upon waking. I've never had such a vivid sex dream before. Like all my dreams of Silvia, I swear I could feel her, smell her, taste her. I was so eager to taste her honeypot too. The memory of her warm flesh beneath my hands and the soft moans she expelled at my touch linger for hours after waking. Neither my hasty morning jerk nor my cold bath after seem to help this growing desire. I need to see her today, but I'm also afraid I won't be able to fully control myself in her presence. The mating urges grow stronger, but I don't want to do anything to scare her away. I feel we are making good progress, and I need to control these desires if I'm going to make this work. I'm a grump as I sit down for breakfast.

The boy is extremely excited for today, which does help to dispel some of my dark mood. Apparently last Market Day, he didn't have as much coin and couldn't buy this knife he really wanted. But today he feels as though he has saved more than enough for a knife, plus some sweets.

"I know you'll want to buy that knife first, so you can tally how much you have left to spend on your treats, but trust me when I say to wait," Emna offers her sage advice to the boy. "If you wait till later in the day, closer to wrap-up time, you'll get a far better price. These merchants and crafters want to sell as much as possible and are always willing to cut a deal at the end. Less to pack up and cart off back home." She knowingly winks and taps the side of her nose.

"Though they are often in better spirits first thing in the day and are eager for the first sale to get the ball rolling," I counter. "Some are superstitious about the first sale too." Les is more excited by my advice.

"Hmm, that's true," Emna adds. "But it only works if you can make sure you are the first buyer that day. Given the time, one would have to hurry indeed to guarantee that spot at this point." I can see Emna trying to hold back a grin as Les struggles to stay in his seat.

"Um, do you think I'd make it if I left right now?" The boy is already halfway out of his chair.

"Mayhaps," Emna looks thoughtful, "but you'd have to be a fast runner to make absolutely sure to get there in time. Why, I bet the vendors are already set up by now." With that last statement Lestien is off his seat and out the door, coin purse in hand. We both laugh after him. "Ah, to be so young and excited. He didn't have to worry though, I told old Pat to keep that knife for next time as I knew the boy wanted it desperately. Would have bought it for him myself, but thought a good lesson about saving for a goal and achieving it wouldn't go amiss," she says with a wink to me.

"So, want to talk about why you were such a grumpy bear this morning? Everything still going okay with your lady friend?

You seemed in such high spirits yesterday when you came back for dinner."

"Just had an interesting night's sleep is all." I'm trying so hard not to feel embarrassed about my dreams last night. Silvia's my Mate and there is nothing wrong about having those kinds of dreams, but it is private.

Those delicious dreams of our Mate are only for us. I'm quick to agree with my bear.

"Ah yes, bad sleep can definitely get one out of sorts." I don't correct her assumption. "Glad to hear everything is still going well with you and Silvia. You ever going to give her that gift you've been working on?" My head whips up to look at her. I didn't realize she knew about that, not that I was hiding it, but I am surprised she noticed. "Oh you can't sneak anything past me in my studio. I keep my eyes sharp from having apprentices around. They always seem to find trouble the moment you take your eyes off 'em," she chuckles to herself.

"Yes, they are done. I'll give them to her when the right opportunity comes along." I finished them a day or so ago but haven't found the right time to gift them to her yet. Maybe today is the day.

Emna and I clean up breakfast, make ready, then head out together. It's nice to talk with her; she's always felt like another Auntie and I didn't realize how much I missed her till this impromptu visit. I'll have to make it a point to come by more often once my Mate and I leave Oakveil. Not that I want to rush this, but I am getting a little homesick.

Almost as if the Universe has heard my thoughts, a piece of home materializes in front of me before Emna and I are halfway to the town circle.

"Well, well, well, if it isn't my big brother strutting down the street. How have you been Tory Bory?" I'm instantly wrapped in a hug from my little sister, Mel. Her name is really Melantha, but she hates it so goes by Mel. Only mother calls her by her given name anymore, and only when she's in trouble. Which I have to say is more often than I ever was. She is slight of frame for a member of a bear clan, but her big personality more than makes up for it.

"Please don't call me that," I say again for the millionth time. It never does any good, though I try everytime. I hate that nickname.

"Well, look at you!" Emna interrupts. "Little Mel, all grown up. And your hair! This new style suits you far better than the long braid you used to sport." Emna hasn't seen Mel in some time despite how close we live. My sister prefers bigger cities, so Uncle usually travels to Oakveil when he needs Emna's help or stock.

Mel's straight onyx black hair is cut short into a blunt bob just below her jawline with equally blunt bangs above her eyebrows. It was our mom who loved the solid black braid of my sister's youth. Mel chopped it short the first chance she got, and I haven't seen it longer than her shoulders in years. But Emna isn't wrong, this style does suit my little sister well.

"What are you doing here?" I growl out even though I know the answer. She's here to mettle in my love life, and I don't want her rocking the boat.

"Some welcome! And after doing you a favor by bringing your clothes and such all this long way." She practically throws a bag at me. "Lucky for me it looks like today is a Market Day. So my trip isn't an entire waste."

"Come with me. We need to talk." Grabbing my sister's wrist, I led her back to the studio leaving Emna to continue on alone.

"Okay, okay, I'm coming. No need to drag me," Mel protests. We get back to the woodshop and I toss my bag of clothes inside before turning to my little sister.

"Thank you for bringing fresh clothes. I've been washing mine everyday and bought this set in town so I could change." Swiping a hand down my face, I get to the point. "I know you've really come to meet my Mate, but it's too soon. I told you all in my messages that she doesn't know about the mating bond yet, so I am courting her another way. And I can't have you scaring her off, please." That last part comes out a bit desperate.

"Whoa, whoa there, bro! I'm not here to tell her any secrets or scare her off. On the contrary, I'm here to help you. I have many friends who don't experience a mating bond and still manage to find love. I've seen how it's done and have come to offer my expert advice." She's looking up at me with a smug smile and confidence, but all I feel is dread. "I'm here to be your 'wingman.' I bet you don't even know what that is." I let out a sound of exasperation.

"Hey," she says more gently, "I understand how important this is, okay. But I also know you and how modest and shy you can be around females. Trust me, no one wants this to work out for you more than me. I've always wanted a sister." She playfully punches my arm. I tilt my head back, close my eyes, and breathe through my nose in an effort to calm myself. "But seriously Torben, let me help you. I know how important finding your mate is. It's all I've ever wanted too, and this isn't how either of us imagined it would happen. So let me meet her, talk you up to her as only a sister can. Then once I've convinced her how amazing you are, I'll leave you to it. I promise." Now she's looking up at me with those big puppy eyes that get my parents every time, and I guess they get me too. She is very convincing, I'll give her that.

Taking a deep breath in, I expel it through my mouth as I let my body relax into the inevitable.

"Okay, I'll introduce you. But I'm serious; no talk of mates, or bonds, and especially no retelling of that time I vomited on Ceilia when we were younger."

"Oh, come on," she grabs the finger I've been wagging at her, "that's the cutest story. You were so nervous trying to talk to her."

"No!" I am adamant.

"Alright, alright, I agree. You don't have to bite my head off. Only amazing stories and no embarrassing ones, got it." She links our arms together, and we begin to walk back toward the circle, and my doom. "Now, tell me all about her and everything that's happened so far."

I have to admit that the walk to the village circle with my sister is nice. I must be missing my family and home more than I thought. I tell her all that's occurred so far. Mel seems a little disappointed.

"That's it?! It's been like two weeks, Tor Bear! You are moving way too slow. Have you even asked her out on a date yet? Sounds like you've just been following her around like some child. I mean, surely you asked her to Market today, yes?"

I am an idiot! Of course I should have asked her to Market Day with me. Yet it hadn't even crossed my mind. I just counted on running into her. Honestly I hadn't even thought about the idea of a date, but now it's obvious that's what I should be doing. Maybe my sister will be helpful after all?

"Torben! I can see from your guilty expression that you didn't ask her. Poor girl must be getting mixed signals from you. But never fear, I'm here at last to save you from yourself. Now, where is she? I know you can scent where she is. Lead the way."

I'm not prepared for how stunning my Mate looks today. Well, she looks stunning every time I see her, but today she is exceptionally so. Her wild, curly red hair is adorned with flowers, she has a subtle glamour on her face that shows off her natural beauty, and she's wearing the dress she wore when I held her hand. Its colors also seem to have been enhanced today. Ellis is very good with such magic.

Her eyes find mine in the crowd almost as though she can sense me too. The green of her eyes is lighter this morning with the sun really setting off the flecks of hazel within them. I must have stopped at the sight because Mel is pulling my arm now. My Mate glances over at my sister and a flicker of concern crosses her face for a moment before her eyes return to me with a question in them.

My ever eager and personable sister thrusts her hand out to my Mate as soon as we are within reach.

"Hi, Silvia! My name is Mel, and I'm Torben's little sister. I surprised my brother with a visit this morning, but honestly I've been dying to meet you." I'm already regretting allowing my sister to stay, but Silvia appears relieved to meet my sister for some reason and offers her a truly happy smile.

"Oh, it's so nice to meet you, Mel. I didn't know Torben had a sister, though to be fair, I don't really know that much about him yet. We met recently and have only spoken a few times." My sister shoots me a look that has me suddenly very interested in the booths around us.

"Well, thankfully for you both, I'm here now and can tell you everything about my dear brother," Mel says with a wink.

"No, please don't," I say as she hooks her arm with my Mate's and begins to walk away. I even reach my hand out like I can physically stop what's about to happen. I must look and sound hopeless because they both giggle at me.

"Don't worry, I won't tell her anything too embarrassing, and I'll give her back after a few stalls. Did he tell you that he hoped to walk the Market with you today? If I know my brother he was too shy to ask and probably would have resorted to following you around until you were walking together." She lets out a laugh and my Mate blushes up at me.

"I'd like that, to walk around with Torben, I mean. After we shop some, of course, since you did ask first. Though technically, I guess he never really asked, but you kinda asked for him. Not that he needed you to ask for him, of course. Since it seems you're the more talkative sibling, and you got to the point before he had a chance too. Not that I'm assuming he would have asked me, just that you said he would have." She's so cute when she nervously rambles. I like that I make her just as nervous as she makes me. My sister is staring at Silvia wide-eyed and speechless for a moment, but it doesn't take long for Mel to cut in.

"It's settled then, Silvia and I will look at a few stalls alone getting to know one another. Then, I'll hand her over to you,

Torben, so you can enjoy the Market together. See you later, big bro!" With that, Mel steers my Mate away before either of us agree. This is going to be an interesting visit.

Chapter 12

Silvia

I'll admit, I might have been jealous for a split second when I saw Torben walk up with a beautiful woman on his arm. I mean, not that Torben is mine or anything. But I kind of felt a little hurt that another woman was that close to him when it seemed like, and everyone said, he was very shy around women. And this woman is drop dead gorgeous, physically fit, and confident. I'm a little ashamed at how I felt once I found out it was his sister. But I won't deny I was also relieved. In my mind, there was no way I could have fought this girl for his affection or attention.

Spending time with Mel is actually nice, though it does seem that she got all the talking genes. True to her word, she is telling me everything about Torben. Their family, the home they share, the community they live and grew up in, his favorite foods, activities he likes, and a few funny childhood stories. Peppered in here and there, she asks questions about me, my life, and my exes. She's very to the point, but she is easy to talk to and quite charismatic. I tell her about my loving grandparents and the bees they kept; I tell her I never knew my dad and how my mother was too toxic to be around. And about my longest relationship that ended when I finally realized that I was taking care of a man-child who didn't even really care about me as a person. I was just a warm body who cleaned and cooked and paid for the apartment.

Thankfully, Mel doesn't make me feel judged for staying in that relationship for as long as I did. She actually congratulates me for seeing my worth and taking action for myself. Makes me feel kinda good, and I think I like her just a little bit more. Once we look over several vendor booths, 'oohing' and 'aahing' accordingly, Torben shows back up. He almost appears worried to have left me alone with Mel. Which makes me even more curious about what fun stories she has about him. Oh, I'm definitely going to be hanging out with her again. I can sense some juicy secrets.

"Well, here's your girl, all safe and sound. Geez, you'd think I planned on running away with her myself the way you're acting." Mel crosses her arms over her chest while talking to her brother. "You're worse than a hovering mama bear." Torben grumbles at that, which makes me giggle. "You two have fun now, and don't do anything I wouldn't do." She wiggles her fingers in goodbye then stalks off to look at some lotions.

"She wasn't too invasive, was she?" Torben asks. "I know Mel means well, but sometimes she can be a bit much. I didn't mean to spring her on you; she didn't tell me she was coming."

"Oh no, she was lovely and we had a pleasant conversation. She's probably only wanting to look out for you." There's a brief awkward pause between us before I feel compelled to continue. "Do you want to walk around with me? This is my first Market Day and I want to make sure I don't miss anything." Unexpectedly, he extends his elbow toward me while admiring his feet. How cute is he?! So I take the preferred arm and we walk together to the next stall.

Being this close to him, smelling him, touching him, reminds me of my naughty dream, and I blush. His arm is so sturdy and strong. Strong enough to hold me with ease, I fondly recall. He's trimmed his beard and the sides of his head; his clothes are also quite neat and tidy today, as well. Boots seem cleaner and maybe polished too. He put in some effort for this. Wonder if he did it for me? Mel said he intended to walk with me today.

"You clean up very nicely, Torben. Looks like everyone puts in a bit of effort for a Market Day."

"Thanks," he says while bringing his hand to the back of his head, rubbing it. I can see him blushing slightly. "You look nice too. I love the flowers in your hair, very pretty."

We walk and admire items silence. Somehow this has gotten awkward, and catching his sister spying on us from time to time is only making it worse. Thankfully, I see Ellis talking to her and walking off into their bakery. Bless you, Ellis! They are such a good friend. I'll have to come up with a way to thank them later for that small mercy.

We continue to walk the Market, commenting here and there on items we like or find interesting. There are more booths than I expected, not only on the circle but also down the streets. I'm enjoying people watching, of seeing the different fairytale creatures who are going about their day like it's all totally normal. I guess it is, here anyway. I'm starting to get used to it, seeing a gargoyle walking down a road or a fairy flitting into a store to buy something. But today it's almost too much for me. My eyes don't know where to look next.

Torben buys some taffy for Lestien from a booth, then gives me a few before eating one himself. I'm thankful for this new thing to focus on. The sweet taste, the feeling in my mouth, and the effort to chew all help to ground me.

I feel so awkward! Why does this seem to be so much weirder than our other encounters? This comes across as being so forced when before we'd meet and talk almost organically. Is it because something is expected from us now? Or maybe it's just me feeling this way?

"Can we go off and sit somewhere for a bit? This is a lot of people for me," he quietly admits. "It is a good time for a midday meal. We could grab something and eat somewhere quieter?" Oh, thank goodness, it's not just me.

"Yes! That sounds amazing. I'm also kinda over-peopled right now." We visit a stall that has some baked mini meat pies, buy a few, and walk off down the road. He finds a nice place under an oak tree, off the road, for us to sit. Torben was also thoughtful enough to get us some cider. We eat and drink in silence. Still a bit awkward and forced, but better now that we are alone. Now that we are no longer performing for anyone.

"Sorry, I'm not much of a talker," Torben breaks the silence. "I should have tried more. My sister showing up unexpectedly threw me off more than it should have. I wanted your first Market here to be better than this." He sounds so dejected.

"I'm having a great time! Lots to see and hear and taste. Plus, I get the feeling that your sister is a force all her own." We both laugh at that.

"I, um, made something for you. Nothing big but here." He hands me a plain white piece of cloth with a green ribbon tied around it. "You can open it now if you want. Or wait till later."

"Thank you, that's so sweet." I gently untie the bow and open up the cloth to find two pieces of wood, each about seven inches long that come to a dull point. Hair sticks! He's carved me some hair sticks. One is plainer, with a simple vine design carved at the top and polished to perfection to make the rich wood shine. The other stick has been painted black at the base and topped with a cute little carved bee which is painted black and yellow.

"I saw you had put a twig in your hair the other day to hold your curls up and thought I'd make you a better option. I didn't know what you would prefer so I made two. I can make another design if you don't like these."

"Oh no, they are perfect." This could be the most thoughtful gift I have ever received. I know I'm going to cry. I can feel the tears welling up in my eyes. I can hardly believe he noticed that twig I used and then made these for me because he knew I needed them. "How did you know I love bees?"

"You have a tattoo on your inner arm of a hive. I took a chance. I'm glad you like them." He's trying to hide a smile now.

"I love them!" I say as I clutch my precious gifts to my chest. "I haven't had anyone make me something in a very long time. Thank you so much, Torben! You don't know what this means to me." Tears are definitely running down my cheeks now. "You've been so nice and kind and sweet. Thank you for thinking of me." He's fully blushing at this point and it's even made his ears red.

"It wasn't much trouble. They are easy enough to make." He takes the white cloth they were wrapped in and gently dabs at the tears on my face. "I'm always thinking of you," he whispers. I look into his face, surprised at his words.

"Oh," I whisper back. "S-sorry for crying on you. I know it's a simple gift that I probably shouldn't be crying over. I perpetually seem to feel too much, ya know, and it almost always comes out in tears. Happy, sad, overwhelmed, or anything in between and the waterworks start. I promise I'll try to keep it together better in the future. Not that I expect you to stick around or anything, or that you'll give me more gifts. But I want you to know that it's something I'm working on fixing about myself."

"Don't. Don't be ashamed of crying, and don't try to fix it. There's nothing wrong with how your emotions present them-selves." He tucks a strand of hair behind my ear. "I love that you feel so deeply."

Marry me!

"You, you say that now but..."

"I say that always. I like you just the way you are." I'm so stunned I actually stop crying. He finishes clearing the tears from my face, stands, then helps me up. "Come, let's see the rest of the Market."

And we do. We walk the whole of the Market and even revisit some stalls we saw before, but this time it feels so much better. No more awkwardness or feeling like we are putting on a show. We talk now and then about the things we see, and he haggles for me over a new bodice. I only had one and needed another since I wear it everyday in lieu of a bra. I thought it would bother me, but I actually prefer it now. So much so that I may try to incorporate them into my outfits once I get back to my real life.

We finish the day by having dinner with Emna, Les, Ellis, and Mel at The Bobbing Apple; each of us showing off our new treasures in turn. Lestien has gotten himself a new knife that he's in love with. I wouldn't be surprised if he even sleeps with it in his bed tonight. Mel has gotten some lovely lotions and bought one for me, as well. I thank her profusely as it was sweet of her to consider me.

We part ways at the tavern, and in the chaos of goodbyes with Mel hugging everybody, I sneak in a hug with Torben. I needed one last hit of his smell before bed. Yummy. Mel clocks the hug and smiles widely at me. She has this glint in her eyes as if she has some devious plan in mind. Not so sure I like that look.

My dreams of Torben are again more innocent cuddling. But tonight he talks about building me a cabin to live in. He wants me to choose the spot, though he has a few in mind. I never thought of myself as a 'living in a cabin' girl, but it sounds so nice the way he describes it that I believe I would like that very much.

Chapter 13

Silvia

The next morning I decide to wear the new bee hair stick Torben carved for me. You can just see the little bee poking out of my curls and I think it's so cute. Since Ellis makes a similar compliment upon seeing me, so it must be true. We both know it means more, but we keep our comments to its appearance and function.

"What do you have planned today, Silvia? If you don't have any commitments I was wondering if you would run an errand for me? I picked up a few things Rosy wanted from The Market and baked some treats for her and Pip, as well. Are you up for walking to The Wandering Mead this fine morning?"

"That sounds perfect! I was actually hoping to get out for a while today. I kinda need to recharge my social battery. Taking a long walk through some nature sounds like the perfect thing. And I'd love to see Rosy again. It's been a while."

Ellis packs up a basket and chatters about Market Day as I quietly eat my breakfast. Today, it's a flaky croissant-type thing drizzled with dark chocolate and fresh blueberries on the side. Once done, they walk with me to the edge of town, sending a message to Rosy that I'm on my way before I depart. It's sweet how

much they care about me. I haven't had such good friends in a long
time.

The walk is somewhat longer than I thought it would be. I
mean, I did come here in a cart, so my estimate of distance was
bound to be off. Lingering by the bridge over the river, I enjoy its
sights and sounds for a time. So peaceful and exactly what I needed.
The feeling of cool moist air around me, the melody of the rushing
water, and the light dancing along the surface do much to ease my
mind and restore my inner balance. I might come here more often
and try meditation. Seems like a great place to do it and I've always
wanted to try. But right now, Rosy is waiting on me and I don't
want her to worry.

When I finally arrive at Rosy's tavern, I am immediately greeted by Theodore.

"Why, if it isn't our lovely little human friend! Welcome back,
my sweet darling. Tell us, how was the Market yesterday? I haven't
been to a Market Day in ages. You must recount everything for
me!" I see Theo is still as flamboyant as ever. "Who set up shops?
I used to know all the local vendors personally and some crafters
further afield, as well." He stops to wink knowingly at me. "Come,
sit by the fire, and regale us with the latest news and gossip. Tell me
child, how goes it with the brawny bear fellow who pines for you?"

"That's none of your business, Theodore," Rosy scolds as she
trots in from the back. "Hello, Silvia. Nice to see you again. Looks

like you made it here on your own safe and sound." I nod and smile
up at her. "Dying to know what goodies Ellis got for me. They are
always so good at knowing what ya need and what's good." She
takes the basket from me and sets it on the bar, so I go sit on a stool
near it. "Want some lunch? It's about that time."

"Yes, please! I didn't realize how long that walk was going to
be and I burned my breakfast off ages ago." I wiggle in my eat
as she hands me a lunch menu. I decide to go with a cold cuts
type sandwich with baked tomato slices fresh from their garden
and a blueberry cider Pip makes himself. I think I'm going to start
coming here more often for lunch, and for the company. Rosy goes
through her basket with me as we discuss the Market and how
everything went. She asks to see my hair stick and how I use it.

"Might have to commission a couple of these for myself," Rosy
says as she's handling my new treasure. "I've never used one but it
seems darn handy and his detail work is pretty good. Feels nice in
the hand, as well. I'm actually surprised he isn't here today with
you. Did you have to shoo him away from following you?" she
smiles at me as she hands back my hairstick.

"No, why would he come too? I was only running an errand
for Ellis and coming for a visit. He has his own work today, I'm
sure." For some reason, I'm flushing a little. "He's been working
on something at Emna's studio and showing her apprentice some
things. So he doesn't really follow me around. It's a small village
and we just happen to run into each other, once he is done with
his morning work and taking a break." She gives me an indulgent
yet disbelieving look.

"Yeah, sure, you just happen to be running into each other.
We'll go with that." She winks and the conversation moves on from

there. The place isn't too busy, so she shows me her garden. We talk about what she has planted now and her future plans. All in all, it's a very pleasant afternoon together with only the occasional interruption from Theo.

"Well, if you plan on making it back to the village before it gets dark you might want to head out now," Rosy advises. "Plus, I should start preparing for the dinner rush. Thanks for the delivery and the company." She bends down to hug me then walks me out, handing the basket back to me, now laden with some of that blueberry cider for Ellis and I to share.

I'm having such a pleasant walk that I don't see the bear on the road till I'm way too close for comfort. How did I not notice a big black bear in front of me?! I'm like fifteen yards away from it and, of course, it's on the same side of the road as me. What the hell am I going to do? Are bears the type of animals that you curl into a ball and play dead for, or are you supposed to climb up a tree? Wait, am I supposed to pee on myself maybe?! That might happen anyway, whether on purpose or not.

Shoot, the river is still a good distance away, and it's on the other side of this bear! And the tavern is definitely too far. I feel perfectly trapped, but I know I need to make a decision soon. It appears as if the bear is as surprised as I am since it also hasn't moved at all either. We are just staring at each other now. Me wide-eyed with a racing heart, it way more calm and in its element.

I mean, of course the bear is calm. It has nothing to worry about from me.

I suddenly realize I came here without anything to protect or defend myself with. I've felt so safe in this book-land that I haven't even been taking any kind of precautions which feels very stupid in hindsight.

Wait, did that bear just cock its head at me? It's actually kind of cute, for a giant man-killing beast. I guess we do all have little teddy bears as kids for a reason. It's also sitting on the road in an interesting position. Right on its rump, back legs stretched out to the sides a bit, and front paws together on the ground between its legs. Not exactly in attack position here. But if the Discovery Channel or Steve Irwin has taught me anything, it's that animals can change their demeanor and charge in an instant.

Maybe I'll try walking backwards slowly? I take one gentle step back and the bear lets out a whining sound. When I look at it in confusion, it cocks its head to the other side. Damn, why is that so adorable?!

I decide to try another step back, and this time the bear lets out a sigh and lays down resting its head on its paws. Okay, this is definitely some odd behavior for a bear, right? It whines at me again and gazes up at my face with its big bear eyes. Maybe it was raised by humans and is lost? Or was released without knowing how to survive in the wilderness? I've heard of people doing that to wild animals who get too big to care for anymore. It sits back up again and stretches its neck out to me with an almost exasperated "woof."

Wait! I am in a magical land so maybe this bear isn't like the bears where I'm from? It certainly isn't acting like it. What if it's a person under a curse? Or maybe it's an animal familiar or something? It could be a magical bear like the unicorn I met when I first arrived. I mean, I am here to have an adventure after all. What if this bear needs my help or leads me to my grand quest? It cocks its head again and twitches its ears.

Who am I kidding? I really just want to pet that bear. Every White-woman's instinct within me is aching for it. It's practically begging me to. Gathering up all my nerves I take a small step forward.

"Hey there buddy, what are you doing on the road?" My voice has changed as if I'm talking to a cute dog or baby. "Are you okay? Do you need something?" It whines at me again so I take a few more steps forward.

"You aren't going to eat me, are you? That would really suck if you did." The bear huffs like I've said something offensive. Interesting. I reach out my hand and continue my slow progression toward the bear. This is so stupid! I know this is the exact wrong thing to do, but I can't seem to help myself.

"Can you understand me, cutie-pie? Please nod your head if you can." Then, to my amazement, it does just that, dips its massive head up and down. "Oh shit, really?!" my voice drops back to its actual range for a moment. "I mean, thank you. Sorry, I've never talked to a bear before. Are, are you a friendly bear? You seem friendly." The bear dips its head again.

I can't believe this is happening, I can't believe this is for real happening to me right now! Recalling my encounter with the unicorn, I try to mimic the actions that the shopkeeper took. Bowing my head a bit I bring my hand to my heart.

"Hello there, my new friend. I've never met a bear before, so I'm sorry if I'm doing this wrong. I was wondering if it would be okay to touch you? You look so soft." The bear nods again and stretches its neck out a bit more toward me. I did it right! I can't believe I'm going to pet this bear. I am totally about to boop that snoot! My finger shakily makes contact with the slightly damp nose.

"Boop," I cautiously whisper. When nothing terrible happens I run my hand up the elongated snout of this bear, bringing the other hand up to its ear, scratching just behind it. It closes its eyes and makes a sound of contentment. I knew it! It wanted pets just as much as I wanted to give them. I'm never going to forget this moment for the rest of my life!

A sudden slicing pain and pressure shoots up my arm. I look down to see my forearm is now inside the mouth of this tricky black bear. I should have known it was too good to be true. What an idiot. I'm so stunned that I can't seem to move as the pain really starts to make itself known to my brain and body.

Before I can even utter a sound a thundering roar emanates from the forest on the other side of the road, which is quickly followed by the sounds of breaking branches and running. The black bear immediately releases its biting hold, and we both step back from each other. Well, it steps back while mine is more of a stumble really.

To my horror, another bear emerges from the woods, a Grizzly maybe, running at full throttle. Without slowing, the massive Grizzly bodily slams into the black bear that just lured me in with cuteness only to chomp on my arm. Even though I specifically asked if it was going to eat me! My last sight of them is of a mass of black and brown fur rolling around on the road as I turn tail and run right into the woods. I might be a big girl but it's funny how a life-or-death situation can really put the pep in your step. I don't think I've ever run this fast in my life! Check that, as soon as I hear the sounds of a massive creature running after me in the woods, I manage to find a little more speed.

My thoughts are racing faster than I am as I cradle my throbbing arm to my chest. What am I going to do? Where am I going to go? Is this how I die? Is this how my story ends?! If I'm killed in this book, am I dead-dead or will I appear back in the bookshop similar to a video game start point? I should have thought to ask those kinds of questions before agreeing to this adventure.

Serpentine! Yes, running in a straight line only helps the bear catch up faster. I need to weave. So I do, or at least I attempt to until I trip over a rock and fall forward. Typical. At least my instincts have me twist enough to land on my good side instead of my face or bad arm.

I snap my head up and around to discover that it's the giant Grizzly bear chasing me. Fan-fucking-tastic. Of course, it's the bigger one. As I'm scrambling to stand again, something amazing happens right in front of my eyes. One moment the bear is there stalking towards me, the next I'm seeing Torben running up before kneeling down at my side.

"No, no! Oh Goddess, are you hurt? Did she break the skin? Did she bite you? Let me see." Very gently, Torben takes my injured arm to inspect it. It must be bad because his face immediately drains of color. Suddenly, he picks me up and starts carrying me. "There's a clean little stream over here. Let's wash off the blood and see how it is." He looks so worried and I'm too stunned to say anything or move. I'm probably in shock. From getting bitten, being chased, seeing a bear turn into Torben, all of the above?

We get to the stream, and he sits down in it with me in his lap. He continues to hold me as he shakily washes the blood from my forearm. Yep, those are definitely bite marks. Wonder if they will leave a cool scar? My body starts to shake of its own accord as I'm looking down at my injury.

"Am I hurting you? I'm sorry, I'm trying to be gentle but we need to get this clean."

"No. No, you aren't hurting me. Think I'm just going into shock or something? I don't know, it's never happened to me before." I tilt my head up to look him in the face. "Torben, are you a bear? Pretty sure I saw you turn from a bear into a human. That or I was hallucinating?"

"No, yes, I mean..." he lets out a breath and meets my gaze. "I'm a bear shifter." He says this so calmly, so matter-of-factly. "I guess I should have mentioned it before, but I didn't want to scare you off. I wasn't sure how much you knew about shifters in general. Sorry."

"Um, it's fine. I've gathered through my short time here that people don't typically talk about what they are." I'm shaking even more now, and I feel cold yet flush and a bit dizzy. "Torben, do weird magic bears carry venom or diseases? I think I'm getting a fever, and I feel kinda dizzy too." I know it's not a good sign when his face blanks out, then becomes serious. He lifts me straight out of the stream and begins to quickly walk through the woods.

"It's all going to be okay. I know exactly where to go. Don't worry, I've got you." I'm glad one of us seems sure about something. But his words and the strength of his arms help to alleviate some of my fears. I'm not alone and he knows what to do. It will all be fine.

"Oh wait, I had a basket with me but sat it down on the road. I told Rosy I'd deliver it to Ellis. We should go back and get it before...it, ah...before it..." With those last words dying on my tongue I pass out in Torben's sure and comforting hold.

Chapter 14

Torben

How could she do this? How could she do this?! I'm so furious with Mel that I could rip her fur out. She had no right, no right to do this! No right to take my Mate's choice away. My Mate, my poor sweet innocent injured Mate. Silvia is the only reason why I'm not back there still yelling at my stupid, impulsive, selfish sister. But I have every plan to confront her once my Mate, my Sweet Silvia, is somewhere safe and getting her injuries tended to.

I started running as soon as she passed out in my arms and I couldn't wake her. The Changing Sickness is already taking hold and I need to get her to my village, to my mother, as soon as possible. It is never an easy transition, but the faster we can get her treatment, the easier the change will be.

I hear her before I smell her; my sister is fast. She shifts from her black bear form into her human one and runs alongside me.

"I'm sorry, Torben. I tried not to hurt her too much. I just thought-"

"No! You didn't think and that's the problem!" I yell at my little sister, interrupting her, having no intention of listening to her excuses. "You didn't think about anyone but yourself! Run ahead

and tell Ma what has happened and to prepare." Still not sparing
her a glance I add, "If I see you upon my arrival, I will never speak
to you again!"

"You don't mean that Tory Bor-"

"You had better heed my words, sister, or I will get you
shunned from the Clan for what you have done." I can hear her
shocked intake of breath at my words. "When you leave, take the
basket Silvia was carrying to Ellis. She was worried about it before
she blacked out; it's the least you can do for her right now." Mel
looks at me hurt by my threats of shunning, but I mean it. She, at
least, seems to realize that.

Mumbling a faint, "Sorry," she races off ahead of me in her
bear form toward our shifter community and home. Not exactly
the homecoming I had planned. My sister has just taken so much
from me, and she either doesn't realize it or doesn't care.

*Our Mate will be fine. We will help her get through this. Her
injuries will heal, and we will deal with our sister once our Mate
is passed this. Then, you will help her adjust to her new form.* My
bear tries to comfort me, but will my Mate ever forgive me for not
protecting her? I followed her as soon as I scented that she had left
town. Wanting to make sure she stayed safe, yet I couldn't even save
her from my own sister.

I still can't believe Mel did this! I can't believe my own sister
would force this upon anyone, especially my Mate. I should have
put a stop to the interaction before Silvia got so close. I should have
known Mel had some silly plan up her sleeve. I thought Mel was
only trying to ease any possible fear of bears Silvia might have. Or
perhaps show her that she was a bear shifter? As much as I'd have
rather been the one to divulge that information, if Mel wanted to

be friends with my Mate, who was I to tell her she couldn't expose her shifter form?

I race right up the porch stairs and through the open front door, looking wildly around for my mother. Thankfully, my sister took my warning to heart and has left our family home.

"Ma! Ma where are you?" I bellow.

"Here. I'm in here. Bring her to the guest room." Quickly, I walk into the first floor room and find my mother there getting things ready for this ordeal. "Place her on the bed, but sit her up. I want to get the elixir into her now before I tend to her bite." I do as my mother commands and help as we try to get the liquid down Silvia's throat. We manage to get most of it in her before I gently lay her head onto the pillow.

"Take her boots off for me son and any other outerwear as I treat her wound. We'll get her as comfortable as we can for this." I take my Mate's boots and new bodice off, the one I helped her buy just yesterday. I also remove the hair stick from her curly locks feeling warm inside upon seeing that she wore it today. I make sure to put it somewhere safe for her.

"Alright, arm is wrapped, now out with you!" Ma orders me while motioning towards the door. "I'm going to change her out of these wet clothes and into something lighter so she doesn't sweat through her layers."

"Did we get here fast enough? Will the change be okay? She won't suffer too much, will she?" I pepper my mother with questions as she practically pushes me out the bedroom door.

"I don't know yet dear, but we are going to do everything we can to get her through this. Go fill up a bucket of water, as cold as you can get it. Maybe put some ice into it as well. Now, out! And don't just barge in here when you get back. Knock please."

She closes the door behind me and I'm stuck for a moment, standing there staring at the wooden door. We are home, she is safe and being cared for, and I will not leave her side during this sickness. Well, aside from right now while I'm off to get the cold water Ma requested. But after that, I won't leave her side!

I hastily grab a large mixing bowl and load it about a quarter of the way full with some ice. I then fill the bowl to the top with cold water and make my way back to Silvia. On my way through the house, my father appears at my side.

"Mel told me what's going on. Your mother will get your mate safely through this. She's done this more than any other in the Clan, and she will do so again now. Be strong for your mate, my son." My father is a bear of few words, but when he does talk, it's always something worth listening to. I thank him for his reassurances as he squeezes my shoulder with his rough workman's hand. Pa does have a way of calming people, for that I am very thankful right now.

I knock on the door as instructed and wait as I ready myself to be there in any way I can for my Mate as she goes through the Changing Sickness.

Three days, it's been three days since my sweet Mate was bitten. Three days of fever, of sweating, of sleeping fits, and sounds of pain emanating from my Silvia. And three days of sleepless nights, worry, and anguish for me. Ma assures me that it's all normal, that I got her here in good time to help ease the transition. But it's still killing me inside to watch her go through this while I am powerless to help in any meaningful way. True to my word, I have stayed by her side through it all.

"The fever has broken, and she's through the worst of it," Ma tries to assure me. "I'll watch over her if you want to grab a bath and some sleep. I know your mate would be grateful for both. Sorry to say this son, but you look and smell awful." My mother laughs slightly as she rubs my back. She is sporting some dark circles under her eyes from sleepless nights as well, but has taken better care of herself than I have. Mostly from the urging of my father. I am grateful beyond words to them both. "She'll be sleeping peacefully for another day or so, I'd wager. So this is your chance to take some time for yourself before she wakes. Now go. I'll get you if anything changes."

"Thanks for everything," I say while wrapping her in a big hug which she returns before making faces and pinching her nose at my smell. She winks to show me that she's only teasing me. Slowly, and reluctantly, I leave my Mate's side.

My father has some food waiting for me, which I devour quickly before heading up to my room to bathe. My mother is not wrong about my smell, and I don't want Silvia's first heightened senses to be associated with my body odor. I end up washing everything twice just to be sure.

I must fall asleep instantly once I hit the bed because the next thing I know it's dark outside again. I've slept all day! I jump up and run downstairs to check on my Mate. I find my mother still sitting with her. At my hurried entrance Ma jumps in her seat, then begins to laugh. I'm confused at first but quickly realize how disheveled I am. Catching a glimpse in the mirror shows my clothing all rumpled and askew with my hair standing all over the place. My harried position in the doorway really completes the look of a madman. I laugh with her and feel better for the break in tension. Wiping tears from her eyes, my mother pushes me from the doorway back toward the kitchen once more.

"Sit down and eat some dinner while I find you a comb for that mess on your head. Then I'll pass the watch over to you." She finds said comb and brushes my hair as I eat quickly. Though I don't like leaving Silvia all alone. "Stop fussing, she will be alright in there for a few moments."

"I've instructed Melantha to stay in Oakveil for the foreseeable future," my father begins as he makes a plate for my mother as well. "I have also advised her to stay away till sent for and to take on work from the noticeboard there. It was her actions that took Silvia away from completing their tasks after all."

"I still can't believe that child of mine would do such a reckless thing! To force a change without prior consent or full knowledge of what's to come." The comb through my hair has become significantly more forceful, and painful. "Then to plan to do so, knowing full well what's going to happen to the poor girl, without being close to me or the village, without having any aids for the fever or pain." Ma is holding tightly to a fist full of my hair at this point.

"Why, I could skin her myself! I thought we taught her better than that. And if Torben hadn't been there when it happened, or acted as quickly as he did, it could have taken her well over a week to go through."

"No need to take your fury out on our boy's hair, Mama," my father says with a smirk as he sets a plate of food on the table for her.

"Oh, yes, sorry, Torben dear. Didn't mean to get so worked up there. Here's the comb," she says while slapping the comb forcibly down on the table. Pa walks behind her and starts rubbing her shoulders. "Thank you, Mate. What would I do without you?" Pa kisses the top of her head as he continues to kneed her shoulders and neck. "Once I finish this meal I'm going to offer thanks to the Shifter Goddess and go straight to bed," Ma announces right before she earnestly digs into her plate. She has worked hard to get Silvia through this as painlessly as possible, and I know she is worn out.

I finish my food, thank them both, and get back to my Mate's side. I straighten myself up as best as I can and continue to keep an eye on Silvia. She looks so much better than she did. No more sweat painting her skin, and no more expressions of pain or discomfort rippling across her face. She now sleeps peacefully, her breathing even, her skin as pale and freckled as ever. Goddess, she is beautiful.

I can't wait to see her eyes again, that breathtaking green with flecks of hazel. But for now I am just grateful that she is at ease.

There is much to look forward to now. Our Mate will recognize us at last. Yes, but we still can't push her. This will all be new to her and she won't understand. There is much she must be taught still. *True, but we will be there to help her each step of the way. And now we can stay closer to protect her. I know this is not how it should have happened, and it's not how we wanted it to happen, but there is still some joy in this.*

Anger flares up within me at those words. Anger at my sister, yes, but also anger at myself. What my bear says is true, deep down I find some happiness at this turn of events. At the fact that my Mate is now a shifter, like myself, and our courtship will proceed as it should. Guilt settles over me as I watch my Sweet Mate sleep and wait for her to wake. What will she see when she opens those lovely eyes? A mate or a monster?

Chapter 15

Silvia

My body feels so heavy when I wake up. My mouth is really dry, and I am finding it difficult to open my eyes. Lick my dry lips, I slowly move a stiff hand.

"Easy now, little one. You've been very sick and need to take things slow." It's a woman's voice that I don't recognize but sounds gentle and compassionate. "Are you thirsty?"

Nodding my head slowly, I finally manage to crack my eyes open. Sitting beside my bed in a chair is a woman who truly exudes 'Mom' energy. She has the kindest face I've ever seen and her hazel eyes shine with a combination of patience and happiness. Her auburn hair is up in a loose bun with a few untethered strands to frame her face. Her blue bodice and white tunic are also loose for ease of movement and she is wearing an apron with hand-sewn embroidery embellishments here and there. She picks up a pitcher and pours water into a wooden cup with what looks like a straw made from fibers or plants.

"Here you go. You can have all you want, but don't drink too fast." The instant relief of this water has my eyelids closing in pure bliss. It's cold, fresh, clean, and exactly what I needed.

"Thank you so much," I croak out. "Sorry if I've been a bother. How long have I been sick? Do you know what happened or what I had? Where am I exactly?" I have a million more questions but that will do for now. I still feel a bit slow and groggy, like waking too early from a very deep sleep.

"You were in a fever fit for about three days. It finally broke about a day ago. So in total, you have been sick for a little over four days, but I suspect you are all better now. Rest and nourishment is what's needed. As far as where you are, you are in my home and haven't been a bother at all. I'm always happy to help people go through the Changing Sickness." By the slight circles I see under her eyes, I know she's not being completely honest when she says it wasn't any trouble. I'm going to apologize again but then her words sink in.

"Four days?!" I almost shout as I sit bolt upright. "How...what...I don't...oh gosh!" It seems I'm having a hard time formulating words. Oh no, did this cause some kind of permanent brain damage? I can feel myself spiraling as my eyes dart between this woman and the daylight outside the window, my breathing becoming rapid. What's the last thing I remember? Think, Silvia! You were walking down a road. That's right, you were coming back from a visit with Rosy.

"The bear!" I shout out loud again. "There was a bear, it bit me. Then, then Torben came and he was a bear too? No, no, that can't be right," I chuckle. "That must have been part of the fever dream." Just then a deep and steady voice speaks from the other side of my bed.

"I'm right here, Silvia." Twisting my torso, I find that Torben is on the other side of my bed, looking even more tired than this woman. He puts his hand on my shoulder and I automatically feel calmer. Actually, it's more than that. I kinda feel like I melt into a puddle at his touch. "You were bitten by a black bear shifter on the road to Oakveil, and I am a Grizzly shifter. You will never know how sorry I am that I didn't get to you fast enough." He's sitting on the bed now, looking deeply into my eyes. He seems so sad and worried, but for some reason I am on fire! Must be left over fever. Yeah, that's it.

"You carried me," I say like a lovestruck idiot as I melt a little closer into him. Gawd, he smells so amazing. I mean, he's always smelled good, but right now I want to lick him all over to see if he tastes as good as he smells. I'm not even a little ashamed of my thoughts either, way too turned on to care.

"Ahem." The sound of throat clearing from the other side of my bed snaps me out of my naughty thoughts. I almost forgot we weren't alone. "Yes, Torben carried you here to me as fast as he could, and thankfully he was able to get you to me in good time. I've known the Changing Sickness to last weeks if left untreated or without timely aid."

I am finding it remarkably hard to keep my eyes off Torben, and at some point, my hand seems to have found his of its own volition.

"Son, could you go get Silvia here something to eat? Your father will know what's best." Son? This is his mother?! And here I am sitting in her bed, lusting after her son right in front of her after she's taken care of me for four days. Good job, Silvia.

Torben reluctantly leaves the room, and my heart sort of aches at his loss. I guess it makes sense, he is the only person here I'm familiar with. Plus, he did save me.

"Now, my dear, there are some things I need to make sure you fully understand right away. Are you feeling up for a little talk?"

Oh no, she noticed! And now I'm about to get "the talk" from Torben's mother moments after meeting her. I must have been way too obvious. A new fear creeps in as I begin to worry that I said something untoward about her son during my fever delirium. We are kind of dating, I guess, and I did have that one seriously sexy dream about him.

"Yes," I reply tentatively. "I'm okay enough for a talk." Leaning forward she takes my hand in hers.

"How much do you know about Shifters?" Okay, not where I thought this was going.

"Um, I guess not much really. I've actually never heard that term. Didn't know people could turn into bears either. I thought it was only like werewolves and that they only transformed around the full moon. Well, I guess the full moon part only applies to some types of werewolves, really. I've never met any before and only have heard stories from books and, uh, stuff."

"Oh goodness, that's some very outdated and false information you have there, dear." Great, now I feel like some old Shifter racist. But she squeezes my hand in a reassuring way. "It's okay, dear. I'm not offended. I just didn't realize how sheltered you were back in your human community. I'm glad that you decided to go adventuring and branch out from your home." Her smile and wink make me feel better about my faux pas.

"I'm afraid 'were' is an old term used for Shifters. But don't worry, we don't find it offensive, simply less correct. Shifters can be any type of animal really, though wolves were among the first and once the most common. The stories of only shifting during lunar cycles were never true. Though wolves, owls, and some others do have a strong connection to the moon. There are many books and theories about how that fallacy began, but that's not a discussion for now. Did you ever hear or read any stories about how Shifters or 'Werewolves' were made, aside from being born?"

"Oh yes, you had to be bitten by...one. Oh gawd! Oh no...am I...did I...will I?!" I manage to string out those partial questions as I begin to hyperventilate. Blessedly, she brings a gentle hand to my face and tells me to breathe. "Am I going to turn? Have I turned already? Oh no, have I hurt anyone? They always hurt someone when they first turn. They lose themselves and become all beastly and kill and eat." Tears are streaming down my face now and I am totally freaking out.

A lot of the werewolves in the movies end up killing themselves out of guilt! I don't think I could stand to be Me anymore if I ever hurt someone. I'm having a hard time taking in breaths. Sounds are muffled and I start to hear a high pitched ringing. My vision is black in my periphery. Pretty sure I'm about to pass out, but then I smell him again. His intoxicating aroma breaks a crack into my black bubble of nothingness.

"Breathe, Silvia! Breathe! Please." It's Torben and he's shouting at me. He's holding my face between both of his hands, looking at me with fear in his eyes. His skin touching mine turns the fire back on in my veins, and I am compelled to listen to his commands. Anything, I'd do anything for him. I breathe in deeply, over and over just as he tells me. We breathe together as he helps me through this panic attack. In through the nose and out through the mouth, a slow and steady rhythm. He uses his thumbs to gently wipe away my tears.

It takes some time, but once I'm calmed down enough, his mother hands him a glass of water which he holds as I drink through the straw. I keep eye contact with him the whole time during my episode. Funny, I usually hate prolonged eye contact. Always felt too personal, too invasive, too uncomfortable. But with him, oh, I could stare into those dark-chocolate pools for a lifetime. They're almost entrancing, as if I'm being put under a spell.

"Oh Silvia, dear, I'm so sorry," his mothers voice breaks into my little world. "I should have broken the news to you differently. I had no idea your images of Shifters were so horrid. Once all this is done, I suggest we pay a long visit to that human community of yours and set some records straight. No wonder they are all holed up there if that is what they think of us. I really do feel so awful, honey." She's taken my hand again and is stroking it. "Here, let's try again, okay? We'll dispel some of your notions and replace them with facts. You saw Torben here change, didn't you? Was he a bloodthirsty beast with ill intent?"

"No," I whisper out as he continues to hold my gaze. "He, he did chase me but shifted when he got near. And I guess he was chasing me to help?" Torben nods then moves his hands from my face to my shoulder and unoccupied hand. I reluctantly drag my eyes from his to look at his mother. "The other bear seemed nice and cute, but then it bit me out of nowhere!" My voice rises at that last statement as my breathing quickens again. I hear and feel Torben growling. Snapping my head back to him, I see true anger in his face.

"That was an unforgivable act that never should have oc-curred," he grits out through a tightly clenched jaw. I've never seen

Torben angry, and he's angry on my account. That's kinda hot. No, no, that is not hot. Stop it, girl! You have other more pressing emotions to deal with. We'll analyze that later.

"Yes, that is not a behavior or practice we condone," his mother adds. "The bear in question will face a severe punishment for it. But they were in control and made a conscious decision to bite you, to turn you Silvia. Which makes the act even more upsetting." She looks angry, but also sad. Seems like this was a big betrayal of the social norm that has rocked them both.

"So, so, when I turn, I will be in control of myself? I won't hurt anyone unless I want to, right? Cause I would never want to!" There are only a few scenarios I can think of in which I would want to actively hurt someone but I really hope to never find myself in those situations at all. I guess now just turning into a bear will deter most, if not all. There's a plus, I suppose.

"Yes, once you learn how to shift you will be the one to decide when to shift and what you do in your bear form. And it won't take a full moon to aid you, nor will you feel the need to kill. Unless you are hungry and want to bring down a deer or what have you, but again that will be up to you."

"Will it hurt? Shifting, I mean. Does it hurt? And what else changes? Our stories suggest heightened senses and strength." I'm starting to feel a little better now that the whole bloodlust thing is off the table, but I need to know more. I need to know everything!

"No, no, dear, it doesn't hurt. Though I've heard it can be frustrating to learn for those who are turned and not born. And yes, to a full human, you would have some other changes. Your bear form will be stronger and faster, you'll hear better, and smell things better too. Not sure about taste though. You'll have to tell me if that's improved," she says with a wink. "We've actually already been in contact with a Change Coach in the area for you. You'll be traveling to him once you're up for it. He'll be able to tell you much more than I and show you how to control your new self."

I'm silent for a time, looking down at my lap as I digest all this new information. Well, there's some good news, I'll have a teacher to help me through this.

"And this Change Coach has done this before, I'm assuming? Helped someone transition their life from human to werebear?" As soon as the term leaves my lips, I giggle. Werebear, what a silly word.

"Oh yes, dear, I've called upon him several times after nursing someone through the Change Sickness. Though he usually gets more of a warning as these things are typically planned." Pausing a moment she looks my face over. "How are we feeling now? Better at all?" I nod my head yes and offer her a little smile.

"Wonderful. You are doing so well and are being very brave." She pats my cheek and it feels like genuine praise. Enough to make me perk up and smile a little. "How about we get you something to eat, then a bath, clean clothes, and maybe some fresh air if you are feeling up to it? Does that sound good, Silvia?"

"That actually sounds really great. I am as hungry as a bear!" We all chuckle a little at my silly joke. "And I would love to get out of this bed. Sorry, you've done so much for me, but I'm afraid I don't know your name."

"Oh you can just call me Ma, most people do." With that she pats my hand, stands up, and walks towards the door.

Torben offers me his forearm which I use to get up and steady myself to walk. I'm so focused on touching him, and the warm feelings it evokes, that I run right into the door frame with a smack! How embarrassing. Torben apologizes and I mumble a half-hearted excuse.

"Must still be out of it from the fever," before I carry on. I'm able to keep my concentration on walking after that.

Moving through the house to the kitchen allows me to see how cottagecore adorable this home is. It's a combo of an English cottage meets wood cabin. With exposed wood beams and off-white plaster on some walls, while others are straight-up stacked logs with white joint filler. The whole place also exudes that warm, homey lived-in and loved feeling. Slightly worn but well cared-for, neat and clean. It all helps with putting me more at ease. I'm not alone in this. There are wonderful and kind people here to help me.

In the kitchen itself, there is another bear of a man who must be Torben's father, cooking and setting out food dishes on a big oak table. He's wearing a lovely apron with ruffles on the straps and hem. I notice more hand embroidery on the light blue fabric. He offers me a warm smile through his big beard and hums as he finishes setting out dinner. Torben pulls out a wooden chair for me, I'm noticing a theme, and sits down next to me at the table.

"Everything smells wonderful, sir." And it does. I mean, it really does! I've never smelled such wonderful food in all my life. Maybe it's my new bear senses or the cooks ability or the fact that I haven't eaten in four days but I'm practically drooling over here.

I get a chuckle, another smile, and a deep-voiced, "Thanks," from Papa Bear. Torben leans over to me and I'm drawn like a magnate.

"Pa doesn't talk much. I kinda take after him in that way." He then smiles and moves back. I try to focus on the food, but the only thing that smells better than it is Torben himself. Damn, what is wrong with me? I mean, I know it's been a while but I've never been this bad before. Maybe it's another symptom of the Change? Extreme horniness. I'll have to ask the coach and watch myself around other guys.

We all sit down and begin filling our plates when I notice something missing.

"Wait, where's Mel? Is she not here?" The table goes so still and quiet that I feel as if I've said something wrong.

"Oh no, dear, she's not here right now," Ma answers. "She's still in Oakveil, actually. Helping out the village in your absence. Seems like you have become someone other people can depend on. Torben, can you pass me the potatoes?"

After that weirdness the dinner continues pleasantly. I ask questions about their home and the food. It's just as delicious as it smells. I can't decide if my sense of taste has improved, but I do think I'm better at discerning the different ingredients than I used to be. So that's a plus. However, I do end up bending my fork and spoon, as well as crushing my ceramic cup due to my new strength. I'm both mortified and impressed. I can definitely see why I would need a teacher to help me out. Thankfully, no one seems phased by my destruction. Apparently this is a totally normal part of the process if you were a being without such strength before the Change.

After dinner, I very gently bathe then dress myself, not wanting to break anything else today. Ma shows me her garden while we walk outside together. I can't decide if I'm relieved or disappointed that it's not Torben I'm walking with. But listening to her talk about the different flowers and their medicinal properties does help to keep my mind off myself and my new situation. I do get tired quickly though and am ushered off to bed to sleep myself out.

Unfortunately, now that I'm alone with my thoughts they run wild. My main concern is, if I am now a Bear Shifter will I be able to go back home? Or is this simply a part of the story? Is this even real? And if it is real, will the bookshop owner be able to fix it? I did ask Ma if there was a way to reverse the Shifter change, but she just looked at me all sad-like and said that it can't be undone. But is that true for me and my circumstances? I guess I won't know until I finish this 'story' of mine and see that shop owner again.

Not even my dreams are a relief. Where once I would have found myself snuggled in Torben's arms, I instead find myself running. All night long I'm running through a forest. But not as I am. Oh no, I'm a bear in this dream, because of course I am.

Chapter 16

Torben

I have fitful dreams again tonight, but they've all been that way since Silvia was bitten. The few times I've slept, that is. Like the others I'm running through the woods trying to find her, searching for my Mate. I can smell her and hear her running, but she always eludes me. Sometimes I change and call out to her; others, I'm frantically barreling through the woods trying to catch up. But she never answers me, never comes to me, never slows down. When I wake, I'm left wondering why my Mate is hiding from me. Why can't I get to her? It leaves me feeling sad and alone. Even with Silvia awake now and fully past the fever, the dreams remain the same.

It makes me grumpy every morning, that is, until I see my Silvia. Just being around her makes everything better, and also so much worse. Now that she's a Shifter, my bear is constantly hounding me. Her smell and nearness sets me off every few minutes. I never knew how hard it would be to keep the mating call at bay. Truthfully, I never thought I would have to.

The fact that it is also clearly affecting Silvia is another complication. It's hard not to give in to temptation when I can smell her arousal or when I see her eyes dilate when we are close. I want to tell her so badly, but it's not the right time yet. She needs to learn what she is, who she is, and what it means to be a Shifter. Patience. I need just a bit more patience.

Fortunately, we will be heading to the coach's cabin sooner rather than later. My poor Sweet Mate is having a hard time controlling her strength and speed. She's broken so many things that now she's afraid to touch anything at all. Silverware, cutlery, dishes, door handles, the bed, plaster off a wall twice, three message book pens, and her new bodice. That one made her cry the most, though Ma was able to mend it. I vow to myself that I will buy her a new one as soon as I can. Ma has been helping her dress since that unfortunate incident. It doesn't help that I find it adorable every time she breaks something, and she often catches me smiling at her when she does.

She's been keeping in touch with Rosy and Ellis too, which has been helping her cope. I'm glad my Mate made such friends before the Change. I still find it hard to hold my anger whenever I think of my sister. Mel seems to be behaving and completing tasks at Oakveil still. And though I'm sure both Rosy and Ellis know who bit Silvia and why Mel is really there, they have kept that information to themselves. It feels like lying, all these truths we are concealing from her, and when my sweet-hearted Mate finds out that everyone she knows has been keeping so many secrets, will she ever forgive us? I do not think even Silvia will forgive or forget such a betrayal easily.

"You're up early!" The chipper voice of my Mate is like music to my ears and a balm to my soul. "Excited about traveling too? I had a hard time getting to sleep myself and woke up this morning ready to go. I can't wait to be able to touch things without breaking them. I sure hope the Change Coach can really help. Your mom told me you've traveled there several times before. How long will it take us to get there? Not too long, I hope. I'm itching to get started."

Her rambling talk this morning tells me how nervous she really is about today's journey and meeting her new mentor. But I let her continue uninterrupted. I feel like the continuous talking helps to expel her nervous energy. Plus, I love the sound of her voice.

"It was so nice of Ellis to pack all my belongings for me and send them here. I'll have to think of a way to repay them once I'm safe to be around people again. Not that you and your family aren't people, of course, but well, you know what I mean." She pats my shoulder and I can hear her quick intake of breath at the physical contact with me. I smile at how much I affect her, but then release it when I recall that she doesn't know why.

Soon. We are going to the coach today and he will teach her our ways. She will be in our arms and in our bed in a matter of days. The mating bond cannot be resisted forever. I know, I know. But I'm not as confident as you are about the time frame. Days might be pushing it. *Nonsense, you courted her before she felt the bond. Now she will know we are meant to be, and that you put in so much work and restraint to please her. She will be ours before the Fire Festival, I am sure of it. Then we will have our way with her during the festivities as we should.*

I can't deny that I am greatly looking forward to claiming my Mate during such a rite. A true mating for a fertility celebration is something every Shifter longs for.

"Earth to Torben, are you in there?" Silvia's voice cuts in.

"Oh, yes. Sorry, I was deep in conversation with my inner bear. What do you need, Sweet Silvia?" She blushes instantly and I realize what I called her out loud. I inwardly kick myself. I've been trying so hard to never call her Mate when speaking but just slipped up with this pet name instead.

"Um, ah, your mother is calling you," and she points back inside the house.

"Thank you." Quickly, I get up from the porch step to head inside and away from the awkwardness I just created. I find my mother in the kitchen packing lunches for our trip, along with some goodies for our stay.

"There you are! I've been calling for you. Were you out in the forest?"

"No, I was talking to Silvia on the porch." No need to tell her any more than that. She has already been giving us knowing looks anytime Silva isn't watching. I understand that my mother is happy for me, but it's still kind of embarrassing nonetheless.

"Well, this is the last bit of food so everything is all set. I helped her pack her bag already and I've told Phil you'll be staying this time. He knows about you two being mates and has agreed to teach her about that aspect of Shifter culture sooner than usual." Mom winks at me and I groan back at her. Great, someone else who knows that secret before my Mate.

"Oh, don't be so stuffy, son." She walks over to me and places her hands on my shoulders. "I am so proud of you. You've been so patient and gentle and attentive to her while battling all those mating drives. She's a lucky girl, and that's not just your mom talking." She smiles wide and grips me in an almost crushing hug. Even at my size she manages to squeeze the air out of me. As I'm struggling to breath, Silvia peeks in the kitchen door.

"Ah, Silvia dear," Ma cheerily says while releasing me. "I've slipped some treats into your bag, and Torben has lunch in his for both of you. The trip will likely take you most of the day to get there, but you should arrive before nightfall." Ma helps Silvia into her backpack and sees us both out. Silvia doesn't escape a crushing bear hug from my mom either.

"Thank you, Ma," Silvia gasps from inside the hug. "I hope to see you again soon once I learn how not to wreck your house." They chuckle and Ma uses the bee hair stick to catch my Mate's wild red hair in a bun.

"No need to worry about that, my dear. Phil is an excellent teacher and will have you holding a glass again in no time. And believe me, you haven't done nearly as much damage to my home as my two little cubs did." She kisses us both on the cheek as my dad comes out to offer his goodbyes. A slap on the shoulder for me and a smile with a wink for Silvia. It makes my heart warm that both my parents already approve of my Mate.

We travel most of the way there along some deer paths through the forest. As with most Change Coaches, Phil's training cabin is out in the wilderness, away from towns and communities. Best to keep some distance when training new Shifters, just in case.

He lives in a nearby village with his mate but does belong to our Clan. I see him at gatherings, and festivals and on the occasional trip to his town. I've brought a few students to him before, but I've never stayed more than a few hours. It will be interesting to see how training is done. As children, we have our parents and school to teach us control, shifting, our history, and culture. I've heard he got into this trade after he taught his mate our ways. I haven't heard the whole story and always wondered why he didn't take him to a coach himself. Maybe one day I'll learn, but for now I'm content enough to know that my mother trusts his training, and so will I.

I have us running every now and then, both to make good time and so Silvia can test her new speed. This aspect of her new abilities brings her great joy. She talks about never being a running person before, but how it feels as easy as walking now. She even passes me a time or two which makes me wonder if she'll end up being faster than I am. The thought makes me smile, as does her sheer delight at her capabilities. Though, I make sure she doesn't exhaust herself. If I know one thing about Phil, it's that he'll be putting her through her paces soon enough.

We stop by a waterfall for lunch and Silvia happily eats, absently swaying side to side. Her eyes stay fixed on the waterfall and the moving stream, but she's the view I can't get enough of. The running and excitement has brought a flush to her face and chest. It obscures some of her freckles, but I know they're still there. Her rocking is also doing fun things to her breasts. It's not till she stops moving that I realize she's caught me staring at her chest.

Well, not just her breasts if I'm honest, but that's where my eyes were lingering when she caught me. But instead of being upset or angry as I feared, she's become slightly aroused. I can scent it in the air between us and see it in her eyes. She's also biting that deliciously plump lower lip. I can't help the growl of desire that rumbles out of me. Her quick intake of air only accentuates her cleavage. Oh, it's so dangerous to be alone with her right now.

Very reluctantly, I close my eyes. Just a bit more patience on my part. I can't have her till she understands what this means and consents to it, and me, with full understanding. She's already had one choice taken from her. I won't rush or take another. Clearing my throat I turn my gaze to the waterfall.

"I love this spot. I try to always stop here when going to Phil's training cabin. How's your sandwich? Didn't get soggy, did it?" I've got to draw our minds to something else. She's still looking at me like I'd be a delicious meal, and I would love nothing more than to let her feast. "You, ah, said your grandparents kept bees? When we get back I'll have to introduce you to Old Man Talbet. He's been keeping hives and cultivating honey since before Ma was born. I bet he could show you a trick or two, and his honey is always worth the coin."

I seem to have chosen the correct topic to break those devious thoughts of hers. She shakes her head as if to clear her mind before answering me.

"Yes, I would love that. I haven't been around any hives or bees since Grandma passed. I sold hers to another beekeeper she knew. Grandma often met up with him to trade secrets and discuss bees. So I felt okay about him getting her colonies." There's a slight sadness to her face now that always comes with speaking of her grandparents. I know she loved them deeply and still mourns their passing.

"Then it's settled, once your coach releases you from training, I'll take you to see Talbet. He's always up for talking people's ears off about bees and all things bee related. He once held Ma hostage for an hour talking about candle making with his beeswax." She smiles at that and it warms my heart. "We should get going. Still a bit of traveling ahead of us to go."

With that we head out once more. Lusty crisis averted, for now.

We make good time with our occasional sprints, and arrive at the cabin as the sun starts its descent in the sky.

"Ho there!" I call out in greeting. Phil is outside building a campfire from recently chopped wood. He's solidly built, as most born bear shifters are. Shorter than me but broader of chest and shoulders, his thick black hair is matched by swaths of hair on his chest and arms. I'm secretly glad I'm not as hairy as he is. I have some chest and arm hair, yes, but he has a rug popping out of his shirt. I've got enough to wash sap and wood splinters from as it is. He raises his arm in acknowledgment and we proceed forward.

The cabin itself is a two-story log building with an attached equipment shed for storage. As I recall, the second story is strictly for Phil's use, while the main floor has rooms for students. I can see that some equipment and logs have already been dragged out for future use.

"Hey there Torben, it's been a while." Once close enough, Phil extends his arm to me for a strong handshake. "Good to see you. And this must be my new little protégé." He shakes her hand as well. "My name is Phil and I'll be your Change Coach. I know this wasn't something you planned on, but I hope it's something you can learn to embrace nonetheless."

"Hi, it's nice to meet you Phil. My name is Silvia. I'm really grateful that you agreed to teach me on such short notice. And I think I might be coming around to this whole Shifter thing."

"Excellent! That will make this whole process much easier. Embrace the change and have an open mind. Torben," Phil turns to me with an affable smile, "why don't you take both of your bags inside while I go over a few things with Silvia and get to know my student. Your rooms are on the first floor, of course. Clean linens and such are in the closet in each room. It'd be helpful if you made the beds for you two. That's a good lad." With that, he hands me her bag and ushers Silvia away.

A part of me is upset at being dismissed like that, but the other part understands I can't hover around for all of her training. I suddenly realize that this might be harder for me than I expected.

Chapter 17

Silvia

This Phil guy has me starting work right away. Even though I have been walking and running for the better part of the day, he instructs me on the art of log splitting. Though it's easier with my new strength, I still need to learn control and how to aim. Let's just say, there are a few flying wood moments. But I start to get the hang of it as the sun fully sets for the night.

He seems to be a good teacher so far, I'll give him that. Offering a good balance of advice, encouragement, and ways to improve or tweak my form. He's not as harsh in his corrections as I would have feared from the look of him. All in all, after the first evening, I judge him to be patient and understanding but he definitely has some serious 'don't fuck with me' energy. I also find that I don't want to disappoint this guy.

As I'm laying in bed this first night, I vow to do the best I can. For my new coach, for myself, and for Torben and his mom. They are all working so hard—yes, I include myself in that—it would really be a shame not to succeed.

The next few days are filled with more exercise than I have ever done in my life! Running, climbing, chopping wood, more running, lifting logs bigger than myself. Jumping up and over stones, wading hip deep in cold ass rivers to catch fish with my bare hands, and did I mention running! I found it fun at first, but my enthusiasm waned long ago. I end every day dirty, sweaty, gross, and hungrier than I have ever been.

The first night Coach Phil gave me a pile of rough-feeling, quickly made clothing to exercise in. He passed off several sets of drawstring pants, long tunic-type shirts, and some odd crossbody bra chest wrap situation. It mostly does the job but I still prefer the bodice, and I'd kill for a good sports bra!

"Why do I have to wear these clothes anyway? I know I can move well in them, but they aren't really very comfortable or flattering." I finally find the courage to complain on the third day.

"They aren't for comfort or for style." He chuckles. "They are so you don't rip up your real, important clothes when you start shifting. Speaking of, have you made contact with your inner bear yet?" That has been my one true failing in all this so far. Though we meditate together every morning and evening trying to make contact with this 'inner bear' I'm supposed to have now, I haven't heard so much as a grumble. "Don't look so down, it will happen. It just takes time. I'm not worried yet and neither should you. Your bear has only recently woken up within you. She'll talk when you both are ready."

Speaking of talking when they're ready, I've barely been able to get a few sentences out when around Torben. I don't know what it is, but since we've arrived, every time I get near him or smell him, I'm hit instantly with the lust bug. Day two of being here, Phil and I were in the woods all day. When we came back, I got to witness Torben tearing wood logs apart with his bare hands. I almost came right then and there! And to be honest, it's been a memory I've replayed several times since then. Thankfully, Torben has been giving Phil and me space to train during the day. But he joins us for dinner—which he cooks—in the evenings. I know Coach senses something between us due to all the smirks, but he keeps his mouth shut.

Today is a squat and meditation day, with some history thrown in here and there. During our morning meditation, he again leads me to visualize a heavily wooded forest. I follow the path I find there, but today, instead of just walking through the woods the whole time, I find a cave. I'm so excited and surprised I instantly come out of my meditative state and yell, "A cave! There's a cave! I saw a cave this time."

"That's excellent. Did you go in? Or did you get so excited you stopped?" He's got one of those knowing half-smiles again. I cover my face with both hands, inwardly kicking myself. He chuckles, "It's okay, but next time try to go into the cave and see what's inside. I'll have us do another meditation after lunch. Now it's time for log squats." Oh goodie.

True to his word after lunch he leads the same meditation prompt again, and to my delight, I find the cave once more, quicker this time. I can hear a noise coming from deeper in the cave as I stand at its mouth. It takes me a while to realize it's snoring. I'm hearing very loud snoring coming from somewhere inside this mind cave.

"Hello, is anybody there?" Nothing.

"Hi, my name is Silvia, and I'm looking for my bear." Still nothing but the steady stream of snores.

"HELLO!" I yell. Right as the snores stop, I hear a faint, *Go away, I'm sleepy*, before I am thrust out of my own vision.

"What the fuck?!" I say out loud.

"Guessing something new happened. Tell me about it." Coach offers me some water to drink and sits down closer.

"I think I met my bear, and I'm pretty sure she just kicked me out of my own damn head!" I'm incensed as Phil turns his head trying to hide his laughter, but I can see his shoulders shaking.

"Well, I guess that's a pretty clear 'I'm not ready to talk' message. Let's use this anger energy and do some log lunges." I stare at him with what must be pure horror in my eyes. I did squats already this morning while holding a damn log, and now he wants me to do it again but this time while moving! "Don't give me that look, you'll be fine. Now, up you get."

As I'm lunging around his house, he peppers in some more Shifter history and lore. This time it's about the Goddess of the Shifters. The one who made the first and all others types that followed. How she started off as mainly a Goddess of Weres, now called Shifters, but has increased her domain since then. She branched out into Transformations, Change, and some other stuff as time went on.

I don't pay as much attention as I should. My mind keeps going back and forth between the fiery pain in my leg muscles and the audacity of my bear. It's my mind! How could she kick me out?! What if she dislikes me already and will always decide to sleep instead of talk? Have I ruined our relationship somehow? Does she know I might not be able to keep her when I leave this place?

"That's enough, put the log down, but continue to walk around. Here, drink some water, and once you finish this whole bottle, we'll go stand in the cold river." Phil hands me said water before continuing. "I'll massage your legs before we meditate one last time today. We'll give that bear of yours another chance before you sleep."

The frigid water of the river helps some, and his massage hurts, but helps. An odd combo of relief and more pain. At some point during my leg rubdown I could have sworn I heard someone say, *Yuck,* but no one was around but Phil and me. I mean, yes, it feels weird for Phil to touch me so much, but it's only to help my poor muscles. I certainly don't find it disgusting, more clinical. He is my coach after all. I chalk it up to weird forest sounds.

To my misery, I discover after dinner my legs will no longer hold my weight and have instead turned to jelly. Torben is quick to catch me though, lifting me easily to carry me to my room. I may nuzzle, oh so sweetly, into his neck as he holds me. What can I say, I can't get enough of his smell. He growls deep in his chest, and I realize that my actions haven't gone unnoticed. Oops! He sets me down on the edge of my bed and asks if I need anything. Yeah, I need him in this bed, ravishing me right now.

But instead, I tell him no and thank the universe that I always wash up before dinner. It feels too gross to eat before I get cleaned from that day's workout. As he leaves and closes the door, I decide I may not be as tired as I thought I was. It would be a real shame to waste this wetness and desire that Torben's nearness has inspired. Time for a little self-pleasure.

As quickly as I can, I wiggle up my bed to lean my back against the headboard. Clumsily, I work my stupid pants off, pull my tunic shirt up over my breasts, and untie the binder I use for after showers. It's not as covering or supportive as the others but it's enough to wear around these men while I eat. My girls are too big to be around others without something to support them. Plus, these clothes are too rough on my nipples.

Nipples that are now peaked and begging for attention. A simple graze from my fingers has me gasping in surprised pleasure. Whatever Torben has going for him needs to be bottled and sold. I'd take a lifetime supply of that in a heartbeat. I decide my undies need to go as well and I end up kicking them off to the far corner of the room in my fervor.

The first drag of my middle finger through my pussy folds is heaven. I'm so wet and ready I know this isn't going to take me long. The first one at least, since this now feels like it's going to be a multi-orgasm event. My eyes drift closed and my head tilts back to rest on the headboard as my fingers dance and rub with familiarity in exactly the way I need. I slip the tip of one finger to rest just at the entrance of my opening while another finger circles my clit. My other hand holds myself open for better access. I'm getting so close my eyelids start to flutter; that's when I notice that I'm not alone. A figure is standing in my bedroom doorway.

I instantly snap my legs closed and pull my shirt back down, but there's no way to hide what I was doing. Torben is standing there, frozen like a statue, still staring at where my whole ass vagina was just exposed to him.

"Close the door!" I urgently whisper at him. He instantly complies, but unfortunately he's now standing on my side of the closed door. I don't know what to do with that. I really didn't expect it. As I'm frantically thinking what I should do, I accidentally move the hand—the one that's now clamped in a vice-like grip between my closed legs— in such a way that sends a pulse of pleasure though my body.

I'm surprised that, after I groan, I hear him groan too. Interesting. Getting a better look at him now I see that he is breathing rapidly, muscled chest heaving up and down. His eyes are so dilated they are like pools of darkness. Eyes which are still trained on my now closed legs.

I have no idea where I find the boldness, but I open my legs a fraction. He groans again at that. Oh, I think he likes this? I lift my shirt back up over my breasts and run my fingers across a nipple. He lets out a low growl. Then when I fully open my legs once more, he drops to his knees with a thud. This feels as if I have discovered a very dangerous power. I've never commanded a man like this, and it feels good. Fully exposed now—for his viewing pleasure—I begin to slowly start working myself again. When I finally let a moan escape my lips, I can see his eyes flutter as if in pleasure himself. That's when I notice the huge bulge in his pants. He's hard for me, and I need to see it.

"Take off your clothes," I say in a breathless voice. He immediately rips his shirt over his head as he stands to remove his pants just as effortlessly. His cock is juts straight out toward me—as I hoped it would—and like the man himself, it's a big boy. Definitely the biggest I've ever seen in person.

"Touch yourself," I order. Who is this woman I've become, and how can I keep her around? He takes hold of the base of his cock, a grip that looks to be hard and tight as a slight hiss escapes his lips at the contact. He strokes up his shaft slowly and thumbs over the head when he reaches it. He's got some precum there. I can see it glistening, but it's not going to be enough for that massive cock. Because I want him to fully enjoy this, I reach my hand over to the lotion pot I keep on my bedside table. "Here, use this," I say as I toss it to him.

He catches it easily with his free hand and brings the jar under his nose, inhaling deeply. It takes me a moment to realize he isn't trying to smell the lotion through the closed lid. No, he's smelling me on that jar. I absently used the hand that is now coated in my wetness, and he's smelling it like I'm the most amazing thing he's ever come across. His chest rumbles again with another one of those sexy growls. Effortlessly, he flicks off the lid and scoops out some lotion. His hand now glides more smoothly over that cock, and it is a sight to see. My hand has made its way back to my folds and is rubbing away with abandon. This is the sexiest thing I have ever done, and it's really getting me off, hard.

The music in the room now consists of his grunts, the slickness of lotion over skin, my moans, and our fast breathing, accompanied by the wet sounds of my own pleasure. It's a song I will remember forever.

After some time of mutual self-pleasure and watching each other jerk off, he grits out, "I'm close."

"Me too," I breathlessly reply. And I am. I am so damn close. Still running my thumb over my now swollen clit, I slowly push my middle finger up inside me to lightly graze my g-spot. But that's all it takes for me to come instantly. My mouth opens in a silent scream as my inner walls clench around my finger and my back arches. I continue to work my clit, extending this orgasm for all its worth. There's a small gush of warm liquid that runs past my fingers. I squirted with my first release? It usually takes several before I work myself up enough for that. Well, damn.

"Fuck!" I hear from the opposite side of the room. I look over in time to see Torben, who's on his knees again, leaning forward onto his free hand to come on the wood floor. And come, and come, and come some more. Wow, this guy really had a lot to let loose. Wonder if it's always that much or if it's just been a while? Both of our bodies are shaking, and we're still breathing quickly. My poor legs are spent and have knocked into each other for support.

It's Torben who recovers first. While keeping his eyes fixed on me, he slowly stands and begins walking toward me. I start to get very excited and can feel my heart rate increase yet again. I would give anything for him to touch me now, to kiss me now, to take me now. But then he veers and walks into my bathroom. I hear the water come on and he exits shortly after—water still running in the other room—with a cloth in his hand. He then cleans up his mess on the floor.

I start to get up so I can wash up too, but he holds his hand up and says, "Wait," in a very commanding tone. So, like a good girl, I wait. He throws the dirty cloth by the door, walks back into the washroom, then returns to my side with a new wet cloth.

"Open your legs," he says in the same firm tone. Yes sir, I think right before I let my legs fall open. The rag is warm, and his hands are gentle as he cleans my naughty bits, then each of my fingers. "Do you want to change the sheets?" His voice is all gravel right now and skates across my naked body.

"Oh, no, I didn't really get them that wet,"...yet. But it was so sweet of him to ask. Actually, I don't think I've ever had anybody take such good care of me after intimacy. Oh girl, I might just be falling in love with this man. He finds my nightgown and pulls it down my body, tucks me into the covers, and kisses my forehead oh so softly. He grabs his clothes and the dirty rags, then opens the door to leave.

"Goodnight," he whispers, and before I can reply in kind, he's gone. Closing the door behind him.

I still can't believe that just happened to me. Me! And when I think about everything that went down, I get turned on all over again.

After coming several more times, and yes, having to change the sheets after all, the fire in my veins is finally cooled enough to sleep. The last thoughts I have before I drift off are, *Now that's worth waking up for.* Which is odd because I'm not waking up, I'm going to sleep.

Chapter 18

Torben

That was unexpected. Amazing, glorious even, but unexpected. I hadn't realized she was playing with herself till I had already opened the door. The smell of it hit me first, and if I had been walking slower, I would have noticed it before barging in there. But I had just left and she had been so tired. I wanted to get back to her before she fell asleep. Why had I gone in there again anyway? I'm having a hard time remembering what was so important. Everything dropped from my mind once I stepped into her room and saw my Mate spread out before me enjoying herself. I'm hard again just remembering what she did, what we did. I'm glad she wanted me to stay, because it would have taken all the strength I had to leave in that moment.

I make it back to my room in time to hear, and smell, my Mate again. She's pleasuring herself once more and I can't help but take myself in hand along with her. I want so badly to go back to her room to enjoy the sights, sounds, and smell of her. But I know if I do, I won't be able to resist touching her, kissing her, burying myself deep inside her. So I stay in my room and listen to her as I jerk myself off. I vowed not to claim her till she understands what that truly means. But, there's no harm in this mutual enjoyment, right?

I'm leaning on my forearm, resting my forehead on the wall we share. I took her undergarments I saw on the floor on my way out, so I'm holding them and the tantalizing lotion jar in my hand close to my face. The aroma from them makes her feel closer. I finish shortly after she does. As I'm about to clean off my mess from the wall, I hear her begin once more, which gets me ready to go again too. I'm going to owe her a new jar of lotion after tonight.

The next morning I wake up and head outside before my Silvia awakens. I find Phil out there enjoying the sunrise with some morning tea.

"I need you to teach her about mates, now," I say by way of greeting. Last night was a sweet kind of torture and took all the restraint I had. I was almost relieved when she was finally satisfied for the night and made ready for bed and sleep. I won't be able to endure another night like that, being so close but not nearly close enough.

"Good morning to you, too. I've no need to ask why since I was able to hear and smell more than I cared to last night." My cheeks heat at his words. I didn't even think about that at the time. I was too caught up in it all. "No need to feel embarrassed, she's your mate after all. You are showing more discipline as a newly realized mating pair than I've seen in some who've been mated for a decade. You were doing so well at resisting The Call that I believe I've put the Mating talks off longer than I should have. And I'm sorry for that." He dips his head at me and I'm grateful for his words. "We'll be covering that today while I'm putting her through the egg challenge." He grins maliciously as I groan.

"Not the egg challenge. Haven't we found a better way to increase gentle handling skills?" We all end up hating the egg challenge as children. I went a whole year once without wanting to ever see, smell, or eat another egg again!

"Sometimes the old tried and true methods are still the best. Hope you'll be up for scrambled eggs tonight." He laughs and I join in. This will make my poor Mate very upset and irritable tonight. She doesn't like failing, and this test is basically designed for you to fail, and fail often. It sounds simple enough, transfer eggs from one basket to another, one egg at a time. But when you are learning to control and truly understand how strong you are, it's quite the challenge indeed. As a born shifter I've been through the egg challenge several times in my life. You need to be reminded as your body grows and changes.

"Do you have enough eggs? I'd be happy to make a trip to the closest town if you need more. There's an errand or two I need to run myself." I've used almost all of my Mate's lotion and need to replace it for her soon.

"I'm sure I've got enough for today, but I might take you up on that offer tomorrow. We'll see how it goes," Phil says with a wink. With that, we part ways to start the day. Him to training and me to cooking breakfast, then doing laundry. It's shaping up to be a nice sunny day, and I know there are some sheets that could use a wash.

My Mate is very shy around me this morning and is having an even harder time than usual looking me in the eyes. But to be fair I'm feeling pretty shy myself. For one, I barged into her room. Two, I've never done that with any of my sexual partners. And three, I don't know if she realizes I continued with her after I left her room. Phil has spared her a run this morning, so I get a chance to talk to her before her meditation.

"I'm sorry I barged into your room last night," I blurt out before I lose my nerve. "I really should have knocked and had no idea what you were doing." My burning cheeks could set my beard on fire.

"Oh, no, yes, you definitely should have knocked, of course. I, for sure, wasn't expecting to see you back. Well, obviously I wasn't expecting you to come back and see me doing that. Not that I didn't like you seeing me, but some warning would have been nice. Though I totally wouldn't have let you in if I had had some warning. So in a way I'm kinda glad you barged in because what we did was amazing. Like, it was the hottest sexiest thing I've ever done. I hope you liked it too because I really liked it. I mean, obviously you saw that I liked it. And, and I'm sorry I kinda ordered you around. I don't know what came over me, to say such things out loud." She laughs nervously and finally looks at me, this whole conversation she's been looking everywhere but at me.

"I liked it very much too," I say while holding her green eyes with mine. "I liked it all, Sweet Silvia." I grin at her reaction. She had been twirling her hair and swaying, but at the use of this pet name she stops completely, smiles up at me, and gently places her hand on my chest.

"If you two are done chatting, we've got some work to do," Phil calls from outside. My Mate's ears go scarlet and she moves to follow her coach's commands, but I stop her by holding the hand on my chest in place. She turns her eyes back to mine, her eyebrows hold a question.

"May I kiss you sometime?" I ask in a whisper. "I'd really like to kiss you soon." Her cheeks now match the red of her ears and she nods.

"Yes," she whispers back, "yes, I'd like that too." She has glanced down at her feet, but I lift her chin with my other hand so her eyes are on my face once more. I need to tell her one more thing before she starts her training.

"Don't be too upset or hard on yourself with today's lesson. It's meant to be difficult, and you will fail many, many times before you succeed. Then you will fail more and only succeed occasionally." She looks so confused but I continue, "We've all been there, even me and Phil. Good luck." I kiss her forehead and release her hand.

"Thank you, I guess. But now I think I'm even more worried." She laughs and leaves while I get to cleaning.

I listen in as I do my house chores. Sounds like her bear is still being contrary and wants to sleep. Her frustration makes me laugh. Phil then has her change tactics, suggesting that perhaps attempting to Shift will coax her bear out. The reward of freedom and fresh air may help the situation. Of course, nothing happens except a lot of funny faces from Silvia with a few grunting noises. She is again discouraged, but Phil assures her that a shift rarely happens before person and bear have met and come to an understanding with each other.

Apparently, several meetings and conversations usually occur before a shift. I've been shifting since I was a toddler and don't remember any of this.

We have always been, my bear reassures me. *Our Mate is working so hard. She is strong and patient. I have chosen well.* Oh, are you taking credit for finding Silvia? *Of course, if not me then who?* Hard to argue with that, I guess.

"Alright, time to move on to the dreaded Egg Challenge," Phil declares while rubbing his hands together. "As our friend Torben has already stated, this will not be as easy as it seems. You are about to break a lot of eggs. But don't feel bad, because we are eating them tonight. Here you will see that there are two baskets, one filled with eggs and one empty. Your task is to transfer all the eggs from one basket to the other, one at a time, without breaking any. You will fail. Now sit on the ground and start moving some eggs."

"That, that's it? The whole challenge is to move eggs? I mean, I did break a lot of stuff while at Torben's parents house, but I've been doing really well since being here. I think I just had to get used to the increased strength, ya know? Since it was all so new and overwhelming."

"First off, I believe I'm the Change Coach here and have been successfully helping people adjust to their transformation for many years now." Phil is ticking off fingers as he gives my Mate a dressing down. "Second, you think I've been running you ragged for the fun of it? Using your new strength purposefully helps you feel when you are using it, and reversely lets you realize when you are not. Plus, making you tired has the added benefit of lessening the strength you have to expel from your system. And thirdly," Phil is now bending down and eyeing his student right in the face. "You think I haven't reinforced this cabin and everything that's within it, down to the spoons and sheets?" He stands back up to his full height once more. "Now, get to crackin!"

"Sorry sir," my Mate mutters and does indeed get to cracking some eggs. She crushes her first ten eggs thoroughly, placing the eggy remains in the ceramic bowl Phil placed in front of her between the two baskets. But by the time I have hung all the sheets on the lines to dry, she is only causing slight cracks to the eggs. She may not realize it but this is quite a feat for her first try. Especially considering Coach Phil didn't run or exercise any strength out of her this morning.

Our Mate is so gentle and perseverant. She will be a good partner and maybe even a mother someday. Whoa there, we haven't even completed the mating bond nor built a home. Let's not get ahead of ourselves. I want to enjoy my time with my Mate for a while yet before having children. *Don't get all worried. I'm talking about future plans*, my bear reassures me.

"Good, good," Phil praises, "you are doing very well. Now, let's add in some Shifter learning while you continue to move those eggs. See if you can listen and keep your control."

My ears perk up at that and I decide to sit behind a tree to listen in without interfering with the lessons. Phil starts off by talking about clans. Starting with our Clan and touching on others in the area. How we are like a family and many are indeed related but an outsider can be welcomed into a clan. Then he brings up the different types of Shifters and how their systems vary or stay the same.

"As an example, one thing all Shifters have in common is Mating Bonds or having, what we call, True Mates. Other beings have this also, but for today we will stick to Shifters. Have you ever heard or learned about Mates or Mating Bonds?"

"Hmm," my Mate looks up and away thinking, which ends up with her breaking her current egg. "Oh shoot! I was doing so well too. But I guess that's the point, isn't it? Not worth it if I can't talk or do other things while I'm handling stuff." Wiping her eggy hands on the rim of the bowl she continues. "Let's see, I think I've read that Fae have mates, right?"

"Yes, that's true, they do. Have you ever heard what it means to have a mate or find your mate?"

"Isn't it like finding your soulmate or something? Like the person you are meant to be with?" She then scrunches her face in an adorable way. "Oh wait, or is it all about making babies and your mate just means you are compatible and will create good offspring? You could not even like each other, but this thing compels you to have sex and make babies! I remember hearing about that too. Is that the kind Shifters have?! I don't want that. Having no choice who I make babies with." Oh no, she's gotten the wrong idea. "No, no, I have this cuff here so it shouldn't happen to me, right? Since I can't have babies unless I take it off. So no mates for me unless I remove it, and I don't think I ever will if that's what's going to happen." She's freaking out now. Phil needs to get her back on track, she's broken each of her eggs while on this tangent.

"Hold on, hold on, there Missy. Let's not go off down a rabbit hole just yet. While yes, procreation is a part of it and some beings' mating bonds are akin to that, this is not the case for Shifters, and certainly not for Bear Shifters. Now, slow down and collect yourself before I go on. We are trying to hold a conversation without breaking eggs, remember?"

My Mate eventually calms down so Phil continues.

"I'll stick with Bear Shifters for now since that is what you are and will concern you the most. For a Bear Shifter, a True Mating is about finding your perfect partner. This can eventually lead to children and often does. But since True Mates can be of any gender, it's less about that and more about finding your 'soul's mate' as you initially suggested. My Mate is also a male, by the way." He winks at her.

"Oh, I'm sorry. I didn't know. Now I feel really awful. I-" Phil holds up his hands to stop her before she spirals again.

"Don't feel bad. You are new to all this, and we haven't really talked much about me and my life. This training is about you, after all. Now back to the lesson at hand. Having and finding a True Mate is a sacred and unbreakable bond. Every Shifter, no matter the species, will respect this bond. And even in death, the bond will remain. You may take new lovers, but you will never have another True Mate. Do you understand?"

"Think I'm starting to, yeah. It sounds kinda romantic, actually." My heart skips a beat at her words. She's not fully opposed to the idea and may even like it. Thank the Goddess!

"It can be, at least after the mating lust dies down. At first, when or if you find you have a True Mate, you both will be quite overcome with the need to...how shall I put this...have sex everywhere, all the time, basically." He chuckles at his own words and experience. These are things I've heard all my life, and am currently experiencing myself, but she appears quite shocked to be discussing this with Phil.

"I see that I may have been too blunt, but it's really kinda the truth. Your animal desires will win out eventually, and you will be 'making love' like rabbits till all parties are satisfied that the bond is strong and secure. There can also be bonds between multiple people, though that's a bit rarer in Bears. Mates can be from any Shifter type, race, magical creature, or even non-magical creatures as you once were. A True Mating doesn't care who or what you are in order to form."

"Oh, I think I've read about those kinds of stories, as well. Where a Fae found their mate amongst humans and took them away." She looks a little embarrassed yet dreamy talking about what sounds like kidnapping to me.

"Yeah, the Fae are known for taking humans. Or luring them away from some other land. They say there isn't magic in that place anymore, but that's just what they say. Anyway, back to Shifter True Mates." Phil tries to get the lesson back on track, but my Mate's eyes have gone very wide at his words and have a look almost like alarm. She quickly schools her face before Phil notices. Wonder what that was about?

"How do you know? How do you know when you've found your True Mate?" My whole body has gone still and rigid at her words. Now we come to it. Will she realize once he explains it? Will she be angry with me, or will she jump into my arms? I've almost certainly stopped breathing.

Chapter 19

Silvia

I was a little shocked at first when Phil spoke about a land without magic and that the Fae sometimes take people from it. But that is what happens in legends sometimes, so such lore is bound to be in this story of mine too, right? They can't be talking about my actual-for-real world. I shake my head in an effort to clear it. To stop it from thinking. I can dig into that thought experiment later once I'm alone. I can't start freaking out right now, wondering if I was actually kidnapped by a Fae, if I'm actually in another world right instead of the book I was told I'd be in. So I keep the topic on mates and ask how one knows when they have found their True Mate.

"Well," Phil says while scratching his beard, "there is the aforementioned lust for one. You will be instantly drawn to them, and it will be unlike any sexual attraction or desire you have ever felt. They will smell better than anyone else has ever smelled before, and you will be able to scent them further away than anything else. In their presence, your body will heat up, your eyes will dilate, and you will be drawn closer to them like a magnet. Touching them will only increase these effects. There is also a sort of 'knowing' that you feel. It's hard to explain that part, and some people feel this 'knowing' more strongly than others. I find those who trust their intuition already trust their 'knowing' more easily and readily. But once you touch, once you kiss...oh, you'll understand immediately. Your body and your beast will let you know and won't let you forget it." His chuckling at the end makes me suspect he's speaking from experience on that last part, and it makes me smile.

I kind of love the idea of having a True Mate actually. Someone who's meant for you and you for them. Awfully romantic and safe at the same time. It would be nice knowing that something is certain, true, and real.

"Does every Shifter have a True Mate out there? Do you think I will have one someday?" I hear what sounds like someone scoffing very loudly near me and whip my head from side to side. "What was that?! Who did that? Did you hear someone?"

"No," Phil shakes his head at me. "I didn't hear anything, and my hearing is outstanding, even by Shifter standards."

"I...I thought I heard someone scoff at my question. Like it was a stupid thing to ask or something?"

Phil glances off toward the tree line but shakes his head and turns back to me with a quizzical expression on his face. He gives me a shrug before moving on.

"As far as your question goes, yes, most Shifters do have a True Mate. It is rare not to have one, and that usually only happens to those who truly do not wish for such a thing or find no interest in sexual activities. And of course, since you were a human, your mate could be someone you already know or met before you went through the Change. You're doing great with the eggs, by the way; you haven't broken or cracked one in some time."

"Really?!" I shout, and then proceed to absolutely crush the egg I was holding. "Damn it!" I glare up at my coach, "Did you do that on purpose?" He chuckles in reply.

"Gotta keep you on your toes." I wipe the egg off into the ceramic bowl and continue moving eggs from basket to basket. "You really are doing very well though. So before I end the lesson on True Mates, do you have any other questions for me?"

"Only about a million." I let out an exasperated sigh. There really is much more to learn than I thought there would be, and now I feel so under prepared for all this. Wish I had a voice recorder or something since these lessons usually happen while I'm doing tasks, so taking notes isn't an option. "Is all this Shifter information in a book or two somewhere? I'd love to be able to read into it more. I feel like I'm only getting the highlights from you."

"Ah, yes, there are books and stories a plenty out there. I'm really just here to give you the 'highlights,' as you say. Making sure you get the information you need to know to survive. Once I'm done with you, feel free to read up all you want." He then brings his hand to his beard, drawing his eyebrows together in thought. "Hmm, actually now that I think on it, I'm sure you could get your hands on some books and read at night after I'm done with you. Torben!"

As Phil shouts his name a tree off by the clotheslines shakes as if it were surprised and Torben steps out from behind it. Was he listening to us or was he taking a nap? Phil waves him over while I move the ceramic bowl of crushed eggs in an effort to hide how many eggs I've decimated.

"Torben, you still up for going into town tomorrow for more eggs?" I wince as Torben nods. "Good, our student here wishes for more scholarly knowledge about Shifters. When you're there, see if you can find her anything at the bookshop or library. Only bring her one book though, I won't have a sleep-deprived pupil." Torben nods again, and I can't help the smile that spreads across my face.

"Really?! Thank you! I would feel so much better and more prepared if I could study the subject a bit more. I still feel like a fish out of water with all this."

"I'll try to find you one that gives a good overview," Torben adds, "and I'll write down the names of some others I find that you might want for next time, so you can choose yourself." I'm over the moon. It sounds amazing and very thoughtful!

"Wonderful," is all I reply with, and it comes out all wistfully on an exhale.

"Let's pause egg cracking and try to contact your bear again," my coach interjects. "Torben, will you stay here and sit with us this time? Maybe having more bears around will coax her out." I'm excited and nervous at the prospect of Torben being here as I meditate. But dread starts to fill me as I realize I'm probably about to fail again in front of him. Great, just great.

He plops down near me on the dirt then moves the egg baskets away. Grabbing my water cup, he gestures for me to hold my hands out so he can pour water on them. I rinse my hands off as best I can before he hands me the small towel he keeps in his belt while cleaning. Why are all these small gestures of care and kindness making me swoon so hard today? Oh yeah, it probably has something to do with what we did last night. I instantly start to blush as the memories invade my mind's eye.

"Now," Phil barges into my daydreams, "go back to the woods again and try to start closer to that cave your bear is in." That's right, we aren't alone out here, and I'm supposed to be meeting my inner bear, not having naughty thoughts about the man beside me. Clearing my throat, I close my eyes and try to bring back the vision of the forest.

It's proving to be quite difficult. I can feel the nearness of him. Every inhale is full of that intoxicating smell of his.

Delicious. My eyes fly open, "What?!" Both men stare back at me as I hear, *I said he smells delicious.* I can feel my jaw hanging open. Torben moves closer in concern, but Phil is smiling.

"You're hearing a voice in your head I take it?" I nod yes and stare at Phil wide-eyed as he chuckles at me. "Don't look so scared. That's how you are meant to communicate with your Inner Bear. It's how we all do it. Though normally those who were changed make contact and talk in visions first."

We have met in a vision, I hear, clear as day.

"She says we have met in a vision. I guess that's technically true."

"Hmm," is Phil's dubious reply. "See if she'll meet you in a vision now, so you can talk face to face."

Why would I want to do that when he's right here smelling so yummy? This is so weird. *No, it's not. He said this is how we are supposed to talk. Now move closer so we can touch him.* No, we are supposed to be talking to each other. *I think we should be doing what we did with him last night.*

I am blushing so hard it feels as if my whole body has turned bright red. She saw! My Inner Bear saw what we did? What I did! Oh gawd.

Why are you so flustered? It was wonderful and we enjoyed it very much. Wish he had stayed to do more though.

"Pardon me!" I shout loudly as I stand straight up and quickly walk away, toward the river. *No, don't leave. Wait, tell him to follow us. We could have him in the river.*

Instantly a mental picture of Torben bending me over a large smooth river stone, taking me from behind, flashes in my mind. Then one of Torben holding onto me with his hands threaded in my hair and my legs wrapped around him. Holding on as he pushes deep into me stifling my cry with a kiss. Now Torben is looking down at me as I wrap my hands and lips around that massive cock.

My whole body is on fire now. I have to stop this. I have to take control of myself before this she-bear inside me takes over and I jump that wonderfully sweet man behind me.

I think he'd like it very much if you did jump him. Remember how he reacted last night? Yes, I do, but you still can't go around hopping on a man's cock all willy-nilly. There's a process, a courtship, social rules to follow. *Not with him. He's ours now.* No, no, he isn't 'ours'. I mean, we haven't even kissed yet. *We could change that right now. He did say he wanted to-*

SPLASH! I leaped right into the cold waters of the river before she could finish her thought and sway me.

Spoilsport. I dunk my head under. Even below the water, I can hear them running after me. I breach the surface and hold a hand up before they make it to the bank.

"Stop right there! I need a minute alone, please. No need to worry or help." They glance at each other in confusion. "Please, just leave me alone!" Poor Torben's eyes cast downward at my plea.

"I'll go check the laundry." He sounds so dejected, but I can't go to him right now. Not till my bear and I can come to some understanding about who's in charge.

"You get a fifteen-minute break. Then come back and we'll continue the Egg Challenge and discuss what just happened." I open my mouth to protest because I have no desire to tell anyone what just happened, but he stops me before I can even start. "We will discuss it, student," he says firmly. "I can only help you, lead you, if I know what's going on. No need to be embarrassed. Trust me, I've seen and heard it all. I won't press for details, only the highlights." He's got his arms crossed in front of him as he stands there looking at me waiting for my reply. I nod my agreement.

"Excellent, see you in fifteen." He starts to walk away but stops. "You understand that getting up and walking straight into the river during a meditation is odd behavior, right? I only need to make sure everything is fine. You aren't in any trouble. I'm only worried about you is all." I give him a genuine half-smile, which he returns before he leaves.

My thoughts seem to be mine again since I haven't heard my bear in a hot minute. 'Hello,' I say in my head, 'you still there?' But only silence greets me. Great, it seems as if my bear runs hot and cold, all or nothing.

I stay in the river for a little longer, splashing the cold water on my face. I go over what went down in my mind and sift through what I feel would be okay to tell and what I for sure do not want to reveal. I slosh my way back to Phil who's thankfully sitting by a fresh fire.

"Come sit by the fire with me. Between it and the sun you should dry, mostly." He offers me another wink, gesturing to the log across from him. So I take my seat and prepare to be embarrassed. "Alright, what happened?"

I take a deep breath in through my nose and release it through my mouth. I can do this. We are both adults and he can't help me if he doesn't know. Taking a look around to make sure Torben isn't near, I launch into the interaction. I leave out some details and any mention of what happened last night, but I still make sure to express exactly how lusty my Inner Bear seems to be. I do feel slightly better as I catch my coach trying not to laugh. I guess from an outside perspective it would be funny. But I didn't much appreciate the lack of control I had over myself. And now, I find the prospect of actually shifting to be scary. Will it be like taking a backseat in my own body while this she-bear inside me drives?

Once I'm done, my mentor strokes his beard while thinking over the interaction I described for him.

"Unusual as it is for your bear to speak to you so directly without meeting first, it's nothing to worry about nor is it unheard of. She has things to say to you when she needs to say them. Feelings, thoughts, and desires that need to be addressed." He looks me full in the face. "Now, I know we have been discussing and talking about your Inner Bear as if she is a separate entity from you, but I need you to realize that she isn't. She is you, an aspect of yourself, a part of you and who you are. She has her own voice, yes, but what she vocalizes are actually your own thoughts, needs, emotions, instincts, et cetera. Do you understand?" He's still staring right at me, so intensely I find it to be quite uncomfortable. Meanwhile, I'm over here looking all around and squirming under his gaze.

"But I would never...I mean...the things she wanted...suggest ed..."

"Are all things you also want, deep, deep down or just below the surface. Oh, you may not be as bold about it as she is, but she is still an aspect of you. What you want, she wants. And it seems she's going to be very vocal and clear with you when there's something you really want. She is your mirror. Opposite to you in some respects, yes, but in a way that balances you. Reflecting your trueness back at you."

I know I have some kind of horrified expression on my face. That can't be a part of me. I'm too shy to ever...I mean, I like Torben a lot but she...she wants him wants him. Okay, I want him too, but damn. Pretty sure I'm going to be thinking this over for days, weeks, the rest of my life? Well, the rest of my time in this book, that is. If I really am in a book. I now have doubts about that too.

"Okay, I can see you are now lost in your own thoughts. Up you get, time for something physical." He claps his hands and stands up; my body automatically follows his actions. "Since you wore your legs out yesterday, let's get that upper body some action. Know how to do a push-up?"

What follows is an intense lesson on proper push-up form. Followed by more push-ups than I've ever done in my entire life. He also has me do chest and shoulder presses with various logs and something called an overhead tricep extension with stones. I end up hitting the back of my head many many times with those damn rocks while trying to perform that move. The exercises did clear my head for a time, which was the purpose, I suppose. But now my arms are noodles, my head hurts, and my mind is filled with thoughts once again. I might have to spill my guts to Ellis and Rosy tonight about all this. That is, if my arms will ever work properly again. Phil really knows how to push a girl to her limits, that's for sure.

We did end up having eggs for dinner. Along with a whole breakfast offering. Torben really out did himself tonight with this spread. When I praise him, his ears turn pink as he smiles down at his plate. He's so dang cute. I try to keep my inner bear's desire for this Shifter to the side and instead try to focus on what I like about him. He's more than just a piece of man-meat after all!

Since I'm having a hard time even moving my arms at this point Torben takes my dishes to the sink for me. We then all go outside to enjoy the fire and sounds of nature before bed. Phil sneaks in another lesson designed to help me focus my newly heightened hearing, which turns out to be quite fun and educational. I never knew there were so many things in the woods, and now I can hear them all. Smell them too, though I'm not as good at distinguishing things based on smell yet. Never needed to know, or had an occasion to smell, a squirrel till now.

Our little guessing game of sounds, direction, and distance is over once I'm yawning so much my eyes are watering. Phil orders me to bed despite my protests and Torben walks me back to the cabin like the gentleman he is. I really am lucky to have him in my life right now.

Chapter 20

Silvia

We walk together all the way to my bedroom door. My Inner Bear has been blissfully quiet the rest of the day. I was afraid she would chime in again once back around Torben, but it seems she is asleep once more. Or as asleep as a branch of me can be?

"I, um, understand if you want to wait on trying out kissing." Torben mutters once we are inside the cabin.

I'm so shocked at this topic coming abruptly from my shy Shifter that I just look up at him wide-eyed with my mouth agape for several moments. My eyelids blink rapidly as my brain seems to turn back on. All I manage is an "Oh" in reply. Very eloquent.

"I'll, ah, leave you to the rest of your night. Good, um, good night." He starts to turn to leave, but thankfully my hands are faster than my mind, or mouth. Luckily for me, he's standing close enough in the hallway that I only have to move my arm a fraction to touch him.

"Wait, sorry, you caught me off guard is all. I...I may be up for a little kiss. I'm feeling much more like myself now." Which is true. I have been wanting to kiss him; I said as much this morning before my bear got all frisky. And since she seems to be dormant once more, what's the harm in a little good night kiss?

"I actually would very much like a kiss from you Torben, and I'm really glad you brought it up. I think it would have taken me days and lots and lots of pep talks before I ever mentioned it." I laugh nervously at the floor. Copying his actions from this morning, Torben lifts my chin to meet his face. When did he get so close? His smell is enveloping me again. I can feel my heart rate kick up several notches, and this hallway has gotten incredibly warm all of a sudden.

Slowly, he bends down then plants a kiss on my forehead, which was not what I was expecting. I'm about to say something but then he kisses my right cheek, followed by my left. I know I'm breathing faster than I should be, but this is so damn exciting! Now I'm thinking I might be in one of those Romance books after all. Then his lips are there, dusting lightly over mine. So soft at first, like he's just testing the waters, before he pulls away slightly.

"How was that?" His voice rolls through me. I giggle like a shy schoolgirl.

"Wonderful," I whisper. "May I have another?" He growls in his chest, then kisses me more firmly this time. Still innocent, still sweet, but with a bit more contact. An "Mmm," escapes me as he pulls away again.

"What a wonderful first kiss." I smile up at him. "Your beard doesn't feel the way I thought it would at all." Reaching up, I stroke his facial hair. "I've never kissed a man with a full beard before. Only stubble which was prickly or like sandpaper. But this, this is nice against my face." I stretch up and rub my cheek against his.

In an instant, I'm backed up against the wooden wall, Torben towering over me with his arm placed over my head.

"May I have one more kiss good night, Sweet Silvia?"

I didn't know his voice could get any deeper, but now it's so low I can feel the rumble in my bones. A finger from his other hand is running along the underside of my jaw. My body is on fire and my eyelids are fluttering. I feel as if I'm softening into a putty for this man. It's hard to even form a coherent thought, let alone speak, but I know I need to give him my answer.

"Yes, please," is all I manage and then he's there. Lips against mine once more, but this time it's no longer sweet, no longer restrained. This kiss is all passion, all desire, and I need more. I open my mouth to invite him in, and in he comes. I've never been kissed so deeply in all my life. Usually the first open-mouth kiss is awkward, but there is nothing awkward about what's happening now. It's as if we've been kissing this passionately for years.

Torben presses me fully into the wall as he leans into me. The enormous hand that was once tracing my jaw now holds the back of neck and side of my face firmly, possessively. Both of my hands are tightly gripping the front of his shirt, like I'm holding on for dear life. He growls while inside my mouth and an unbidden moan of pleasure escapes from me. Which in turn has him pressing even more firmly into my body, and oh boy, is he happy to see me!

Wrap your legs around him. Oh, that sounds like a wonderful idea. He's so strong too; I bet he could lift me. I've never been picked up by a lover before. *He's so strong! I bet he could fuck us against this wall.* Gawd, that sounds so sexy. Wait, what?!

Breaking the kiss, I push on his chest. He immediately moves away.

"Sorry, sorry." he pants. "Was that too much? Did I hurt you?"

"No, no," I quickly cut in, "it wasn't you. You were amazing, it was amazing. It's my damn she-bear! She's speaking to me again, trying to talk me into things. It's too much all at once. I'm sorry."

I look up at him while on the verge of tears. I don't want him to be upset with me, I really really like him. At least, I think it's me that likes him. Ugh, I'm so confused now! It's too much; it's just all too much. I can feel the tears starting to run down my face, and his face becomes concerned.

"It's not you, it's not you," I quickly reassure him, "it's me. You are perfect. I cry when I get overwhelmed. I don't mean to be so emotional, and I swear I'm not trying to make you feel bad. This is all just me and my issues."

"Hey, hey," he coos while taking my hands. "Everything is fine. I'm not upset with you. If anything, I'm upset with myself. I...I shouldn't have pushed you like that. I took it too far."

"No, no, you didn't." I'm shaking my head vigorously. "Please don't blame yourself for my crying. That is exactly what I don't want." The urge to fall apart is making it hard to talk now. I've got to get away, I've got to control myself, I've got to-

"Shhh," is all the warning I get before I am wrapped up in a warm and all consuming hug. "It's okay to cry. There is nothing wrong with crying. Ma says sometimes it's the best thing to do."

That instantly releases the tiny dam I had holding the rest of these tears back. All I can do is hold onto his shirtfront again and press my face into his chest. We end up on the ground, me sitting in his lap, his arms enveloping me, gently rocking while rubbing my back. He is silent and just lets me cry and cry until the tears let up on their own.

"You have been going through so much," his rich voice rolls over me. "You have been so brave and strong and smart and patient." I laugh-cry at that part. "There really is so much changing for you all at once. I shouldn't have pressed." I try to protest but he continues over me. "No, I know you had a trying day, and I should have thought about that before I asked for that last kiss. My bear likes you very much too," he whispers in my ear.

"Really? He, he doesn't think I'm too-" but before I can even start listing my flaws, I'm squeezed so tight I probably couldn't talk if I wanted to and all that comes out is, "ooph!"

"We think you're perfect." Be still, my heart. This sweet shy quiet man sure does have a way with words sometimes. "Feeling better now?" I rub my cheek up and down his chest in a yes. And it's true, I really do feel better. I don't recall having had a good deep cry since I was changed and now that I let it out I feel as though a weight has been lifted. "Good, I'm glad. Guess Ma was right about crying. Do you want to stay here for a little longer or do you want to go to your room now?"

"Room, I guess," is what I say, but I could happily stay held in his arms for hours. Hallway or not, I feel very safe and comfortable right where I'm at. He smoothly stands up while still holding me in his arms, then gently sets me on my feet and brushes the hair out of my face to look at me. I know I'm an ugly crier but I don't shy away from his appraisal. He doesn't care how I look, just wants to make sure I'm really all right. He kisses my forehead oh so sweetly once more and opens my bedroom door for me.

"Need anything? Water, food, something sweet?" I shake my head no as I slowly go into my room.

"Thank you, Torben. You've been so sweet and nice to me. I do appreciate it. That was a really really good kiss, by the way. Despite how it ended." With that, I shut the door and press my forehead against it. From the other side of the door comes a soft reply.

"It was the best kiss I've ever had." I stand stunned and listen to his footsteps walking back outside. I take a few deep breaths to calm and compose myself before throwing my body into the bed in frustration.

Well, are you happy now?! I yell at my bear in my head but get no response. Of course! Next time keep your nose out of my love life and maybe I'll have one.

I stomp off into my bathroom and vigorously splash my face with cold water. I'm so angry I don't know what to do with myself. After drying off, I pace back and forth in my little room. It started off so well and then devolved into...that! Oh, I could strangle that bear inside my head. Why did she have to chime in? Why did she have to make me doubt myself?

I can't think through this alone. I need to talk to my new friends to help me sort through this tangle of thoughts and emotions. But I have to calm down first or I'm going to snap yet another pen to my message book. Grabbing a pillow from my bed, I press it against my face as tight as I dare, and yell into it with all my might.

There, that's better. A perfectly normal thing for a grown-ass thirty-six year old woman to do.

Opening the drawer to my side table, I pull out my forest green message book before flopping back onto my bed belly-first. This position and situation reminds me of writing in my diary as a teen, but now my pages will respond with advice and encouragement from my new friends. I really need to do something nice for them once I'm fit to be around the public. Are there such things as spas or nail salons in this realm? I want to do something for these two wonderful people. What would a pedicure look like for a centaur anyway, a farrier? I shake my head of those thoughts and get down to the business at hand. Thinking about other more enjoyable topics isn't going to help me with my current situation.

Going to the page between Rosy, Ellis, and myself, I start with a simple message.

"Hey, I know it's kinda late, but are you two up? Some things have gone down. I'm really confused, and I could use some outside perspective." END.

What feels like only milliseconds go by before Ellis replies,

"I'm here. Tell us everything!" -Ellis

Rosy takes a bit longer but soon I see her scrawl.

"Yes, I'm here too. What happened? Are you ok?" -Rosy

"Yes, I'm ok. Well, mostly. Physically anyway. But my mind is spiraling. Sorry, I'm being so selfish. How was your day? Rosy, did you get your sugar peas planted in your garden? Ellis, how's the Fire Fest baking preparations going?" END.

"Oh no you don't! You are not being selfish, our days were fine, and preparations are on track. Now spill the tea, and no more stalling." -Ellis

A smile cracks my face. Their straight to the point, no-nonsense attitude is exactly what I need in my life.

"Yeah, what they said. Peas are planted, now out with it. Never pegged you for a tease Sil." -Rosy

So I launch into today's events. Since they already know my bear is sleeping and the struggles I've been having contacting her, I start by explaining the Egg Challenge, which they both find funny. I briefly touch on the True Mates lesson, which they are oddly quiet over, and move on to the entire interaction with my bear.

"Woah, wait. What did she mean by *we should be doing what we did with him last night***'?' And when did you two talk about kissing?! I think you've left out some developments between you and Torben." -Rosy**

Crap, I hadn't meant to tell them about the mutual masturbation session between Torben and I. So I simply say.

"Due to an interesting set of circumstances, we ended up pleasuring ourselves in front of each other, and I would like to leave it at that. Then the next morning, this morning actually, we talked about how we want to kiss at some point. Which we, in fact did, just a little while ago. It's one of the reasons why I'm writing you two now." END.

"Those must have been some circumstances, but we won't pry. Please continue." -Ellis

Thank you, Ellis, you Beautiful Androgynous Deity!

So I continue the story of the evening. First, the sweet kisses, to which I can practically feel the high-pitched squeal of joy from both of them. Then, the not-so-sweet kisses, which brings warmth to my cheeks —and other places— to explain on paper. And finally, my bear's reappearance and the meltdown that ensued.

"Then, he told me through the door that it was the best kiss he'd ever had. And I know it was the best kiss I've ever had, but now I'm so confused! Is it me that wants him like that? Is it the bear that wants him and is swaying me,

making me feel this way? Or is there even a difference? Phil said we are one and the same, but I certainly don't act like this bear. Are her feelings overriding my own? There is just so much going on, and I don't feel as though I'm handling it well at all. I mean, I cried so hard for so long in front of him! Any advice?" END.

I decide to leave out the part of my day where I learned I may or may not have been tricked and abducted by a Fae. It's either that or I made some kind of deal with an immensely powerful woman to have an adventure in a fantasy book. And how do you tell your friends that they may not even be real? For now, best to just ask for help regarding the relationship and Shifter stuff.

"So let me make sure we have everything straight. You have found yourself to be 'overly' attracted to a very nice and caring Shifter Male. You have had sweet moments and passionate moments, but you are afraid that these passionate moments are incited by your Inner Bear, and that said Inner Bear is perhaps making you feel this way, yes? And you are afraid to pursue or indulge in these feelings until you know if they are truly yours or not, correct?" -Ellis

"Yes? I think that is a good summary of the situation with Torben. I mean, I have never felt this strongly about anyone before. What if it's not my feelings at all?" END.

"Sorry, I'm just over here shaking my head at you girl. Ellis, will you please handle this?" -Rosy

Ouch, Rosy, damn!

Then Ellis begins to scrawl.

"Let me ask you some more questions, Silvia. Didn't you have feelings for Torben before you became a Shifter?

You had several meet-ups and even a real date. You're telling me that you never had any sexual desire for him, no naughty dreams perhaps?"

How did they know about that?!

"If I've gauged the situation correctly, you had the hots for Torben before your bear ever came into the picture. And from what I understand about Shifters, their animal is really just a vocal part of their deeper selves. A part that is able to speak up about what they, or you, actually want or need or dislike. They give voice to the things you might otherwise push away. Hasn't Phil told you the same thing? It seems to me that you and your bear are of the same mind about Torben. She is simply more vocal and true about her desires, which are actually your desires. You are not a human anymore my friend. You are an Animal Shifter and your animal instincts are closer to the surface than they have ever been. I know you would prefer a little more control over the situation, especially given how all this came about for you, but the heart and body want what they want. And both of yours want Torben in a bad way." -Ellis

"What they said! Exactly! Speaking the truth. Even on that second day at my tavern, you were so flustered at how attracted you were when you bumped into him shirtless in the hall." -Rosy

"First of all, I was not flustered. Secondly, he was only wearing a towel and it was very low around his hips. Who wouldn't be turned on?! I'm only human, well at least I was."
END

"The point we are trying to make is: you liked him when you were still human, you like him even more now, and your Inner Bear is in agreement with you. She seems to be trying to help move things along is all. So tell that she-bear of yours that you'll handle it. Then actually handle it." -Ellis

"Yeah, go for it girl!" -Rosy

"Ok, well when you put it like that I feel stupid now. Thanks for helping me work all that out. I owe you big time." END.

"You aren't stupid. These are confusing times for you. Taking a step back from a situation helps you gain perspective, as does consulting your friends. I'm glad you talked to us instead of stewing in your own mind." -Ellis

"Now that that crisis is averted, do you know what you are doing for the Fire Festival? Are you staying there, coming back to Oakveil, going back to Torben's family?" -Rosy

"Yes, we haven't seen you since the Change. I'm eager to see if you look different now. I bet you are at least a bit beefier and toned with all that running and log lifting you described. Glad it's you and not me sweetie." -Ellis

"I don't know what the plan is actually. I'll ask Phil and Torben about it tomorrow." END

"Well, be sure to sneak away and message us the answer at some point tomorrow before it gets too late. We need to know ASAP!" -Rosy.

"I promise I'll ask at breakfast and report back right away." END

We chit-chat a little longer, then sign off to sleep. I feel so much better now, better than I even thought I would. And now I have some actionable steps!

Step 1: Find out about Fire Fest plans and message friends. Step 2: Tell Torben how I feel and that I want to continue to pursue a relationship and more kisses. Step 3: Meet up with my bear and tell her I will be dating Torben but at my own pace and that she needs to take a back seat on this.

Nothing goes according to plan the next day. I ask Phil about the festival but the plans seem to still be in flux. They depend on how well I do with the egg challenge today and what Torben has planned. But we can't ask Torben because he has already left on errands in town and won't be back till this evening. So now I can't even talk to him about our relationship, even though I am ready with a carefully thought-out script.

The icing on the cake, my bear is again refusing to talk to me! I go to my mind's forest and find the cave with the snoring bear inside. But when I try to wake her to have our serious discussion, she snorts, throws a pillow at me from the darkness inside, and kicks me out of my own damn vision. *He's not here. You don't need me,* is all I get. I break a lot of eggs after that interaction. .

Chapter 21

Torben

After leaving my Sweet Silvia at her bedroom door I quickly make my way back outside. I need to go for a run. I need to get out of my skin. That kiss still has me on fire. The memory of my body pressed against her soft flesh, molding into mine. Then the crying, the confusion, and the conflict. The overwhelm she is facing because of me. All I could do was hold her, comfort her as best I could.

It hits me hard when I realize that I am mostly to blame for her troubles. If I hadn't pushed for that last kiss, if I hadn't sat back and just watched as my sister approached her in bear form...if I hadn't been her Mate at all, none of this would be happening to that wonderful creature in the cabin behind me.

I shift as soon as I hit the tree line and run and run and run. I don't stray far from the cabin. The need to be near my Mate is too strong for that. But I careen around the forest in wide circles, not caring much for anything that's in my path. All I can think about is her.

Eventually, I tire myself out enough to sit by the river and watch the water in the moonlight.

I'm sorry, my bear chimes in. *Our Mate cried because of me. Because I pushed you to do more than she was ready for.* It's not your fault, I knew better. Well, I should have known better anyway. I was the foolish one. *We are both to blame then. I didn't realize what our Mate was suffering. We have always been. I have never thought what it might be like to have a new voice pushing you, confusing what you once were. To have everything about yourself change, both physically and mentally. We were just so happy to have found her, our Mate at last. I didn't consider her side of things once she went through The Change. Only our own gain, our own joy.*

There is a long pause after all that. He usually doesn't talk so much when I'm in my bear form. Goes to show how deep the feelings of guilt and shame are.

We need to be a better Mate for her. We will not push again. We will simply be here to support her while she adjusts to her new form and connection. Agreed. *We will be the best of Mates,* my bear proclaims. *The most understanding and patient.* I snort at his overconfidence. *And we will not push or expect anything during this Fire Festival.* I can feel him sadden again. *I was not thinking of her when I thought she would be in our bed by then.* No, no you weren't.

Tomorrow we will get our Mate her lotion, the best book, and a surprise gift to cheer her up. Now, time to sleep. We will need to leave early tomorrow to be back in time for dinner with her. Getting up, I lumber my way back to the cabin, only shifting back when I hit the porch.

My dreams are filled with me holding my Sweet Silvia tightly in my arms as I apologize to her over and over again. She says I'm not to blame, but that's not how I feel.

My bear wakes me very early the next morning, too early in my opinion seeing as the sun hasn't even started to lighten the sky. But I get out of bed with minimal grumbling and opt for a cold wash in the river to help wake me. It does the trick all right. I leave Phil a note, grab the empty case he uses to carry loads of eggs, and head out as the sun starts cresting the horizon. I shift and run most of the way to Havensted, the town Phil actually lives in.

My first stop is to the farmer Phil gets his eggs from. I'm not surprised at all to see them out feeding their animals already this morning.

"Ho there, Farmer Gael!" I shout over the ruckus of farm animals eager for their morning feed. They look up, smile and wave as I approach.

Their ancestry appears to be a mix of Dryad and Fawn. Their skin reminds me of fine ebony hardwood. Pointed ears poke out from the hair scarf they wear, and the only thing that shows their old age are the wrinkles on their face and hands. But I know from past experience they are far faster than their age or size would suggest. They might only be four feet tall on a good day, but I've known them to travel great distances in no time at all. How they frequent Rosy's place so often is a testament of their quickness. Maybe the hooves help in some way?

"Phil sent me to collect more eggs for his new student," I begin once I'm closer. "I've got some errands to run in town. Is it okay to leave the case here and pick them up before I leave, around noon?"

"Ah, Torben, good to see you! Yes, Phil sent me a message yesterday letting me know. Follow me and I'll show you where you can leave the case. I'll have it filled up for you by noon, no problem." They walk over closer to the hen house and wave a hand at a little table there. I unload my burden just as Gael says, "So, heard you've got yourself a new mate. How's she doing with the Change?"

I miss the table completely and the container falls to the ground. I stare at them wide eyed, frozen.

"How did you know all that?" I ask, astonished. They chuckle at me as they bend over and set the egg case on the table. Leaning in close, they put their hand on the side of their mouth in mock whisper.

"Trees are terrible gossips," they wink exaggeratedly before straightening back up. Cackling, they walk over to start feeding their chickens. "Don't worry lad, I'm not one to go spreading people's business. It's not common knowledge yet. Congratulations, and have fun in town!" With that I seem to be dismissed.

I start my walk into town still in shock. Do trees gossip? If so, why would they want to talk about me and my life? I guess it did all happen in the woods, the discovery of my Mate and the bite. And here I thought I had a pretty good relationship with the trees. I'm a carpenter, yes, but I always ask permission and only use the trees that agree. Should I try talking to them more?

Trees will do what trees will do, comes my bear's sage advice. *I bet it's boring staying in the same place all the time. So they would need stories of what's going on in other places.* My bear makes a good point, but I'm not sure I'll ever feel alone in the woods again knowing the trees are not only watching and listening, but telling other trees too. My whole body gives an involuntary shiver.

Making it into Havensted without issue I head to buy Silvia some lotion first. Thankfully, they have the exact same type in stock so I buy two. One for now, and one for emergencies.

I then head to the library and ask the librarian for suggestions related to Shifters, Bear Shifters, new Shifters, etc. To my astonishment I'm able to speak with her without much difficulty. In the past, I would have had a big problem talking to a female I don't know, but today I'm almost normal when talking with her. Is it because I have now found my Mate, or is it because I'm on an errand for her? I'll have to test it out again later when I'm not a male on a mission.

The librarian doesn't currently have a copy of the book suggested as a first read, but thinks the bookshop might. So I head to the bookshop with a list of about twenty books, with one at the top.

Sometime later I leave the bookshop with a new copy of 'So, You've Become a Bear Shifter: Now What?' by Ursulon Major wrapped in a flower-pattern fabric and tied in twine. I slipped the list of other books into its pages before it was wrapped, so it wouldn't get lost. Now, what type of special gift should I get my sweet Mate? It shouldn't be so big that it makes her feel guilty or put on the spot. Something small but thoughtful.

I'm slowly walking down the street peeking into shops for ideas or inspiration when a male I've never met runs up to me. I may not know him personally, but I recognize his smell; this is Phil's mate.

He looks to be taller than Phil but not as wide across the chest and arms, slimmer but still quite muscular. His shoulder-length hair is white and tied back loosely with a blue ribbon. But the thing that surprises me the most is that he doesn't smell like a bear, he smells like a wolf. I knew Phil got into being a Change Coach by helping his mate after he was bitten, but I always assumed he was a bear, as well. Wolves usually stay in their packs, but there isn't one near. It's odd that a new wolf was left alone during a Change.

This isn't our business, we shouldn't pry. I know. I already feel like I know more than I should.

"Are you Torben?" he asks once on the same side of the street as me.

"Yes, and you're Phil's mate?" He gives me a nod of confirmation.

"Are you going back to the training cabin? If so I, um, have a letter for the new student there." He's looking a little flustered. With his hand rubbing the back of his neck he continues nervously. "I heard she was bitten against her will?" I glance down as shame fills me.

"Yes. My younger sister thought she knew better than the rest of us. I was not quick enough to stop her actions; never thought she would do such a thing." A low growl escapes me, the anger boiling up again.

"Something similar happened to me. I wrote her a letter in hopes that it will help her come to terms with her new form and her new life. Would you pass it off for me? I'm not sure when I'll get a chance to meet her, and these are things I wish I had heard or knew sooner during my transition." I stare at the letter in his hands and feel a lump in my throat.

"I would be honored to deliver it for you. This will mean the world to my Mate, thank you." I hold out my hands and take the thick envelope. He must have much to say.

"I hope it helps her, even a little bit." He turns his head but I can see that he has wiped a tear from his eye. He clears his throat and offers a hand. "My name is Wilhelm, but everyone calls me Wil. It's nice to finally see you again. You probably don't remember me but I stayed at your mom's house for a while when going through the Changing Sickness. She really helped me out there. You were only a kid at the time."

"It's very nice to see you, Wil. I tried to never bother Ma's patients. Knew they were going through enough already. And I was so busy following my uncle around in the woods and studio, I didn't take as much interest in my mother's craft as I should have."

"Pah, from what I hear, you have a natural talent and the wood calls to you. Is it true you can hear the trees?"

"Not as well as some folks, apparently, but I can feel them. Get an answer when I ask if they want to be crafted into something else, something new."

"That's pretty incredible for a Shifter, Torben. The Goddess must have blessed you herself," he slaps me on the shoulder. I can feel my ears start to heat from the praise. "So what were you doing before I interrupted you?"

"I was looking around trying to find a little gift for my Mate. She had a difficult day and I made it worse. I want to get her something to help cheer her up and apologize. She needed a lotion refill so I got that, and she wanted me to look for a book on being a new Shifter, which I also found." I hold up the wrapped book. "But I want a little surprise too."

"You got her a book on becoming a Shifter? That's really thoughtful." The way he says this is so sincere I have to look away. "I know Phil doesn't really offer books or opportunities for note-taking during his training lessons. Though to be fair, people usually know before the Change happens giving them a chance to research it beforehand."

"Oh, it wasn't my idea, though I really hope I chose a good one. I also got a list from the librarian of about 20 others for her to check out after this one. The librarian here is very knowledgeable and helpful."

"No matter whose idea it was, you still went through a lot of trouble to get her a good one and I say that's sweet." Wil glances up and down the street with a finger on his lips, thinking. "How about you pick her up a journal or something to write in. That way she can take notes from the books she reads. Or maybe she'll want to keep track of her experience of becoming a Shifter?"

"That sounds like a great idea. She did mention wishing she could take notes. Thank you, Wil." He waves his hand dismissing my thanks.

"No thanks needed. It was merely a suggestion, after all. Now, I'll leave you to finish your errands. Thanks for delivering that letter and tell Phil I miss his snoring." He smiles and walks back the way he came, while I make a trip back to that bookstore.

After a quick bite to eat, I pick up the eggs from Gael's farm, then get back to the cabin and my Mate in time to start cooking dinner.

Despite how last night ended, she seems very happy to see me upon my return, which has me smiling like an idiot the rest of the night. Wonder if she missed me? There aren't as many broken eggs today as I would have thought, so I offer her my praise. She blushes at this while thanking me. What a beautiful Mate I have, inside and out.

I pass on the message from Wil about Phil's snoring over dinner, but I wait till after we eat to give Silvia her items from town. I know that once she gets the letter she'll want to read it in private, but I needed to make sure she ate well first. I grab the bundle as she and Phil clean up the table.

"Here are the things I got you from Havensted." I set them on the kitchen table. "There's a refill of the lotion you let me borrow." We both blush slightly, so I quickly move on. "Here's a book on becoming a Bear Shifter. The librarian suggested it, but their copy was checked out, so I bought you your own. There's also a list of other books she recommended for you in there. And I got you a journal so you can take notes or write about your day or whatever. It has a forest green cover to match your message book."

"Thank you so much!" She quickly wraps her arms around my torso in a tight embrace. "You didn't have to do all this for me." I'm so surprised, and she moves away so quickly to unwrap her books, that I don't get a chance to return the hug.

"Wow, this title really says it all, doesn't it?" she says with a laugh. She skims the list of other titles with glee and unwraps the journal. "Oh, Torben! This is a beautiful journal. I almost hate to actually write in it." She thumbs the pages and takes in a big breath through her nose. "Hmm, it smells perfect."

"Wilhelm, Phil's mate, also asked me to deliver this letter to you." I finally pull out the letter. "He went through an unplanned Change as well and wanted to pass off some things he hoped would help you." I hear a faint rumble from Phil but keep my eyes on Silvia. She's staring at this note like it is a thing to be treasured. She extends both hands to receive it then clutches it to her chest.

"That's so nice of him," she whispers, but we can hear her clearly.

"Go read it now if you want; we'll finish cleaning up here," Phil says gruffly. Silvia looks at me questioningly, and I nod my head in agreement. She quickly gathers her items, squeezes my hand, and swiftly walks to her room before shutting the door.

"That letter couldn't have been easy for my mate to write. But if anyone was going to appreciate it, it's that one." I think I see a glint of moisture in Phil's eyes, but he quickly turns and continues to wash the dishes. "And for the record, I don't snore." I chuckle and start rinsing plates.

I don't know what's in that letter, but I know it makes her cry. It makes her cry for a long time.

Chapter 22

Torben

I fell asleep to the sounds of Silvia turning pages and writing. I know she stayed up far too late for her own good. Now I'm thinking Phil might have been right to limit her to just one book.

As soon as I walk into the kitchen, Phil welcomes me with an order.

"I've got some news for you two. Get Silvia up for me and I'll tell you together." He's making breakfast so it must be something urgent.

"Everything alright?" I ask hesitantly.

"Yes, you worrisome bear, now go fetch your mate." The use of the word so near Silvia has me flinching and looking around to make sure she didn't hear. This only makes Phil chuckle and return to cooking.

Walking back down the hall, I gently knock on her door.

"Silvia, you awake yet? Phil wants to talk to us. Some kind of news." Nothing. I knock again but louder. "Silvia?" Finally hearing movement and sluggish steps coming toward the door, I wait. When it opens, I am greeted with the sight of my sleepy Mate. Her clothes disheveled, she has wisps of red hair escaping her silk headscarf, and her fist is actively trying to rub the bleariness of sleep from an eye. I now realize I needn't have worried about Phil's 'mate' comment.

"Everything okay?" she asks with a yawn.

Our Mate is adorable in the morning. Indeed, she is.

"Yes, Phil says everything is fine, but I think time might be of the essence."

"It is!" Phil calls from up the hall. "Now put on your real clothing and come to the kitchen." My Mate's eyes are fully open now.

"Real clothes? I haven't worn those since we got here." I shrug, so she closes the door to make herself ready.

I help with the last of the breakfast preparations, and Silvia arrives a short time later wearing the outfit she wore when I first saw her. But this time there's an addition, the wooden hair stick with the bee I carved for her. I can't help the smile that leaps to my face, the pride that fills my heart, or the fiery heat that rises in my pants. I quickly sit down before anything becomes noticeable.

"Right," Phil starts, "I'll get to it. We are all going home today." He then proceeds to take a big bite of bacon on toasted bread. We both just stare at him in confusion for a moment while he chews. But he's looking at us both as if that's all there is to say.

"Am, am I done with training already?" Silvia asks with a puzzled expression on her face.

"No. But you are far enough along that I feel you can safely attend the festivities with Torben's Clan. I've already spoken to Mathilda, so she knows to expect you two."

"Who's Mathilda?" is my Mate's first question, but I can feel a million more on its heels. I have a few myself.

"That's Torben's mother's real name," Phil answers with a slight smile. "I'm smart enough not to call her that to her face though. She hates it, but I refuse to call her 'Ma' if I don't have to."

"You really think I'm ready to be around others? I don't know if I think I'm ready. I'm still breaking eggs, haven't had a proper talk with my inner bear, and haven't shifted so much as a hair, or fur, rather. I've only started reading my new book, which is amazing by the way. It has so much good advice and information. Not that you haven't been a great coach! You've been awesome, but it's nice to have some things written down for reference when you need it." Her rushed babbling betrays how concerned she is by this news. "I can't believe that you don't have a mini library of Shifter books here. But I guess not everyone needs them like I did."

"Silvia," Phil calls, trying to stop her nervous rambling.

"Oh, I'm sorry I'm being selfish. This Fire Festival must be very important to you guys, and I'm just worrying about myself. I bet your mate really misses you when you are training new Shifters. I bet Ma would love to see Torben for the holiday too. Maybe I should stay here by myself? I could read my book and still try the eggs. Get some good one-on-one time with my bear."

Like I would leave her here alone.

"Silvia," Phil tries again but to no avail. I hide a smile from him as he eyes me across the table. My Mate must be very, very nervous about this.

"It's perfect! I'll stay here, and you two will enjoy the holiday with your families, or Clan, or whomever. I promise not to burn the cabin down. What is the Fire Festival anyway? I've never celebrated it before, which is why I don't mind being left out. Not as important to me, ya know?"

I get the feeling that Phil is going to be louder the next time he tries to stop her, so I decide I had better step in. Reaching my arm across the table, I gently cover her hand with mine.

"Silvia," I say in an octave I know she likes. She's immediately quiet and turns to me. "There is no need to be so anxious, my Sweet. Phil wouldn't have suggested it if you weren't ready."

Her breathy "okay" in reply sounds euphoric, and it stokes to life the fire from earlier. I'm thankful for this table once again.

"Torben is right. I wouldn't have made this plan if I thought you couldn't handle it. You'll be perfectly safe with the Clan. Plus, you're doing better than you think you are with the training so far." He starts ticking off his fingers, "Your bear is already communicating with you directly. It may not be what you want to hear, but you hear it. You are claiming and controlling your new strength remarkably well. Bears are exceedingly strong little lady, and you are doing damn well with the Egg Challenge. Maybe better than any student I've had before. Lastly, you are taking all this very seriously. That right there is one of the most important aspects of this. I trust you, and you need to learn to trust yourself too." With that, he begins to eat again with gusto.

"You, you really trust me? You think I'm doing well?" He gives her a deadpan look over his plate of food, then continues eating. "Right, silly question. You wouldn't have said it if you didn't mean it."

All I can do is smile in my happiness and begin eating as well. My Mate is doing so well and we'll be with the Clan for the festival. This is a good morning.

We all eat, clean up, and pack. Since Silvia can't change, we won't be there as quickly as I am usually able to make the return trip, but she's been running so much that I have faith we'll make good time anyway. We say our farewells to Phil while agreeing to be back here in three days time.

I set a steady pace for our return trip, which my Mate is able to easily keep. She has come so far, and I'm glad to see she still enjoys her new running abilities. She smiles and laughs as we travel, still marveling at her ease in running. Especially now after her training with Phil.

We stop at the same waterfall as before to rest and grab a snack, choosing to sit on a large boulder together. I am glad that my Mate enjoys waterfalls as much as I do. There's a place not far from a little waterfall that I've long thought would be a perfect spot to build a home. Wonder if she will like that location too?

"Torben, I want to talk to you about our relationship, if that's okay?" I almost spit out my food. All I can manage is a nod in agreement. "I know I've been a little weird," I try to deny that but she holds up her hand. "Please, let me get this all out. I know I've been a little weird, what with this life-altering change and new voice in my head." I swallow a big gulp of food not sure where this is going. "But after some time to really mull it all over and reflect," my heart has stopped and migrated to my throat, "I realized that I really want to continue building a relationship with you. Not because some voice in my head wants me to, but because I want to. So, if it's not too big a leap too quickly, I was wondering if we could make it official? Torben, would you like to be my boyfriend?"

All I can do is blink at her for a moment. I must be silent for too long because I can see a bit of panic in her eyes and can sense a torrent of words is about to bubble out of her.

"I don't know what a 'boyfriend' is?" I quickly blurt out to stop her. "I mean, it sounds like a male you are friends with by the title, but your reference to 'official' and 'building relationships' makes me think that is not what you mean. I am already your friend." I feel confused and embarrassed that I don't understand what she really means, though I know it's important to her.

"Oh, yes," she laughs nervously, "um, a boyfriend, or girl-friend, is an official title. It means you are dating, it's a commit-ment thing. That you're building a romantic relationship together and possibly a future. It's a part of the courting practices where I come from. It's the next step."

"Ah," is all I can manage at first. I'm a little sad that she still hasn't realized we are Mates, and it must come across in my tone because her face falls slightly. "Sorry, yes, yes! I very much want to be your boyfriend. I am honored that you want to share your courting methods with me. I'm eager to officially take the next step with you. What must I do to gain this title of 'boyfriend'?" She giggles at my response.

"You don't have to do anything really, just accept. Then you are my boyfriend, and I am your girlfriend. We'll call each other that, and you will introduce me to new people saying 'This is my girlfriend, Silvia' or something like that." She smiles mischievously at me, "I will also expect you to perform your boyfriendly duties."

A rumble of pleasure escapes my throat at that. I inch closer to her on the boulder.

"And what types of duties comes with this new title?" I ask, returning her playful smile. "I wouldn't want to disappoint my new girlfriend." She giggles and inches closer too, mimicking my movements.

"Well, I will expect more real dates, of course." I nod my head, leaning in. "Maybe a small thoughtful gift every now and then. Holding my hand when we are close enough." I take her hand in mine and hold it, which elicits a smile from her. "You'll tell me about your day, your worries, your successes." I place the back of her hand on my cheek while still holding on. She licks her lips and inhales deeply.

"And um, I really enjoy parallel play." I arch my eyebrow in question while still rubbing her hand on my face. "Oh, it's like, when two people are in the same room together doing different activities." I can hear her heart rate increase and can smell her desire in the air. Her words are soft dreamy whispers now. "Like, you would be carving wood and I would be reading. You know, that kind of thing."

"Any other duties you would want me to perform?" I slowly turn my face to gently kiss the back of her hand. Her whole body shudders and more of her delicious aroma fills my nose.

A sweet soft "oh" escapes her lips. I am liking these reactions, so I turn her hand over and kiss her palm, then her wrist.

"Kissing?" she whispers, then clears her throat. "Kissing is often part of the boyfriendly duties."

"Is that so?" She nods her head vigorously. "Should I kiss you now to seal this new bond we have forged?" She nods her head even more emphatically. "Hmm," I rumble, now a mere inch from her lips. "I wish to hear my girlfriend's voice in agreement on this."

"Yes," she responds quickly, "I would very much like a kiss from my new boyfriend." I place her hand back on my cheek, smoothing it flat to lay there, and reach mine to cup her face, then lightly stroke her lower lip with my thumb.

"Then a kiss my girlfriend shall have, but only one. For now." I lightly hold her chin and jaw and close the short distance. I start soft then slowly increase the pressure. I'll only give in to one kiss, but I intend to make it count. When she opens her mouth to me I tilt my head, grab her waist with my free hand and pull her into me as my tongue sweeps into her freely.

I breathe in her scent deeply, wishing to ingrain it onto my very being. I know it's time to stop when her moan of pleasure brings a possessive growl to my throat. As we part, she lightly nibbles on my lower lip, which causes my whole body to shudder. My Mate is testing my resolve at every turn. As she's panting from being released, I kiss her forehead then leap from the stone.

"We should probably get back to our journey, my girlfriend. I want to make sure we get there in good time."

The rest of the journey continues much the same as the start. Though there are some stolen glances and much smiling.

We have made great progress. Though I do not understand this new term and wish she knew us as Mate. It is still progress. Indeed it is, and she requested it! *This makes us very happy, to know she wants us too.*

It's when we hit the edge of my Clan's village that I first smell her. My sister is here. It's hard to stifle my anger at this intrusion and mean to confront Mel as soon as I am able. But I won't do so with my Mate so near. I must come up with a way to distract Silvia while I find my meddling sister, but how?

"Hey, I think I smell honey!" my Mates excited voice breaks in. "Oh and now I definitely hear the sounds of a hive! You have no idea how awesome it is to have all these heightened senses. Sure, it's sometimes hard to tune things out, but that's something I've always struggled with anyway. I should ask Phil about that, or maybe there's a section in my new book. Are there others in your Clan that went through the Change; maybe I can ask them?"

"Yes, of course," I reply distractedly before all her words actually sink in. Bless the Goddess that Old Man Talbet and his hives are on this side of Clan lands. "The Talbet bee yard is very near here, and since I did plan to introduce you to him we'll go now before everything gets too chaotic," I say while changing our direction. He'll keep my Mate occupied for me while I deal with this mess.

"Really?! Are you sure it's alright? I know your family is expecting us and what if he's busy getting ready for the Festival? I don't want to bother him."

"Do not worry, my sweet girlfriend. We made excellent time getting here and Old Man Talbet loves nothing more than speaking about his bees to anyone who is willing to listen. He will be delighted to speak with someone who actually wants to hear all about them." My Mate giggles and takes my hand as we continue on the path.

We reach the rows of hives and, as I expected, Talbot is out talking to his bees. A wizened old male with pure white tufts of hair at the sides and top of his head, he walks bent over with his hands clasped behind his back. His overalls look about as old as he does with multiple patches dotted here and there. I remember as kids we would try to count how many wrinkles he had on his face if we were ever trapped in conversation with him. I almost feel sorry for what I'm about to do to my Sweet Silvia, but I need to get Mel out of here before they meet. I only hope that my Mate is truly as interested in bees as she's made it seem.

"Ho there, Talbet!" I call out loudly to make sure he hears me. He raises his hand in return and quickly shuffles to his fence line. I can see the wide smile on his face from here. He loves visitors. "I hope today finds you well, sir." I ask once we reach the fence.

"Oh, well enough, well enough," he says eagerly. "Springtime is always good on these old bones, till it rains that is." He cackles. "And the bees live for the spring. Now step aside, boy! I can't see who you've brought to see me. Ho now, is this the pretty young lassy I've heard talk of in town? Hair like fire and sweet as pie. I see the rumors were true. Nice find there, boy, a nice addition to the Clan, a fine new Shifter indeed. Been up there training with Phil I take it? Good lad, that one. Miss seeing him around more, but after everything with his mate I don't begrudge him the move. We do anything for our mates now, don't we boy?" He gives me a knowing wink, and I feel I need to take over the conversation immediately.

"Yes!" I quickly interject "We have been up at Phil's training but are back for a few days to celebrate with the Clan. This is Silvia, and her grandparents once kept bees themselves." The hungry look on Talbet's face tells me I have chosen the correct topic to divert him from continuing on about mates. "Ever since she expressed her love of bees to me, I knew I had to bring her to see you as soon as I could." Old Man Talbet can not hide his excitement at my words. He's bouncing around like his birthday has come early.

"Indeed, indeed, is that so?! Tell me now, did you ever help them out with their hives and such?" he directs at Silvia.

"Oh yes sir, every chance I got. It's been such a long time since I have though, but I do miss it." My Mate could not have said anything more perfect at this moment.

"Is that so now? Well, come, come with me and I will show you my lot." He's waving emphatically at her and walking down the fence to the gate. "And you'll tell me what you remember of how your grandparents did things. Every beekeeper has their own ways and tricks, of course." He cackles again as we follow. Once we come to the gate, I decide to make my escape.

"Here, let me have your pack. I'll take our things home and let Ma know where we are. I'm sure Talbet will keep you entertained while I'm gone." She hesitates, seeming to not want to part from me even for that long. I swell with happiness but push it back.

"Are, are you sure?" she says looking between myself and the bee master.

"Don't worry, my dear. I won't bite and he's never been interested in my bees," Talbot interjects. "He'll be back very quickly, I'd wager, and his Ma would be glad to know you're safe. Oh, that reminds me, I have a special jar of queen's jelly for her. Here, let me get it and you can take it to her for me." He quickly shuffles off to a work shed as I take my Mate's pack. I can see the questioning in her eyes as she hands it to me. This almost feels as if I am lying to her again and I don't like that feeling at all.

I shoulder her bag, then take her hand and kiss it.

"I promise I will be as quick as I can. This is really brightening his day and I'll be able to come back with an excuse to snatch you away blaming my mother." She lightly laughs covering her mouth. "Plus, now that you've met him, you'll be able to come discuss bees anytime you desire." I see the old male hurrying back so I lean down to kiss her forehead and whisper, "I'll be right back, Sweet Silvia." I straighten in time to see a blush starting to rise to her cheeks.

"Here ya go, my boy," he hands me a plain, glazed ceramic jar. "Now scoot! We've got bee talkin' to do." He links his arm with Silvia's and turns her away, heading back to the work shed.

I inhale the sweet scent of honey and my Mate, stealing myself for the confrontation that's about to occur, then quickly turn around and run for home. Because that is where Mel's scent is the strongest and where I'll get the answer to the question that's been hounding my mind since I smelled her. Why the fuck is she here?

Chapter 23

Silvia

T orben sure was acting odd. I know him well enough now to realize that, at least. I want to think about it more, but this friendly old beekeeper at my side is so excited and chatty that I'm fully distracted from those thoughts in no time.

"So was the boy pulling this old timer's leg, or did you really enjoy helping your grandparents with their bee colonies? I get it's not everyone's cup of tea, despite my best efforts." He chuckles at himself there.

"Oh yes, I started helping them as soon as I was able to. Must have been six or seven years old the first time I suited up and smoked for my grandpa. Since then, I was hooked. Processing wax, harvesting honey, setting boxes for the seasons. I was heartbroken having to sell their colonies after they passed, but I really didn't have the space or time. I lived in the city and had a full-time job by then. I sometimes wish I had the courage to stay and take on beekeeping as my career instead. What I was doing certainly wasn't my calling." A lump grows in my throat, remembering that time in my life. If I knew then what I know now, I think my path in life would have taken a very different turn. I shake my head and clear my throat. "How long have you been keeping bees?"

"Oh Goddess bless me, more years than I can remember. Inherited the trade from my mother and continued in her footsteps alongside my mate, Glory. We dreamed for a while of passing it on to our little ones, but our only child had an unfortunate accident when he was still quite young and we never had the heart to have another." Even after all these years, I can feel the sorrow of that loss radiating from him. "You remind me of Glory actually, wild red hair and freckles. I bet our grandchildren would have looked a lot like you." Oh no, the way he's gazing at me and that meaningful statement has me on the verge of tears. Thankfully, his eyes dart away as he clears his throat.

"So, what trade do you find yourself in these days, since it isn't beekeeping?" He levels an almost disapproving gaze at me.

"Oh, um, I'm actually between trades at the moment. I hastily quit my last job and am trying the whole adventuring thing. I have just been assisting people with tasks on the noticeboard in Oakveil." We've made it around the other side of his work shed, and there's a little table and two chairs there. He motions for me to take a seat as he claims the other chair.

"Hmm, a noble endeavor, to be sure. Adventuring and helping those in need. Do you plan to return to that, once you're done training with Phil, that is?" Before I confess that I have no idea and hadn't really thought that far ahead, he continues. "Not to interfere but one does typically stay with the Clan for a time after the Change, forming bonds, growing relationships, and whatnot."

"Oh, I didn't know that. Makes sense, I guess."

"Yes, yes," he quickly interrupts me. "If you were to stay, I could certainly use the help. My old body isn't what it used to be. I've found it to be an impossible task to find myself a competent and eager apprentice. I think the whole Clan I'm going to go on living and producing their honey needs forever." He stretches his legs out in front of him and leans back with his hands behind his head. "Not meaning to sway you or anything, but if you were to stay on here, I'd be willing to take you on as my apprentice. My only apprentice," he says that last part with a wink. I know there's more meaning behind his offer but it feels rude to ask and I also don't want this man to think I'm stupid. I'm also somewhat shocked by his offer.

"You, you would really want me as your apprentice? But you just met me! What if I'm not what you really wanted or expected? What if I'm terrible? It's been so long since I've worked with bees; what if I've forgotten everything?" I can feel worry starting to build up inside me. I really hate disappointing people, especially kind people.

"Oh, well, that just means I'd be able to teach you my way all the better." He waves his hand in dismissal. "I know people, and you're a good one through and through, no doubt about it." I'm speechless. I'm sure my mouth is hanging open, waiting for a bee to fly in it. "Plus, you have what really matters already." He leans over the table conspiratorially. "You appreciate and care about the bees. You have a love for them that's tied to family. I couldn't have asked for a better match. And don't think I missed that carved bee hair bobble poking out of that mane of yours nor that hive tattoo you're sporting on your arm there." I touch my gift from Torben, then the tattoo I got in memory of my grandparents and smile. "Yep," he quickly snorts in through his nose as old men are wont to do, "knew as soon as I clocked those the Goddess herself sent you to me."

"Are you sure, like a hundred percent sure you want to take me on as your apprentice?" I'm starting to get excited by the prospect. An old childhood dream of mine pushed aside for more practical options brought back and laid before me on a silver platter.

"Of course, I'm sure! I'm no wishy-washy youngster. If I say it, I mean it. And I mean it! So girl, what's your answer?" He tilts his head in thought, "I suppose you'd like some time to stew it over and discuss with-"

"YES!" I stand and blurt out before he finishes. "Sorry, I mean, yes. I would love and be honored to be your apprentice." The largest smile cracks his face and creates even more glorious deep wrinkles there. I take hold and violently start shaking his hand.

"Oh, thank you, thank you, sir! You won't regret it. I'll be the best apprentice you've ever had. And I won't flake out on you, no sir. I'm a diligent and dedicated worker." I realize I'm still shaking this poor old man's hand and quickly release it. "Sorry about that! I'm just so excited. I've got to go tell Torben, right now!" I suddenly long to see him and tell him this good news. I want him to be the first person to hear it. Now that I'm thinking of him, his scent fills my nose and I know where he is. Well, which direction and roughly how far anyway.

I instantly break out into a run and end up leaping over the fence. Wow! Phil did have me jumping over and on rocks and boulders, but actually jumping a fence puts it all into perspective.

"I'll be right back!" I quickly turn and shout. As I start to run once more, I can hear Old Man Talbet laughing. Glad to know he's not upset about me ditching him. But I can't seem to help myself, I need to see my boyfriend right now!

I run all the way to Torben's family's home, finding it by following his incredible scent. I am again thankful for all the training Phil has given me. I should find a way to thank him, as well as his mate. That letter Wilhelm gave me has been a blessing and a balm to my mind. I read it three times last night and plan to read it again soon. I actually brought it with me in my pack, even though I'll be going back to the cabin. It simply didn't feel right to leave it behind.

As I near the house, my heart full of excitement for the future, I begin to hear raised voices. I slow down to a walk as the voices from within become clearer. I can just make out, "It's not fair," from a woman. "The council will summon you when it's time." That's Ma and it sounds like she is trying to keep her cool. The voice that says, "Leave, now," with absolute venom is a deep male voice. A voice I recognize but can't believe it could ever utter any words with such hatred. Torben.

Again, I hear the female, "Fine! But I'm not going back to Oakveil to slave away on meaningless tasks." A great BOOM comes from the back of the house and I can hear someone walking quickly to the woods, being immediately followed by a much heavier set of footsteps.

I'm so confused and curious that I tiptoe to the side of the house to see who has angered my sweet bear. Pressing my body as flat as this chubby girl can against the wooden walls, I peek my head around. They are only a few yards into the woods but I can still see them. Torben looks just as mad as he sounded and his rage seems to be directed at...Mel? What could have happened between the siblings? Whatever it was must be bad if Mel needs to be summoned by some council.

Torben catches up to Mel and grabs her arm roughly, turning her to face him.

"You will go back to Oakveil, and you will continue to take on tasks from the noticeboard there, since you are the one who deprived them of Silvia. And you will do all this gladly until the Council decides what your punishment will be." My brain is starting to put the puzzle pieces together now, but my heart is resisting.

"I don't understand why I would need to be punished at all!" Mel replies, her own voice raised while ripping her arm from Torben's fierce hold. "I was doing you a favor, stupid!" I feel my own anger quickly rise to my chest at the insult to my boyfriend. How dare she call him stupid when he's the sweetest, gentlest, most caring and observant partner I've ever had.

"You had already confirmed that she was your mate." Everything in my body freezes in an instant, my own fury stopped quickly in its tracks by her words. His mate? "You didn't even tell the poor girl! You were going about the whole thing so slowly, and for what? To follow her inefficient human customs?"

"You had no right to take that choice away from her!" Torben's voice is booming. "I would have waited till the end of my days for her to choose me! Followed all her courtship expectations of me. She deserved the chance to understand what a mate is, what it means to be a Shifter, before making a decision. I would have been with her as a human or bear, never pressuring her either way. She didn't have to suffer the Change just to be mine!" I can feel the tears streaming down my face unbidden. "You were not here to see what she has suffered due to your selfishness! The physical pain, the mental anguish, her struggles and sorrow. I'm unsure if I will ever be able to forgive the hurt you have done my Mate." These words strike his sister like a blow.

"You...you don't mean that. I did this for you, for both of you. So you two can get to your 'Happily Ever After' faster. Let me talk to Silvia. I know she'll understand and forgive me." Mel turns to start walking toward the house but Torben moves so fast to stand in her way I'm amazed.

"You will go nowhere near my sweet-hearted Mate." The way he says this makes goosebumps spring up on my skin and his ire isn't even directed at me. "You will go back to Oakveil. Now!" He levels his whole arm in the direction the village must be.

"But I can't go back there!" Mel practically whines. "Ellis has been practically cruel to me, giving me the cold shoulder and refusing to speak to me unless it's some snide comment. And Rosy has been even worse. I tried to explain to them why I did it. I mean, they both already knew you were mates, so I thought they'd see reason."

I can practically hear my heart crack. They knew? They knew this whole time? That Torben was my mate, that Mel was the one who turned me, and neither of them said anything.

Betrayal, resounds as a snarl in my mind. They must have laughed at me and my silly feelings, all the girl talks about Torben. I feel like such an idiot. Who else knew? Who else knew I was Torben's mate? Thinking back on interactions with people, his parents, Phil, even Old Man Talbet, they all knew. Everyone, and no one told me. *Lies! They lied to us, kept things from us. How dare they?! How could they?! We thought they were our friends.*

I'm so stupid. How could I not have known, not have put the pieces together that were right in front of me? Phil was practically spelling it out for me that day during the True Mate's lesson. I thought they were all my friends. I thought they all cared for me. And Torben, that he of all people kept these things from me hurts most of all.

My breaths are coming in quick and fast. My heart is racing and breaking all at once. I press my body to the sturdy wooden wall of the house behind me and squeeze my eyes shut. It's too much. It's all too much, and I'm about to break! I open my mouth to scream, but what comes out is a roar! The roar of something big, angry, and fierce. I hear the ripping sounds of fabric and feel the tightness around my body give way to my flesh. My teeth become massive in my mouth, canines enlarging and elongating. I find myself towering over the rocks and bushes, wobbly on my feet, so I fall to all fours. I feel strong, I feel massive, and I feel hurt.

Shifting into bear form has helped my overwhelming feelings, but only slightly. So I run.

Stupid, stupid, stupid! The thought repeats as I barrel through the woods. *Betrayal, lies, secrets,* says another voice inside my head. This is not the fun adventure I thought I'd be having. I'm truly hurt by all this. I want it to be over; I want to go home. I can't even have imaginary book friends, it seems. The thought brings a new wave of sorrow, of old wounds and new. I can feel tears run down the fur on my face.

I hear the sounds of something following me, running to catch up, so I put more effort into my running. Looks like I'm much faster than my pursuer, than my mate. Good! I don't feel much like talking. I only want to run and run and run. So I do just that, leaving him far behind.

I try to turn my mind to other things, to feeling the here and now, the world all around me. My senses are even more pronounced in bear form, especially my nose! Feels as though I can smell for miles and miles. Most things smell good and as they should, except a few things further off. Whatever that is, it smells bad. So I angle away from that direction.

I'm loving the feeling of running, the sounds of me thudding on the ground and crashing through the brush. I find deer paths every now and then but keep off them to shake off my mate.

We are much faster than him and clever to not make this an easy pursuit. He will have to work to earn us. He's not earning us. I'm just not ready to talk about it and confront his stupid face. *His face isn't so stupid. We quite like it, actually.* Okay yes, he does have a nice, kind face. Makes sense we were tricked by it. *Hmm, I do not think that we were tricked.* What do you mean?! He lied to us. *No, he kept secrets from us, which is unacceptable. But maybe some were things you were not yet ready to hear?*

WHAT?! Are you really taking his side? *I do not take his side, only making a point. When you were a human, how would you have reacted to a big strange male walking up to you and saying that you were his Mate?* I mean, well, probably not the best. *If I recall, you thought our Mate 'creepy' at first and he hadn't even spoken to you yet.* How do you know about that? I hadn't been bitten yet. *Pfff, I have always been here, only asleep. I am a part of you, remember? But now I have a voice.* Yeah, you do. I hear her chuckle.

I liked how fierce and angry our Mate was on our behalf. I feel a ripple of pleasure and heat run through our form. *He was very upset for us and defended your lack of choice in the matter.* Yeah, that was something to see for sure, and kinda sweet. He said he would have waited for me and even that he didn't care if I became a Shifter or stayed human. *Being a Bear is pretty nice though, yes?* I mean, I do like the benefits so far, but dealing with my new tendency to break things has been hard. As have you, if I'm being totally honest. *I am new, and you were being silly. He was so often right there near us, smelling so good, ready to be claimed. I did not understand why you kept fighting the mating urge.* I come to a full and abrupt stop.

You knew too?! You knew he was my mate, our mate, whatever. *Of course I knew.* I'm sputtering with rage inside my own mind and begin to run again, changing direction.

How could you not tell me? Why didn't you tell me? *I did not know it was a thing that needed telling. I realize my mistake now. For this, I am sorry. It was pretty obvious though.* Don't start with me. I already feel stupid enough as it is.

You are not stupid and you need to stop telling yourself that. You are exceedingly smart. I can see how your mind works, the connections you make, quick to figure out new tasks and master them, and your desire to learn more. You have emotional intelligence too; you're able to read people and their needs, pick up on their little details. Aww, thanks. That's kinda sweet. I guess you're right. It's not really good for me to tell myself I'm stupid. Grandma would tell me not to put myself down too. 'No negative self-talk in my house' she'd say. *Grandma was wise.*

I come to a big old tree, the biggest I've seen so far in this forest. Its massive roots are popping up out of the forest floor all around.

"Yeah, she was," I say out loud. It's not till I speak that I realize I'm back in human form again. Human and naked and full of so many emotions that I fall to my knees at the mossy base of this ancient tree and weep.

Chapter 24

Torben

S he shouldn't have found out that way. I shouldn't have let it happen like that. I ought to have told her sooner. I didn't even know she was near till I heard that bellow of anguish. I was so wrapped up in my anger, my anger and fear. The fear of her finding out exactly like this. My selfishness has hurt my Mate yet again.

I find her clothes in tatters at the side of the house and catch a glimpse of reddish fur disappearing into the forest.

"Was that Silvia? Did she hear all that?" I ignore Mel's query and shift to follow my Mate, leaving Mel to her own devices. At this moment I don't care what she does. I only have one concern and that is to find my Sweet Silvia.

My Mate proves to be faster than me, as I suspected. But I'm able to follow her scent without issue. This reminds me of the dreams I had while she was sick with the Change Fever. Always running, never catching, just out of sight. It scares me. What if, like in my dreams, I don't find her? What if she leaves me? What if she hates me? What if I do find her and she never forgives me?

Those thoughts are not helpful, my bear chides me. *Keep her in focus, find her, make sure she is safe and well. Then we will do what we can.* He's right. I push my fears and doubts aside. I instead focus on following her, on finding her. That is the first step.

I scent that she has changed back to her human form, and I also taste her tears. I growl at myself for causing this. I know she hates to cry, and I have made her cry so much. I find her curled in a ball under the Ancient Tree, naked, shaking, and sobbing. Shifting, I run up beside her, unbuttoning my shirt to throw over her bare flesh and I stay near on my knees.

"Oh my sweet, sweet Silvia, I'm so... I never meant to... I should have... it's all my fault!" I slam my fist into my thigh in anger and frustration. "You should not have heard it like that. I should have been the one to tell you. And I should have told you right away, or at least much much sooner." She sits up, shifting my shirt over her shoulder and clutching it shut in front. Even crying, she is still so beautiful to me; hair wild and untamed, cheeks red with a smear of dirt and salty tracks running down her freckled face.

I mentally prepare to be yelled at, to grovel for forgiveness, to be spit at and pushed away. But when she looks up at me with her big watery eyes, I am not prepared for her to whisper, "Hold me," before another sob rips from her lips. I'm so shocked that my mind blanks for a moment, but only a moment. I quickly do as she asks and lift her to my lap as I did once before. I rock her and rub her arm while apologizing over and over again. Promising to never keep a secret again. To tell her anything and everything that happened and I confess to her what a stupid, stupid male I am.

"Don't call yourself that," she croaks out. "You aren't stupid, and she was wrong to say so." Again, not at all what I was expecting and far more than I deserve from her.

"Okay, not stupid, but at least a fool. A fool for thinking my resilient, strong, and amazing Mate wasn't ready for the truth."

"Agreed, you were a fool. And an asshole!"

"Yes, yes, a very foolish asshole. A big, big ass." I squeeze her a little tighter to me. "Thank you for letting me hold you. I know how angry you must be with me."

"I'm not angry with you," she muffles into my bare chest.

"How can you not be angry with me? I'm furious with myself."

"Well, maybe a little angry," she concedes. "I'm angry you lied to me, angry you kept so much from me, and angry that you didn't trust me with the truth." My heart hurts at her words. She's right. I should have trusted her with it all. "But," she sniffs several times, then looks up into my face, "you also said that you were willing to wait for me. That it didn't matter if I was a bear or human. And you were so angry on my behalf about not getting to decide for myself." She places her hand upon my bearded cheek, "How could I not love you after hearing that?" New tears fall from her eyes.

I hug her so closely that I almost fear breaking her bones. She loves me. She loves me!

"Oh my Mate, my Mate." I chorus while holding her tightly. "How did a male ever get so lucky? To have such a kind, forgiving, and loving Mate as you. My Mate, my Sweet Silvia, my sweet Mate. What do you want, my Mate? What do you need, my Mate? Ask anything of me and it will be yours." I'm so full of happiness I feel I might burst. I shall light all the candles and give many offerings to the Shifter Goddess for such a blessing.

"Well, first," she says while struggling in my embrace, "maybe ease up on the grip there, Bear Man." I quickly comply. "And then maybe just hold me a little longer. Still tight, I like the pressure, but maybe not crushing." Placing my cheek atop her head, I hug her.

"I would hold you till the end of days." She giggles and snuggles into me.

"I like that," comes her whispered reply.

We stay like this for a time, under that big and ancient tree. With roots and moss all around us. I listen to the bird songs and watch a few squirrels running along branches. I'm so happy and content holding my sweet Mate that it takes me a moment to pick up the scent, and it's a smell I know all too well. An involuntary rumble comes from my chest, quickly followed by a small gasp and a stronger release of arousal. It's now that I realize she is curled up in my lap practically naked.

Dropping my voice down low, "Mate," she wiggles that delectable rump in response. "May I kiss you?"

"Yes," is the quick reply I get before our lips meet and our tongues collide. No soft start now, we are fully enveloped into each other upon contact. One arm wrapped to support her torso as I lean her deeper into the cradling hold. My free hand tightly grabs a handful of curls. This gentle tug has my Mate moaning in my mouth.

I feel my shirt that was covering her fall from her shoulders and body. As if on its own, my hand leaves her mane to rove down her side and firmly grab that squeezable ass. It's just as soft and malleable as I thought. She brings her knee up to my side and slightly twists to give me better access to knead her flesh there. I move that hand lower and my fingers graze the area where her desire is beginning to slicken. She moans even louder at the brief contact, which spurs my boldness to fully trace her wet seam.

At this touch, she breaks our deep kiss to arch her back, issuing even louder sounds from that sweet mouth. Lucky for me, this new position practically offers up her delicious and ample breasts. Her nipples are pink and peaked. How could a male resist? I bend over and swipe my tongue to gently flick a nipple. With a sharp intake of breath, her hand quickly grabs my hair to hold my head in place. No need to guess what she wants from me. I gladly succumb. Taking the whole nipple into my mouth, I suck and flick and graze my teeth upon it. All the while lightly stroking the tips of my fingers through her arousal.

She's making some truly amazing sounds now. My cock is so hard that my pants are causing me physical pain, but I would not move for all the world. I shift her and continue my ministrations on the other breast bringing my hand up to continue to work that first nipple. That was a big mistake. Now the sweet aroma of her desire is so close to my nose that I can practically taste it. In an instant, I'm licking my fingers as if they are covered in the sweetest honey, and to me they are. I close my eyes and rumble deep in my chest.

"Oh my Mate, you are too delicious. I need to taste you at your source."

She can barely get out a, "Wh-what?!" before I lay her upon the mossy ground and kneel between her legs. I place my large hands upon her bent knees to push them open, to expose her yummy honey pot.

"You, you don't have to do that," she stutters as her hands try to hide her sex from me.

"Have to? Oh Sweet Silvia, there is nothing I long for more." I bend my head lower and kiss the tops of her hands. "Please, my Mate, let me taste you. I need to drink you in."

I inhale eagerly through my nose and growl possessively. Slowly, she moves her hands and I take a grateful first lick. I growl more deeply as she moans on my tongue. Moving to lay flat on the ground I hook my arms under her thick thighs while holding her generous hips. Then I feast. I bury my face into her slit, my tongue exploring all her folds with a need to familiarize myself with every inch of her. I swipe my tongue over her clit till it buds. Then use my nose to continue playing with it while my tongue finds her entrance.

My Mate struggles in pleasure, but I hold her firmly in place. Her thighs are tight around my head, squeezing, but I'm in heaven. Her new strength might harm a full human, but for me it's only a tight embrace. My tongue traces circles around the entrance of her core, then I move it back up to run circles around her clit once more.

"Oh gawd!" my Mate yells and I redouble my efforts, gripping her hips even tighter as she bucks. "Please, please," she calls, "please put a finger inside me. I need it now!" I quickly release one hip and run my middle finger through her sweet nectar. Moving my tongue to her clit once more I slowly press the finger inside. The effect is immediate, and she comes with a silent scream, back arched, thighs tight, and hands tangled in my hair. It's the most beautiful thing I have ever seen. And I want to experience it again, right now.

I continue to work her through her orgasm with plans to ride it right into the next. I back off her clit and watch her body shake, her chest heave with exertion. But I continue to slowly work my finger in and out. I gently bite her thigh, letting a bit of fangs brush along her flesh. A slight twitch of pleasure and excitement courses through her body. She looks at me and I do it again, letting her see the fangs.

"Oh my," she whispers.

"You are so beautiful wrapped in pleasure. Let me see it again."

Before she can reply, I bring my mouth to her clit and plunge my finger deep inside. Her moan of pleasure is all the permission I need. I suck and lick her bud as I add a second finger inside her. She tilts her pelvis and my fingertips brush a different texture of flesh deep within. A guttural, almost choked noise comes from her throat.

I pull my fingers out then make sure to swipe the area once more when I press them in again. Her moans have turned deeper than before so I know I've found a good spot. I don't let up, I hit that spot over and over making sure to continue to lick, suck, and even gently run a fang over her clit and folds. Her hands are scrambling along the ground now, digging in the moss and dirt, searching for something to hold. She must manage to grab a root because I hear the breaking and splintering of wood as her hands lock into it.

Knowing she must be close, I continue my actions with the same pace and pressure. I place my free hand on her abdomen to keep her locked where she is, and as soon as I apply pressure there, my Mate comes with an enthusiastic moan and a fountain of warm delicious honey.

I got to smell her sweet release that night, but to taste it, to have it fill my mouth is an ecstasy all to itself. I lap it up, drinking it down as I continue to pump my fingers into her. She eventually stills and releases the root. So I remove my fingers, but can't help licking up her sweetness from them. She's trembling all over and I can't help the swell of pride.

"Geezus Krist!!" she says breathlessly. "I don't think anyone has ever made me come so hard in my life." I playfully bite her thigh once more and smile wide. Oh yes, my Mate is well-pleased.

I sit back on my knees and realize at some point I came as well and released into my pants. Seems the combination of her scent, the sounds she made, and her delicious cunt were too much for me to stand. I chuckle to myself as I run my hands along her knees, down her thighs, over her stomach, and up to squeeze and cup her breasts. What a soft and malleable Mate I have. I want to bite her everywhere.

"What are you laughing at?" she asks with an eyebrow arched

"That my Mate is so sexy, beautiful, and delicious that I can't even wait for my own release while she is having hers." I glance down to the now wet patch in my trousers.

"Oh!" she exclaims, then giggles behind her hands. "Well, I guess I can wait for you to get ready for the next round. Being the kind and patient Mate that I am."

I flop to the ground and gather her in my arms to lay along the side of my body. One of my hands goes to her hair as she uses my shoulder as a pillow, the other holds her thigh across my abdomen. She laughs and snuggles into me, hand playing with my chest hair.

"With you draped around me like this it won't take long for me to be ready again. How are you doing? Was it too much? We can be done; we don't have to continue. I don't want you to miss the whole festival." I squeeze her to my side.

"Oh, I'm doing wonderfully." It comes out almost blissful. I smile even wider with pride, burying my nose into her mane of curls, now sporting leaves, moss, and some fresh wood splinters.

SNAP!

"Well, well, well, look what we have here, boys," comes a slimy and crude voice. "If is isn't a couple of lost little bears all alone, fucking in the woods."

I sit bolt upright, pushing my Mate down and behind me. Goblins! What are goblins doing here, on our Clan lands? There's five of them riding giant boars as mounts. These goblins have truly seen better days. Their long pointed ears are marred with cuts, scratches, and chunks missing. Dull, patchy hair dusts their shoulders, hands, and feet covering sickly green skin. Their typically shiny black talons are dulled and some are even graying. Their bared teeth and fangs are yellowed and decaying, and none still have all their teeth intact.

"Shoo-eee, boss, it smells something awful. Does bear fucking always smell this bad?" They all cackle as they leisurely circle around us, slowly closing in.

"Can't say I've ever had such a snout full before," the one they call boss replies. "It may indeed." More cackling. I can feel my Mate shaking and smell her fear. It's a scent I do not enjoy nor wish to ever smell again.

"What are you doing in Clan lands? You have no right to be here. Speak your business or be off before the entire Bear Clan of the Oaks descends upon you." I boom my voice as loud and threatening as I can while I rise to my full height. A few steal glances of concern at each other. Good, they should be worried.

"Speak our business, you say, or the Clan will be upon us, ay?" the ring leader says in a teasing tone. His confidence bolsters the doubtful ones. "Our business is you Bear Shifter, or at least the parts of you that will sell." Sell? What does he mean by that? "And I don't think anyone will be coming, little boy," the goblin sneers. "You are far, far, far from your little clan and today is a festival day. But not just any festival, one where couples are expected to wander off from home for little dalliances in the woods." My eyes go wide because he is right. "No one will come looking for anyone for quite. Some. Time." They all cackle once more.

Before their stupid laughter dies down, I leap toward the leader and shift into my Grizzly Bear form while in the air. I land on both goblin and boar with a satisfying crunch. I know I'm a big male in my human shape, but nothing could have prepared these idiots for how massive I am as a bear.

For good measure, I make sure to wedge this goblin's head within my jaws and squeeze down till I feel his brain matter and skull upon my tongue. I spit it out as best I can as I barrel toward the next goblin. Thankfully, they are all still surprised and have yet to get their startled mounts under control. I dig my claws deep into my new target. As blood gurgles from his mouth, I fling him hard directly at the one closest to my Mate, knocking him from his seat. Hopefully, I also broke or injured him enough for now.

I feel two sharp hits to my shoulder and torso. Seems the others have recovered enough to attack me. I look down and see that something is sticking out of my ribs. A dart. Appears they wanted us alive, big mistake on their part. But this does mean I need to hurry before whatever this is overtakes me. My bear rages at the injury, and I surge into the next goblin. I'm hit two more times before I reach him and slash his face and throat. Only two more to deal with and one is already down, for now. I can feel myself becoming sluggish. Another hit, this time to my rump. What an asshole move!

I can hear the wild beat of hooves quickly approaching me from behind, but my body isn't responding fast enough. I whirl around trying to meet my enemy, but I know I'm too slow. He's going to hit me. Probably with a crude club I've noticed dangling from the saddles of the others. I turn my head in time to see a blur of cinnamon-colored fur ram full speed into the attacking goblin. I hear a crunch of bone and the ripping of fabric and flesh. My Mate has shifted once more and has killed for me. She has saved me, but at what cost to her sweet spirit and kind nature?

My legs betray me and I fall hard to the ground. The poison is swiftly taking its toll. My adrenalin and rage are losing out. I manage to stumble back up, trying to make my way to the last of the goblins. I have to make sure he is down. I can't leave my Mate until I know the threat is gone.

"Hey, hey, are you okay? What's wrong?" There's so much worry in her voice that it's heartbreaking. Our bond hasn't been sealed yet so she can't hear me in this form. So I shift, though it saps the rest of my strength.

"Need, to kill, last, goblin," I manage to say.

"It's okay, it's okay, he's dead already. His big pig fell on top of him when you threw that other guy. Must have punctured a lung or something. He was wheezing, and gurgling, then died," she says that last part in a whisper. Though I am sad she had to see that, I'm more relieved than anything. I let my body rest upon the forest floor. "Wait, wait, don't lay down." She's crying again, her voice is choked. "What's wrong, what can I do?"

"Darts for sleep." I pause for two breaths. "Leave me." She's shaking her head violently side to side. "Go home." With that, my world becomes black nothingness as I succumb to the sleeping potion.

Chapter 25

Silvia

"Wake up! Wake up, Torben! Please wake up! Don't leave me!" I yell while crying and shaking his body. He's out like a light and softly snoring. But he's alive, so that's something.

These goblins smell awful, and I recognize the smell as the bad one I encountered while running. At least I know what vile goblin smells like, I guess. I frantically look around the woods trying to think, weighing my options. Stopping, I take a moment for a calming breath, promptly wipe the tears from my face, then get to work.

First things first, I put on Torben's shirt and button it up. Then I check and make sure all the goblins are actually, for sure, dead. If movies and TV have taught me anything, it's to double and triple check. Once I verify that all assholes are very, very dead, RIP, I check to make sure Torben is still breathing, then turn him on his side. Pretty sure I read that somewhere. Better safe than sorry, right? Now, what to do?

I'm having a hard time smelling if there are more goblins or big boars in the area because these are all around me, filling my nose. Plus, the boars that could escape ran off in several directions, making this even harder for me. Torben told me to go home—his home, I'm assuming—so I sniff around to see if I can tell where it is and how far.

Bad news, I smell that it's really far. Even worse news, a rain storm is moving in. I can both smell and hear it, and it's coming fast. So, home is too far to drag this man by myself before the storm hits and way too far for me to leave him all alone not knowing if more kidnappers are around. The storm releases a resounding crack of thunder that reverberates through the woods. I can hear animals and birds moving quickly to safety.

Think, think, what's the best course of action? I need to make a decision and I need to make it soon. I instantly decide I'm not leaving him alone, obviously. I'll walk all night in the rain carrying him over my shoulder if I have to. Though I would prefer a better way to haul him. A sled! I saw Torben use one while in Oakveil to transport wood. I can make one now to carry him. I quickly find some smaller trees and easily tear them out of the ground. Being strong is awesome! I use the straps from the boar saddles and belts from the dead goblins to tie the wood together. I've never made one before, but I only need it to last for a short while.

Torben weighs a ton! Even with my new impressive strength, I find it difficult to roll him onto the travois. Maybe Phil should have had me carry this guy around. Another crack of thunder and a whoosh of wind reminds me of my need for urgency. I take a belt knife from one corpse and grab its pack too, for good measure. I'll look through it later. Now, it's time to move, and move I do. Hoisting the makeshift sled, I begin to drag my Mate away from this crime scene. A few yards from the ancient tree and dead bodies, I find a new smell in the air. One that brings me hope.

To my right, and not far off, I get a slight whiff of his Clan. I got a good nose full of what his town and several members smell like earlier. This scent is similar, though faint. I don't know if some are up here for the festival, or if there's a community cabin, or even a shrine of some kind? I do know that whatever it is, it's theirs and it's closest. So I turn us towards the scent and start walking.

It takes a hot minute to get to it, and unfortunately it involved dragging my behemoth of a man up some inclines. My calves are killing me, but we finally make it to a cave right as the rain begins to pour down.

"Of course, it's a cave!" I yell into it as I drop the man I love onto the ground. I take a moment there, bent over with my hands on my thighs, catching my breath. I'm a Bear Shifter, not Wonder Woman.

The cave looks cozy enough. There's a big palette-type bed on the floor covered in furs and blankets. I see a pit near it for a fire, pots and pans, and baskets that smell of food. There's also stuff painted on the walls, but I can't make any of it out in the darkness. A nice cozy fire will help with that.

I pick the handles of the travois back up and drag Torben closer to the bed. First, I'll light the fire; second, I'll get Torben in that bed, and third... Well, I'll worry about that once I finish steps one and two.

I thank my lucky stars when I find a familiar red crystal that I've seen Phil use to start a fire. I've watched him several times now, but never asked how it was done. From what I've seen, he rubbed his thumb over it and then a fire would spring to life. The pit looks as if it's already set up to start a fire. There's wood and twigs and some dried wood shavings.

Wonder what this place is for? Maybe it's someone's vacation cave, or maybe it's like a hotel for the weary Shifter in need? I sure hope it's that last one. Grabbing the red crystal, I mimic Phil's actions near the shavings, and a fire does indeed leap from the stone and onto the kindling. I'm totally shocked for about two seconds before I remember that, yes, magic does indeed exist in this place. And here I thought Phil had this special skill. I laugh at myself and shake my head.

Once I get Torben situated on the pallet, I snoop around the place. I start with the baskets on the shelves. Some have food and spices for cooking, others have towels and robes, and one is filled with several types of oils I'm unfamiliar with. There's also books, cards, and what might be board games. Now I'm starting to think I've just broken into someone's vacation cave after all. Oops, but it was an emergency, and we'll replace anything we use.

Further back, I discover a pool of water that turns out to be a natural hot spring. There's also a trickle of cold water running into it. A nice hot bath and cold fresh water, amazing! My delight continues as I find there's actually a functioning toilet and sink tucked in the very back around a corner. Now this is camping! Or maybe it would be called glamping? Either way, I'm getting in that water. I look in the baskets by the pool and find more towels, sponges, and several kinds of soaps for body and hair. Hmm, not going to trust my hair to any old shampoo but the soaps for skin should be fine. I race back, check on Torben, fling his shirt off me, grab a robe, and head back to the little pool.

Once I'm done washing and picking forest debris from my hair, I stay in the warm waters and relax my poor limbs. Bear strength or not, I've put my body through a lot today. Running from Phil's cabin to the Talbet Bee Yard, Shifting for the first time, running as a bear, hard crying, some mind-blowing oral sex, intense fear, shifting again, and killing a goblin. Then finally, dragging an unconscious bear man around the forest. I'm impressed with myself, that's for sure. Take that, high school PE coach! I do have endurance!

One thing strikes me as odd though; my Inner Bear has been silent since we made up with Torben and I'd like to know why. Dragging myself from the bliss that is this natural tub, I dry off, put a robe on, then walk to sit by the fire. It's time to meet my bear.

In my mind, I open my eyes to the forest and cave where my bear resides. Just outside is a campfire with a log to sit on, so I take a seat.

"Okay you in there, time's up!" I call out. "Come and talk to me face-to-face. No more napping."

I hear the shuffling of leaves and the padded steps of a very large animal within the cave. A grown bear, with fur the color of cinnamon, steps into the sunlight and slowly walks to the fire in front of me.

"Wow, you're beautiful!" I instantly blurt out without intending to.

"Yes, we are beautiful," the bear replies with confidence, though her maw doesn't move. We are in my mind after all, makes sense I guess.

"Is that how I look when I shift?" The bear gives a little nod. "Cool," I say with a big smile. At least my bear form is awesome. "Why have you been so quiet?" The bear breathes deeply, then sits down too.

"Because it was time we had our real meeting, and I had hoped my silence would bring you here when you had a moment. I think I shouldn't have been talking to you like that before you accepted me. And I know we shouldn't have shifted till you did." She looks almost guilty.

"Oh no, it's okay. You didn't do anything wrong. We were having some real big feelings that first time, and the second was to save Torben. Please don't feel bad."

"No, if I had gone about our meeting, our connection, the correct way, much of this would have been avoided. If I had talked to you first, instead of pushing the mating urge upon you, you would have known about being mates and would not have felt that betrayal in the first place." My bear bends her head down. "I am sorry I put the mating connection before our blending."

"Please don't be so hard on yourself. You were new and from what Phil told me the urge to mount your mate is very, very strong."

"Yes, it is very strong, and once we fully accept each other, you will feel it even stronger than before." My bear surprises me with that reply.

"What now? I feel it pretty strong already."

"No, once you and I connect completely, there will be no doubt who your True Mate is. You wouldn't even have to know what a mate is to be all over him." She chuckles before adding, "It will be almost impossible to resist."

"Oh my," I say while fanning myself. "Now I'm even more excited and scared. So, what do we need to do next? You mentioned blending?"

"You still wish to do so? Now?" the bear communicates while cocking her head to the side. "I would understand if you needed more time. Or even needed to forgive me?"

"Of course, I still want to connect with you, silly goose."

" I am not a goose, I am a bear."

"Yes, yes," I agree while waving my hand dismissively, "It's just an expression, a term. You don't take it literally."

"Oh, I see." She pauses for a moment then continues in a serious tone. "Thank you for not being cross with me. I promise to be the best bear to you. Truthful and honest and forthright." Confidently, I get up and stand in front of my bear.

"And I promise to listen to you and take your thoughts and instincts seriously." She reaches out and grips me in a snug bear hug, which I return as tightly as I can. The vision of the woods swiftly fades and I open my eyes. Was...was that all we needed to do to blend? Have we really merged?

Hmm, I don't feel any different. Sitting here by the fire I slowly take a mental inventory of my body but it all seems the same. I test out my senses but they don't appear to be anymore enhanced than they were after the Change. Maybe fully merging with your bear takes a little time?

While I wait, I decide to clean Torben up a little. He still has some goblin blood on his face and hands, as well as a few pinpricks from the darts. Grabbing a bowl full of warm soapy water, I wash his face, neck, and beard as best I can. Then, I move down to clean his little wounds with a fresh bowl.

Man, that fire is really putting off a lot more heat now. While loosening the robe and fanning myself I realize that his pants are covering the rest of his injuries.

We should take his pants off then. What?! *So we can clean him up and nurse him.* Oh, yes, yes, of course. I start with his boots and socks. Easy enough, though this heat from the fire is getting to be a bit too much. Now his pants. I swallow the extra saliva that has congregated in my mouth.

No peeking, I hear with a laugh.

"I'm not going to peek or peer or ogle. I won't look at his impressive manhood without his permission. Consent is very important."

Who are you talking to?

"You, him, the world at large, an invisible audience. I Don't Know! Just covering all my bases here." Whoa, this temperature is making me crazy.

I don't think it's the fire, my bear says in a sing-song way followed by more snickering.

"What?! Oh! I see. Damn, okay." I fan myself with my hand to no avail. As quickly as I'm able, I yank his pants down to his ankles and throw the covers back over him. There, that will do it. Easy-peasy.

But you still need to wash his injuries and at least one was on his butt. Now she's giggling.

"Nope, nope, I can't be trusted!"

Hands raised over my head, I walk away toward the front of the cave. The cool wet air helps my growing heat a little, a very little. I take some deep breaths in and attempt to go back to sit by his side, but as soon as I draw near, his scent washes over me and sets me ablaze. Hot damn, she wasn't kidding. This is nothing like I was experiencing before.

I tried to warn you. Yeah, yeah. So I grab a quilt and one of the sitting pillows, then station myself to sit at the entrance of the cave. To protect my man from anymore goblins, but mostly to protect him from me.

I must doze off at some point because I'm startled into wakefulness by a violent clap of thunder. My neck is slightly cricked from the angle it was in as I leaned against the cave wall. As I stretch it out, another great boom sounds making me jump, and I see a twitch from the palette followed by a groan.

"Hey there, sleepy head, you awake?" Another groan of pain issues from the palette, followed by more movement.

"My head feels like I've been drinking nothing but Pa's home-brewed mead for three days straight." He's got both hands over his face, fingers pressed into his forehead.

"Anything I can get you to help with the pain? There's some cold fresh water here."

"Yeeeessss," comes the muffled reply. I laugh and fetch him a big cup full. Thankfully, my mate being in pain lessens the urge to mount him. At least enough to get near. He lurches up and slouches over his lap, still kneading his head. I sit on the bed and hand him the water. He drinks it down fast. Suddenly he jolts and looks at me while grabbing my shoulder. "Goblins! There were goblins. You were in danger."

"Shh, shhh," I croon while patting one of his hands. "We killed them all, remember?" He eases his grip and nods his head, but winces in pain at the movement.

"Where are we? How did we get..." he asks while looking around, then freezes and begins to blush for some reason.

"Well, you got shot with all those tranquilizer darts and were out cold for a while. I couldn't tell if there were more goblins in the woods, what with all that blood and those boars running around all crazy. And I couldn't very well leave you alone there all defenseless. Your home was so far away, and a storm was coming too, just my luck." He's staring straight at me and blinking more than usual, probably trying to keep up with my speedy babbled explanation.

"I pieced together a crude sled to drag you behind me, like the one I saw you with that one time in Oakveil when you startled me and I spilled all those metal bits. Anyway, I started walking us toward your home preparing for a long, wet trudge, which I would have totally done for you. But then after I got further away from the terrible reek of those assholes, I smelled something that was like your clan. Weighing my options, I risked this closer smell, hoping to find some of your people or any type of help or refuge. And let me tell you, it was a slog to get here. You are one heavy fella. Especially up hills and over annoying rocks."

At some point during all this, I scooted closer and started running my hands along his chest. I notice what I'm doing, but don't care enough to stop. Plus, it's helping to calm me as I continue my story.

"We made it to this cave right as the storm hit, which I am so grateful for because all I was wearing was your shirt. I don't even have any shoes!" I wiggle my toes to emphasize my point. "I lit a fire in this pit, which was already prepared, but I did figure out the red stone trick on my own. Got you into bed and explored a bit. I think this is someone's vacation or camping cave, so we'll need to wash and replace the things we use." He's gazing at me so sweetly with a hint of a smile playing at one corner while playing with my hair. What an awesome guy, letting me get all this out without interrupting.

"There's a real toilet back there and a hot spring pool that's absolutely divine! After my bath, I finally had that meeting with my bear because she had been suspiciously quiet and I wanted to find out what was up."

"You met with your bear? Congratulations, my sweet brave Mate. I know you've been trying hard to do so. Glad she decided to come out of her cave for you."

"Aww, thanks sweetie. That means a lot. But we didn't just meet. After we talked things out, we hugged and I guess bonded or melded together? Something like that." He paused his stroking when I mentioned bonding. "I don't fully get what that means. I'm sure Phil would have explained it had it happened with him. But what I do know is that we are talking better in my head and, um..." Now I feel heat creeping up my cheeks and onto my ears as I'm about to admit this next part. I lick my suddenly dry lips and press on, "and um, I know for sure now that you are my Mate. I can feel, oh, all kinds of things, especially when I'm near you. I honestly can't fathom how you put up with this for so long. I had to stop cleaning you up and move away. I felt as if I couldn't completely trust myself around you. Especially being mostly naked and all." He resumes playing with my curls.

"Is that why my pants are around my ankles?" he remarks in a teasing tone.

"I didn't see anything! I was only going to clean where they shot you on your butt, I swear." He's silently laughing at me, trying to contain it but losing. "I really was!" comes out at a higher pitch than I intended. Clearing my throat I continue. "I was going to anyway, but I was getting so very hot. I grabbed the sides of your pants, pulled them down quickly, and instantly threw the covers back over you. After that I realized I should probably stop and leave you be."

I'm getting even hotter than before now, with him awake and looking better. But he's not okay, I remind myself. With a tremendous amount of mental fortitude, I remove my hands from his chest and scoot back a bit on the bed. Then a little bit more for good measure.

"Um, how are you feeling? They shot you a lot and you had to fight four of them. Are you hurt anywhere else? I'd feel so bad if you were and I didn't know." He moves a little closer towards me again, but as he opens his mouth to answer I cut in. "You should really take a bath!" He freezes instantly, hand mid-air about to resume the contact I broke.

"I don't think I got all that goblin blood off you, under your nails, in your beard, and such. And, and it can't be good for you to have it on too long. Unsanitary and all that. Plus, the hot spring back there is amazing!"

I gently pat his knee in an attempt to take the sting out of my comment that sounded an awful lot like 'you smell.' He hums and slightly bobs his head in reply.

"Oh, and there are all these different oils and things around too," I add. "Thought one might be nice to rub into my poor sore legs but I wasn't sure which would be best. Goodness, is everything alright?"

Torben's whole body has gone beet red, his eyes are darting everywhere, as if not knowing where to look. He can't look at me, he can't look at the bed, and for some reason he can't look at the walls.

"What's, what's wrong with the walls?" I ask. His eyes are back onto me now and wider than I've ever seen them. So I turn my head to get a better view. I know there are murals and writings on them, but I didn't really examine them once I lit the fire pit. They are old and fading, but once I actually decide to inspect them I realize what I'm seeing. The walls are full of images of bears and people in various sexual positions and acts. There are a few other animals and fantasy creatures thrown in the mix as well. My eyes begin to do that rapid blinking thing again as my brain processes this.

"Torben, what kind of a cave is this exactly?"

Chapter 26

Silvia

I am also having a hard time finding a place for my eyes to go. The walls are a no, back at Torben also no, the baskets full of what I now guess are sex oils, definitely not. I settle on the rainstorm raging outside. Yeah, there we go, that's safe.

"This is the Mating Cave," comes the deep rumbling timbre of Torben. It washes over me making my body shiver in delight. "This is a place where newly mated shifters of our Clan can come to be alone while the mating bond is running rampant and being formed."

"Oh, that's nice." My reply is high pitched again.

"Yes, things can get a bit...loud." Oh, I'm going to combust from embarrassment and need. "Sometimes shifters can get possessive, though not as often with bears. It's mostly for privacy. Giving them time alone with each other without worries."

"That's very considerate and smart." I'm hopelessly fanning myself, still keeping my eyes firmly on the rain outside. I've even turned my body in the direction of the cave mouth. I find I'm currently torn between leaping on the man behind me and running right out into that storm to cool off.

I hear Torben quickly say, "I should go bathe," moments before I hear a splash of water. Guessing I'm not the only one having a hard time. For some reason that thought makes me smile. He's been feeling this way about me, about my presence, the whole time. Makes me feel a little giddy, like I was some kind of sexy vixen. I inwardly giggle at myself.

We are sexy! We are sexy, and he has wanted us since he saw us. He has yearned for us. And now we yearn for him. Can we please finally have him? My inner bear pleads with me. *We are Mates, he made all efforts to woo you the human way, we are in the Mating Cave, and he is naked and almost clean.* All very solid points and hard to argue with. Let's let him get a little more clean, then we will make him all dirty again in a different way.

Yes, yes, a great idea. Oh, we should sneak over and surprise him. I like the way you think, She-Bear. Wait, you aren't going to be talking to me while we're making love are you? I don't know if I can handle that honestly, no offense.

Oh no, we will be together. No need for words. Perfect.

I slyly look over my shoulder at Torben who has his back to me. From the smell, I know he's already washed his hair, and now I can see he's started to rinse off his body. Excellent. I slip my robe off and slink away from the pallet as quietly as I can. Thankfully, Torben is splashing water onto his face. As calmly and confidently as I can, I stalk over to my Mate. He's washing his face and beard again. Good call there, seeing as I have plans for that face. As he's rinsing the soap away, I strike what I hope is a sexy pose.

"Got room for one more in there?"

His eyes turn to me, then he freezes. Perfect response. I don't wait for an answer. Instead I step into the pool, slowly sinking lower and lower into the hot water.

He's watching me the whole time, eyes roving all over me, body still as stone, hands frozen in place mid-splash. While I still have the nerve, I walk right up to him, place one hand on his chest and use the other to move one of his to my hip. He squeezes as soon as it makes contact, which has me leaning into him. Removing my hand from his, I place it on his cheek and I look up into his eyes.

"So my Mate, are we going to use this cave for its intended purpose?" I ask with a sultry tone I've never used before.

A low rumbling growl is the only warning I get before he wraps both arms tightly around my body, lifting me up for a kiss. Following his lead, I hook my legs around his waist and grab his face between both my hands. He shifts his to my ass and grips tightly.

The kiss is deep with tongues twisting in, out, and around both our mouths. I suck on his lower lip which makes him hum in pleasure. He sinks into the water, sitting down on a smooth stone bench I used earlier. This time I have a much more exciting seat.

Straddling his lap as I am, I can now feel that wonderfully hard and massive cock I've glimpsed once before. It's wedged perfectly in between the two of us so I begin to rub it against my clit and pussy folds. I moan loudly in his mouth at the sheer delight in that contact. But I want more.

I lift up higher and attempt to maneuver the head into my opening, but he grips my hips firmly, moving me back down along his cock instead. I whine at this and he laughs, breaking the kiss.

"Not just yet, my Mate. We'll get to that soon, but first..." he suddenly stands up, lifting me again and places my ass on the cold rim of the pool "...I need a taste of that sweet honey of yours."

He kisses me again as he lays me back upon the cave floor. Legs still wrapped around him, he moves his hands up my thighs slowly as he releases that breathtaking kiss to lightly bite my neck. This sends shivers through my body all the way down to my now curled toes. Hands continue their upward caresses as his kisses continue to trail downward, meeting finally at my breasts. I'm breathing heavy in anticipation which is making them heave like in those naughty romance novels. I guess I'm in one of those spicy books now. I have a fleeting thought that I hope nobody reads it before my brain is stolen away.

The first lick of his tongue upon my nipple has me gasping for breath and digging my hands into my own hair. I've always enjoyed nipple play but it usually takes some working up to feel this good. I don't know if it's the whole mating thing or what, but whatever it is, I'm not complaining.

His hand comes up to cup my other breast, gently running his thumb over that nipple as that agile tongue of his swirls the other. I can hear my moans of pleasure reverberate off the walls of the cave. As my hips start to buck and wiggle with their own desire, I feel his hardness again. Grabbing his shoulders, I angle myself so that it grazes my pussy. He instantly gives my nipple a hard little pinch, which sends shocks down to my core.

"I said not yet," comes his throaty response.

Leaving my breasts, his mouth and hands travel down my body. Nibbling and squeezing as they go. With strong hands he parts my legs wide then moves my ass closer to the edge of the hot spring. I can feel the warmth of the water curling up to gently caress my most sensitive parts. He gives my thigh a love bite before turning his attention where I desperately need it.

With both his massive hands holding my thighs open, he lowers his head and begins to devour me. It feels as if his tongue is everywhere all at once. Delving, parting, flicking, and swirling in all the places I need it. And when he starts to suck on my clit, my eyelids begin to flutter. I move my hands from my hair to his, needing to feel more of him. As soon as I get a solid grip, he brings a finger to slowly trace a circle around my opening. I come almost instantly, much to my surprise and his.

"Already, my Sweet Mate?" he asks while lifting his head to look at me, a smile on his face.

"S-sorry, felt soooo goooood," I manage to get out.

"No need to apologize, Sweet Silvia, you may come as often and as quickly as you please." I smile at him, but before I can reply with a 'gee thanks' or some such, he slowly pushes that finger all the way inside me while his hungry eyes lock onto my face.

Oh my gawd, that's so sexy—is what I think—but what comes out is a nice long "Fffuuuuucckkk!" as he twists that finger while pulling out. To my surprise, he adds a second finger right away and pushes them both deep inside, slowly. I bring my hands to my breasts and begin to play with my nipples. Since he's teasing me, I decide to start teasing him. The dangerous growl that emanates from him lets me know my plan worked.

"Don't stop doing that. I want to see what you like," he rumbles so deeply that I shiver at his words. Oops, seems my plan might have backfired. He continues pumping his fingers into me as his other hand moves to work my clit. Oh no, I'm already close to breaking again. Until he starts talking to me, that is.

"At some point during this mating, you may feel the nearly uncontrollable desire to bite me. It's the Mating Urge seeking to complete the Bond between us. You have my permission to bite me if or when this sweeps over you."

"Wh-what?" I ask breathlessly, confused at this new topic while on the edge of an orgasm.

"I know you didn't get to that part of your lessons," he continues, just as his fingers find my G-spot. Oh goodness, how am I supposed to hear words right now while I'm in this state? "So I wanted to warn you, but also give you my permission to complete our Bond on your end if you so choose. No more keeping things from my Mate." He curls his fingers even more while within me, making me cry out in pleasure.

"Yes!" I exclaim while nodding my head, "I want you to bite me too! I want you to make me yours." And I do, I really, really do. I want to be his, and I want him to be mine. We are Mates and I want to complete this bond that ties us together.

He stops his movements which makes me whine and move my hips.

"Are you sure? We don't have to do so now, the first time. I can explain it to you better later. So you can decide once you know everything." How did I get so lucky?!

"I understand and I want the bond, I want to be your Mate, completely. I want to be connected to you forever. Now bite me or fuck me, but please do something, NOW!" My final word comes out in a voice bassier than I've ever spoken before, and more commanding than I thought possible. Torben's hands pick back up their movements with gusto as a cavernous rumble begins to emanate from his chest.

"Where?" comes his question in a voice deeper than the Mines of Moria.

Look him right in the eyes and whisper, "Anywhere."

With that one word, his mouth suddenly clamps down on my inner thigh once more, but this time four fangs puncture my flesh. There's a little pain, but it is quickly washed away by the waves of pleasure that overcome me. My eyes roll in my head as the intense pleasure of that one bite sends me skyrocketing over the edge and into utter bliss. My mouth is painfully wide open but no sounds will come out; my back is contoured in an arch that you would think only a gymnast could achieve. Flashes of light dance in my vision as I ride the roller coaster of undulating pleasure. There's nothing I can do but hold on and enjoy.

Eventually, I blink back from my daze of ecstasy to find my Mate licking the new mark upon my thigh.

"Will it scar?" I manage to croak out.

"Yes, but it will look more silvered upon your skin. It will be slightly raised as well. Marking you as mine." A smile of satisfaction accompanies those words.

"Good," I say breathlessly and smile back at him. "You chose a good spot too. It's kinda sexy."

"Very sexy. Seeing my mark upon my Mate's flesh so close to her honey pot will fill me with overwhelming desire."

What a wicked answer, and the way he's looking so possessively at it has me getting hot again all over. I almost can't believe I'm ready to go so soon after that mind-altering release. This whole mating thing is intense. I roll my hips slightly to get him to look there instead. And look he does.

"Oh my Sweet Mate, I'm afraid I need to claim you right now." He suddenly stands and positions the head of his cock at my entrance, slowly rubbing it through my slick folds. "So perfectly wet for me. I had wanted to get three fingers into you before I took you, but I think with how soaked you are, I will be able to fit into you just fine. But I'll take it slow." He winks and bends slightly to kiss my knee.

Slowly, he pushes the head of his cock into me, making me moan and squirm in pleasure. I wrap my legs around his hips, wishing for him to push deeper.

"Patience, my sweet. It's hard enough to control myself without you egging me on. I want this to last."

He pushes in a little deeper before pulling back out again. I'm so sensitive at this point that I can feel the ridge of his cock's head sliding in and out of me, and it feels amazing. So I let him take charge, moaning loudly each time his head passes through my opening.

"Play with your breasts again, I want to see your pleasure."

I do as he wishes, strumming my peaked nipples with my fingers. I'm starting to feel stretched now. He must feel it too. Bringing his thumb to his mouth I watch as he takes a nice long lick before bringing it down to my clit. Perfection. It's exactly what I needed to open myself more for him and accept the slight sting that comes when he finally fully seats himself within me. With one final push, he's there. His head hitting my g-spot, his thumb working my clit, and my fingers pinching my nipples, I come for the third time, squeezing even tighter around him as my warm release rushes out of me and dribbles down my ass.

He's got his eyes squeezed shut, shoulders rounded, and hands tightly gripping the edge of the pool at either side of my hips.

"You said I could come as often as I wanted." This makes him chuckle.

"Indeed I did. And I am blessed to have such a Mate. But it makes it very difficult not to come myself, and I do not wish for this to end so soon. Especially right after I finally got myself inside you."

Now it's my turn to chuckle which has him throwing his head back and inhaling quickly through clenched teeth in a hiss.

"Oops, sorry. How about you bend down here and kiss me till you're ready, my Mate." He leans down and kisses my forehead, kisses both cheeks, then lightly dusts his lips against mine just as he did that first time. "Hmm, lovely. May I have another?" to which he obliges.

This time it's him who nibbles my lower lip and opens his mouth to me first. Just as I am getting into this kiss, he picks me up and sets us back down into the water, shifting his cock deeper inside me as I straddle him once more. I let out a cry as I throw my head back, grabbing his shoulders.

"You did that on purpose," I say breathlessly.

"I did, but didn't it feel good?" he says while nuzzling my neck. I nod my head because, yeah, it did. "I want you to ride me, my Sweet Mate. And if you feel the urge to bite me, I would like mine upon my neck for all the world to see." Oh damn, why is that so sweet? "But fair warning, I may not last long."

"Oh honey, that's more than okay," I reassure him as I look into his face. "It's about time you had your turn."

Before he can reply or protest I begin to move. I rise up slightly and let myself slowly sink back down. He makes a noise deep in his throat while closing his eyes, grabbing my ass with one hand while the other grips my hair at my scalp. Oh, I like this. So I do it again, but this time I rise up slightly more, then accelerate my fall back down with a bit more vigor. This makes both of us shout. I continue to ride him, up and down. He holds my ass and hip now, helping me move. With the way his cock is hitting me so deep inside, I might not last long either.

All I can hear is the slosh of water, his grunts and moans of pleasure, and my own heartbeat. It's growing louder and louder as I bounce on his lap. Taking his dick over and over again. My dick. My Mate. Both are mine forever and no one will ever take them from me. I can't even hear the water anymore. Only my Mate, my heart thumping in my ears, and a thought repeating over and over: mine, mine, Mine!

My mouth is filling with saliva. I start to come down harder on him. Grabbing a fist full of his hair, I pull his head to the side and breathe into his neck. Mine, mine, mine, I chorus each time I fill myself with his cock. His grip is hard on me now, almost wanting me to stop or slow down, but I can't. He is mine and it feels so good.

"Silvia," he grits out my name and I know he's close. This thought makes me smile wildly. I'm going to make my Mate come inside me, filling me up, and I'm going to claim him.

Before I even know what I'm doing, I find my mouth clamped tight on the side of his neck, teeth buried deep. No, not teeth, fangs. I continue to move his cock in and out of me till he finally stops my movements with his strong and powerful arms. I can feel him coming, cock pulsing and warm liquid bursting deep inside me. The force of his release was all I needed to push me to completion once more. I scream my orgasm into his neck while still biting down. With my arms now clamped in place at my sides, it's the only thing I have to hold onto.

Breathing rapidly through my nose as I come down from my orgasm, my fangs seem to retract on their own accord. So I do as Torben did, as my instincts command, and lick his wounds. He's still holding onto me for dear life and twitching. But I am content where I am. My Mate marked and fully seated within me while in the tightest hug of my life. What bliss.

Torben insists on drying me off himself and actually carries me to bed, after I make a quick bathroom visit that is. He feeds the fire, setting it up for the night then comes to cuddle up beside me under the furs and quilts. It's not really cold, but it feels nice to snuggle in. Like earlier today under the big tree—gosh was that only just today—he holds my thigh across his torso as I use his shoulder and arm as a pillow. I'm absently playing with his patch of chest hair as he winds a ringlet of my hair around his finger. My body is too tired to do much else, but my mind is running wild.

"Why do you have clothes on when you change back from your bear form but I'm naked? Aside from this period bracelet I was gifted, that is. I could feel my clothes being torn to shreds, but you are always fully clothed once you're human again."

"It's because we haven't gotten your clothes magically tailored to you yet."

"What?!" I instantly lean up. "You have your clothes magicked to do that? It doesn't just happen? It's not an automatic part of being a Shifter?"

"Nooo," he drags out his reply with a puzzled expression on his face. "Why would they do that? I've never heard of that before. I guess some Fae can change their shape or form and return with clothes on, but that's due to their magic changing them, I think. Our bodies are changing and it's not really a fully magicked change. Though some magic does come into play, I guess." My mind is whirling and all I can do is stare at him, dumbfounded and blinking.

"You have to go to a Tailor Mage to get them done. But it can't happen till you are able to shift at will since the Tailor will need to see and measure your animal as well as your human form. That's why Phil has you train in those inexpensive clothes. He knows they will get torn at some point and doesn't want his students destroying all their garments." I've laid back down beside him but am still trying to process this. "We'll go into the city for that. Ma has a Mage in Avenston that does most of her dresses and such. We can all go there soon."

"Thanks, that would be great. Not a big fan of walking around naked personally."

Oh, but I like it very much, a gravely male voice replies in my mind. I spring back up to look Torben in the face.

"What was that?" I ask almost panicked, but Torben is grinning ear to ear.

I said I like it when you walk around naked. Your unclad body is a beauty to behold.

"Is, is that you?" I ask while pointing to my head. "Are you talking to me in my mind?"

"Yes, my Mate," he concedes out loud. "Now that our bond is complete, we can speak to each other in our minds. It's very handy when in our bear forms. And once you formally join the Clan and undergo the Linking Ritual, you will be able to hear anyone within our Clan while in their shifted forms and also speak with them while you are shifted. Though I will be the only one whom you can mentally speak with in both human and bear forms."

"Oh," is all I can manage in reply as I lay back down. I guess that would be handy. Deciding to test it out myself I bring Torben to mind; thinking clearly, strongly, and as focused as possible. *CAN YOU HEAR ME?* Torben winces at my side.

Yes my Mate, there is no need to shout, comes the reply.

"Oh, I'm sorry. I didn't mean to yell at you." I squeeze him tight. "Just wanted to try it out." He squeezes me back and chuckles.

"It is okay, my Sweet. You may practice on me anytime." I snuggle back into him and could easily fall asleep quickly if it wasn't for one last burning question.

"Last question, I swear. But I have to know, what exactly is the Fire Festival?" Torben's body instantly goes stiff next to me.

Chapter 27

Torben

How is it that she doesn't know about the Fire Festival? Do her people not celebrate it? She did ask about it at Phil's during her nervous rambling this morning. I've never met anyone who didn't, and I've never had to explain it before.

"Do your people not celebrate the Fire Festival?" I ask. "I thought everyone did."

"No, we don't, and I can't think of any holiday that falls at the end of April, or is it May already? I've kinda lost track of time since leaving home. So what happens during these festivities? What's it celebrating? Those goblins made it sound as if it's a day for couples like Valentine's Day or something, but that happens in February."

I'm unfamiliar with some of her words. Perhaps they are things only humans celebrate, or maybe just her secluded region or culture? I'll have to ask about her celebrations later though. Right now I'm trying to remember how this event was described to me as a child and changed as I grew into adolescence, then adulthood.

"I'll do my best to explain it to you, my Mate. Let's see, the Fire Festival falls in between the Spring Equinox and the Summer Solstice. Much of the festivities will take place tomorrow: lots of feasting, kids playing tricks or pranks, dancing around a

Hawthorne Pole, and some competitions." I pause a moment to think as I play with her hair. "Oh, someone will be crowned the Flower Queen for the day. They'll lead the ribbon dance around the Hawthorne and be the Judge for events. The Queen is always someone very feminine and usually young, but not always. The night before, which is tonight, we light the bonfires which will be fed throughout the night and into tomorrow."

Now I can feel myself heating. How do I explain this next part to her?

"Oh!" she exclaims while sitting up. "That sounds like a May-pole! I believe there is something similar called May Day that's celebrated in Europe. I remember watching a show where the main girl was crowned May Queen for the day and I've seen pictures of Maypoles all wrapped in colorful ribbons. Will I get to dance around the Maypole and weave the ribbons around it too?! Or is that just for kids?" She looks kind of sad at the thought of not getting to participate, so I quickly reassure her.

"Fear not, my sweet Mate, Clan Members of all ages are welcome to dance the Hawthorne. My grandmother would rage if someone ever told her she couldn't. She eagerly awaits it all year." My Mate is visibly relieved and then surprised.

"Your grandmother is still around and dancing? Will I get to meet her?"

"Oh my Mate, I don't think anyone would be able to keep my Gran-Gran from finding and welcoming you to the family. She'll be very pleased to show you the dance steps. All my grandparents still live in the Clan, aside from Ma's father who passed away long ago. Both of Ma's mothers will be there though. They probably will enter one of the baking competitions. They were a Grouped

Mating of three," I add when Silvia looks up at me with confusion on her brow.

"Gosh, I'm going to need a more in-depth breakdown of your family before we head back to the Clan. I don't want to mess up meeting them. Don't want them hating me, ya know." I laugh out loud at this absurd statement.

"My Mate, I can't even imagine a way for you to accidentally make them hate you." Holding her tight to my chest, I continue, "They will love you as I love you. You are my Mate, and we are now all family."

I hear her silently whisper, "family," as she squeezes me just a little tighter. Seems that my poor Mate has not had a family in a long time. I feel hot tears fall upon my chest and kiss the top of her head. I am sad that she has been alone for so long. But immensely happy that I can now provide her with the loving and welcoming family she deserves. Well, there may be one amongst them that she didn't deserve thrust upon her, but I have no wish to think of my sister now. With a sniffle, my sweet-hearted Silvia changes the topic.

"Why do the kids play pranks? That sounds more like Halloween or April Fools."

"I believe that hearkens back to a more Fae or Fairy influence. When they used to slip through the Veil and into another Realm. They would play tricks on humans there or take them for a time. I've heard they would grant them wishes sometimes too."

"Interesting," comes her quiet reply. "So, where does the couple stuff the goblins mentioned come from?"

"Ah, yes, that comes during the bonfire times tonight and until dawn. Some of the bigger aspects of this celebration revolve around fertility, love, attraction, sacred unions, and, um, sex." I feel the surprise in her body and I quickly continue. "Couples, mated or not, tend to slip away during this night into the woods. To celebrate privately, and sometimes not so privately, the more sensual and wild facets of the Festival."

"Oh, well then, I guess that means we chose the perfect time to finally mate and bond, right?" She tilts her head upon my chest to look up at me with a smile. My heart squeezes and I find myself returning her smile without pause.

"I suppose you are right. Going forward this celebration will forever hold more meaning for us. Though I'm not sure if 'we' is quite right. I was simply trying to take a bath. I'd say that you chose the most perfect time, my Mate." I rub my face into her curls, inhaling her new scent, forever changed to mark her as mine. But it seems Silvia has taken some issue with my statement as she is now sputtering at me.

"What? No, I didn't...I don't think...I mean..." I smile as I turn and fold her into my body, wrapping both arms around her form.

"Yes, my Mate chose the most perfect of days to claim me. Dragging me into the Mating Cave herself, then pouncing on me as I bathed, to mark me as hers forever." She is mumbling sounds of indignation into my chest but I'm having far too much fun teasing her to stop. "What a lucky male I am to have such a dominant Mate who takes what is hers." Now she's full on grumbling and I can't help but shake with suppressed laughter.

She finally pushes her face away enough to clearly speak.

"Ha, ha, ha. Yes, you're very funny." Her words and sarcastic tone only makes me laugh more. I no longer hold it in and my joy fills the cave and echoes back to me. She joins in, laughing into my chest. Once we stop she tilts her face up at me.

"Should we do it again? How many times is the usual to celebrate with? Wait, does that mean you have sex every year on this night? How many years have you been participating? Wait no, that's not appropriate to ask and I don't want to know really. Wow, I bet that means there are a lot of February babies. That would make them...Aquarians? Don't quote me on that." Her rambling seems to be purely of curiosity and not nerves this time. "Do you think anyone will come here to use this cave since it's still kinda raining? Is there, like, an occupied sign or something we can use? Or do you suppose the rain would really stop anyone? Should we go outside and do it in the rain? You know, to really get into the spirit of it."

"Shhhh, my Mate," I say while gently stroking her back. "There are no expectations or requirements placed upon you or us in this. We have Mated and Bonded which trumps all else. No one will come to use this cave, and any who come this way will smell that it's currently occupied. Now, I think you should rest as you have had a very long day. I only wish to hold you in my arms. Plus, if you have any hope of keeping up with my Gran-Gran tomorrow for the dances you'll need all the rest you can get. Sleep now, my most precious Mate."

"Okay, I'll try," comes her glum reply. It doesn't seem to take much trying as I soon feel her breathing even out and body fully relax against mine. I don't know how long I lay there, touching my Mate and watching her sleep, but eventually the day catches up to me as well. And despite my earlier poison-induced nap, I also drift off and dream of cuddling a beautiful cinnamon-colored bear.

Despite the sweetness of my dreams, I am awakened with pleasure and a need so urgent my eyes snap open instantly. It's then I realize that my Silvia has both her hands wrapped around my cock.

"Oh good, you're awake," she whispers with a wicked grin.

"How could I possibly sleep with a sexy Mate such as you doing that to my cock?" She giggles and starts to scoot herself further down into the coverings. "What, what are you doing?" I ask surprised.

"It's my turn to taste you. I haven't gotten to yet, and it's past time my Mate got some TLC of his own. I've been wanting a closer look at this amazing monster in your pants since that night you caught me masturbating."

My eyes drift shut from the memory of that night and the way her hands are twisting around my member. I roll onto my back and she positions herself more comfortably under the covers between my legs. No, this won't do at all. I whip the covering off us both so I can watch my Mate as she plays with me.

"One favor though," she continues, holding me with one hand while the other sweeps her mass of hair to one side, "could you not come in my mouth? I'm not a fan of the texture. Just give me a warning if you can."

"My Mate, I would love nothing more than to paint those big glorious breasts with my seed," I say while gently stroking her cheek with one finger before taking hold of the curls now gathered at her shoulder. I get no warning before her eager tongue darts out and slowly licks the underside of my shaft from base to tip.

"Sweet Merciful Goddess!" I exclaim, which makes her chuckle before doing it again. I've been told that the touch of previous sexual partners doesn't compare to the touch of one's mate. But being told a thing and experiencing that thing are very different indeed.

I hold her hair tightly in one hand, careful not to pull it, while my other comes up to grip the pillow under my head. But my eyes, I keep my eyes focused on the sight before me. Never has a partner explored my cock like this, with hands and tongue and eyes. Never has anyone ever looked at it the way my Mate does now, with a mixture of hunger and excitement, like it's a great puzzle she plans to solve. And never has anyone made me feel this incredible, this desired. She makes eye contact with me and speaks in a voice still raspy from sleep.

"Tell me if there's anything you want more of or don't like, okay? Right now I'm just kinda exploring you, but I want to know what you prefer, what you need. I want you to enjoy this. To get it right for you like you did for me." What a prize I have been gifted in this female!

"I think I'm going to love anything you do to me, Sweet Silvia. But I promise to speak up. If I can speak at all," I tell her truthfully. She quickly smiles at me before directing her gaze back to my extremely hard cock. More precum has gathered at the head during our exchange.

"Hmm, you're much bigger than any I've ever had before." My chest instantly swells with male pride. "There's no way I'll be able to get all of that in my mouth, but that's what hands are for," she proclaims while squeezing her hands tighter around my shaft. Gripping my cock with both hands, she bends down and swirls that lively tongue of hers around and around my head. As I'm beginning to wonder how long I'll be able to last under her care and attention, she pops my head into her mouth and begins to suck and lick with new fervor. The answer to my question is: not long at all.

She takes me deeper into her mouth while continuing to suck. Her tongue is now on the underside and undulating in a way that makes my toes curl. Just as I think it can't get any better, she begins bobbing her head up and down slowly, while her hands move in tandem. Her saliva and my precum have mixed to create the perfect combination of lubrication. I can't take my eyes off her. She is an artist.

It is an excruciating pleasure. I want to take her now, to plow into her and make her scream my name. But I also want this pleasure to go on forever, to watch her and feel her and smell her. Her own arousal fills the air making this all the more enjoyable. Not only is her aroma intoxicating but it also shows how excited she is by what she's doing to me. That thought alone, that she too is enjoying bringing me such pleasure, nearly pushes me over the edge.

I try to settle my mind on other things. My go to for such situations is how to create effective and precise dovetail joints for wooden drawers and such. I close my eyes and mentally begin to walk myself through the steps. But I am finding it increasingly difficult to keep my mind anywhere but here and now. Her scent is all around me, the noise of her working me echoes slightly in the

cave, her soft hair gripped in my hand, her warm body between my legs, her mouth...

Quickly squeezing my eyes shut and turning my head to the side, I desperately reach for anything to divert my mind and body from the soul-alteringly amazing sensations coursing through my body. I land on the last project I was working on. The now almost late tub I promised Maggie Farris. A ping of guilt shoots through me for a moment, though I know she'll understand. I hate that I won't have it done in time for the anniversary. Right when I finally bring to mind where I left off on the project and recall what my next step would be, a delicious moan from my Mate vibrates up my cock and shatters my woodworking world.

My eyes pop open and I steal a glance down but quickly realize what a mistake that was. My Mate's full attention is on my pleasure. One hand gently playing with my balls, the other wrapped around my shaft moving in tandem with her head up and down as her tongue invisibly works some magic within her mouth. Goddess help me.

"Almost there," I manage to grit out. That marvelous tongue stops and the suction ceases as she removes her mouth, but her hands continue. With one hand pumping me and the other moving up and over the head of my cock, I only last three passes before I finish. I can feel my balls pull up and tighten right before I begin to spill all over my Mates hands. Quickly, she angles herself and my shaft so that my seed does indeed paint her chest. What a sweet and amazing female I have. She keeps her hands in motion, slowly milking me of all I have. I bring the hand that just had a death grip on my pillow to gently touch her wrist, stopping her movements. I can't seem to form words or catch my breath.

After releasing me, she sits up, her breasts on full display, and begins to rub my cum all over her chest. A possessive growl escapes me which has her looking down at me.

"How was that?" she asks coyly. "Okay?"

With renewed energy I gained from that sassy little question, I bolt upright, pin her onto the bed, caging her body with mine. I kiss her in a devouring way. I'm about to show my Mate just how good a job she did. I will have her screaming so loud in pleasure that it will take a moon cycle to fully recover her voice. There will not be a speck of her body unknown to me. Despite my earlier promise of dancing and festivities, my Mate will not be leaving this cave today or for several days to come. She is mine, and I intend to keep her all to myself until we are both fully sated.

"Ho there, Torben!" comes a call from outside the Mating Cave, putting an abrupt stop to all my delicious plans.

Chapter 28

Silvia

Squeaking out an "Eek!" of surprise, I quickly grab Torben tighter to me as I wildly look at the cave entrance. I'm one hundred percent naked and was just giving my man a BJ. Not the best time for company.

"Sorry for interrupting this sacred time between new mates, but we must speak with you urgently," comes the same voice from outside the cave. At least it sounds like they aren't right at the entrance. "It is of grave importance," the voice yells at us which has me instantly worried.

"Those kidnapping goblins! Do you think they got anyone?" I ask Torben, wild-eyed and full of worry.

"Give me a moment," my Mate tells the guys outside before turning back to me. "I'll go out and speak with them. You can get cleaned up and dressed in here." He gently kisses my forehead, grabs his pants, and strides outside before even putting them on. Seems as if his Clan is a little more comfortable with nudity than I'm used to.

As quickly as I can, I wash up, dry off, and wrap a robe around myself. Aside from Torben's shirt, it's the only thing I have to wear. I haphazardly throw the covers back onto the palette bed and walk to the cave entrance. A group of three, two men and a woman, are down the slope speaking with Torben who thankfully is now wearing his pants.

Though I'm still mostly in the cave, I can hear their words clearly. Another couple was almost taken last night but were rescued by other Clan members who heard the commotion and smelled the intruders. How search parties have gone out to locate everyone of the Clan and warn other villages. How they discovered us safe in the Mating Cave early this morning but let us alone until any news was confirmed. All members of the Clan have been accounted for, except Mel, who nobody has seen since we all ran off yesterday. And how they finally found her scent mingled with goblins heading away from Clan lands. Mel has been taken.

I gasp when I hear the news, and Torben turns to look up at me. The heartbreak etched across his face rips my heart to pieces, and white hot tears leap to my eyes. Before I even tell my body what to do, I find myself already in motion, running down the incline to stand next to my Mate. I hardly notice the rocks under my bare feet as my need to comfort Torben overrides everything else. He's breathing quickly in and out of his nose, looking down at the ground, opening and closing his fists. Once I reach him, I slip a hand into one of his and hold his arm. He relaxes a little, glances at me briefly, then returns his focus to the shifter trio.

"We tracked her scent all the way to the river near Oakveil, but lost her after that. I think they may have taken her a ways down the river. We have trackers searching for the trail along the riverbanks. I'm sorry I do not have happier news for you, my friend." The guy shifter that's been talking grabs and squeezes Torben's shoulder. "We will find her," he says while releasing his hold. "When was the last time you saw her? Do you know if she knew about the goblin raiders?" Torben can't seem to form words, all his effort is locked into not breaking down. I can see it in his body and his face.

I've got this, I mentally send out to him. I know he receives the message because his eyes quickly turn to me, somewhat surprised.

"The last time we saw her was yesterday afternoon," I calmly tell them. "We had a disagreement which led me to shift into my bear form for the first time unexpectedly. I ran into the forest and Torben quickly followed. I smelled the goblins while I ran but didn't know what I was smelling at the time. I never saw her following us as we ran, did you?" I ask Torben as I look at him. He shakes his head no while keeping his eyes on me, squeezing my hand as if I am his lifeline. I gently squeeze back and face the group once more. "We were attacked at the big oak tree that way," pointing in the direction.

"Yes, we found the goblin bodies there. You two did a good job of it all alone. Those goblins must have been desperate to attack Bear Shifters on Clan lands."

"Torben handled most of them. Saved us, really." I flash him a small smile as my pride in him shines through. He squeezes my hand again. "Unfortunately they did hit him many times with some kind of tranquilizer darts. He was out like a rock and I couldn't drag him all the way back to the Clan alone. Plus the storm was about to hit hard. So I got us to this cave. I should have thought of a way to get a message back. But I couldn't leave Torben all alone in his state and didn't know if there were more goblins around." Before I can continue my apologies, the lead Shifter holds up a hand to stop me.

"No, you did well. No one would expect you to leave your unconscious mate with that storm and unknown dangers within it. Especially since you are new and unfamiliar with these lands and the Clan. Right now we need to move forward and do all we can to find Mel and any others that may have been taken. After the storm, there wasn't much left on the bodies as far as clues to their den's location."

"OH!" I shout and raise my hand like I'm in school. "I snagged the leader's bag, just in case. It's in the cave. I never had a chance to go through it." Everyone is looking at me in shock. "Come in, we can search it together," I say with a wave as I begin marching back up into the cave, dragging Torben behind me.

My clever Mate, rings in my mind which makes me smile.

The three race up after us with enthusiasm. Inside, I quickly find the bag and pass it to the head guy.

"My name is Silvia by the way," I say as a way to try and get his name.

"Yes, we all know. Sorry, my name is Quinn, and this is Brianna my mate, and Ash my brother. Wish we were being introduced under better circumstances."

I nod in agreement and watch as he takes everything out of the bag to lay out on the ground. Torben comes up and holds me from behind as we all look at the contents. There are a handful of empty vials and one with a strange black liquid in it. It smells weird and the Shifters sneer at them, quickly releasing the vials as if touching them is gross. There's some food, more darts, a small coin purse, a necklace with a symbol I don't recognize on it, a message book, and a notebook. We also find some crudely drawn maps of several areas, one I recognize as Oakveil.

Quinn releases an audible exhale while looking at the maps. His eyes quickly scan over them all before passing them off to his mate.

"This was a much bigger operation than we realized. Looks like it was planned for last night specifically and ranged over several towns, territories, and Clans. We need to get in touch with these areas and tell them about this in case no one has noticed their missing yet. Or if any goblin raiders are still in those areas." He quickly scans through the message book then stands up. "We need to get all this to the Clan Council. If there's information in here it's written in a code I don't know."

"Hey, isn't this the crest of the Grath Family?" Ash, I think that was his name, says after picking up the necklace. Quinn glances up at it and nods in agreement. "Appears to be purposely defaced too. Might be someone who left or was cast out." Ash must notice the questioning expression my face has morphed into because he continues with, "The Graths are a particularly powerful and well-known goblin family."

"Outcast or no, they won't be happy to find out one of theirs was involved in a scheme such as this. Or that they were taking Iynk." Brianna sneers down at the veils. "The slave trade is long dead and gone as far as I know. Why would they plan to take so many people and in one big sweep?"

"Well, the goblins did say something about selling our parts," I offer. "Is there like a Black Market organ trade or something?"

"Hmm, I've never heard of this Black Market, but I have heard of the sale and trade of parts from magical beings." Quinn has started pacing around as he continues to speak. "Those who lack magic of their own or wish to gain more believe certain parts from different creatures and beings offer some perks or advantages or powers. And while some do, like unicorn horn, phoenix feathers, blood of a God and such, most have been proven to be totally benign or magically inert. I can't even imagine what these people think they would get from a Bear Shifter." Coming to an abrupt stop he turns to face me, "Do you know where this Black Market is? Where we can find it?" He's asked me this so earnestly that I very quickly have to suppress a giggle.

"No, sorry. I don't imagine it's actually a real place. It's more like a term you use or a place in made up stories. You know, like the Boogie Man or -" but before I can finish explaining, everyone visibly tenses up and Torben quickly places a hand over my mouth.

Hush, my Heart! Do not speak of the Boogies out loud. You might summon one here, and we have enough to deal with right now.

WHAT?! I reply mentally, looking up at him wide-eyed. *Are you saying The Boogie Man is real?* He nods in the affirmative and I can hardly believe it. Not only is it real, but all these big strong Bear Shifters are genuinely afraid of it. I've got about a million follow-up questions but tuck them away for later.

"Sorry, everybody. Where I come from we use that as a term for an unknown scary thing. Didn't realize it was real." They all continue to look at me horrified. "So, ah, who or what is the Grath Family? Should we talk to them about what we found and see if they know anything?"

Changing the subject back seems to help snap them out of their moment of apparent fear that I might have summoned up a Boogie Man. Though I do catch Ash glancing around and into any shadows.

"Yes, we should definitely find a way to communicate with the Graths about what we have discovered. They will take it as a slight if we don't. Plus, they may be able to help. But I'll leave that up to the Council." Quinn gives a nod to Brianna who takes out a message book and begins writing. "We should all return to the village now with this new information and get the two of you back to your family."

Torben insists on carrying me all the way back to the village.

"My Mate, you have no shoes and can't control your shifting yet. So I will carry you. It's only fair since you carried me here." He says with a warm smile down at me. But I can still see the sadness in his eyes, though he is trying to hide it.

We will find her, I mentally send him as I snuggle into his arms. He holds me a little tighter but doesn't respond.

The search party stays with us till we reach the edge of the village, departing with nods and waves.

We are both immediately wrapped in tight, long bear hugs from both Ma and Pa when we step inside Torben's family home. I think Torben is even lifted off the ground an inch. There are many people in the house, other family if I had to guess. Thankfully, Ma ushers me into the guest room to change into some real clothes as soon as the hug ends. I briefly clock that my pack has been opened but set that little detail aside as I put my clothes on. I'm surprised to find that my boots are in one piece. Odd considering

I was wearing them when I shifted and all my other clothes were shredded. I remember hearing and feeling that. Guess these boots from the Bookshop Owner are magical in some way. I'll have to remember to ask, if I ever see her again. I also find that my bee hair stick has been placed on the bedside table. I am utterly relieved to find it unharmed.

Once dressed, I quickly throw my hair up, using my carved bee to hold it all in place. While alone in the room I take the opportunity to send a message to Rosy and Ellis, who have been frantically messaging me already this morning. I let them know I'm all right, telling them briefly about our goblin encounter, listing what we've found out, and asking if they have heard anything about Mel or other abductions.

They both reply how glad they are to hear I'm safe and unharmed. That there are other confirmed abductions in the area and Oakveil itself. But Ellis's message regarding a Grath Family member living in Oakveil has me dashing out of the guest room and into the kitchen where the family has congregated.

"A member of the Grath Family is in Oakveil and Ellis thinks she'll help me!" I blurt out as soon as I see Torben.

Ma and Pa quickly pack their bags as other members of the family wrap up some food for us. Not sure we'll need it, but better safe than sorry, I guess. That is what people do to show support in times of trouble, isn't it? Make sure you have food. The four of us make good time running to Oakveil. I find myself thanking the Universe that I'm a Shifter now, or else this running from place to place wouldn't be happening. But I'm still quite winded when we reach Ellis's bakery.

Ellis doesn't seem to care or take that into account when they sweep me up into a hug. They are way stronger than they appear, that's for sure.

"I am so glad that you are safe and sound, my friend." Still holding me they continue, "Any news regarding Mel? Last we heard her scent was lost along the river outside of town."

"That's the last we heard too," I hear Ma reply as I continue to be crushed against Ellis's front.

Finally releasing me, but only as far as arms length, Ellis begins to thoroughly look me over head to toe, spinning me around several times.

"You've completed your Mating Bond!" they say somewhat surprised.

"Yes we have," I say proudly with maybe a hint of pink touching my cheeks. "And once all this is over, I have a bone to pick with you and Rosyyyy!" The last part comes out in a screech as I'm picked up from behind and hugged by the stealthiest centaur ever to exist. I seriously do not know how I didn't hear her clop up behind me. I have super hearing now, and she has hooves!

"You can be angry at us all you want later," Rosy says while I flail my arms and legs in vain, eventually giving up to hang in her arms like a rag doll. "We're just so glad you're safe and unharmed. For a while we thought you were taken too." The last word comes out in a sob as Rosy begins to cry. I gently pat her arms around my middle as she buries her face in my hair. Then, just as suddenly,

I'm released and Rosy wipes the tears from her face. "Okay, what do we need to do now to get Mel back home?"

"The next step is to get our dear Silvia inside the bakery. There's someone in there who might be able to help who owes our friend here a favor." Ellis links arms with me and begins to glide us into their shop.

"Wait, who owes me a favor?" They outright ignore my question, but I don't have to wait long before finding out.

Sitting alone at one of the smaller tables, holding a steaming teacup between her hands, is a woman who looks familiar. It only takes a moment for me to place her. She had a request on the job board and I painted her fence. At our entrance, she turns to face us and gives me a sad smile. Now that I know what they are, I can place that she is part goblin. Her skin is a lovely shade of light green, and her long nails are black with rounded tips. Her pointed ears are long, but not nearly as long as the other goblins were, and poke out of beautifully shiny black hair that has a streak of silver running through it.

She stands up from her table to greet us and reaches up to take my hands into hers. The top of her head comes to my hip level, so she has to crane her head up to address me.

"I am so sorry to hear about what's happened," she says with true feeling, focusing her gaze on both myself and Torben, who is right behind Ellis and I. She then looks at the rest of our party with the same sad smile before gesturing for me to join her at the table. I sit down across from her in the too small chair, while everyone else grabs seats and carries them to be closer to us.

"As soon as Ellis told me that a former Grath Family member was involved in this horrible situation, I contacted my nephew in

Avenston. And when I told him that it concerned the family of the lovely young lady who helped me out by painting the fence of his favorite Aunt, he insisted on helping you personally." Sliding a folded piece of paper across the table and into my hand she continues.

"Here is the address where you are to meet him as soon as you reach Avenston. He will be putting you, and any who accompany you, up for the night and for as long as it takes to finish this nasty business." She squeezes my hand and gives me a crooked smile. "I assure you that he is doing everything in his power to find your sister and will be seeing to the punishment of any goblin mixed up in this." Releasing my hand she stands and brushes away any folds that appeared on her skirt while sitting.

"Thank you, thank you so much," I stammer out. "I don't know what to say."

"There's nothing to say dear, and no thanks are necessary. You did an amazing job on my fence when no one else would, and we can't have these miscreants giving goblins a bad name. Now, if you want to make it to Avenston by nightfall, you'd best be on your way." As she exits the bakery, she stops briefly to look Ma in the face and squeeze her knee reassuringly. Ellis rises to walk her out and lock the door behind her.

"Well, you heard the lady, you should hit the road as soon as you can. I'll stay here in town and pass on any information that comes my way." Ellis glides over to deftly pick up the cup that was left and pushes the chair back under the table. They then glance around the room, clearly wanting to hear everyone else's plans. To my amazement, Pa chimes in first.

"I'll head back home, let the family and Counsel know what's going on, and be there in case our girl escapes and comes back on her own."

"Then I'm going to Avenston with Torben and Silvia," Ma says while standing up, a fire in her eyes, fists clenched. "I'd like to see them try and keep me away from my child." Full mama bear mode has been activated and I almost feel sorry for these creeps. Almost.

"I'll come too," Rosy chimes in. "I've got a friend who's a fellow tavern owner there and a part of the Taverns Guild. He'll get the word out and all the tavern, inn, and bar owners will be on the lookout. People discuss all kinds of business openly in such places. Maybe somebody has heard something."

"Then it's settled," Ma proclaims. "We'd make better time in our bear forms. Silvia, do you think you could shift?"

I feel so put on the spot and unsure that all I can do is stare back at her blinking, unable to form any words. I honestly don't know if I can shift but it looks like I might have to.

"Silvia can ride on my back." Rosy states. "I'll be able to carry her and keep up with two bears, no problem. Though I left my passenger saddle at the Wandering Mead, so you'll have to ride bareback."

"Oh goodness, are you sure, Rosy? I don't want to put you out. I can try to shift."

"No, you still need shift training and I'd rather you wait till Phil is around to help." Torben steps in close to me and runs his knuckles down my cheek. "I don't know what I'd do if anything happened to you too, my Sweet Mate." The care in his eyes, the touch of his skin, and the scent of him has me weak in the knees. If we weren't surrounded by people, I'd kiss him so hard right now.

So caring, so tempting, my inner bear chimes in. Tell me about it, I reply.

"Here, let's redistribute our packs and rework what we're taking now that Pa is going back home," Ma says, taking charge. "Torben dear, bring me yours and Silvia's." With a half smile just for me, Torben takes my pack and walks over to his parents who are using one of Ellis's tables to sort things on.

Joining Rosy and I by the counter, Ellis gives Rosy a sly look.

"So, this tavern owner you know wouldn't happen to be that handsome Minotaur you've spoken of before, now would it, Rosy? The one who's helping you to finally get over that Mermaid trash who broke your heart?" Looking over at Rosy in surprise, I can clearly see she's blushing deeply and begins sputtering while shaking her head. "That's what I thought," Ellis says coolly. "You'll have to tell us all about it when you get back."

"And start from the beginning, I want to hear about this bitch who hurt you." I add which makes Ellis laugh a little.

Chapter 29

Torben

We make good time running to Avenston, and true to her word Rosy keeps up with us just fine while carrying my Sweet Mate. Guilt and anger consume me from all sides as we travel. I swing back and forth between thinking of my sister and of my Mate.

I regret the harsh words spoken to Mel, the way I treated her since she bit Silvia. How scared she must be, if she still lives. I shake my head each time that thought pops up. The rage I feel toward those that took her fuels my speed. I've never felt this kind of anger before, and it almost scares me. When it becomes too overwhelming, I think of my Mate to take its sharp edge off.

But that only helps till I recall how all this is affecting her. This was not how our Mating should be going nor how her first Fire Fest should be spent. I should have lavished her body with love and care for hours this morning. She should have met my extended family and my Clan, our Clan. She should have eaten till she was bursting and danced the Hawthorn with my Gran-Gran. Then, we would have returned to the Mating Cave and spend days alone together there, forging and strengthening our bond. Instead we've spent the day running around, carrying fear and anger and loss.

My Mate deserves so much better than this. The dread that she deserves better than me is a pit I can't look into.

I feel her periodically gently touching my mind as we race onward, but she never says anything to me and I say nothing to her. I am grateful for both her silence and connection. Knowing she is there is more of a help than even I can say. Once this is past us, I'll forever try to show her just how much having her at this time has meant to me.

Ma and I shift back to our human forms once we hit the edge of town, and I help my Mate dismount her friend. Given the way she walks, rubbing her legs and backside, I take it she's never ridden a centaur before. Her silly walk does bring a brief smile to my face, though I am quick to hide it when she whips her head to scowl at me.

I can feel that through our bond you know, she mentally chides me while making the cutest angry pouting face. I hold my hands up in surrender and walk by her side, resting my hand upon her lower back. The nearness and connection to her helps to keep all these swirling feelings at bay.

Thankfully, Rosy is pretty familiar with Avenston and she finds the way to our meeting location with ease. What I hadn't expected was for the place to be a mansion. A gated mansion with tall stone walls surrounding it and guards posted at the entrance of a tall wrought iron gate. But it seems the goblin guards out front are expecting us and usher us in without a word. Their eyes, black pools of obsidian, constantly scanning the street and anyone upon it. Who is this nephew exactly?

We walk along a brick path through a perfectly manicured lawn with box hedges and at least three fountains. I can see more

goblin guards walking along the front porch and upper two bal-
conies, pacing and eyes sharp. Some carry knives, short swords,
clubs, maces, and I think I even see one with a wooden wand. I
bring my Sweet Mate closer to my side and move my hand to her
shoulder. Why does this nephew live in a place with such security?
It makes me both nervous and relieved.

The front door is opened for us before we can even knock.
What I can only assume is a butler, given his outfit, ushers us in.

"Please enter and follow me, the Master of the house is expecting you. He wished to speak with you immediately upon your
arrival." Thankfully, the door frame accommodates not only my
height, but also Rosy's. Not too common in the home of a smaller
being.

The whole front parlor and staircase seem to also be built with
larger folks in mind. I even notice that there are two sets of stairs,
one bigger and one smaller to accommodate guests of various sizes,
with a lift between them. As we are guided down a long hall, I also
see that many of the doors have knobs all along them at different
levels. This is something one usually only sees in public buildings
and such, not in a personal home. They must have visitors or
entertain all kinds of creatures and beings here.

A set of double doors at the end of a hall are opened for us by
another pair of guards flanking them. These are only part goblin
and stand taller and broader than the other guards I've seen. They
both hold spears, which seems at odds with their fitted and tailored
garb. Before we pass them, Silvia leans into me and whispers "Are
those guys wearing suits?" in a surprised and perplexed tone. I can
only shrug in response as I've never worn such an outfit. Thinking
back, all the guards I've seen thus far have been wearing surpris-

ingly similar clothing. Though all of theirs had been black, while these are a muted ruby red with black shirts under their jackets.

Passing the doors, we enter a large room that is split in half by a rug running down its length. On the left side is a large roaring fire with couches and chairs of varying sizes fanning out from it with plenty of end tables and such. All look expensively upholstered and lush. The entire back wall looks to be made of glass with glass doors that open onto a porch overlooking a garden and pool area. Velvety evergreen curtains are gathered on each side, held in place by golden tassels. Finally, a large and ornately carved wooden desk occupies the right side of the room with the wall directly behind it filled with fully loaded bookcases.

Many goblins are gathered around this desk, focused on maps and papers scattered about it. But only one goblin is seated, that one is clearly the goblin in charge. He sits in a high-backed wooden chair, upholstered with dyed green leather. While all the goblins here are also clad in the 'suit-type' garb, his is clearly the most well crafted. A suit of sapphire blue fits him as if molded to his form, bejeweled rings glint on each finger, and gold loops and jewels run along his long pointed ears. I see a flash of a gold cuff on his wrist as he takes a sip of amber liquid from a small glass.

It's then that he notices us filing into the room. With a nod and wave of his hand, the party around the desk silently leave us alone with him. Though one, a personal guard I assume, stays at his side. Once the office doors are closed, the goblin behind the desk addresses us with a voice that's gruff yet sophisticated.

"Please, make yourselves comfortable around the fire. I know you all have had an exhausting day." He rises from his seat to join us on the other side of the room, making his way to another green chair closest to the fire that is clearly his. I sit perched on the edge in the middle of a long couch across from his chair. While Ma and Silvia sit on either side of me, leaving Rosy to stand directly behind us all.

"First and foremost, as head of the Grath Family, I need to apologize to you and yours." He says this with a solemn yet earnest face, adorned hand coming to rest over his heart. "We all take this affront to the Grath name very seriously. Be assured that we are doing everything we can to correct this grievous error that any former family members have been a part of. We do not condone nor associate ourselves with any form of magical being chop shop." He ends with a slight snarl to show his disgust at the trading and selling of body parts. Ma responds before I can even think of how to reply to that.

"Thank you, sir. You have no idea how much my Clan and I, my family and I, appreciate your assistance in this. But please, have you heard anything? Any news of where my daughter was taken? Do we know if she's still..." My mother falters and I can see tears forming in her eyes, her chin quivering.

"Unfortunately, I don't have any updates for you about those taken. We were able to quickly find their base of operation, thanks to the intel your Clan provided. But it seems they knew it had been compromised. So there was nothing but old information to be found there. My people search this city as we speak in hopes of finding their backup location." He then turns to face my Mate. "I believe it is you we have to thank for acquiring much of our information, including the link to exiled Grath members being involved." He bows his head slightly to her. "I was greatly surprised to also discover that you were the lovely young lady that assisted my

Mother's half-sister when others had not. It's not everyone who is willing to help Goblinkind, and from what I heard, she had posted that request some time ago. I was in the middle of arranging to have some of my people go down and paint the fence ourselves when she wrote to inform me about you."

My sweet, sweet Mate looks to be quite flustered now.

"Oh, there's no need to thank me really. I was new in town and looking for work to earn a little money. It, it was no problem, really. Your aunt was very nice and already had the paint and brushes ready. I'm actually from a human-only city and didn't have any bias against goblins or any other being actually. Not, not that I have a bias against goblins now or anything. You and your aunt have been nothing but kind and courteous and helpful. I mean, we all have family members that we aren't too proud of or don't want to be linked to. Not that I'm assuming anything about how you feel towards these exiled members, of course. Drugs are a slippery slope, and people aren't really themselves anymore when they get addicted to them, ya know?"

The goblin's eyebrows continue to rise upon his forehead as my Mate quickly rambles on, I even see a smile tug the corner of his cheek at her nervous oversharing. He raises his hand gently to stop her once she pauses to take a breath.

"Be that as it may, the Grath Family pays its debts, and we intend to return the favor in kind. Now, my butler will escort you to the kitchens for some much-needed food and then to your rooms. I insist on lodging you here for your safety and to inform you of any updates as they come. I assume you may wish to assist in any rescue efforts. Having Bear Shifters join us could prove useful. And I hear your mother is also a gentle healer." He inclines his head toward her in respect. "I pray we won't need your skills, but I fear we will." He snaps his fingers and the doors swing open to admit the butler. "If there is nothing else, I need to get back to organizing the search," he says as he stands and begins to walk back to his desk.

"Um, actually," Rosy speaks up for the first time, halting the head of this goblin family. "I am friends with a member of the Taverns Guild and plan to head over to speak with him as soon as possible. See if he can get the feelers out and about. People tend to feel free to talk and plan in such places, so I'm hoping someone has heard something." Rubbing his chin, the goblin nods his head.

"Yes, that could be quite beneficial. I'll have one of my men accompany you and station themselves nearby in case you get any information." As if summoned, a female goblin, also clad in a black suit, appears to stand near Rosy. Clearly her new escort.

Parting ways with Rosy in the hall, we are then taken to a bustling large kitchen. Seated at an old and well-used table off to the side and out of the way, we're showered with food and drink. Lots of loud conversing and shouting in the goblin language makes an almost comforting backdrop. It really feels like a big family gathering to cook a meal for the house. The smells are amazing and everything is delicious. I wish I could appreciate it more, and looking at Ma and Silvia, I can tell they are feeling the same way. Waiting for news is not something that is going to be easy.

I eat as much as I can, though I know it's not nearly as much as I usually consume. We are then shown to our rooms. Taking the lift up to the third floor, we are given rooms across from each other. I hate to leave Ma alone tonight, but she turns down the offer to stay with Silvia and I in our room.

"No no, you two are still a newly mating pair, and it would just be uncomfortable for all of us." I try to interject that we have no plans for any such thing this night but she waves me off. "I have something to help me sleep, and I'd rather cry in private as I message your father. Now, you two try to get some sleep and what comfort you can from it and each other." She pats my arm before disappearing into her room, leaving my Mate and I to enter our own.

The wooden four-poster bed is large and looks comfortable. Silvia must be impressed with it given the way she's running her hands along the comforter. The room is also fitted with a desk, large wardrobe, window seat, small fireplace, and an attached private bathroom. My Mate has already thoroughly inspected the room and has informed me about the bathroom amenities while I have stood frozen at the door. I don't know what to do with myself. I'm too overcome with feelings, and have been for so long, I seem to be stuck. I'm almost startled when my Mate speaks and she's right in front of me.

"Come on, let's get you in the bath. That way if we get any word, you'll be ready to roll. Plus, I bet a nice warm bath will feel good on all those muscles. You've been running all day. At least, I got to ride here." She takes my hands and tugs me slightly towards action. Her sweetness, thoughtfulness, and caring for my well being opens the dam.

I begin to shake as fat tears roll down my face. Throwing my arms around her I hold on for dear life as wave after wave of sorrow and despair rack through me. She rubs my back while reassuring me that everything will be okay. She even attempts to move us to the bed, but I'm rooted to the spot. So she stays with me, letting me hold and squeeze her. Giving me all the comfort I know I don't deserve.

You're far too good for me, my Mate. You should have been paired with someone better.

"Oh hush, you big silly," comes her muffled reply. She pushes her face off my chest to look into my eyes, bringing her hands to frame my jaw. "Now, you listen here," she begins sternly, "nobody talks bad about my Mate in front of me, not even my Mate! You are kind, gentle, and patient. You are a talented craftsman, a caring brother, a thoughtful boyfriend, and a giving lover," she proclaims with a wink. "What has happened is out of your control. Yet you are doing everything you can to help. I am lucky and proud to be your Mate. I only hope that I..." but before she can even finish that thought I crash my mouth down upon hers while lifting her body so her face is level with mine.

I bring a hand to tangle in her mane of hair, holding her head in place to deepen the kiss. She's melded against me and has wrapped her legs around my waist. My other hand cups her ass as she moans in my mouth. That moan has me instantly hard and I need her now. The bed is way too far away, so I take her over to the desk along the wall next to us.

I set her ass upon it, then sweep my arm across, knocking the items off the top. I definitely hear some things breaking, eliciting a gasp from Silvia, but I don't care right now. That's a concern for later, right now all I can see or hear or smell or feel is my Mate, and I need more.

"You'd better undo that bodice now before I tear it off," I declare against her neck as I begin to pull up her dress. Her reply is a cute little noise and a shiver along her body, but she quickly complies and soon the bodice is gone. I throw it across the room, vaguely hearing it knock into something else. My Mate offers a nervous giggle.

With the bottom of her dress now bunched in my fists at her hips I quickly pull it over her head in one swift motion. Her glorious breasts bounce as they escape their confinement. My eyes are instantly drawn to them, and soon my mouth follows. More surprised sounds issue from my Mate, but they quickly turn to whines of pleasure.

While my mouth and tongue feast upon her left breast, my hand squeezes the other, thumb playing with her nipple. Her notes of pleasure deepen which has me growling low in heated hunger. The need to be buried deep inside her is almost overwhelming. My inner bear driving me to claim my Mate, to cling to this refuge and be lost within it. Taking her underwear in hand, I rip them off—with the help of my claws—and toss them over my shoulder. I briefly think she should never wear panties again before the intoxicating smell of her arousal sends my eyelids fluttering. Oh, she should definitely never wear anything to cover that up, ever.

She's taken the opportunity to hike up my shirt, so I assist and fully remove it. Unfastening my pants I let them fall to my feet where I leave them. There's no way I'm taking the time to untie my boots and kick them off. I can now see the appeal of males who wear kilts or other pantless garb. Something to try out for myself later perhaps.

I'm swiftly brought back from my clothing thoughts when Silvia takes my now free cock in hand and guides it to her slick opening. My surprise and delight to find her just as eager as I am for me to claim her is only overridden by intense need. Holding one hip, I kiss her earnestly again and push myself fully inside in one deliberate movement. I swallow the moan she gives me and begin thrusting into her hard and fast. She's holding onto my shoulders and back for dear life, causing little scratches. But I can't stop or slow myself. She feels far too good tightly wrapped around my shaft. Just as I think I could spend eternity like this, I hear the breaking of wood and feel the desk shift.

"Hold on tight," I warn before I grab handfuls of that malleable ass and lift her off the table. Quickly, I shimmy us over to the wall and pin her to it. I almost feel bad for the person whose room shares this wall with ours, almost. Before I can resume pounding into my Mate, she whispers to me in a husky voice.

"I've always wanted to be fucked against a wall," then nibbles my earlobe. I could have come right there, but my Mate has a wish and I plan to see it fulfilled. And more than once, if I have any say in the matter. I begin driving deep into her again, more restrained than before, testing the sturdiness of this wall. A picture does fall off, but once I'm satisfied it will hold I ramp up my efforts.

When I find a rhythm that has her chanting 'oh my, oh my, oh my,' I know she's close and dare not alter it. Everything about her in this moment is mesmerizing. The sounds she is making, her face with eyes squeezed shut, the way she's fully escaped into and is consumed by the sensations. Her wild mess of rich red curly hair bouncing as I take her roughly. Speaking of bouncing, her breasts have never looked better.

Suddenly she arches her back, as much as she can in this position, and her inner walls clamp down on my cock like the most amazing vise in existence. Her release is a warm torrent between us that helps lubricate my strokes as I continue to ride her through her orgasm. Mine follows soon after, its own deluge that floods my Mate's sweet tight cunt. A final few thrusts before I press my weight upon her, leaning us into the wall as we catch our breaths and I try to remember how to exist again. She's quicker at coming back to her senses.

"Oh wow," she gasps. "Oh wow, that was amazing. So intense but in the best possible way." She then begins to lightly pepper kisses all over my face, breathlessly saying "amazing" between each peck. My chest fills with pride and a slight smile tugs at one side of my face. "I wasn't lying when I said I've always wanted to do that. But no one has ever been strong enough to even try before. Given how heavy I am."

"You weigh nothing, my amazing Mate," I interrupt her, then begin nuzzling her neck and shoulder.

"Yeah, nothing to you, Mister Strong Bear Man. I mean look at you, you're still holding me up here even though you must be exhausted. And you broke that desk over there with your mighty surges." I'm fully smiling now and I feel as though my chest might split wide open if she keeps praising me like this.

"Come my Sweet Mate, let's get you cleaned up and into bed." Still firmly inside her, I shuffle us both to the adjoining bathroom, eager now to tend to my Mate's needs. For a time, she helped me get lost in the deep ocean of pleasure that is our Mating Bond, but I can now feel the current of thoughts pulling me back to reality. Focusing on her is the only way I'm even able to function for the rest of the night.

Chapter 30

Silvia

I wake this morning with a smile on my face, all warm and snuggled into what is perhaps the best bed I have ever slept in. The scent that is pure Torben still wrapped all around me. After that surprise and intense love-making session, he lavished me with attention till I fell asleep in his arms. Torben showered with me, insisting on washing my hair and body himself. He was so gentle and caring. It was perhaps the most intimate thing a partner has ever done for me.

He even dressed me in my nightgown and had me teach him how to treat my hair after a washing. He did every step with that same care and focus. I've never felt more cherished. Once all was complete he wrapped my hair in the silk the bookshop owner gave me and literally carried me to bed. I laid my head on his chest as his arms enveloped me in a tight hold. I know he needed the distraction and I was more than happy to let him focus on me instead of the current situation.

Remembering that instantly sucks away all the warm glow and fuzzy feelings I was basking in. We aren't here on vacation; this fine bed isn't in some grand hotel. Mel is still missing, taken by some body part trafficking ring. And Torben is beside himself with grief, amplified by how he left things with his sister.

Speaking of Torben, I now realize I am all alone in this big old bed. I sit up and search around, using my new senses to try and locate him. He's not in the bathroom as I had hoped, and I don't even think he's on this floor anymore. I can smell Ma is still across the hall in her room, cleaning up if I'm not mistaken. Well, I guess I had better get up and face this day too.

I quickly dress in my most action-ready outfit, it's just the plainest skirt and top options I have, and fix my hair up with my bee hair stick. I then pace around the room a little bit, waiting for Ma to be ready as well. I'd rather walk down with her than alone. Plus, she might have some news already. I walk out of my room when it seems like she might be almost ready.

"I'm nearly done, Silvia. You can come in here if you like," I hear her through the door say. Ah yes, she has bear hearing too and is more versed in using it than I am. Then my cheeks flush red as I think about all the sounds she must have heard last night. Too late now, I guess.

I walk to her door, gently tapping it before turning the knob and walking in. She's all dressed and is braiding her still damp hair. I can tell from her eyes that she's been crying, but she's got on a brave face now as she looks over at me.

"There hasn't been any news so far, dear. Torben is downstairs now with Mr. Grath, and he didn't want to wake you without any kind of update."

"That's sweet of him. Though you two are the ones who really needed the extra sleep, not me. Of course, if I were in your shoes, I wouldn't be able to catch a wink at all." Oh no, that sounded heartless, didn't it? "Not that I'm not also stressed and worried! It's really all my fault that she's missing anyway, if you think about it." And then I make the colossal mistake of doing just that, thinking about how this is all really my fault.

If I hadn't overheard that private conversation, if I hadn't run away, hell, if I hadn't even accepted the shopkeeper's offer in the first place, none of this would have happened. I look up at Ma, horrified, knowing that I'm the reason her only daughter is missing. And now I'm crying about it, great. I have no right to cry to this woman.

"I'm sorry. I'm so, so sorry," is all I can get out before she rushes over and wraps me in a comforting hug.

"Oh my dear, none of this is your fault at all. No one is blaming you, not me, not Torben nor Pa, and not Mel. The only ones to blame are those that took her and those in on this scheme." She holds me tight and pats my back as we sway there.

"I shouldn't be the one crying right now. I'm sorry. I should be the one offering you hugs and thoughtful words," I say through my sobs. Gosh, I'm a mess.

"Hush now and stop apologizing. You're going through some-thing too. Though you aren't that close to Mel yet, she is your new sister, a member of your new family, and your Mate's sibling. You have been so strong this whole time for my little Torben, and you have no idea how much I appreciate that he has you right now when he needs you most."

We are both crying now, and in a strange way, it feels nice. To be together in this mixture of emotions, getting support and love while being supported and loved in return. I haven't felt this since

I lost my grandparents. I didn't realize how much I both missed and needed this kind of connection. Family.

A mighty grumble chooses that moment to issue forth from Ma's stomach, startling us both. I stand back in shock, looking at her also shocked and embarrassed face, before we both burst into laughter.

"Well, I did use a lot of energy running yesterday and couldn't eat much at dinner. Seems like that's catching up to me," she says while patting her tummy. Quickly wiping the tears from her face and eyes, she continues, "Shall we wander down to the kitchen then and see what we can grab for breakfast? If last night's meal is any indication, I'm betting it's going to be delicious." Then, arm-in-arm, we set forth to find that Magical Goblin Kitchen once more.

Torben finds us eating breakfast soon after we were given a bounty of food to feast upon. Ma looks up at him hopeful for any news, but he quickly shakes his head indicating nothing has come up. Then we practically have to force him to take a seat and eat something with us.

"Mel will need her big brother at full strength when we find her," Ma guilts him. "So please, eat something for her and us, if not for yourself." He eats a little more earnestly after that.

"Ma said you were talking to Mr. Grath this morning. What were you talking about?" The way Torben suddenly goes still has me wishing I hadn't asked. Then when his neck begins to turn red, and he avidly avoids looking in his mothers direction, I really really wish I hadn't asked.

Taking a big gulp of juice, he mentally tells me, *I went to apologize for the things I broke in our room yesterday when we....*

"Oh!" I say out loud. Now I'm getting red in embarrassment.

"Mr. Grath has commissioned me to make a smaller desk to match his own. His little girl enjoys playing 'head of the family' with her dolls."

"Now isn't that sweet," Ma chimes in. "Nothing like a parent who takes an interest and supports their child's endeavors." We both nod in agreement, thankful that the awkward situation was averted. "I'm guessing that's how you are paying him back for what you did to that room last night." We both become stone still and stare at Ma wide-eyed. "I don't fall asleep that fast, children, even with aid. And don't look so mortified, it's perfectly natural. Seeking the solace of your mate in trying times. Plus, you two are newly mated and still bonding. I'd have been surprised if you could have resisted the urge. I remember how powerful they were." Then leaning a bit over the table closer to me she adds, "His Pa and I still break things on occasion." She sits back with a wink as I smile. But Torben sinks down into himself, deeper into his chair.

Just then, one of the taller goblin guards in red enters the kitchen and walks over to us. I don't think any of us breathe while he makes his way to our table.

"We have gotten a few leads that may pan out. Mr. Grath has asked that you put a list together of any supplies you may require in healing efforts, anything that may be needed to stabilize before transport to Healing Facilities, and anything to patch up less-wounded folks. We won't know their conditions till we find them, so whatever you think is best we'll get you."

He then hands Ma a notepad and pen before stealing a piece of bacon from the serving tray, munching away as he waits. Ma quickly writes her list and passes the notepad back to him. But before he can leave, another goblin guard, one in black, rushes in.

"The leads seem solid. Boss wants the Bear Shifters to come with us." In a flash, both Ma and Torben are on their feet, while I pop up right after them.

They both turn to look at me, then at each other, and my stomach drops. They don't want me to come. Of course, they don't want me to come. I'm not really family after all, and I'm not strong or trained well enough to really help. I'd probably be a hindrance. I know that, but it still hurts. I want so desperately to be stronger. To be helpful.

"Silvia, I think it would be best if-" but I interrupt him before he can say it.

"No, no, I get it. You're right I shouldn't come. I'd just be in your way. I know I'm the weak one here, and I don't have any useful skills that would be a benefit." Don't cry, don't cry, don't cry. Now is not the time, stupid feelings. There are bigger things going on.

Before I know it, Torben is in front of me, holding my cheeks as I'm holding back tears.

"You are so fucking strong, Silvia." He tells me while making direct eye contact. "I could not have gotten through this without your strength to hold me up and keep me going." He then kisses my forehead, before wrapping me up in a fierce embrace. "If anything were to happen to you, I think I'd lose my mind completely.

I need to know you are safe in order to do what I need to do." *And I don't want you to see what I might become or what I might do in order to save my sister. I'm a little afraid of myself and can't have you looking at me with fear in your eyes.*

I could never be afraid of you, I reply. *I know the real you. I've fallen in love with the real you. I've already seen you go berserk on some bad guys and am still around.* Pulling back I dash the tears from my eyes. "Now, you go get your sister and bring her back safe and sound. Even if you have to go full beast mode. Just, please be safe. I can't lose you either." He kisses me quickly, but passionately, before he turns to leave. Ma gives me a nod, then they are both gone.

"Why don't you come with us, dear?" A voice coming from somewhere around my mid-thigh scares the living shit out of me. I look down to see an older goblin woman. She takes my hand in hers and pats it. "Sorry about that, love. Didn't mean to sneak up on you. Old habits die hard, you know." I just stare down and nod my head yes, though she's got me wondering what kind of old habits she's talking about. "We don't have some of the items off the Shifter's list on hand, so we need to go into the market to get them. You'll come with us, be useful, and carry things. A Bear Shifter like yourself can carry far more than a little old goblin like me." She starts to walk off, still holding my hand, so all I can do is follow.

Turns out what we needed were some types of medicines or plants or something. Not really clear, but the two goblins I'm with seem to know, which is how I found myself standing in an honest-to-goodness apothecary. But as cool as it is, and it really is amazing to inspect all the things, my nose can't take it. I've always been pretty sensitive to smells, especially too many and too strong. Now with my new enhanced sniffer, the sensation is overpowering. So much so that the goblins immediately notice my problem and send me outside. I end up having to cross the street completely, not even able to stand in front of the shop.

The busy street itself is a marvel all its own to behold. So many people and creatures of all shapes, sizes, and colors. There are some types I think I recognize: like the little fairies flying here and there, a Bigfoot who just ran around a corner, and I even witness a Sphinx gracefully strutting down the road. I notice everyone very obviously giving her a wide berth and giggle. Then, there are others I couldn't even guess what they are. A tan man with a large set of black feathered wings, a family who all have slightly pointed ears but also fish scales in places, and one woman who looked as if her hair was made of fire. Now this is definitely big city fantasy. I find that I'm quite glad I came upon the little village of Oakveil instead of a massive place like this. I would have been so overwhelmed. Plus, I probably wouldn't have made such close connections so quickly.

My fingers itch to message Ellis and Rosy, but I feel weird since we haven't gotten to hash out the whole 'keeping secrets from me' thing. I mean, I kind of understand the why, but I still need to hear everything from them.

Don't let them off so easy. They said they were your friends, and friends are supposed to have each other's back. My bear, who is clearly still upset, speaks up for the first time in a while.

And where have you been this whole time? I ask my she-bear. *I am always here with you. We don't have to speak to connect, you know. Plus, you could seek me out first. It doesn't always have to be me starting conversations.* Touché. Inner Bear one, me zero.

You're right, on both counts. Guess I'm not used to communicating with another voice in my head yet or utilizing you. And if you're speaking up about what Ellis and Rosy did, then I guess I'm still more upset about it than I realized. *Good,* is the only reply I get.

I glance around for a place to sit, intending to continue conversing with my Inner Bear, when an old woman catches my attention with a wave. And when I say old, I mean old. I don't think I've ever seen someone more wizened in my life. She's bent over her cane so acutely that she'd fall over without its support. She's wearing an all black robe with attached hood, and wisps of white hair poke out around her face here and there. If there was ever a being that matched the description of an Old Crone, she's it.

I whirl my head to either side of me, assuming she must be trying to get someone else to notice her, but there's no one around me right now. Looking back at her she points right at me, waves me over, and begins to hobble away. Realizing she must need someone to help her, I quickly follow.

"Ma'am, do you need something?" I call out as I continue to follow her. "Um, do you need something from me?" I ask again louder, but all she does is raise her arm and wave me on. It's only after I turn down the second alley that I think this might have been a bad idea. Not only do I not know this person or where she is leading me, but she is also way faster than any Crone should be. She quickly rounds another corner, so I put on my new Shifter speed intent on catching her before we go any further into this maze of a city.

WHAM! I run into something hard and also moving incredibly fast. I slam down right onto my ass, head ringing and slightly dazed. As I rapidly blink my eyes and shake my head, I could swear I hear a cackling laugh behind me. But that cackle is quickly forgotten as my eyes focus and I get a good look at what I ran into. It's Mel! I almost can't believe it, and given the expression on her face, she can't hardly believe it either.

"Silvia?!" My name passes her lips in a croak. All I can do is shake my head before she crawls over to me and wraps me in a powerful hug. "Silvia, Silvia, Silvia," is all she says as we rock back and forth, holding each other and crying.

"I found her! She's over here," comes a shout behind me that has Mel frozen in place. I glance back to see the goblin guard I came to town with and the older goblin lady quickly behind her.

"It's okay, it's okay," I hurriedly reassure Mel as I stroke her head. "They're good; they're with me. The Grath Family has been helping us find you." There's fear written all over her face, her eyes are wide as saucers. But she eventually shakes her head and relaxes a bit against me.

"It's Mel!" I shout to my goblin companions. "I found her! Well, we sort of ran into each other." The guard gives me a nod and pulls out a mirror compact from her pocket, then begins to speak to it. That's an odd thing to do.

"I've let Mr. Grath know, and he's informed your family. They will be meeting us here shortly." The guard tells me quickly as the older goblin walks over to us. I guess that was some kind of communication device? I'll have to find out later. Right now, caring for Mel is more important.

"Here's some water for you sweetie. Drink it slowly now," the old goblin says while handing her a glass bottle of water. "Your Ma is on her way." Mel eyes the bottle with suspicion, which is totally understandable. So I take the bottle and gulp down a mouthful, showing her it's safe, before passing it off to Mel's trembling hand. She's sitting fully in my lap now, like a little kid, crying softly. So I rub her arms and back as we rock there in silence.

The bottle of water is almost gone by the time Torben and Ma arrive. The only warning I get is Ma shouting, "Melantha!" before two bodies crash into us and hold us both tightly. The next few moments are filled with tears, many apologies from everyone, and soul-crushing hugs. It's Ma who gets herself back together first.

"What happened? How did you get here? You weren't at the location the others were held. Are you hurt anywhere? Let me look at you. How are you feeling? What did they do to you? Did they give you anything?" The barrage of questions comes so fast that even my head is spinning. But before Mel can answer one of the red guards walks over to us.

"Perhaps it's best to continue this back at the Manor," he suggests and holds out his hand to assist Ma up. A very clear message to maybe not have this discussion out in an open alley.

Once back at the Manor, Mel is plied with food, then ushered up to a bath. After Ma gave her a good once-over, that is. We were told Mr. Grath wanted to hear Mel's story and none of us wanted to make her tell it twice, so we all patiently wait for Mel to get her needs tended to and for the Head of the Grath Family to return. But before he does, we all get a surprise when Pa, Rosy, and Ellis arrive. More hugs and crying ensue when Mel comes back from her bath, looking shaken still, but far better than she had in the alley.

Not long after, we are all ushered into Mr. Grath's office where he is already sitting by the fire in his green chair. His suit jacket is thrown over the back and his shirt is slightly open. He raises his hand to forestall all the thanks we are trying to give him and motions for us to take a seat.

"Now, I've heard many stories today, but yours, young lady, is one I am most keenly interested in." With that he steeples his fingers, awaiting Mel's account. I get the feeling he's not the type of guy who ever needs to ask twice for something. Rosy, ever the bartender, has already poured Mel a drink of some kind and hands it to her with a quick reassuring wink and smile. After taking a sip, Mel finally fills us all in on what happened.

"Well, I guess I'll start with running after Torben and Silvia into the woods." She glances over at me then with an expression of deep remorse before continuing. "Pretty quickly, I caught the scent of goblins on our lands, though it was a bit off. But since it seemed to be moving toward our village, I decided to go investigate." She makes a face to show she knows that wasn't the smartest thing to do alone.

"I've never had any issues with goblins so I just kinda ran right up to them, to ask if they needed help or something. They looked and smelled so off I thought they were sick. It wasn't until much later I learned that the smell was some kind of drug they were all hopped up on. Anyway, they shot me with sleeping darts right away; it's kinda embarrassing how quickly I went down, to be honest." She does indeed seem quite embarrassed confessing that part of her story. "When I woke up, it was night and I was in a cage with some others, some still asleep and some awake but groggy like me. We were on a cart being taken somewhere, but when we came to a stop at this big warehouse, our captors got a message that upset them." Mr. Grath shakes his head knowingly, putting pieces together, but says nothing.

"I guess too many of us were waking up at this point, so we all got darted again, even those who hadn't even moved yet. When I woke up again, I was in a small cage by myself and could tell it was daytime through the small dirty window at the top of a wall. I was pretty sure I was in a basement or cellar of some kind. It was cold and damp, for sure."

Mel takes another sip from her drink and nervously rubs a hand over her thigh. Ma takes her hand and squeezes it reassuringly.

"I could tell there were others in cages or chains around the room, but most of us were still pretty out of it. Every now and then someone would come in and put us back to sleep. I woke up one last time to find that they were moving us again. It looked and sounded as if I was the only one awake. I really don't know why I was still awake though. Maybe I got missed or something, but I decided to pretend I was asleep anyway." She sits up a little straighter, taking pride in her quick thinking.

"Once they carried me out the door, I shifted, crushing the guy who was carrying me, swiped at a few others, then ran like Sleipnir. When I got to a place I thought I recognized, I shifted back and started making my way to a market space I knew about. Just hoping to find as many people as possible to help. That's when I plowed right into Silvia in that alley." She turns to face me. "I could hardly believe it was you at first. Of all the people to run into! It was like fate or something."

I plaster a grin on my face and nod in agreement. Yeah fate, that was it. Not a sly old crone of a woman leading me to my doom or anything.

"Hmm, that's quite an adventure you had." Mr. Garth offers. "We must have arrived right after your daring escape as we found those very wounded goblins still in shambles. We have seen to the rest of the victims at that site, plus the two others we found. Seems after their original space was compromised, they had to scatter you all about in different hiding holes before regrouping. Rest assured that we plan to viciously purge this blight from our city." He stands and grabs his jacket. "Now I have much to attend to. You are all welcome to stay here tonight if you wish." But before any of us can answer Mel looks over at Pa with big puppy-dog eyes.

"I really want to go home now." That was the end of the discussion.

Chapter 31

Silvia

My two friends go out to prep Ellis's cart for our return trip. While Torben, Ma and Pa go upstairs to collect our things. I start to follow Torben but Mel stops me, asking to speak with me alone. Torben kisses my forehead and tells me he'll pack my things. Since he is the one who unpacked for me last night, he knows what is mine. What a sweetheart. Now alone in the foyer, Mel begins.

"Here, I need to give this back to you," she says quietly while handing me an envelope. "I...I took it out of your bag after you and Torben ran off. I went to your room to get your new Bear Shifter scent off something in your bag, to help track you. I smelled Wolf Shifter and took this. I'm so sorry I shouldn't have." I realize now that it's the letter Wilhelm wrote to me, the one about being turned without choice. I look up at Mel and tears are running rivers down her face.

"I'm so, so sorry, Silvia!" she wails at me. "I read it, while I was in that cage. Oh Silvia, I never should have done that to you. Bitten you like that without your consent. Without you understanding what it really meant. I've always been a Shifter and never even stopped to think. I never even thought to see what happened from your side." She's holding my hands so tightly now, crushing them and the letter. "I'm the villain in your story, just as that Wolf Shifter is to Wilhelm, and those goblins are to meeee!" She is shaking in her tears, and her voice is beginning to really carry now.

"Shhh, shhh, you are not a villain, Mel." I try to soothe her, but it only seems to make it worse.

"Yes, I am! I'm a horrible person and sister. I don't deserve how nice you are being to me. I was so relieved when I found you. I didn't want to die before I had the chance to apologiiiize!" Oh no, she's super loud now. "And you were being so amazing to me in that alley, and I couldn't even say it then."

"Mel, you had just run for your life and escaped capture. Plus, you'd spent like two days drugged out. I did not expect an apology on sight." I start to wipe tears from her cheeks. "But I greatly appreciate the apology now. Though you probably owe one to Wilhelm for reading his private thoughts and personal story, okay?" She nods yes before throwing her arms around me. "I'm glad you are safe, and I'm glad you understand now why what you did was wrong."

"I didn't realize how painful it would be, Silvia. I knew about some of the physical pain but I never paid attention to how danger-ous and bad it could be. And I never even considered there being emotional pain, as well. I think Torben was right about me being selfish." She breaks the hug and looks me in my eyes. "It's time I grow up a little more and become a good sister to you."

Not knowing how exactly to reply to that statement I pat her hand, "Um, thanks."

Shortly after that slightly uncomfortable, but much needed conversation, I find myself riding in the back of a cart once more. Rosy trots beside us telling her side of the story. Apparently it was her contact in the Taverns Guild that helped find two of the locations. Sounds like ale, drugs, and resentment make for loose lips. Listening to Rosy and Ellis banter back and forth about this handsome Minotaur helps the trip pass more quickly and easily. The feeling of normalcy is welcome after days of fear and worry.

Torben holds me close to him the whole ride, while Mel is firmly sandwiched between her parents. But I get the feeling she doesn't mind in the slightest. I can't even imagine what she's been through and what it's going to take to work through it all. I'd have nightmares, for sure, no doubt about it. I wonder what kind of therapy they have in this world.

What is on your mind, my Sweet Mate? Torben asks me privately.

Worrying about your sister and how she's going to work through all this trauma. He chuckles slightly beside me.

Of course, you are. My Sweet Silvia is always thinking of others. But how are you feeling? Ah yes, how am I feeling?

Hmm, let's see. I'm relieved Mel and the others are safe. Content with Mel's apology and remorse. Anxious and nervous and slightly queasy at the thought of finally talking to my friends about keeping things from me. I'm not a fan of confrontation. But, my Inner Bear has let me know that we are still bothered by it.

You don't have to do it right away. We are still in our Bonding time, giving us the excuse to make our way back to the Mating Cave as soon as we like. We glance and smile at each other, knowing full well what that means.

While that offer is very, very tempting, I know I'll only build it up in my mind if I push it off. I'd rather be distraction and guilt free once I get you all to myself again. I bump my knee into his thigh.

"You two are so stinkin' cute, silently flirting over there." Mel is looking right at us with a smile on her face. "I'm glad you two have worked things out despite my stupidity. Everything is good, right?" There's a bit of worry in her expression and question. So I take Torben's hand in mine, lacing our fingers.

"Everything is wonderful," I say beaming up at Torben. And it's true. I have honestly fallen in love with this sweet and caring bear man who is my Mate. I've inherited an amazing new family and am pretty sure I have a dream job waiting for me. After I finish my Shifter training, that is. And I have two new good friends, who have shown up for me in a way that no other friend ever has before. At least, I hope they're still my friends after a little heart-to-heart.

We are met with an amazing surprise once we reach the Clan's Village. All the Fire Fest decor is still up and a great bonfire is burning. The whole Clan has gathered, and it smells like a feast has been prepared. From what I hear, they felt they couldn't continue with the celebrations while a Clan member was in danger. So everything was held off until we were back safe and sound with Mel. I catch Mel furiously wiping away her tears upon learning this. Ellis and Rosy are asked, or more correctly pressed, to stay and celebrate. It's later, during some wild dancing around the fire, that I am able to get them aside to talk in private. It's actually Rosy who begins before I can even bring it up.

"Silvia, I, well, we really want to apologize for keeping the whole Mate thing from you. At first it simply wasn't my place to tell you, it was Torben's. I also didn't want to scare you away knowing humans don't have the whole True Mates thing. But I knew poor Torben couldn't talk to females, and I should have made it more clear to him that keeping this a secret was so close to a lie. That's no way to start a relationship. But then that's how we started ours with you, keeping this big secret from you."

"Yeah, lying isn't really the best way to start something." I begin. "And I get that it wasn't for you two to tell me. But you were supposed to be my friends, in my corner. Then, after I found out, it made me feel so stupid." Oh, there's the anger at feeling humiliated. The angry and hurt tears soon follow, but I push through, needing to get it out. "Discovering you two knew as I poured my heart out to you both and asked for advice. It really felt like you two were...laughing behind my back, at the stupid human."

"Oh honey, no," Ellis appears truly horrified, hand going to their chest. "We never laughed at you. Never ever, you hear me? And we certainly do not think you're stupid. I am very sorry we ever made you feel that way." I catch a glimpse of a single tear glisten on their cheek. Damn, why are they still gorgeous even when they cry?! "All we wanted was for you two to find happiness in each other. We honestly thought we were doing what was best to support you, but I can see how it might feel as if your new friends betrayed you from the start."

I look over at Rosy, who's crying as much as I am. She's been nodding her head in agreement with all that Ellis has said.

"What do we need to do to make this up to you?" Rosy asks earnestly through her tears. "I really love having you as a friend. You're so kind and easy to talk to and funny. Feels like you are the perfect fit for our little friend group. Please tell me we haven't lost the chance at still having you in our lives."

"This, this right here is what I really needed." I sob out, rubbing tears from my eyes. "Just no more lying or keeping big life-altering secrets about myself from me, okay? I don't think my heart could take that again."

What follows is a group hug with more crying and apologies. Eventually, we move on to drinking and lots of dancing with my new best friends and Gran-Gran.

When the festivities start to wind down, Torben and I say our goodbyes and return to the Mating Cave. The next two weeks are spent alone together, kind of like a little honeymoon. We fill our days in a variety of ways. I learn about my new Clan, we have sex, he shows me the Clan lands, we make love in a river, he demonstrates how he finds the right tree for his craft, we fuck in the woods. It's bliss really, and I'm the happiest I've ever been.

At one point, Emna writes Torben to let him know she finished a tub project for him and what day it's set to be delivered. He felt truly grateful to her and mortified at how he let the project slide from his thoughts. So I gave him a blow job to cheer him up, which led to him going down on me, then more cave sex. This whole mating lust thing is no joke, but I'm not longer complaining.

Torben insists on installing the tub for Maggie Farris himself. I know he really wants to apologize to her some more and also check Emna's work. Not that he doesn't trust her craftsmanship, but more wants to put his own mind at ease. I give him a long and passionate kiss at the entrance of the cave, showing him how much I'll miss him. I'm making it even harder for him to leave by doing so completely naked, wearing only the menstruation cuff gifted to me at the beginning of my adventure. I simply want to make sure he comes back to me as quickly as possible.

Once I can no longer see that biteable butt of his walking away, I decide it's time to sink into the natural hot spring in the back of the cave. The warm mineral water feels so good on my sore areas that I just sit there for a time with my eyes closed.

"Well now, doesn't that look relaxing." I'm so startled that I let out an actual screech before inadvertently dunking myself under and breathing water into my lungs. I clumsily reemerge and begin coughing up said water. Throat burning and eyes streaming tears, I continue to cough as I look to see who the hell nearly killed me.

My struggle instantly stops as I behold a vision of womanly beauty and wonder once more. The Bookshop Owner is here, trying to hide a laugh behind her hand, while sitting on an ottoman that was most definitely not in this cave before. If it had been, Torben and I would have totally used it at some point. Probably several times.

She appears to be even more wondrous than I remember, sitting there laughing at me. Her mahogany brown hair draped loose over one shoulder and falling into her lap. Amber eyes that sparkle when filled with mirth. Her quiet laughter is like the melody of a music box. All I can do is blink as I drink her in once more.

"Oh dear, it was not my intention to scare you, little one. But how you did flail about!" More melodic laughter. "Here, let's get you out of there and dried off so we can have a little discussion." An all too familiar big white soft towel is once again in her hand being offered to me. Why am I always dripping wet when I meet her? Covering myself the best I can with my hands and arms, I grab the towel and quickly wrap it around me.

"Goodness, those delightful freckles really are everywhere, aren't they?" I can feel my whole body turn red in embarrassment.

"Yes, yes, um, why are you here exactly? Now, that is?" I ask once I'm out of the water and reaching for my own robe, suddenly wishing to be as covered as a nun in front of this woman.

"Why, my dear, to take you back home, of course." My entire body freezes. I can't think, can't breathe, can't move. And she's said it so casually, like it hasn't rocked my entire world. "You've had your grand adventure. Helped people who were in need, learned new skills. Found friendship, and the family you so desired to have. Made yourself a love match and even have a lovely new career all lined up. You've reached your Happily Ever After, and I congratulate you." She raises her hands and gives them a delicate little clap.

"But, but I'm not finished yet!" Surprised I can even speak right now, I grab hold and continue. "I haven't finished my Shifter Training with Phil. I, I haven't met the whole family yet. Torben and I are going to be building a lovely house by a waterfall. And, and there's the beekeeping apprenticeship I, I haven't even started that yet. So, so you see there's still lots to do, lots more story to come." My heart is racing, fluttering like a butterfly in my chest.

"Yes, yes, dear, that's all the 'happily ever after' part. The boring bits of a life continued after the story. And nobody really wants to read about that, especially in a Romance. You've got your man, you two have resolved your issues, planning for a perfectly normal future. The End."

But I'm not ready. I'm not ready at all for it to end.

Standing, she sweeps her hair over her shoulder to fall elegantly down her back then holds both hands out to me.

"Now, take my hands and I'll get you home. Back to your real life."

I instinctively take a step back from her. Torben, where's Torben?! I need him to come back right now. I can't let her take me, not yet, not without a goodbye. I start furiously shaking my head as tears begin to fall down my cheeks.

"What's this, my dear? I'm not going to harm you."

"I can't leave. I can't leave him. Not like this."

What about me? my Inner Bear speaks up. I clutch my hands to my chest.

"My, my Inner Bear. Will she still be with me? What will happen to her once I return to the real world?" The shopkeeper gives me a look that's full of pity and I know the answer. My bear will be gone too, there are no Shifters where I'm from.

"My sweet child, I thought you understood. This was a single story to help you learn and grow. To be an adventure for you, something you reflect back on." There is true concern in her eyes.

"But what if I stay? What if I choose to stay?" I've stepped closer to her now, looking up into her eyes pleading. "Can't you come back later? I need more time. More time with Torben, more time with my new family, and my new friends. More time to learn, to be this new me, and to be happy. Please, please come back later." I'm full on sobbing at this point, clutching my robe tight to myself.

"Oh Silvia, come and sit down with me by the fire. I didn't mean to cause you so much distress." She's taken my shoulders and is walking us over to the fire pit. Her ottoman has moved over by it, and a second has appeared. "This is not typically how people react to being done with their story and sent back home. The Horror folks can't wait to return home, poor souls." She helps me take a seat before gracefully descending upon her own.

"Here, have some nice warm tea to calm yourself." She hands me a cup and saucer, the same ones she let me use once before, with the ivy rim. And of course it's filled with the same tea that brings back all my fondest memories. "Now, take a few sips and breathe for me. We need you all collected for this conversation." She tucks a piece of my damp hair behind my ear as I comply. Secretly, I feel the need to buy myself some time before Torben returns.

"Now Silvia, I'm going to need you to listen to me carefully and really think about what you want out of your life. Because what you decide now will affect you for the rest of your days, and there will be no changing it." She's speaking to me calmly but firmly while staring right into my eyes. I nod my head in acknowledgment before she takes a breath and continues.

"Before you are two choices and two choices alone. Option one," she holds out her right hand, "you stick to the original plan and come back home with me. You return to your apartment and your cat and live the rest of your days as a normal human woman. Changed forever by your experiences here. There will be no Shifting, no Inner Bear, and no Mate. But hopefully you will take what you have learned here and apply it to your future. Any questions about option one?"

"What about Torben? I'm his True Mate, what will happen to him, to his future?" The bookshop owner holds up a hand to stop me.

"This is not about Torben or anyone else here. This is only about you. Do you understand me? I need you to contemplate what's best for you and not make a decision based on others." I nod my head showing I heard her, so she continues. "Now, option two, I leave you here in this story of yours for you to live out the rest of your days. There are no guarantees that it will play out as a 'happily ever after.' There may be more trials, those you love will someday die, and you will forever be altered as a Bear Shifter. But most importantly, you will never be able to return home again. This here, this moment is your only chance to ever go back to your world. You will be stuck here forever as I can not come back for you." I'm nodding my head to show I've understood her.

"I mean it now, young lady. No more fast food, no social media or movies. You'll never find out how any of your shows or book series end." She's ticking off her fingers as she lists everything I'd be missing out on. "I really need you to consider what you'll be forever giving up. Any questions?" she asks again. I take a deep breath and ask the only question that really matters. The only thing that could sway my decision.

"Could I bring my cat here?"

Epilogue

Harvey

My human should be home soon. Which is good because I am starting to get hungry. It's been a good day though. The rains have been off and on, which are pleasant enough to listen to. But my favorite part is watching all the birds that gather on the grass through the window. I love to watch them. The predator in me knows that, if I was out there with them, I'd be bringing home a prize. They are indeed lucky that I do not need to hunt them for food. If ever given the chance, I would certainly hunt them for sport though. The killer instinct and drive still remains in me, passed down from my noble ancestors.

The sound of the door being unlocked makes my right ear twitch, but something is off. The all too familiar sounds of my human's keys are absent, as is her unique scent. In its place is silence and no aroma at all. I leap down from the bedroom windowsill and casually walk to the small hallway. There I sit and wait. Eventually, a tall woman comes into view, but I know before I even see her that she is no human. She is real and tangible, unlike some of the other things I see in here from time to time. No, not human, but some-thing much grander, something with more power. Something I've never encountered before.

"Am I to assume that you are Harvey, cat companion of the human Silvia?" She knows how to speak to me correctly, without the use of that 'baby voice' some other humans have insisted on directing at me. I give her one slow blink in response.

"Perfect," she states with a smile. "You have a choice about your future you need to make. Please join me in the living room when you are ready to discuss." With that, this woman turns and walks away.

Given the countenance of this person, I doubt very much if it's going to be a choice about my dinner. How interesting. I sit there for a time, using all my senses to try and figure out what this person might be, but come up with nothing. I have never encountered anything like this before. So, after an appropriate amount of time, I saunter into the living room, tail held high and swaying with confidence. This is my territory, after all, my space.

I round the corner to find her sitting in a chair I do not recognize. A chair that smells of fire, books, leather, and tea. Once close enough to not be a show-off, I leap onto the coffee table to sit and gaze upon her.

"First I must offer you my apologies. Your human Silvia will never be coming back to this place nor to you. But be at ease knowing that she is safe and exceedingly happy." I grow concerned at this news.

My Silvia needs me, needs my companionship. She is often lonely, and I see it as my duty to comfort her, be with her. She is my caregiver, and I love her. She rescued me when I was a kitten on the streets. She was patient and kind to me, I care for her well-being deeply. I narrow my eyes at this creature in my home. But she merely chuckles at me.

"She is not alone, little one, and has many others to watch over her now. Consider your duty to her fulfilled." I sit completely still, I do not move my tail nor my eyes. She shall get no reaction from me till she continues. "Oh, I do like you Harvey, which is why I've come to offer you a choice. Since I cannot bring you to where she is now, your human has asked me to find you a safe and comfortable home. Made me promise this, in fact. In point, you are the only thing that she was concerned about leaving behind in this world." I move my head slightly at this comment. If my human is not in this world, then where is she? But the powerful being does not elaborate on that point.

"The choice is this, little Harvey. I can do exactly as Silvia had intended when asking this of me. I can find you a new home, one that is safe and comfortable. A new human or humans, if you prefer. I'll even make sure you like your new situation before fully relinquishing my duties. Or," she pauses for what must be dramatic effect, "you could choose a different kind of life. You see, I own an exceptionally unique bookshop. I've got it trimmed out to appear as any bookshop should, but I find myself missing one thing. That's where you come in. I wish to offer you the position of Bookshop Cat."

I blink at her again, indicating that she should elaborate on this.

"Now I know that not all bookshops have a cat, but I think you could be a real boon to me. People seem to be drawn in by such things and I feel that your presence can help with the authenticity of the place and put people more at ease."

The more she describes it, the more I feel as though I would become a glittering jewel in this trap she's set for humans. I narrow my eyes again to show her my displeasure at being bait for other poor humans like my Silvia.

"Oh, don't get the wrong idea, Harvey. The people whom I deem worthy or in need of what I have to offer are always given a choice, akin to the one I am giving you now. They are all drawn to my establishment seeking a change, and a change is what I give them. If they are brave enough to accept." She moves to sit closer to the edge of her chair. "You, my dear Harvey, have the exact qualities I've identified as requirements for my Shop Cat. Intelligence, reserve, a striking visage, and a caring nature to those who are in need of it. In return you will never lack for food or treats, you will have the run of the bookshop, and I have fine bay windows for you to peer out of. You will see places you've never seen before and meet interesting people, not too many of course. I only ever have one customer at a time." Her mouth curves into a not altogether pleasant grin at that statement.

I have to admit I am intrigued by her proposition. I do not believe I am ready to open my heart to a new human right now, not without mourning the loss of my Silvia first. And despite what this lady says, I may one day get to see my human again, if I stay around her. I am also very curious to find out what this being is, what she is doing with these humans, and why she's doing it. Plus, I am not immune to flattery, especially when all she claims about me is true. It could be fun to unravel her secrets and meet these humans seeking change. A new view to look out upon would not go unappreciated either. Decision made, I offer her another slow blink.

"Excellent. I hoped you would agree." As she stands, the chair she was sitting in disappears. Not even a lingering odor left in its wake. In its place now sits a cat carrier, door open, ready for me to willingly walk inside. "Feel free to bring anything you wish from here with you, though I promise all your needs shall be met."

I begin to pile my favorite toys near the carrier; I couldn't leave without my little plush banana, Mr. Nan, of course, and I include a few balls and a small blanket Granny made me. Last into the pile, I take a scrunchie that belonged to my Silvia, her scent still infused within it. I offer this woman a meow to show I am ready. Once all are swept inside, I confidently walk into the carrier.

"All settled and ready for your new adventure, Harvey?" the woman asks me, and I believe I am. Ready for some change myself, and to get some answers.

The End

Acknowledgements

First and foremost, I'd like to thank you for reading my debut novel. You have no idea what it means to me. Thank you for taking a chance on me and my ability to tell a good and entertaining story. I hope you enjoyed my silly little book because I loved writing it.

Second I have to give a gigantic thanks to my co-workers and personal Hype Team, Lauren and Levi. I don't think I would have even written a book at all without them. They heard my harebrained idea for a series of romance books, then encouraged and pestered me to write them so they could read my stories. They were indeed the first to read this novel and really stroked my ego into thinking it was a real book. Guess they were right?!

A huge shout out to my Beta Readers: Thai, Kim, and Letha. They really helped reshape and begin the polishing process of this book, as well as adding their own encouragements. Thank you so much for all your time and energy. You have no idea how much your input helped me along this debut author journey.

The amazing talents of my wonderful Cover Designer, Lisa, cannot be stressed enough. She accepted all my little, and sometimes vague, critiques with a can-do attitude. Thank you for working with me in the creation of this cute cover.

Big thanks to my patient and speedy Copyeditor Jesslyn. She really helped to add the final polish to my debut novel. And through her efforts I know this story is better than it was before. Even if it was challenging, and not always fun, it was well worth it.

And a special thanks to my super loving, patient, and encouraging partner, James. Thank you for always standing by me and supporting all my crazy endeavors. You are truly my other half.

Lastly, I do need to recognize my crazy, weird, and wonderful neurodivergent brain. Without it, I wouldn't be who I am, and though we are at odds sometimes, I know it is way more of a help than a hindrance at this point in my life. Without it, I truly would not have had the audacity to think I could learn to write a book. Thank you.

Ella Outlaw Books

The Magical Bookshop Series

About the author

Ella Outlaw is a nerdy, witchy, neurodivergent girlic, with one of those invisible chronic illnesses. Currently living in the DFW area of Texas, though desperately seeking to leave as it's far too hot here! She loves to game, cross-stitch, and read smut. While her love of writing may be 'new,' her joy of storytelling has been with her since childhood. Who knew her maladaptive daydreaming would be turned into such works of art!?